LETHAL GAME

Charlie Gallagher was a serving UK police officer for thirteen years. During that time, he had many roles, starting as a frontline response officer, then a member of a specialist tactical team and later as a detective investigating the more serious offences. His books are a series of thrillers and, rather unsurprisingly, policing is central to the stories. He lives with his family on the south coast of Kent.

Also by Charlie Gallagher

The Friend

LETHAL GAME

Charlie Gallagher

avon.

Published by AVON
A division of HarperCollins*Publishers*
1 London Bridge Street
London SE1 9GF

www.harpercollins.co.uk

HarperCollins*Publishers*
1st Floor, Watermarque Building, Ringsend Road
Dublin 4, Ireland

This paperback edition 2021
1

First published in Great Britain by HarperCollins*Publishers* 2021

A catalogue copy of this book is available from the British Library.

ISBN: 978-0-00-844554-6

Typeset in Sabon LT Std by Palimpsest Book Production Limited, Falkirk, Stirlingshire
Printed and bound in UK by CPI Group (UK) Ltd, Croydon CR0 4YY

For Julia James.

Prologue

Shannon pushed herself back against the wall firmly enough for the exposed brick to dig her in the back. Her buttocks were lifted, her feet out in front of her to scrabble in the straw, pushing it away in clumps towards the mud-flecked boots that had appeared under the weathered door. She held her breath, silently praying that those boots would turn on the spot to face away in any direction and then walk on. Her hands flailed like they were controlled by someone else and her fingers caught on the wire that had been tight around her waist from the moment she had arrived, holding her against that wall.

The door made a clacking sound. The acoustics of an open barn made it sound like a gunshot that bounced around the exposed metal rafters. The door shook too, the movement slight but enough for her to know it was unlocked. She still held her breath, staring at the door with such intensity that she might almost expect it to burst into flames.

The boots did turn and then they were gone. They scuffed and scraped away, the sound of a pair too large for the wearer. He was not coming in. There were to be no more instructions, no more threats or promises.

The final part was about to begin.

The clanging of the first bell confirmed it. This was louder still, its echo making it impossible to determine the direction of the source. Shannon scrambled upright. It seemed more difficult somehow; the wire was suddenly slack around her middle and she couldn't lean on it to pull herself up. She managed a few paces before the wire halted her again, tightening all at once to pinch her hips. She was a metre closer to the door, a metre of ground that had to contain something useful.

She dropped to her knees into a frenzy of movement, tearing at the dry straw that had formed a layer on the floor of the pen, searching for anything that could help. Her bare hands disturbed solid clumps of animal dung that she discarded, plunging her hands back so hard her nails and fingertips scratched and scraped on the concrete base. Nothing.

The bell clanged again. Two out of five. *Could that really be ten seconds already?* Her restraint slackened again to allow another few steps and she threw herself forward towards the door, stumbling in her haste. She might have toppled over but the wire caught her again, forcing a breath from her, and this time pinching her stomach. She went back to searching the floor, bending her fingers back in her haste, registering the pain, but there was no time to stop. Her fingertips bumped something. She scooped it up and it kept coming: a belt; leather with a small buckle. Not what she wanted but it could be of use. She slung it round her waist, her sore fingers fumbling in her urgency to fasten it, her eyes already back to the task of searching for something else. The third ring of the bell forced a whine as her desperation peaked. She was scrabbling round the edges of the pen now, where the straw was firmer, trampled flat and mixed with more dung to solidify. But there was something else, something with some weight. Her nails caught and scraped as she pulled it clear. *A hammer!* This time her whimper was one of relief. This was something she could use, something that might give her a chance. It was only small, a hammer for glass, the type she had seen on buses to use in emergencies. It didn't matter. It would be more effective than her fists. She got back to her feet and stumbled forward, one step, two, the third just a half step, and was caught again with a clunk that left her balancing on one foot with the other knee raised while she flailed for a moment at the door in front of her.

The bell clanged for the fourth time.

Ten seconds left.

The time for searching was over; the wire that had been gripping her fell slack. She moved back, now with time to realise just how hard she was breathing, gasping to fill her lungs. She needed to get that under control; it wasn't the exertion so much as the fear, anticipation of what she knew was coming next. Her fingers hurt as she pulled at the wire loop that now fell apart to drop at her feet. She stepped out, fixing her gaze on the closed door, knowing the outcome if she dared leave before that final bell. She felt for the wall with her bare foot, using it as something solid to push off, to give her the best start. She leant forward, her hands resting on the floor, her right foot dragged up to complete the stance of a sprinter on a starting block. She had a moment to glance down her tensed body at the belt hanging loose off her waist and at the hammer that was uncomfortable in her right hand, squashing her knuckles into the floor – but she dared not let it go, even for a moment. She was wearing a loose red dress made of coarse material coated with a layer of filth. The thigh that was lifted was stained with animal faeces and dirt too.

She lifted her head for one last look at the solid stone lintel above the door. She was sure the pattern and the row of numbers scratched into it were also scratched into her mind and with such ferocity that that she would never forget them, but what if they left her just when she needed them? *What if she didn't remember?* She shook her head, trying to put it out of her mind. It wasn't just her mind that turned over with doubt and anticipation; her stomach churned too, while her chest burned with the strain of holding her position. She dropped to one knee, a moment to rest. The last clang of the bell was taking longer, she was sure of it – the time should be up by now. She was being toyed with.

Then the fifth bell filled the space.

Shannon threw herself forward, her right hand gripping the hammer. Two strides and then a jump and turn, and the door burst open with such violence that its clamour slammed her eyes shut and the blow knocked her off balance, so that she dipped her head as she stumbled into the noise of a second door thrown open to smash off the wall directly opposite. She lifted her head and saw another terrified young woman who had emerged. Their worlds stopped for a moment, a silent exchange before the other woman twisted left and sprang towards the entrance that glowed a scorched white: daylight.

'Shit!' Shannon was already behind. She broke into a sprint. The other woman made the sunlight first and the bright sun distorted her white dress as she fled. And she was fast too. 'Shit, shit!' The instant Shannon was out of the barn the terrain changed – still concrete but broken up, stained too, with something that made it slick. The stones jabbed at the underside of her feet and this time when she stumbled it turned into a fall that she took on her knees and palms. There was no time for the pain. She bounced back to her feet. She kept her eyes down, desperate to pick out patches of ground where she could plant her feet. The woman in white was still ahead and faring better. She was already onto a track that twisted away to become a steep hill. And she was still running.

Shannon made it to the track too. It was kinder on her feet, since vehicles had cleared two clear lines among the stones. The terrain changed again at the top of the hill to smooth tarmac and here she could see country lanes meeting at a crossroads fifty metres ahead. The woman in white was there already. But she was hesitating, had even stopped, long enough to glance back. Then she seemed to make a decision, bursting back into a sprint. She went straight on.

Shannon slowed for the same crossroads, thrown into doubt and confusion by the other woman's actions. The scratched diagram had shown a left. *But had it?* She stopped, her chest burning from the hill. Her mouth was full of excess phlegm and she leant over to spit it out. She walked a few paces left. She was too far behind the woman in white to go the same way anyway. She had to believe she was right, that the other woman had made a mistake. It was her only chance.

Shannon was back to a sprint. It was flatter here at least, the road stretching out in front of her with solid mud banks on either side. The woodland ahead arrived with a change of sound, her footfalls bouncing back off the underside of the tree canopy. There should be a dog-leg next: a quick right, then a left. The makeshift map hadn't made it clear how soon the turn should be. But there should be one; if it didn't arrive then she was wrong. And she couldn't be wrong.

The right turn appeared as a violent slice through the woodland, cutting the mud banks in a sharp angle. She turned into it. A left turn followed almost straightaway and she dared to hope she had been right.

She was struggling now. Her chest burned brighter and her heart thumped. Her legs were close to cramping and she knew she was going to have to slow. She opted for a fast walk, her strides long to aid her recovery like she had been taught at her running club. She should have time. She pushed her hands into her hips, pulling her shoulders back to take gulps of air, aware of the hammer pressing against a hip bone. Shannon threw a look over her shoulder. A woman in a loose white dress was moving towards her. Fast.

'Ah, dammit!' Shannon realised she was too tired to run, that she could intercept the woman instead, hold her ground here. She gripped the hammer tighter, but now, as she fixed on it, it seemed smaller in her grasp – lighter even. What if the other woman had found something else? Something better? From the etched map she should be nearly there. She picked up her feet to run again.

Those few moments of rest had done her good. She was faster – stronger. Another right should appear. It did. This time she could see it coming from a long way off. The scenery was back to fields, and the high banks either side were now gently dropping away. When she cast another look over her shoulder the other woman was scrabbling up the bank on the right side – *trying to cut the corner!*

Shannon reacted by veering right too but she stayed on the road, terrified of falling if she attempted the bank. The right turn seemed to take an age, but it did come and she leant into it. The other woman had gained on her but Shannon was on the last straight. The field on her left flashed past as a vivid yellow, the rapeseed filling the air to coat her nose and throat as she sprinted past it. But all her attention was in front of her, to where she could see the bright red of the phone box in the distance. It added strength to her stride. *She was going to make it and she was going to be first!*

The door to the phone box opened outwards. It was heavy and she was exhausted. She had enough forward momentum for the door to bang into her shoulder and the side of her face. The impact shook the hammer from her hand and she had to scoop it back up, looking down the road as she did. The other woman was ten metres behind and shrieking her desperation, her eyes wide, her hand raised. There was something in it.

Shannon shut the door behind her. The phone box was a steel construction that was at its thickest in the four corners, the glass panels on all four sides criss-crossed with thinner steel. Much of the glass was missing, pushed out or smashed to leave jagged remnants. She turned on the spot to see the other woman almost upon her. Shannon needed more time.

A sudden idea had her fumbling with the belt she had

wrapped around her. It came free and she pushed it out through a glassless panel and round the bottom corner of the door where she could tie it shut. In her haste her wrist caught on a shard of the glass; it split her skin to spill blood but she didn't flinch; she barely even felt it. Shannon had to calm hands that shook with adrenaline as she wrapped the belt three times round then, more slowly, fed the end through the buckle. The door frame was too thick for three times round, and the belt's metal pin fell short of the punctured holes. But only just. There was no time for correction. She yanked on it, leaning backwards to use her weight. The leather creaked and the pin edged closer.

'Come *on!*' Shannon begged.

The other woman hit the phone box so hard it rocked, and rusted red fell in pieces from the roof. A glass panel higher up smashed inwards, the sound merging with the woman's shriek and the noise of her rattling the door. The belt still wasn't fixed. It started to unravel as the door was pulled. Shannon leapt to her feet and swung the hammer at a remaining piece of glass near the top. It popped outwards, showering shards on the woman outside, whose reaction was to shriek again, her hands lifting instinctively to protect her head, revealing a similar glass hammer in her right hand. Shannon dropped back to her knees, tugging again at the leather belt, wrapping the excess up in her fist for better grip. The belt tightened, crushing her injured fingers. She used the pain to fire herself up, to fuel one last pull. The pin's movement was agonising but it did drop into place. The woman outside was back to shaking the door but the sound of the rattling was muted; the belt looked like it was going to hold. There was no time to wait and see. Instead Shannon spun away from the door to face the handset. She could hear screaming behind her, pitiful and desperate, tailing off into a wail. Then the sound of more glass shattering that fell into her hair and spilt onto her bare feet.

Shannon lifted the handset. There was a tone – *thank God*

there was a tone! The door rattled again behind her, then a hand reached in and she felt a firm pinch in the fleshy part of her back. She spun to the pain and her right hand came down on instinct, the hammer still in it. Shannon felt the impact through her own hand and wrist and the woman in white leapt away, now wailing with pain.

The phone's keypad faced her. A silver coin lay on top of it just like she had been promised; it was freezing cold and the sensation cut through her panic. The wailing woman was soon back, trying to lash out through the gaps in the steel. The phone box shook and glass still smashed – she felt it nip at the underside of her feet with every movement – but she had to focus, just for a moment while she recalled the line of numbers that was scratched into that lintel right below the map. She'd known it was a phone number the moment she had seen it. Shannon could remember the first part clearly. She typed it in . . . 07652 . . . and now she hesitated. When she had tested herself she had been getting the second part wrong a lot; it just didn't seem to want to stick, and she was wrong at least half the time. There was only one coin.

'Fifty, fifty,' she muttered while the door rattled and another shriek filled the space. Shannon was receiving blows in the back, on the arms. She was just out of reach of anything with any power but it didn't help her focus. She typed what she thought was right and got a dialling tone. She held the phone tight to her cheek. The mouthpiece had a tight stretch of film over it that brushed her lips as she mumbled the same word over and over: *please, please, please!*

She turned back towards the woman in white outside, whose assault had paused at least. Now she was still and silent, her right hand gripping one of the slats tightly enough to suggest it was helping her stay up, her knuckles bleeding freely. The two women were locked in a stare. Then the woman outside started to back away, her head shaking, thick tears suddenly spurting down her cheek.

'Hello!' Someone answered the phone to Shannon. The panic and dread were instant, the word more like a rushed breath than a voice.

Shannon froze for a moment; the phrase she was supposed to say wouldn't come. *'Hello?'* the voice said again.

'I had to win,' Shannon said. The words burned all the way from her heaving chest to her thorny throat. The woman outside reacted to the words like a shove that made her stumble backwards, finally tearing her away to turn full circle and scour the rural scene.

'Oh God, no! Please!' The voice down the phone was mournful and desperate and Shannon didn't want to hear it anymore. She dropped the handset for it to bump against the side and swing above where she slumped to sit on the floor. Shards of glass bit and tore at her buttocks and back and dripped from her hair. Her feet out in front of her bled freely over a layer of filth. But she didn't care.

For her, it was over.

Chapter 1

The first blow with the left was a guide for the hard right that landed with a satisfying thud to launch the punchbag up and away before another satisfying noise where it was caught by its rope, then the squeaking of its mechanism made it sound like a wounded animal in retreat as it wiggled and twisted, first away, then back for another blow. This one was heavier still, enough to shake sweat from the brow.

'Detective Inspector Joel Norris!' The voice boomed through the space, carrying enough authority to halt Joel's attack on the bag all at once, but not enough for him to turn towards it. It was 6.30 a.m. and he was in the gym. This was not the time of day when he needed to answer to his full working title; he wasn't on the clock for more than an hour. 'If you were to attach a face to that, would it be anyone in particular?' the voice persisted. Joel didn't recognise it and threw another punch like he wasn't even interested. Which was a lie. He still kept his back to the voice as he moved to his water bottle, taking a deep drink and risking a first glance at his interrupter.

A man in his early fifties, hands on his hips, a stance and smile that communicated a casual confidence. His dark hair was neat and short but with grey taking hold to spread up from the sides in patches, like disease in a conifer. He had a drink too, hot and in an insulated travel cup, the steam that rose from it visible as individual droplets in the strong sunlight that arrowed down at an angle between them. He wore a shirt and tie, his sleeves already rolled up around thick arms with a faded tattoo on his right forearm that was faint enough to look like a youthful mistake. He was tall too, maybe even taller than Joel at six foot one.

'I spoke to my union rep, he told me that any PSD contact needs to be official. This doesn't feel official. You need to announce yourself at least,' Joel said, his hands finding his hips.

'I really need to sort out my tie–shirt combinations if you think I'm from the Professional Standards Department. From what I hear, you've met the whole department anyway.' The stranger's reply kept up the impression of casual confidence.

Joel shrugged. 'There's always more to come out of the woodwork. What do you want?'

'I'm your boss, Joel.'

'My boss?'

'Detective Chief Inspector Jim Kemp. Your new DCI.'

Joel took another swig from his bottle, using the time to further size up the man stood in front of him. 'I might have preferred PSD. At least I can tell them to fuck off.'

DCI Kemp reacted with a half-smile and a shrug. 'You're not on shift 'til eight – technically you could tell me to fuck off if you wanted to. But I can offer you a few reasons why you shouldn't.'

'One will do.'

'I'm not out to get you, Joel. I've worked with a lot of management in my time, some good, some not so good. You know what a good DCI should be?' He gestured with his cup. 'A punchbag. The higher you go, the less power in the hits they can throw. Unless you really mess up, that is. I spoke to PSD yesterday, someone at my level. I told them that anything they need to speak to you about, they speak to me first.'

Joel took another swig to delay the need to reply. This wasn't the first person who had emerged to offer support since the conclusion of the last case he had worked, but even among the supportive voices Joel had managed to pick out an undercurrent of blame. Innocent people had lost their lives and the hindsight brigade had come up with two different summaries of that case in the two months since: it was either a successful arrest and conviction of a very dangerous man, with lives saved due to his fast and brave actions, or it was a shit-show that had cost lives – including that of a serving police officer and an innocent teenage girl.

Even Joel hadn't settled on a version to believe.

Successful or not, the one thing he couldn't argue about was his lack of experience. That had been his first murder investigation and, two months later, it was becoming clear that it might have been his last.

'Whether they speak to you first or come see me in the gym before my shift, I won't be talking to PSD. Not anymore. I told them that.' Joel adjusted his stance so he was stood square on to Detective Chief Inspector Jim Kemp, happy to make it obvious that he was sizing him up.

'Then I'll tell them the same. If you get any direct approaches, take their names and pass them on to me. I'll deal with it.'

'And deny me the chance to tell them where to go? I'm not working for a living anymore – all that's left to look forward to is the occasional ability to swear at PSD. Don't take that away too.'

'Why aren't they working you?' Kemp flashed a smile that died on his lips. He was sizing Joel up too, watching closely for his reaction.

'You tell me, *boss*. I'm currently sat up in an office that I've rejigged to create this professional-looking investigations area, I've started recruiting . . . and for what? Jobs have come in that we could have got involved with and Debbie Marsden's been waving them goodbye on their way to Major Crime. I want to do police work, otherwise what am I?' Debbie

Marsden: the woman responsible for pushing Joel to move from a job he knew and loved as a sergeant on a uniform Tactical Support Group to the rank of inspector, running a team of detectives. She being a superintendent meant there was always going to be someone recruited that would sit between them, but no one had told him it was imminent. Joel's passion was spilling out as anger, something that had been happening more and more recently. Most people had been stepping back from him as a result. Jim Kemp held his ground.

'I spoke to the superintendent at length. Yesterday. She speaks very highly of you.' Kemp found a more permanent smile this time. He was certainly saying the right things.

'Which only makes my position more bizarre. If she rates me and my team she needs to put us to work.'

'Debbie said you were having trouble getting experienced detectives—'

'I don't know if I want experienced detectives,' Joel snapped to cut across his new DCI. 'All I've been hearing about is how I made mistakes. The only mistake I made was trying to be someone I'm not, to be like them. I'm not like them.' Joel's step from passion to anger was complete.

'You're not. You know that's why Debbie put you in this role in the first place?'

'Then she needs to stand by that decision.' Joel suddenly felt like going back to his workout.

'That's exactly why I'm here. Major Crime don't like you but they don't know me. I've made myself a fly on the wall and I've read through everything that has been written about your last case. I also talked to coppers you've worked with before, people who know you. Do you know why the likes of Major Crime don't like you? It's because you're different. It's because you're in the gym at 6 a.m., it's because you have the balls to kick in a door when you probably shouldn't, to threaten the skipper in source handling who wasn't giving you what you needed and to step out in front of a loaded shotgun.

Do you think they would have done that? Not a chance. Every one of them would have waited for the firearms team to come take all the risks.'

'The right thing to do, according to PSD.'

'The right thing to do to preserve your career. Something *experienced* detectives become expert at, better even than catching the bad guys. You spend enough of your career following protocols, leading textbook investigations, and you might forget the most important promise you make when you sign up for this job: *Protect life and limb.* Nothing is more important than that. You did that, the very best you could. And of course you're different in other ways, you're built solid so you look after yourself, no drink problem that I'm aware of, you don't look much like a smoker . . .' He paused for a reaction. Joel shook his head, having let the beginnings of a smile form on his lips. 'First marriage, I'm told, too, and two young daughters, neither of which are bastards?' Kemp's smile was brighter.

'Not in the technical sense of the word.' Joel's smile couldn't be concealed any longer.

'And no mistress, no sordid office-party stories or gambling addiction?'

'No. Is that where I'm going wrong?'

'If you want to be accepted into Major Crime, absolutely. You really are nothing like them.' The DCI swigged from his travel mug. It was gripped in his left hand so that Joel noticed the absence of a wedding ring and wondered how much his new boss had just described himself.

'These last couple of months I decided that I'm not going to change. I was trying to be like them, worrying what they thought of me – wasting my time. I don't give a shit. I know what I'm good at and I'll play up to that, Lucy can fill in the rest.'

'DS Lucy Rose,' Kemp said like he approved. 'Another interesting prospect.'

'The only person who's stood by me and a fine detective. I'm lucky to have her.' He meant it too. There had been a rocky start; Lucy had moved over from a role in Child Protection but her reasons for doing so were a little unusual. The murdered police officer at the centre of the case was a friend of hers and she openly admitted to being appalled that someone with Joel's lack of experience was leading the response. In their first conversation Lucy Rose had mouthed off about how she didn't rate him. He couldn't have known it then, but that conversation was the foundation for a very effective relationship, one that Joel had been hoping to build on. For that to happen, they would need a job.

'What do you need, Joel? From me, I mean?' The increase in Kemp's intensity was marked.

'We just need to get back to work. That's it.'

DCI Jim Kemp burst into a wide smile that caught in the sunlight as he turned away and started towards the exit doors.

'I was hoping you would say that!' he called out, stopping to lean on the door. 'We have a classic Major Crime investigation. It just came in. Dogwalker spots dead body. Victim's a young woman, the injuries sound pretty horrific. I printed the CAD, it's on your desk. The FCR are aware you're heading up first thing and Major Crime have got the Major Hump. Night duty response have the scene. I've already told them that the A-Team will be on their way.' His smile was now heavy with mischief.

'Just came in? How do you even know about it?' Joel said.

'First thing I did was to let the FCR know that anything serious comes to me first, although, as it happens, I heard this one come in on the radio so I was already one step ahead. But they did call. The system worked.'

'You were sat up listening to your police radio in the early hours of the morning?' Joel said and Kemp shrugged.

'It was about an hour ago, hardly the early hours. And I don't sleep well. That's what a broken marriage, a gambling problem and kids by two different women will do to you.' His grin was wider still as he pushed through the door.

Joel threw another punch. His blows had been laden with frustration and disdain just a few minutes earlier, but now the bag squealed and squeaked from a hit powered by hope and excitement. A new case and a new boss. And both had the potential to be pretty interesting.

Day 1

Chapter 2

'Ah, DS Rose, we were just talking about you!' Joel pushed a cup of coffee towards his colleague as she entered the Serious Crime Investigation Team office situated in Kent Police Headquarters. They were in the central building of a network of mostly smaller buildings that were just a couple of minutes' walk away from the Kent Police College and the sports hall where he fancied that punchbag might still be swinging. 'And I made you a coffee.' He pointed up at the clock. 'Six fifty a.m., like clockwork. So predictable.'

'One man's predictable is another man's reliable,' Lucy Rose grumbled and swept up the mug. She took it over to her desk, dumping a rucksack and light jacket before falling heavily into her seat. 'And *DS Rose* again, really?'

A sharp Lucy Rose would have recognised a deliberate attempt to wind her up. 'If ever anyone looked like they needed a coffee. Rough night?' was Joel's reply.

'I didn't sleep well.' DS Rose rubbed at her eyes as if to back up her words. Joel and Lucy had only been working together for a few months but already he knew better than to press her for anything more. Still the only thing he knew about her that wasn't on her personnel file was that she couldn't stand being called DS Rose. Something he had done consistently for their first month together and she had finally reached the point where she had practically burst in front of him, telling him how she hated it, how she had always hated it and *could he not just call her Lucy?* She was a closed book who had the potential to let things build until they exploded. That could certainly make things interesting.

'What's with your mood this morning anyway? I think I prefer you miserable,' DS Rose continued.

'We have a job. We get to do something!'

'A job? Someone trusted us with a job?'

'Our new DCI,' Joel said.

'We have a new DCI?' DS Rose scowled.

'We do. And we have patrols waiting for us out in the Maidstone rural. Victim's a young woman, two types of injury: possible gunshot and stab wounds. Sounds like a messy end. Dog-walker found her body in a phone box.'

'Phone box! They still have those?' DS Rose peered out over the top of her coffee cup.

'Of all the things I just said, that was what you picked out?' Joel said.

Lucy got to her feet. She was noisy as she gulped her coffee. 'Come on then, let's go see this phone box.'

Joel stood in an oppressive heat that seemed to make a mockery of the time of day. The directions had taken them to a place that was much like the rest of the county of Kent: vibrant under the bright light of the sun but thirsty for a drink. The long grass coating the verges on the way in was browned and patchy, while the solitary B road that pushed past the *Welcome To Lenham* sign had a layer of baked-on mud that now looked like a permanent feature, remnants of a winter that seemed like a lifetime ago. The phone box was in the middle of a sloped bank that was sliced in half by a stone pavement and the grass either side was different, resplendent in vivid green. The lower half of the bank that sloped towards the road had a teardrop-shaped bed of colourful flowers dug out of it, with soil that was a deep brown, to fuel suspicions that the whole area had recently been watered. No doubt a local was keeping it going; no way the council were out wasting water on flower gardens when an official drought had been declared. Which local, however, was anyone's guess. The few houses Joel had seen were set back from the road, peeking out from under huge trees or behind squared-off hedges to offer nothing more than a glimpse of a thatched roof, of crisp white render or a shaped window. Joel reflected that if the phone box in the middle of the police cordon was still operational it was surely because someone had forgotten it was even there.

'Hard to believe we could be in the eye of a storm come the weekend,' Joel said. He was referencing 'Storm Andrea', a windstorm that the national news was tracking across Europe, claiming it was on course to cross the English Channel and coming with an amber warning for disruption.

'I heard it's going to miss us completely,' Lucy said and stretched like the journey had been far longer than the fifteen minutes it had taken from the centre of Maidstone.

'Morning.' A patrol officer took a few steps towards them. His marked car was skewed across the road with the *POLICE DO NOT CROSS* tape starting from its closed passenger door. The livery was so bright in the morning sun it was painful to look at. The officer seemed to eye them suspiciously at first, relaxing visibly when Joel produced his warrant and completed introductions. Another uniformed officer was visible further along the path where he was talking to an elderly-looking woman who was doing her best to control a bucking spaniel.

'Is that our witness?' Joel said.

'No, she's at the nick for a statement. We're talking to anyone we see about, just in case.' He shrugged like he knew the chances of anyone being of use out here were slim to none.

'And it's just you two here?' Joel said.

'Just us two.'

'Anyone else on the way?' Joel said. Despite the isolated location, he would need control of a far larger area.

'The early turn are aware. Our lot on nights have been tucked up just about all night. The skipper was coming out with two other patrols at first but they got diverted. An RTC and a 136 both came in together and what with waiting for traffic to get off their arse and all the secure mental health units being full . . . But like I said, the early turn are on now . . .' He faded out, stopping short of voicing what they were both thinking: the early turn would still be round the parade table necking cups of tea, waiting for an emergency call to give them an excuse to stay the hell away. No one liked scene preservation.

'We need to make this cordon wider,' Joel said. 'And close this road from the other end.'

'We've put a sign out at the other end. No one's come past it since we've been here.'

'It's still early. Once people get an idea of what's going on we'll get the usual stream of murder tourists. I'd rather we made it a little more difficult. Can you call up on air and put a rocket up the early turn? Has it been tagged for CSI?'

'First thing we did, sir. There's no one in from CSI to speak to yet. There's no night-turn cover anymore.'

'Of course there isn't!' Joel smiled, he couldn't help it. Sometimes the extent of police cuts was such that all you could do was smile and shake your head. He moved away, calling out his assurances that he would make some calls to the early-turn skipper himself, see if he could get him and his mate off-duty. The lack of resources was an issue for Joel too, although for different reasons. He actually had a budget to recruit more personnel to his team, but that meant DCs who were willing to move from another part of the business, who could be released by their current team and who were good enough to make Joel's team better. This holy trinity of needs was making recruitment just about impossible – for everyone.

Superintendent Debbie Marsden had sold this role to him by telling him *policing was changing* and that he could be a part of that. Major Crime were part of the old guard and had a team on each of the three areas. They were viciously territorial: when a murder was reported in the northern part of the county, two of the three teams had remained sat on their hands, keeping their desks clear, waiting for something to happen on their 'patch'. Joel's team were a centralised investigative team out of Headquarters. They went where they were needed and took the lead, then pulled on the local resources as needed. This was the theory at least. The resistance to change had been stronger than he might have anticipated, but, standing out in the fresh air with a new investigation to get his teeth into, and buoyed by his conversation in the gym that morning, Joel dared to think that they might now be over the worst.

'What time are CSI in?' Joel knew the answer already; he was thinking out loud. DS Rose indulged him anyway.

'Eight. Same time as the rest of our team.' There didn't seem to be any irony in her tone any longer when she said *team*. Nothing was getting done for an hour at least. At least it gave them time to survey the scene before CSI arrived and took over.

The phone box was in a poor state. Joel was a keen cyclist, a hobby that had him exploring villages and rural roads in the county. So he knew there were still red phone boxes hidden among small villages. Generally, however, they were extravagant garden features for the wealthy, or book-swap hubs in the community garden of some well-to-do village. This one seemed different: operational. It even had a handset, though it was hanging down, visible through a door that was wedged open by a protruding leg.

He focused on the victim, a young woman. She was lying on her side, her left leg tucked under her outstretched right.

Joel stepped closer, snapping on a pair of disposable gloves to pull the door open as wide as it would go to get a better look. DS Rose stood just behind him.

'Jesus,' she uttered close to his ear. 'Someone meant it.'

Joel could hardly disagree. He now had a clearer view of a young woman who had never stood a chance. She looked to be in her mid-twenties, pretty too, with an athletic build and long blonde hair that was loose, falling over part of her face. The leg that was pulled up under her was badly damaged by what looked like a blast injury. A chunk of flesh was black and ragged where it surrounded an exposed shin bone. The bone itself was splintered just above the ankle, and with a sizeable piece missing. Her bare foot was connected by just a flap of skin and bent back under the knee. Joel's gaze moved higher up her body to where more injuries were visible. She was wearing a loose white dress that had rucked up enough to reveal a series of ugly puncture wounds in her abdomen. Joel leant in closer.

'Do they look like they're in a row to you?'

'Yeah. I would say they do,' DS Rose agreed.

'Like a sausage on a barbecue,' Joel said.

'If you mean pricked with a fork, then yeah, that would make sense.'

'Only in our world could a woman stabbed to death with a giant fork in a phone box make sense.'

'So, a pitchfork then? Is that what we're saying?' DS Rose said.

Joel took a step away to study where the ground was freshly disturbed. The phone-box door opened out towards the road. The pavement that passed across its front was slim, while the incline looked far more slight than it had from the road. The grass was long enough to show a flattened trail that continued across the edge of the flower garden to snap a few Sweet Rockets and to reinforce the image of the young woman being dragged. The stems all had a uniform bend that gave a sense of the direction: from the road up the incline to the phone box. The thin layer of mud baked onto the road surface wasn't the only substance here; there was blood too. A lot. Its first appearance was in the centre of the road and here the surface looked different. The baked-in mud was gone, removed by a method that had left a fresh looking white scar, like from a directed blast. More blood was stretched out across the road, towards the phone box, gluing strands of grass together as it continued across the bank. Joel and his DS looked at each other.

'So a young woman dressed in a white dress and barefoot has her lower leg blown off by, what, a shotgun? Then she is dragged over a road and finished off in the phone box with a pitchfork in her chest. Is that what we're saying?'

'I don't think so,' DS Rose said. 'Not quite, at least. Look at the blood.' She pointed down at the road. 'There's a pattern, points where the blood's pooled and then where it's smeared in a line.'

'Meaning?'

'I think she dragged herself.'

'With her foot hanging off?' Joel said.

'Adrenaline mixed with desperation – it's possible, we've all seen what people can do. She must have seen the phone and she was trying to get help.'

Joel sighed, long and heavy. 'She would have been slow, very slow. She only makes it to the phone box if the shooter lets her. There's a risk to that, it's a public road. What if a car came along?'

'Look where we are. I don't think that's a problem. Not in the dead of night.'

There were lampposts – three of them – equidistant and jutting out of the grass bank. They seemed to cover this part of the road only. Joel knew that the fact the area would have been lit only mattered if there was someone here to see it. He pulled the phone-box door back open. 'Would you mind holding this for me?' DS Rose took the door, her hands also protected by forensic gloves. Neither detective had used the handle; DS Rose was squatting a little to hold the door near the bottom. Joel reached in for the woman's chin and pushed his fingers into her neck for a pulse.

'They already did that,' DS Rose said.

'Old habits,' Joel replied. He changed his grip to try and lift her head up by her chin. A human head is a heavy item but he couldn't move it. Joel didn't want to force it and abandoned his attempt. Next, he moved on to her left arm, which lifted with no resistance. 'What do you know about rigor mortis?' he said.

DS Rose shrugged. 'Takes a couple of hours, different for everyone and can vary massively depending on temperature, position of the body . . .'

'Extremes of temperature, we don't have that here. The way she's sat it would start in the jaw and neck. Two to four hours is the normal time for it to take effect. Her neck feels pretty rigid, but her limbs still have flexibility. The extremities are the last to be affected.'

'Someone's been reading their murder manuals!' DS Rose scoffed.

'I considered I might have some catching up to do.' Joel still studied the body. He was desperate to see what other injuries she had. She was filthy, her hands particularly, and Joel knew he could be staring at key evidence trapped under those nails. CSI would be here soon, but patience was not his strongest asset. 'The handset,' Joel said, standing back up to stop his thighs burning, 'I can't see a way she could have got that off the hook – adrenaline or not.'

'So someone else did? The killer, you mean?'

'Maybe . . . or maybe she got to the phone first to be dragged back out. But I think . . .' Joel hesitated, his mind suddenly rushing with horrendous images that had no place on a picturesque country lane, 'I think she was being toyed with at the end.'

Chapter 3

A few hours earlier

Margaret Marshall watched the beginnings of a new day from her kitchen window. It wasn't so much a sunrise as a gradual brightening, the source seemingly a strip of light across the top of the opposite side of the valley. She had always felt so lucky to live here, with its sprawling views that, at this time of the year, were a patchwork of greens, browns and corn yellow. She could almost fool herself that the valley she could see, and all the nature contained within it, was the whole world. That she was all alone and completely safe.

But she had never felt more terrified.

Her phone was ringing.

At first, she just stared at it, her terror freezing her rigid while her screen showed a row of numbers that started with her local area code. She had been told that if a call was to come it would be a local call, it would be at first light and she would need to answer it. Those instructions were the reason she had spent the night sitting right there, watching the big, bright moon slowly glide across the valley, praying it would stop, never to give way to the dawn.

She took hold of the phone, almost dropping it, her hands were shaking so badly. She clamped her eyes shut.

'Hello!' Her voice came out shaky too. The reply was delayed, it needed another prompt and was delivered by a stranger who sounded out of breath.

'I had to win!'

Instantly Margaret felt numb. The only feeling left was a sensation of ice starting in her chest and moving out to encompass her whole body. Then her own voice sounded like it was coming out through sound-deadening, like it was someone else doing the talking, someone else begging.

'Oh God, no! Please! Please just don't hurt her!'

There was a thumping sound from the other end. Margaret was so tense it made her jump, her lips making a whistling sound where she sucked in a breath so fast. 'Please!' she tried again but her throat was closing all the time and it came out as a squeak. She could hear a voice now, distant, low and shouted. A man's voice. Then a creaking sound like a door in a horror movie. Another sound took over, dominating so it was all she could hear. It was a shriek, long and powerful until it fell away to a whine. Then came a shout, a woman's voice this time; this one she recognised. It was Kelly. And she was begging for her life.

Margaret forced words out: 'Kelly! KELLY!' It was no use, Kelly sounded like she was some distance away from the phone, too far to hear. Then everything was drowned out by a *BOOM!* Margaret held her breath. There were more shouts, then Kelly's voice again. This time there were no words, no begging, now it was just anguish. Shrieks of pain. The shrieks got closer. Slowly but surely, like Margaret herself was dragging a wounded animal towards her on a rope. She had the phone pressed so hard against her ear that the pain registered through her horror. She heard the same creaking door sound. Now Kelly's cries were much closer, close enough that she might hear her.

'Kelly! KELLY! KELLY, talk to me, Kelly . . . KELLY!' The voice she heard wasn't a reply, it was begging again, but now it was just one word repeated. 'No'. Louder, quicker, each time with more fear. 'No. No, NO! NOOOOOO!'

Then the voice stopped. Margaret took the phone away from her ear to check the display, to check the call was still live. When she pushed it back to her ear there was something. A sort of cough that she was still able to recognise as Kelly, like she was failing at clearing her throat. Then the sound changed again.

Now it was the sound of her drowning.

Margaret held the phone tight against her right ear, her left hand just as firm over her mouth, tight enough that she couldn't breathe through it. Then a click that made her flinch and all sounds were gone.

The call had been cut.

Chapter 4

Joel, accompanied by DS Rose, swept past the two rows of empty desks that were closest to the door to make for the front of the office where there was some life at least. He had been promised a brand-new team in a brand-new office. So far, he had a stolen office space, two detectives and an intelligence-officer-cum-analyst who was brand new to policing. It was his intelligence analyst that he wanted to speak with and, as usual, she was the only person around.

'Eileen . . . tell me you have something. I think we just found the only public spot in the whole country where someone can take their time committing the loudest murder possible and then disappear into the night.'

'Loudest?' Eileen Holmans sat back and shook her head with accompanying blinks. She had half-sized glasses. Joel was convinced that she didn't need them at all; they were just something to peer over when she was looking at him, to make her seem more disapproving. She was doing it now. 'Is that what you want me to put on the log? That DI Norris's first impression of the scene was that it *would have been loud?*'

'You can jazz it up a bit. Something like how the *good-looking and charismatic detective noted scarred tarmac consistent with a shotgun discharge . . .*'

Eileen still peered out over the top of her glasses for a deadpan response. 'I think I'll word the log if it's all the same to you.' And Joel laughed. He couldn't say that the glasses didn't fit with the rest of her. She habitually wore a long skirt and heavy cardigan: dowdy perhaps, comfortable for sure. It would have made it difficult for Joel to guess her age had he not seen on her application that she was only fifty-six. She had done nearly thirty years' teaching before illness had come out of nowhere to claim her husband and tear up their plans for retirement. The reaction had been changes in many aspects of her life. One of those changes was her career, where, after doing what she needed to get her full pension from teaching, she switched to work for Kent County Council after applying for a role investigating and enforcing fly-tipping incidents. It seems the excitement of forcing the scum of Kent to clean up their own mess wasn't enough to hold her and, as she described in her interview, she was desperate to take the thrill of the chase up a level. Working for the police was the obvious choice, but the carpet slippers in her bag for her to change into on her first day suggested, to Joel at least, that she was still keen to tightly control the excitement. No one else on the interview panel had picked her out as a candidate but Joel had adored her immediately. He spotted someone with an incredible attention to detail, computer and analytical skills that belied her background and a natural ability to get what she wanted. It didn't matter to him if she was wearing carpet slippers when she did it. It also suited Joel to have someone on his team he could rely on to be sat at a computer screen with access to all police systems whenever that was required. The job as his intel analyst was hers the moment she first held him in that glare over the top of those glasses.

'Fair enough,' Joel said.

'Definitely a shotgun?' Eileen asked.

'That's how it looked to me. Close range, possibly adapted

or sawn-off due to the size of spread, fired downwards at her ankle.'

'I'll put early signs *suggest* the use of a shotgun. And she was on the ground when she suffered this wound?' Eileen asked.

'Early signs suggest it.' Joel couldn't hold back his grin, but it fell away as he continued. 'She had plenty of bruises and marks on her arms, face and upper body. CSI will give us a fuller picture when they've done a body map, but I would say she was beaten to the ground.'

'Beaten to the ground, her foot just about blown off and then she dragged herself into a phone box where she was stabbed with a pitchfork.' DS Rose gave her first input, the shock in her voice thickening with every word.

'OK, all presumption at this stage, of course,' Eileen said, without breaking stride. Joel spoke next.

'A horrific end, whatever happened. That's why we need you to tell us all about the breakthrough you got when you looked at the phone records, so we can pop out and nail this bastard.'

Eileen stopped her typing to peer up and over at him again. 'Not sure you'll be popping out to nail anyone, nor am I sure that sort of language is necessary. We don't know for sure that our offender is from a broken home, after all. Unless you would like to me to insert that description on the log, also as a presumption?'

'And the phone records?' Joel said, ignoring his telling-off.

'I'm afraid I may not be able to offer much at this stage. I got onto BT. They confirmed that the phone box is functioning, though earmarked to be decommissioned once a new mobile phone mast goes live nearby to extend the network coverage. They were quite happy to provide records of its use. That phone box has ten phone calls listed in the last three months. I am in the process of acquiring the details. My focus however is looking at the call that was made today at 5.10 a.m.'

'Go on?'

'I don't want to get your hopes up, Inspector. Someone dialled out to a mobile phone, but it is what is known as a *burner*. As a stroke of luck the SIM for the burner was provided by BT too – a different department but they were able to fast-track me through to the person who could help me the most. They matched the number with an IMEI and—'

'Is there a short answer in there somewhere?' Joel cut in, well aware that Eileen was incredibly thorough in all aspects of her work – perhaps more than she needed to be when it came to updates. She huffed.

'As I was saying, it's a burner phone. Not shop bought. Probably eBay or a market stall – and old enough to have been in circulation a while.'

'So, untraceable.'

'Yes.'

'Mast triangulation?'

'There is some good news here, at least according to the expert I spoke to at BT. There's only one mast involved.'

'Meaning?'

'Meaning it was a local call. From a location point of view at least. Phone masts work by passing calls from one to another, it would seem – they sort of hand a call over. This one didn't.'

'So we have a radius? Something to narrow it down to?'

'We do, but this is where the good news runs out. A mast servicing a rural area can easily cover 10 square kilometres, which, from that location, would stretch to cover Maidstone, including where we are right now. Densely populated and with no way of narrowing the search.'

'What about an active trace? If it's still talking to the mast then we can get the location.'

'It is not.'

'They switched it off.'

'Switched off, destroyed, dropped down a drain.' Eileen shrugged. 'We just know it is not talking to the network.'

Joel had been resting on one of the numerous empty desks. Now he began to pace. 'Suggestions then. A call was made at or around the time our victim was murdered. Why and by whom?'

'That call had to be linked to the victim,' DS Rose said. Joel stared at her to prompt further explanation. 'There's only two reasons to make a call that I can think of: you're either calling someone on your side, someone who might be able to help you clear it up . . . or you're calling someone linked to the victim.'

'To tell them what you've done?' Joel said.

'Maybe?'

'Or the poor girl made the call? She was the one asking for help?' Eileen was back to staring over her glasses, this time waiting for a reaction.

'Why call a mobile phone number? If you're in peril like that, you'd call 999, wouldn't you?' Joel was thinking out loud. At that point there was no answer to that question. 'And you're monitoring the FCR, seeing what calls have come in to us?' Joel referred to another task he had given Eileen over the phone.

'I am. No one's called 999 to tell us they've received a call from a woman in distress, or anything like what we have. I had a look at mispers in the surrounding areas too and there's nothing that matches the description of our young woman. I can have a look at reports of threats or stalking cases that have been called in, even domestic violence reports, but we're talking of a lot of time-consuming work that might be for nothing. I assume work is ongoing to get the poor thing identified? Once I have a name I can be a lot more efficient with my time.'

'I get that. We put her through the lantern while I was there and it came up with nothing.' The lantern was effectively a mobile phone with a fingerprint scanner strapped to its back. The memory of the woman's cold, dead fingers being manipulated against the glass was still fresh in Joel's mind.

'So she isn't known to police,' Eileen said.

Joel shrugged. 'Her prints aren't. Every day more drop off our database though. Another win for data protection legislation in the battle to make our jobs as difficult as possible.'

'If it was our killer that used that phone then the handset might have something for us. DNA loves a hard plastic surface,' DS Rose said.

'It does,' Joel sighed then took back to pacing.

'But . . .?' DS Rose said.

'Nothing's making any sense. A fit young woman with no police record in the arse end of nowhere, wearing a dress that looked . . . I dunno, I don't understand fashion these days but it didn't look right, it certainly wasn't fitted. And she was barefoot. Her murder wasn't quick either. Someone knew they had time. This phone call too . . . I agree with Lucy, that call had something to do with our victim. If it was the offender asking for help to dispose of the body, to clean up, why hasn't that happened? So why . . .' Joel rubbed at his face, his words falling away for DS Rose to complete his line of thought.

'Why haven't we had anyone come forward to tell us they've just had the worst phone call of their life?' she asked.

'Exactly.'

'There's only one explanation I can think of.' DS Rose was shaking her head, her eyes glazed like she was inside her mind. 'This murder, that scene we have out there on that country lane, it's only part of the story.'

Chapter 5

'There's really no need for you to wait here, Billy. Who knows how long these things can take.' Margaret spoke to her friend Billy Easton, whose discomfort was becoming more and more obvious. They were both sat out on the solid plastic chairs of the waiting room of Maidstone General Hospital Accident and Emergency Department and on another day she would have been squirming and huffing just as much as her companion. But today was different. Today she could barely feel the firmness of the seat, or the fact that the stiff plastic back was angled just right to dig into the loose skin under her arms. Today she could barely feel anything.

As glad as she had been to see a friendly face, she was now beginning to wish he would just go. Billy was Margaret's next-door neighbour. They had struck up a close relationship right from the start, having moved in at around the same time. Margaret had been struggling with some mobility issues from a broken foot that had taken its time healing and Billy had immediately been a great help. Even with a removal firm, moving house is a physical activity and he'd spent the first week putting up shelves, reassembling furniture – even taking care of the food shopping – all before sorting out his own place. Margaret had felt bad at first; she wasn't keen on using people like that, but he had never seemed to mind in the slightest, even insisting that he liked helping her out, that it made him feel useful. They had a few things in common. Both had suddenly found themselves alone when their respective partners had announced their wish for a divorce. Hers she had seen coming enough to be prepared, but she had the impression that Billy had been a little more caught out. Both had been left with a bad taste in their mouths and with a general feeling of being too bitter and too beaten to look again for a happily-ever-after. Margaret was on her own and determined to make the best of it, and the move to a remote country cottage was an important step. She had yearned to be somewhere quiet, somewhere to feel safe.

The serenity had lasted almost four years, but the chaos of the outside world had still found her and it was the reason she was here now. Her breathing was still shallow, her pulse still racing, and at first the doctor had suspected an angina attack. The early test results however had been communicated by a chuckling nurse as 'nothing more worrying than a panic attack'. Margaret hadn't laughed; it didn't make her feel any better. She had played it down, told the medical professionals how it had just come from nowhere and that she was fine. The medical staff and Billy, with his leathery hand holding hers, had all smiled together as they had agreed that anxiety can just come on, that there doesn't have to be a reason.

But there had been a reason. A shrill phone call had cut through an unobstructed sunrise view to enter the one place she had come to feel safe. But it didn't now. Even there, evil had found a way in. It had come right to her door, laid out her very worst nightmare and then confirmed its completion in the uttering of a single sentence:

I had to win.

Chapter 6

Joel broke into a jog to cross the four three lanes of traffic choking the life out of Maidstone's town centre. He was heading towards a grey multi-storey car park, the bottom two levels of which were grandly labelled as "Chequers Bus Station." DS Rose was waiting under the sign on the pavement.

'I told you we could have parked at the nick and just walked from here,' she grumbled.

'Have you tried parking at Maidstone nick? You need a signed permission letter from the Chief Constable and a shoehorn.'

'Someone was supposed to be here to meet us,' DS Rose said. Joel took a moment to take in their environment. The whole area was bustling. The only other people standing still were those forming the queues for the rumbling busses that rattled and whined, locked in a constant one-in, one-out conga. Everyone else had their head down. The bus 'station' was more a two-way road cut into the Chequers Shopping Centre. The left side was assigned as the waiting area for passengers and an extra wide corridor offered facilities such as angled, plastic bases jutting out of the wall to masquerade as seats, tiled floors with filth for grout and whole sections of wall inexplicably made of thick, translucent glass. Its design was surely to combat the lack of any natural light, but it only seemed to serve as another place to show up a layer of grime. The ceiling that came close to the top of the double-decker buses also served to amplify the hissing hydraulics as they came to a stop and threw open their doors. It was enough to make Joel flinch as he walked deeper into the throng.

'Do we have a number to call again?' Joel was running low on patience. From the moment Eileen Holmans had spotted a significant call being put onto the system by an operator in the Force Control Room, Joel had been anxious to get answers. It was the first possibility of any sort of lead, something that might give them a clue as to what the hell had gone on overnight in the village of Lenham. A call had come into the non-emergency number from a bus driver who might not have called had his ex-police-officer-colleague not told him that he should. He had called at the end of his shift about an incident from his first loop where he had picked up a young woman who was filthy and upset and had needed to beg for a lift with no money and no phone. Of course he had agreed that she could ride back to the station; she seemed really scared about something and, the weirdest part of all, she had been wearing a dirty-looking dress with no shape, described as looking like a red sack. Joel had been on his way out of the door before Eileen had even finished reading out the part where she was also barefoot.

'Officers?' An employee of the bus company emerged from the crowds and greeted them cheerily. He wore a clip-on tie over a short-sleeved shirt that had creases ironed into the arms to the point of looking dangerous. He held his hands in the small of his back to rock onto his heels. He was mid to late fifties with a moustache up top, a pot belly for the middle and highly polished Dr Martens shoes for the bottom. His name tag announced him as Norman Kepple but he still repeated it in his introduction. The name of the bus company was sewn at an angle into the triangular part of his tie.

'Retired and topping up your pension!' Joel voiced a hunch he had. 'Kent?'

'Met for the first half, Kent for the second. Traffic mainly and I know that's not always the popular choice! Did my thirty though. I must still have that copper vibe!' He seemed delighted.

He would be the 'ex-police-colleague' mentioned in the call then. He stank of ex-job: *eau d'ex copper*. It was a scent that lingered on them all. 'There's definitely something about you. Are you the man that can help us with our enquiries today?'

Norman gave another rock on his heels, his face still the absolute picture of delight. 'Best I can, any police enquiries tend to come through me. They worked out pretty quick that I might know both sides of the fence as it were. I've been here a few years now. Started as a driver but I've been taking on more and more of the security elements and now it's pretty much my bag.'

'We're definitely speaking to the right man then.'

'Let's hope so! So, you've got a young woman gets on a bus out at Lenham looking a bit bloodied and beat up. It's not Henry's normal route but I guess it would look out of place to anyone. Good lad is Henry. He wasn't sure what to do, bless him, so he came and spoke to me. I told him to call it in straightaway, but by then a fair bit of time had passed. Still, I assume you would like to have a look at her.'

'Yes, if we can.'

'Right this way!' Norman set off at a pace. He aimed for a set of double doors that was signposted *Shopping Centre / Toilets*. The CCTV room was one of the first rooms inside the shopping centre and the door to it could easily be missed between two blinking wall-mounted cash machines and a vending machine. Joel was just glad to be away from the din.

Access was gained by a coded lock and two further keys that extended out on a bungy from Norman's pocket. Once inside, the room was laid out with two monitors next to each other in the middle, a chair on wheels in front. One side of the monitors had a neat stack of folders, the other a stack of writeable DVDs still sealed in their packets. It was every bit the environment to be expected of an ex-traffic officer.

'The buses all have internal CCTV, you see. Henry was in earlier so I burned all his footage over to this . . .' He pointed at a memory stick that was stuck in the front of the computer tower. 'Once I knew where she got on I was able to run the footage to the exact minute when he should have been there, and . . .' Norman pressed something on the keyboard and both monitors came on at once. One was a blue screen with icons arranged in a neat pattern, the other was a still image of a bus door, viewed from the inside. 'Here we are: 6.34 a.m. Henry's one of our more reliable drivers. Been doing it a while, he knows how to make a timetable work. This would have been the first bus from that location.' Norman's excitement was peaking. He pressed play and the footage showed the bus doors opening. An elderly woman was first on. She was pulling a trolley behind her; it caught on the lip of the floor and there was movement behind her as someone came to help. A young woman dressed in a plain red dress with thick shoulder straps stooped forward to ease it over the lip. The elderly woman didn't even seem to realise; she barely turned around. The woman in red was next on. Her hair had a red tint to it too, although in a far lighter shade than her clothing. She stood there talking to the driver for several minutes; Joel could see the people waiting behind her. They seemed to be keeping their distance.

'She stands out.' It was Joel's first reaction. The CCTV was good quality, good enough that he could see the layer of filth on her neck and the tops of her arms and chest. It looked like she had pushed it around on her face a little, maybe where she had tried to clean herself up. Her exhaustion was clear even from the way she was standing. She was gesturing in an increasingly agitated way.

'There's no sound?' Joel asked.

'Afraid not. However . . .' Norman lifted a piece of A4 paper to give to Joel. The first few sentences were in a format that was instantly familiar – *on day, date, time* – the standard police statement opening. It went on to give a detailed and chronological account from Henry from the moment his shift started. Joel skimmed it to note the registration of the bus was included, and descriptions of other passengers, and then the detail increased when it got to the part that covered the driver's conversation with the woman in red. The handwritten account even had Norman's initials at the end, and he had ensured that Henry had also signed it as 'correct to the best of my knowledge'.

'This is fantastic. You don't fancy a return, do you, Norman? I happen to have a couple of spaces on my team.'

'Oh no, thank you very much. Thirty years was just about enough for me. I figured I might be able to save you some work.' Joel was done skimming and he passed it to DS Rose. Norman summarised the content anyway. 'She didn't have any money. Some drivers I know might've left her there but Henry's one of the good guys. He said he took one look at her and saw that she might be in a bit of strife. He offered to call someone for her straightaway, but she said she was OK, said she just needed to get back to here.'

'And she definitely said *back* to here?' Joel said and Norman pointed at the written statement.

'I asked the same question and it's in there. She said *back*.'

'And she got off at this bus station?' Norman's response this time was to work his mouse. The screen changed to external CCTV. Instantly the quality was worse. It looked like the footage was from a camera hovering over the walkway they had just taken. It showed a single-decker pull up and its double doors open to let a steady stream of people emerge. The woman in red was the second to last one out but now she was wearing a different top. It was light grey in colour, hooded, with sleeves that were too long for her. The angle of the camera allowed a glimpse of her feet when she stepped out; they were still bare. She stopped momentarily, turning back to the last passenger to exit – a man, tall and slim, white-skinned, dressed for an office and with a holdall-style bag heavy enough to cause a visible dip in his shoulder. There was a brief exchange between the two and then they left in different directions.

'Is there any other coverage? Anything that might give us a clue where she went next?'

Norman was shaking his head before Joel had finished his sentence. 'Nothing that I've got. I can tell you she took the Romney Place exit, which is away from the centre, but you could go anywhere from there. The council have their own cameras up; she might have walked onto them if she stuck in the town. You'll see from Henry's account that he gave her a fiver, it was all he had in his wallet. He said she could go and get some breakfast at least.'

'And did she say she would?' Joel glanced back over to where Lucy was still reading through Henry's statement.

'No, but you see someone dirty, half-dressed and barefoot at that time of the day and I s'pose you just have them down as hungry. Henry said that if she didn't eat with it, at least he knew she could make a phone call.'

'He is one of the good ones.'

'He is. You see things on buses, a lot of things. The company has a policy for the drivers not to get involved; just report it. Be a good witness, they say. But things like this you can't ignore. Is she OK?'

'OK?'

'The woman? With respect, in my day you wouldn't get a Guv'nor and a skipper out on enquiries unless it was life or death. I know times change but I don't reckon it's changed that much.'

'You're right. We're part of a team that investigate crimes

where serious violence is involved. I can't tell you details, Norman, but trust me, mate, you wouldn't want to hear them anyway.'

'You're right about that. Thirty years of seeing those sights and hearing those tales was enough for me. I don't even watch the news anymore. She's walking OK though . . . Henry said she had scrapes and bruises but if he thought she was seriously injured he would have—'

'He did the right thing, more than others might have.' Joel cut him off before the inevitable follow-up question came. 'I don't think she's seriously hurt, seems she was lucky.'

Norman narrowed his eyes to fix on Joel. 'Someone else wasn't so lucky, were they?'

'That's exactly what I want to ask her. Are you *sure* you don't fancy a return, Norman? We're always looking for good detectives.'

Chapter 7

For Margaret Marshall, the approach when coming back to her house from the hospital had been entirely alien. This was a place that had always been warm and bright. Its position high up the side of the valley meant that when the sun was out it would drench the Kent Peg tiles unabashed, accentuating the different shades of browns and orange. Even a rainy day did little to dull its impact; the moisture would darken the browns but lighten the orange to stand out, so driving towards it conjured thoughts of a cosy fireplace; the last embers before bed.

Today the sun was bright but the moment she was inside with the door shut, the overriding feeling was cold and empty. The hall that stretched out before her seemed dark and foreboding, despite the light that poured into her lovely country kitchen at the end – the one she had commissioned a local kitchen fitter to make bespoke for her with the money left over from the move. She'd never had a brand-new kitchen before. It was a little treat to help with the transition. But that was then.

And this was now.

This was 3 p.m. on the day her life had changed forever. This was the deathly silence of being alone, a silence that confirmed that Kelly wasn't here waiting like she had dared to hope, to say she was sorry for the misunderstanding and they would never have to leave the house again.

Margaret leant against the front door and slid down to the floor. Her mobile phone was in her bag. She took it out and bit down hard as she skipped past the screensaver – two young women beaming out at her – to bring up the keypad. Three tones for three taps on the screen. She lifted it to her ear.

'Police . . .' she said, her rasping voice reverberating down her own hallway. 'I need to report a missing person . . . I'm really worried.' The voice on the other end of the phone was male. He was talking and she detected a question but got none of the words as she started to break down. 'Please . . . just send someone . . . It's my daughter . . . She never made it home.'

Chapter 8

The trees grouped together in the basin of the valley gave way to reveal rolling fields sloping gently upwards. The reveal also included a row of cottages. It was a beautiful scene; the sort of place where you might be forgiven for believing that the world was only waving trees and pleasant sunlight. Joel hated this part of the job, the part where he needed to be the one bringing the darkness.

'We're sure, aren't we?' It was a rhetorical question, a sign of his nerves.

'I am.' Lucy's response was just what he needed to assure him they were in the right place, that Margaret Marshall was the person they needed to speak to. Hers was the life that was about to feel an awful lot darker.

The name had come from Eileen. She had been interrogating the systems for current mispers when a new call had come in. Margaret Marshall had phoned to report her daughter missing. She had given a description, one that loosely matched their victim, and Eileen had taken that as a starter. A few minutes on a couple of social media platforms and, using the profile pictures of a smiling young woman, she was able to confirm what they had. They had a name for their murdered woman: ***Kelly Marshall***. Eileen had written it up on the whiteboard in the incident room, followed by ***Victim***. They had all fallen silent and stepped back to take it in. They all knew what it meant.

Once they had a victim, a person to tell was quick to follow. Kelly Marshall was on the police system but as a VCO – Victim of Crime Only – when she had made a burglary report a few months earlier. She couldn't identify if anything had been stolen, it was more that items had been moved in her flat and a back door found unlocked when she was sure she had locked it. There was nothing she could prove and, from reading the closure report, the attending officers hadn't been sure anything had happened at all. But Kelly's actions were those of someone far more convinced. She would stay somewhere else that night. The officers had recorded it, noting it as her mum's address: the cottage now drenched in sunlight in front of them.

Joel took a deep breath. The house was the middle of a row of three with obvious clues that it had previously been a single large farmhouse. The divisions were crude and looked relatively recent with some windows and doors bricked up by a newer stock to stand out like scars. The neighbour on the left side had a curtain that twitched. A man's face appeared behind it, overrun with wrinkles that bunched up into a look of concern. Joel ignored the neighbour to knock on Margaret Marshall's door.

She looked tired, as if standing up was a conscious effort. Joel was aware that he was wearing a lanyard that, combined with his shirt and tie, would make it obvious whom he represented. Still there was no sign of the energy he might expect when responding to a call from a mother missing her daughter. Instead, the first impression from her seemed to be one of resignation.

'Mrs Marshall?' The woman nodded and stepped backwards into a long, dim hall. There was a glimpse of daylight at the far end and he and DS Rose were led towards it. They were greeted with a country-style kitchen with skylights providing shafts of light through a sloped roof.

'Do you have news?' Margaret's voice rasped, like her words were forced through a dry throat. She watched him intently, her misery held back by a stoic face and a layer of foundation that seemed a shade too light and added gauntness to her look of exhaustion. She was wearing a white scarf that looked to be silk and also did nothing for someone flushed of all colour.

'Perhaps we might move into the living room, somewhere we can sit down and talk.'

'Bad news then.' Margaret somehow managed to droop even more where she stood. Her eyes glazed over, and the focus still didn't return when her front door made a sound like someone was lifting the knocker to let it fall in a pattern. There was no reaction at all, like maybe she hadn't even heard it.

'Are you expecting someone?' Joel said.

'It's Billy's knock, he lives next door. He took me to the hospital earlier. He'll be worried about me.'

'Should we let him in? It might be good to have someone here with you.'

'Just tell me. Tell me where my Kelly is. You've found her, haven't you?'

Joel made eyes at DS Rose who got the message and moved away to answer the door. 'I'm very sorry, Mrs Marshall, we have found her. I'm afraid she was deceased when we did.'

That was it. The standard police delivery when breaking bad news: tell them straight, then deal with the fallout. Joel had been the officer delivering bad news more than enough times, but it was rare he would have to say the whole sentence. People just knew. Parents especially. Maybe today it was the lack of any props – no hat to take off and tuck under his arm, no radio strapped to his chest to turn down, so his attention was undivided. Just a lanyard to fumble with awkwardly, a tie to straighten.

The words didn't seem to go in. Not at first. If Margaret Marshall had been resigned to receiving bad news, she showed signs of fighting it now. She even straightened up, pulling her shoulders back to puff out her chest while her hands took on the shape of fists. But she was still looking beyond him, her eyes lacking focus. Whatever images she was seeing now, they were internal. She muttered indiscernible words. Joel stepped a little closer to try and pick them out but they were lost to a sudden noise, a male voice from down that long hall, a question aimed at DS Rose but asked in a voice deep enough to rumble past her and fill the kitchen: 'Where is she?'

'What happened?' Margaret spoke next, her focus snapping back and fixing on Joel. Her fists unravelled, the strength that had straightened her up now seem to leave in a hurry and she rested the flat of her palms on the kitchen side for support.

'She was found on the other side of Maidstone from here, six miles from her home address, in a village called Lenham. The circumstances of her death, Mrs Marshall, they're very concerning.'

'Murdered?' she muttered and her attention was gone again, like she was back to studying more internal images.

'I believe she was,' Joel said. 'How about we move to somewhere where we can sit down.'

'Murdered! Who was murdered!' Joel turned to see the same face he had seen through the window from outside, but with the wrinkles now arranged to show his shock. 'What the hell is going on, Margaret!' the man said. He reached out to take her by the wrist. She shrugged him off to move for the living room.

'I think she could do with a drink. A cup of tea, perhaps.'

Joel spoke to him, positioning himself to block the man from continuing after her. 'It's Billy, right?'

'Yeah. She has coffee.' The shock was still raw on his face.

'Coffee then, perfect. She's going to need you, Billy, more than ever if you don't mind sticking around. But we need to speak to her first, OK? We need to try and work out what's going on here. I'm sure you don't mind?'

'No . . . Of course . . . I'll make some coffee.'

'Great,' Joel said and Billy spun away, looking a little unsteady. A cupboard slammed where he was clumsy with it. Joel was sure he would be OK. Billy wasn't his main focus.

Margaret had sat in a leather armchair that made her look smaller somehow. It had a high back and arms that were carved in dark wood to roll outward with a flourish. Joel sat in the matching three-seater just off to her right. And he waited. The only sound was the loud ticking of a clock to time the silence.

'Murdered. My little girl.' Margaret lifted her eyes to meet with the inspector. 'She would never go out of her way to upset anyone, never to hurt them, that's for sure. You raise two girls like that . . . beautiful, clever . . . just amazing girls and you know you're going to have problems. Creeps and weirdos!' Her face flickered a smile. 'That's what Nicola used to call them.'

'Nicola. Is that your other daughter?'

'Kelly's big sister, not that you would think it. Two daughters is a constant worry – the creeps and the weirdos – but I never worried about Kelly, not really. I just never felt like I had to. She's got real spirit, that one. You wouldn't mess with her.' There was new intensity in her stare now as she locked back onto the inspector. 'Who on earth did this? And how?'

Joel stumbled over his first words. Despite the situation his own mind had wandered – back to the village of Elham, to his own family home, to his own two daughters. 'We . . . we don't know for sure, it's still very early. We need—'

'You've seen her. You said you were an inspector, and your friend here is a sergeant. You're investigating, that means you've seen her. I'm right, aren't I?' Margaret cut in.

'You are,' Joel said.

'So what did you see?'

'Mrs Marshall, I think—'

'I deserve to know. I want to know. You tell me what you saw, you tell me what happened to my little girl and you tell me now!' She pointed with a crooked finger.

'It's not a pleasant thing to listen to. Are you sure—'

'You think anything is going to make this day a pleasant one? You're building up to ask me to come and see her anyway, to identify her. You need me to do that, right?'

'I might.'

'My husband had to do it with his brother. I know how this works, but I will need to be prepared. So what the hell happened?'

Joel sat back a little. He could sense DS Rose staring over at him. 'Kelly was found by a woman out walking her dog first thing this morning. It was already too late to do anything for her. Kelly had a significant injury to her foot, the sort that would have incapacitated her. We think maybe that fighting spirit got her to a phone box where she could call for help. We don't think she made that call. She also received several puncture wounds to her torso. An autopsy will take place that might give us more of an idea . . .'

'Stabbed? What on earth did she do to deserve that!'

'I'm so sorry, Mrs Marshall. I know this is a terrible shock.'

'You've taken your meds, your pills?' Billy's reappearance was sudden, his words abrupt. He pushed past Joel, slopping a coffee down on a stacked nest of tables and leaning in to fuss.

'Yes. Billy, please. I'm OK.'

Billy straightened up and glared back towards Joel, his gaze heavy with accusation. 'She's not been well, not well enough for this. This morning we had a trip out to the hospital. Suspected angina attack.'

'But it wasn't angina, was it? It was a panic attack at best. Nothing more.' Margaret tutted.

'You need to be looking after yourself, that's all I mean, you're not in the right frame of mind for all these questions, all this pressure. Does this have to be now?' Again Joel was the subject of his stare, but it was Margaret who answered her neighbour.

'I'm fine and when I'm not, *I* will be sure to let you know. This needs to be done, Billy. If not now, when?' Mrs Marshall's snappy start faded fast; that spirit might have reached its limits. She took a few deep breaths then was able to reach for her drink. The saucer clattered where her hand shook. She peered over the top of the cup while she drank, taking in the detectives first but settling on Billy. 'Did you not make tea for my guests?' she said.

'I just wanted to make sure you were OK.'

'Would you mind?' she said. Billy hesitated but he did move back towards the kitchen. Margaret opted to hold her cup in her lap, perhaps aware that it might be better to conceal her shake. 'You must be thinking we're like an old married couple. I go to a coffee morning once a week, down in the village. They all say it, they all call us the old married couple, but it's just a very lovely friendship and I must try harder not to snap at him like that. He's very good to me.'

'I'm sure you're very good for each other. The moment we pulled up Billy was at his window giving us the eye.' Joel chanced a chuckle. 'If I was a burglar I would have turned away instantly.'

'He does have his uses. He makes a terrible cup of coffee though.' She grimaced at the cup in her lap.

'Mrs Marshall, are you OK? We're not going to need to run you back to the hospital any time soon, are we?'

'No, don't talk nonsense. I've suffered panic attacks since . . . well, since my husband upped and left. Every now and then they can catch me out. Kelly was supposed to come round today, this morning. She didn't turn up and I couldn't get hold of her and I just knew . . . I knew there was something wrong. She would never do that!'

'Tell me about Nicola. What does she look like?' he said.

'Look like? What does that matter?' Margaret snapped.

'I just want to eliminate her. We might have a witness, someone that was in the area. A young woman who might be a friend of your daughter. I just want to be sure it wasn't her sister.'

'Nicola . . .' Margaret's face took on a hint of warmth for the first time. 'Beautiful. They both are. Softer features, freckles, blonde hair, much lighter than her sister. Shorter too.'

'And her build?'

'I don't know, I guess you would say medium. A little larger but it suits her. She wouldn't look right otherwise. Kelly's always been into her running, biking . . . you name it. Swimming's her latest thing . . .'

'It doesn't sound like our witness. When did you speak to Nicola last?'

'On the phone a couple of days ago but she texts every day. She sent something earlier . . . nothing much, a recipe for cinnamon buns. I was going to reply.'

'Did you want to call her? You could ask her to come round if she is local and I could talk to her. It would save you having to—'

'No!' Margaret snapped again, then came back softer. 'No, thank you. I will tell her. Not tonight, not now. She'll be on her way back from work at this time. She works long hours. I'll talk to her tomorrow. Billy can take me to see her maybe. Please, let me talk to her first.'

Joel met her intent stare with a smile. 'I understand.'

'Mrs Marshall, did your daughter ever talk to you about being stalked?' DS Rose cut across them both. Joel was quick to answer before Margaret could.

'My apologies for my colleague, she's very much in a hurry to get to work finding the person responsible for what happened to your daughter. We have to consider a number of theories.'

Margaret's smile seemed to come a little easier this time. 'Well, a woman after my own heart, and that is what you're here for after all. Stalked?'

'Kelly came to stay with you after she had been burgled, a few months ago,' DS Rose continued.

'April 23rd. St George's Day.'

'You have a keen memory.'

'It was Billy's birthday. It fell on a Friday this year, I always do fish on a Friday. I did fish and chips for Billy and his son. All homemade. Kelly was here in time for me to heat up the left-overs and I sent a grumbling Billy home. He had brought a film round for us all to watch and we never did get to see it.'

'And you talked about the burglary?' DS Rose pressed her.

'Not really, to be honest. She said some stuff had been moved around in her place. She was a little freaked out. She only stayed one night, I said she could stay as long as she wanted but she got the locks changed and went back.'

'Did she think someone entered with a key then?'

'Your lot didn't find any evidence someone had broken in. She said she was due an upgrade anyway. It was a bit of a doer-upper, that flat. She's getting there though. I don't know where a new front door was in her plans but it became a priority.'

'You said "moved stuff". So nothing was taken?' The sergeant was leaning in, holding Margaret's attention; there was intensity between them.

'Like I said, she didn't talk about it much. I don't think she would have wanted to scare me.'

'She didn't tell you if anything specific was taken?'

Margaret sat back, flicking her hand out in an angry gesture. 'I assume she would have told *you* that. She called the police. A couple of knuckle-scraping blokes turned up and basically told her she was wasting their time.'

'Is that what she said? About the officers?'

'Yes. Maybe they'd had a bad day. Do you think that has anything to do with . . . with what happened?'

'And she definitely didn't mention anything that might have been stolen? Or talk about specifically what was moved?' DS Rose persisted.

'No! I told you that already.'

'We just need to be sure,' Joel cut in, his tone soothing, the antidote to his sergeant's approach.

'I know one of the officers that went,' DS Rose said. 'I know how he would look to a young woman, how he could come across, and he was with another male officer, two men staring at her . . . she might not have told them everything she knew.'

Margaret shrugged, 'I can't think why. You call the police, you tell them what happened. Why bother otherwise.'

'The report said that some items were moved in her bedroom. Maybe it was her underwear, maybe it was a sex toy? Maybe this was someone who had an interest in your daughter and not her property. Kelly might not have been comfortable talking to those two officers about that. But she might have been comfortable talking to you?' DS Rose was matter-of-fact; a history of investigating sex offences could make you blasé.

'Sex toys! And you think she would talk to her *mother*

about that sort of thing!' Margaret was a long way from blasé. Her shock was genuine, threatening to tilt into disgust.

'She might not have used those words. She might have told you that some personal items were moved, a drawer disturbed. Please, Mrs Marshall, this could be very important.' Still matter-of-fact, but the appeal element softened it.

'She didn't talk about it. She said someone might have been in her flat, the police weren't so sure. They took her details, told her there were nothing they could do and they left. That's all I can tell you.'

'Did she ever talk about anything else? Like being followed, receiving unwanted communication from strangers . . . Maybe an ex-boyfriend who wouldn't leave her alone?' DS Rose was unrelenting.

'Not to me,' Mrs Marshall snapped.

'Her sister Nicola. Are they close?'

'They're sisters. Of course they're close.'

'So she might, have talked to her about that sort of thing.'

'She might,' she snapped again and DS Rose finally gave her a moment to breathe. Margaret's chest rose and fell in a sigh and she came back wistful. 'Kelly is far more likely to have talked to Nicola than to me about these sorts of things. I don't know when it happens but you get older and you realise that somewhere along the line there's been this complete turnaround. You go from the parent cosseting your children from the horrors of the world to suddenly being the one who is being cosseted – protected. If Kelly was having problems with someone she would never have told me. I'm protective, I overreact. It's only because I know how dangerous this world can be.' She lifted eyes that suddenly looked heavy with tears. 'And I was right, wasn't I?'

Joel was sure to get all the details he needed. He also had assurances that Billy would be staying the night on the sofa and would be ready and able to drive her when she was needed to go and formally identify the body. Margaret said they would use her car. Joel had spotted a blue Nissan Note at the bottom of her garden, but Margaret talked about how she didn't really like to drive if she could avoid it, and he got the impression that Billy had added 'chauffeur' to his list of neighbourly services.

Joel drove when they left Margaret Marshall's address. The road led them downhill and into the basin of a valley that was now mostly shadow. The car was silent.

'We talked about the burglary on the way over . . .' Joel said.

'We did,' DS Rose replied.

'About how maybe it wasn't a burglary at all, how it could have been a stalking incident.'

'We did.'

'I also said we would explore that a little more before we talked to her mother about it.'

'If anyone was going to know, it was her mother. We know she came here straight after.' DS Rose's tone was defensive enough to suggest she knew where Joel was going next.

'She told you that Kelly didn't talk about the burglary at all. The stalking angle is just a theory – not even that yet. All we did back there is make those initial officers look incompetent and fuel a theory that might be nothing,' Joel said.

'Those officers might have been incompetent. And I was pursuing a theory, trying to rule it in or out. That's how it works in major crime investigations.' DS Rose folded her arms in petulance.

'I see. Well, thanks for letting me know how those work.' Joel's reply was instant and then he wished he hadn't. She wanted him to bite and he'd responded.

'You know what I mean,' she said sulkily.

'We're not Major Crime.'

'We're doing the same job. Just with less experience.' This was projected towards Joel, then DS Rose turned away again to stare out of the window.

Joel slowed the car, pulled over and waited until she turned to face him. 'Do you still have a problem with me being SIO on major investigations?' Joel was doing his best to sound calm.

'No.'

'But you think someone more experienced might do it better?'

'I don't know. You work different, you *think* different even, like a tac-team sergeant, and maybe that's an approach that works.' DS Rose unfolded her arms at least.

'And maybe it isn't?'

DS Rose shrugged. 'Time will tell. But I've worked investigations and I've always been trusted to think for myself, to follow stuff up if something doesn't sit right. A lack of investigative experience means you've never worked as a detective before, it means you've never managed detectives before. And I don't want to be the one that suffers for that.' There was a softening; it was always subtle with DS Rose but Joel was learning to detect it.

'I've been managing police officers for more than a decade.'

'On searches . . . warrants. Pre-planned operations to arrest dangerous offenders. That's quite literally leading a team. A warrant is you leading people to a door to supervise them busting their way through it. You have tight control of that team; they may have different roles but you can see every one of them doing it. And when you get through that door to search, every find is brought to you, every prisoner is brought to you, every *decision* is brought to you. Leading a murder investigation is sending your team out to chase down leads, to think for themselves . . . to have the freedom to *investigate*. I'm not here to be told what room I can look in and when.'

'The way you talked to her back there, our only witness, you made her feel uncomfortable,' Joel countered.

'Too right I did.' DS Rose sat straighter to scowl her anger. Joel mirrored her exactly.

'Why would you do that?' he demanded.

'Because I got the impression she was holding back. Because I don't believe that a daughter turns up at her mother's house because she's too scared to stay in her own home and doesn't get the third degree – not from her mother, not from a woman like Margaret. I was trying to make her uncomfortable, angry even. Angry people go off-script.'

'You think she had a script? Why would she not want us to know everything?'

'I don't know. But if she is keeping something from us then it has to be important. Nothing's making sense right now, not the victim, not where she was found, not how she was found, not wearing just some shapeless dress and barefoot . . . And not her mother's reaction when we turned up either.' DS Rose had calmed down. Now she seemed to be thinking out loud.

'What did you think of her reaction?' Joel was calmer too.

'Hope is usually the last thing to go. That wasn't the case back there.'

'And you think her daughter talked to her about being stalked, that she knew there was a threat there but she decided not to tell us about it?' Joel said, trying to conceal the fact that this didn't seem right to him at all.

'I thought she might have been holding something back. It could be about the burglary, or maybe she knows something about the girl that was with her, about our only suspect.'

'So what would you have us do next? You know, if you weren't working with a naive fool choking your every move?' Joel was glad to get a flicker of a smile as a reaction.

'I would go and see the other daughter, Nicola, and I would go now. It's an outstanding line of enquiry and the address is on the way back to the nick.'

'The one I just told her mother we would go and see after she'd had a chance to talk to her?'

'Yes. And for that reason. I want to see her first reaction and this is our only chance.'

'You know it's me she'll be pissed off at?'

'And me who feels like they've been listened to, so a win-win for me.'

Joel took a moment to consider. 'OK then, DS Rose, she's your witness.'

Margaret had watched them all leave at the same time: Billy down the garden path to double back on himself at the gate and the two police officers walking to their silver car. She watched it move away, its clean surfaces taking on the greens and browns of the fields and banks like a giant chameleon as it slunk down the hill and into the shadow filling the basin from the bottom up. She was still watching when they stopped, the car pulled over untidily into a passing place on the left side and she felt her anxiety building again. *Surely they weren't coming back!*

They didn't. A minute or so passed and then the brake lights flickered off and the car continued away. Once it was out of sight she could find a more natural rhythm to her breathing. It didn't last.

Suddenly she was alone. Billy was coming back; he'd gone next door to get a few things but it was temporary, a quick fix. It wouldn't change the fact that Kelly had gone, that she had lost her daughter. She'd been so busy trying to fool all the people around her that there had barely been time to reflect on what had happened, on what this all meant.

The realisation was like the turning of a tap and finally she broke down. When it came it was everything: desperation, sadness and anguish bellowed into the emptiness. Anger came last; it came from the unfairness of it all, from feeling totally hopeless, from lying to her friend, to her doctor and then watching the police wind their way down the hill, knowing she had lied to them too.

Chapter 9

It would seem that DS Rose had led Joel astray when she suggested that Nicola Marshall's house was 'on the way'. They were north of Maidstone – a long deviation from the centrally located police headquarters – at a row of semi-detached houses in an area that had a premium feel, despite a clump of trees being the only thing concealing a short view down into the car park of the Hempsted Valley Shopping Centre. They were closer to Rochester than Maidstone in truth, and in the very centre of Kent.

Nicola's house was fronted by white weather-boarding that was UPVC and new-looking. The house next door looked identical in shape but was still brick-fronted, affirming that the weather-boarding was a recent addition to keep up with a very recent fad. The sharp-looking Audi on the drive, resplendent in matching white, added to a picture he was building of the people who might live there.

Even the doorbell seemed a little above its station. It was a tune rather than the classic *ding-dong* and was still playing when a red-faced man with untucked shirt over formal trousers and slippers answered the door.

'Oh!' he said, his expression contorting to one of confusion. 'You're not from Just Eat, are you?'

'Just what?' Joel said.

'Takeaway. If you don't have a curry on you, mate, then we're not interested.' He started to close the door. Joel caught it in time to shout his name and rank through the gap.

'And we need to speak to Nicola Marshall, please,' he added.

The door pulled back open. 'No one here by that name, mate,' he said.

'When were you married?' Joel chanced. The reaction was slight but enough for Joel to know that he was in the right place.

'It's about her mother. She was in hospital this morning, suspected angina attack,' DS Rose called out and the man pulled the door wider to look at her. Then he half turned to bellow back into the house. 'Nic!' Then he said, more quietly, 'She's a Jones now.'

Nicola Jones appeared. The change in her facial expressions also suggested she would much rather prefer a hot meal over two suits. 'What's going on?' she said.

'The police, something about your mother?' her husband huffed.

'What's wrong with my mother?'

'She's fine, Nicola. I'm Detective Sergeant Rose, this is DI Norris. We've just come from your mum's over in Tonbridge. We just wanted a quick chat if possible.'

'About my mother?'

'Have you spoken to her recently?'

'In person? No. My sister was over there last weekend for dinner. We couldn't make it.'

'We won't take up too much of your time.' Joel stepped forward, upping the pressure, and the couple on the doorstep caved and stepped back. A brightly lit living room was first on the left. No one sat down.

The resemblance to her sister was uncanny to the point of unnerving. Joel had an image of Kelly he couldn't shake. She was on the floor, her head held up by blood-smeared glass to face out. Her blood was everywhere; its presence made the bone of her right leg all the more shocking white, where it had pointed directly towards him like an accusatory finger. As if it was his fault that he didn't get there in time. He had noted the pronounced cheekbones, the small, cute nose and the blue eyes peering out into nothing from under long blonde hair. Now very similar features were living and breathing in front of him, waiting for an explanation as to why they were all stood under the bright white lights of the living room.

'Well? And can you keep your voices down, please, we have two kids upstairs.' Nicola's annoyance seemed to have increased since the doorstep. Her attention was fixed on DS Rose. Joel had been careful to take a step back, to make it clear that his colleague would be doing the talking. It was what had allowed him to look Nicola over. He had to focus on the here and now, replace the image of their victim with a visual assessment of her sister. There was no sign of defensive wounds, no cuts or grazes. She was barefoot in her own house, and her feet didn't have a scratch on them. She had a fuller figure too, not as athletic as the mystery woman who had appeared on the CCTV. She was not the survivor, but her reaction had already told him that. As much as he wanted to find the mystery woman on the CCTV, Joel was relieved; this family had suffered enough.

'This isn't about your mother, Nicola. We were speaking to her about Kelly, about your sister,' DS Rose said.

'What about Kell?'

'I'm sorry, Nicola. She was found early this morning . . .' It took a moment but Nicola's head-shaking started first, then the colour drained. She lifted her hand to cover her mouth, her glazed eyes only finding focus when her husband's arm suddenly shot out to grab her round the middle. This was more like what Joel had seen before. This was someone reacting to awful news in real time. Lucy had been right. The mother's reaction had been wrong and it seemed even more so now. 'It was already too late, she was already gone.' DS Rose delivered the confirmation and Nicola took it like a punch to her gut. She doubled over, the air forced from her in a squeak. Her husband helped her to the long sofa. She took a large breath and almost immediately let it out as a sob. Her lips moved like she was saying words but nothing came. There was nothing the detectives could do but wait for the initial shock to pass.

It was another fifteen minutes. Joel and Lucy moved out of the living room, using the excuse of the doorbell to go and collect the food on the occupants' behalf and to take it into the kitchen, where it sat smelling delicious on the table, reminding Joel that he'd barely eaten all day. The couple took the time they needed and then came through. Nicola's husband called out to a small boy who had appeared on the landing to ask if his mummy was OK. He was told to go back to bed. Nicola pulled out a high stool at a breakfast bar, while her husband moved the food to another surface.

'What happened?' Nicola spoke downward into the table and Lucy was quick to reply.

'Your sister was found in Lenham, a village on the other side of Maidstone and six miles from her home address. She wasn't dressed for the time of day, she was barefoot, out on a country lane and she might have been trying to get to a public phone. I know this is a massive shock to you but we're going to need your help in piecing this together.' DS Rose paused there. She was right to. Nicola's eyes had glazed, her head was shaking again. There was a lot to make sense of, any more information and she would be swamped.

'Help?' The word was choked with tears.

'Your mum said you were close with your sister. I need you to think about conversations you've had, recent or otherwise. Was there any time when she's mentioned anything you think could be relevant?'

'Relevant? Like what?' Her eyes were suddenly larger, the

shock and the moisture combining so they seemed to take up half her face. They were searching too, flickering around the floor with no real focus.

'Any incidents that stand out? Any threats towards Kelly, that sort of thing?'

'Threats?' Nicola managed a focus on DS Rose. 'No! Why would anyone threaten her?'

'Ex-boyfriends, girlfriends, rejected love interests, work colleagues, someone she borrowed money from . . . People fall out, it happens. Did she ever mention anything like that?' DS Rose leant in a little. Now she had Nicola's attention she seemed determined not to let it go.

'You're saying she was murdered though, that's right, isn't it? *Murdered*. No way someone would want to do that to . . . to my sister.'

'So she's never mentioned a falling out?'

'No! And she certainly doesn't owe anyone anything.'

'It doesn't have to be someone owed something, maybe someone she upset?'

'She doesn't *upset* people either, OK!' Nicola's eyes finally snatched away. With the bond broken, DS Rose sat back too.

'It's OK,' Joel spoke, knowing the value of a different voice when delivering something traumatic. 'We're not suggesting this was anything she brought on herself, we just need to understand who she was. That's all.'

'She reported a burglary to us, a few months ago. Did she talk to you about it?' DS Rose's question came like it had been ready to go. Joel sensed his colleague trying to keep the pressure on.

'Burglary . . . She . . . yeah, she went to Mum's. She was freaked out about it for ages, thought she was losing her mind. Does that have something to do with it? Is that what you're saying?'

'What freaked her out?' DS Rose leant back in.

'Someone being in her house! That's enough, isn't it?' A thick tear seemed to catch Nicola out, and she flinched, raising her hand to swat it away.

'And she was sure? The police report suggests she wasn't.' DS Rose reached out now, her hand resting lightly on Nicola's shoulder to emphasis the importance of the question.

'She didn't explain herself very well, when the police turned up. She knew someone had been in her house, she just knew it but she couldn't really explain how. There was nothing missing, nothing really messed up, but stuff was moved, a drawer was open. You would know, wouldn't you? If someone had been through your stuff.' They locked eyes again.

'You would,' DS Rose agreed. She nodded too and gave a reassuring smile.

'But explaining that to a couple of strangers – police officers – she couldn't. You lot want something missing or damaged . . . something you can't mistake, and I understand that . . .'

'Not necessarily. My colleagues should have explained themselves better. An offender doesn't have to steal something to commit a burglary, it's about the intention of the person who enters. If someone broke in to cause criminal damage or to assault someone it would still be rec—'

'Assault! Do you think someone went into her house to hurt her? That's why they were there? That's why nothing was taken!' Nicola was winding herself up with every word and it was for DS Rose to bring her back down. Her tone was softer when she spoke again.

'We don't know. It might not have anything to do with what happened to Kelly but we do need to be thorough, to consider all the possibilities.'

'It's too late now, you should have been thorough then! They didn't take her seriously, she said that. They made her doubt herself and couldn't wait to leave. That's what she said. Made her feel stupid, to be honest . . . and now she's dead.'

'Other than the incident at her house did she ever talk to

you about anything else? About someone following her maybe, or getting approached online, messages to her phones . . . anything like that?' DS Rose tried to move her on.

'You mean like a stalker?'

'Did she talk about having a stalker?'

'No.'

'Do you think she would?' DS Rose said.

'Talk about it?'

'With you, or with your mum?'

'Of course, we're family! A close family too, wasn't so long ago Mum was talking to us both about her creepy neighbour. That was right here, in this room . . .' She suddenly faded out into melancholy.

'Her neighbour?' DS Rose said.

'Yeah, you woulda met him, no doubt. He spends all his time there like some little lapdog.'

'What do you mean by creepy?'

Nicola sighed. 'Nothing really. He looks out for her but, like all men, that means she owes him something, right?' She flicked up to glance at Joel. 'No offence.'

'Sex?' DS Rose said, quick as a flash.

'That's my mum you're talking about.' A smile flickered and died, like it was a joke she would have told in a previous life. 'I'm being unfair. He does a lot for her, but men don't do anything for nothing. We tease her about him a bit but we're both happy she's got someone next door. You can't get anywhere near her place without him knowing.'

'What about your dad? Would Kelly have talked to him about any problems?' DS Rose's change of direction was sudden enough to catch Nicola out a little. Her answers had been instant but now she huffed to give herself time to think. 'I don't talk to him, really, not since he upped and left my mum. She might have told you. It ruined everything.'

'She mentioned it.' Joel answered this one.

'Did she mention that his new bit has grown-up kids herself?

A whole other ready-made family. I guess he decided he was better off with that one.'

'She didn't go into detail, but I will have to speak to him as part of the investigation. Did they fall out? Kelly and her dad?'

'Not officially but she didn't like him very much, not sure I do either. Doesn't mean I don't love him though. He's actually a very difficult fella to fall out with. It's not like he gets defensive or argues his side of things, just accepts that he's done something wrong and thinks he can wait until we're over it. It's hard to explain. Will you be telling him what happened then?'

'Unless your mother gets there first, but she didn't have contact details when I asked. Is that something you would have?'

'Is that what she said? I thought she still had a way to contact him. Me and Kell deleted his number to make a point. We wanted to see how long it took him to get back in touch with us. He's moved recently, I know that, but I don't know where exactly. Still local though.'

'So Kelly didn't talk to him?'

'No, she was more vocal about him than any of us. I didn't want to take sides, not at first, but the more I found out, the more I realise that he's been stringing her along for a long time. He doesn't do confrontation, it was always going to take me and Kell to make it up and get back in touch, and I think we would have, but now . . .' Nicola seemed to take a moment to gather herself. 'Now he's lost one of us for good.' She broke down, like saying the words had reinforced their meaning. Her husband stepped back in to wrap her up in his arms. 'Stuart . . .' she mumbled into his chest, 'what do I do now?'

It was time to leave. DS Rose dropped her card onto the table. 'We've taken up enough of your time. This is my card, you can call me for anything at all. We'll be working hard, day and night, to find out what happened to your sister.

Sometimes people need assurance of that. Just call me.' DS Rose lingered until she got a nod back.

'One last thing,' Joel said, 'we need to have a look round your sister's home address. It could be vital. I already have colleagues in uniform outside her door. Would you happen to have a key? I would rather that than risking damage to get in.'

Nicola wiped at her eyes and sniffed. 'Yeah, we swapped keys. I keep it in my bag.' She left the room, her direction back towards the front door. Her husband looked like he was searching for something to say but opted for a shake of the head.

'It's not here!' Nicola's voice travelled down the hall. When she reappeared she had her bag in her hand. She dropped it onto the table, her movements frantic, items spewing out of it as she searched. 'It was here!' she said, lifting wide eyes to each of the detectives in turn. 'It's gone!'

Chapter 10

Joel clicked to send his last email of the night. It was a form authorising payment of the invoice from the locksmith he had utilised to gain access to Kelly Marshall's flat. Joel could already foresee a problem with the invoice being paid promptly; the finance team would always challenge when a course of action had been taken that wasn't the cheapest available. Joel had opted to have the locks changed rather than smash the door off its hinges and then patch it up with boarding and a cheap padlock. Finance might have their preference, but they were not the people who would need to hand those keys over to a grieving mother or sister when they were done.

Joel had led the search. CSI had been present to hold it up, but only while they determined that there was nothing of interest for them there. There was no sign of disturbance or anything to suggest that Kelly's ordeal had started in her flat. Instead the place had been remarkably neat – almost like a show home – and Joel had to be forceful to get fingerprint dusting carried out on all external doors and windows and all internal door handles. There was a brief discussion about how police had been here before, when a burglary report had been made that might have made it worth the CSI time and effort, and how that opportunity had been missed. Joel knew that, and there was nothing he could do about it; he just had to hope that they got lucky.

CSI did find prints. The officer delivering the news had done nothing to quell her told-you-so attitude when she was able to match them quickly to the victim. Unperturbed, Joel called the senior CSI, a woman named Sandra Allum, to see if there was any update on the scene still being worked out at Lenham. Sandra's update confirmed that she was just about finished there and that the only real development was regarding the clothing. Their victim's white dress looked handmade, crudely so, of cheap denim that had been bleached white. Sandra also said that the body would be moved at first light and a detective would be needed to travel with her for continuity reasons. Joel had suggested it would probably be him. He wanted to go back out to the scene in the morning anyway, if only to make sure the search team set off in good time rather than giggling and gossiping over a mobile tea urn. Joel was still a qualified Police Search Advisor – or PolSA – himself, and he knew the process well, but he knew the mentality of a search team better. The key was to keep the team interested. The search briefing for a victim found outside and in a rural location would be wide and generic; the area to be covered was large and the chance of finding anything of relevance was remote. CSI officers would cover the initial search of the body and immediate area. In the morning the role of the search team would be to work away from the body to look for 'anything of significance'. Joel wanted to be sure they knew what that meant and that it wasn't an excuse to while away a shift with a walk in the woods.

Joel still had a map of the area spread out on one of the spare desks. He had divvied it up into sectors to save the PolSA in the morning. The area wasn't just large but complicated too. In the first square mile alone there were bodies of water, thick woodland, domestic gardens, ponds and outhouses; and then there was the rolling farmland that he remembered being mostly thick with rapeseed. He sat back and sighed while taking in the screensaver image of a giant clock: 11.20 p.m.

'Penny for them.' DS Rose placed a mug of tea on his desk. He noted she didn't have one for herself and now sat on her desk rather than at it. They had both been in a blur of activity since getting back from seeing Nicola Jones. Joel's focus had been looking ahead to the next day while DS Rose had updated the policy log with all the actions already concluded, which meant detailed summaries of all the conversations from that day. In the morning, Eileen would need to transfer it all over to the Home Office system – HOLMES – which Joel had never really understood and avoided like the plague.

'Sandra said the phone box was wiped down and they got nothing. She's snipped the receiver to take apart in the lab in case there's something microscopic caught in the mesh but she didn't sound hopeful. She now thinks that the dress was homemade, which means we won't be able to trace it back to a shop or a town with CCTV coverage or match it with a credit-card transaction. That tells us something, doesn't it?' Joel said.

'The killer's intelligent, aware of our processes,' DS Rose replied.

'And this has been planned in some detail, well in advance, which means the phone box was always part of it.'

'You mean this isn't someone who was attacked and ran to the nearest phone?'

'Exactly. Kelly Marshall doesn't belong where she was found, not in what she was wearing. She was taken there. This other woman was too.'

'Our suspect?' DS Rose said.

'Is she?' Joel stood up from where he had been gazing down at his map.

'Until we can prove otherwise. She has similarities to the victim and got the bus from the area around the time Kelly Marshall was murdered. The bus driver saw blood on her; we don't know that was hers. And still the same question: why hasn't she called the police?'

'So we think the team doing the route search in the morning will find the two different types of weapon that she used and discarded?' Joel said.

'I very much doubt it. I don't fancy her as a murderer either,' DS Rose conceded, 'but she's all we have right now.'

'So what are you thinking?'

'Survivor.'

'Go on?' Joel prompted.

'That what happened to Kelly Marshall was supposed to happen to her too but she got away. Somehow.'

'So why *hasn't* she called the police?'

'I don't know,' DS Rose admitted.

'There is one possible explanation, one I just can't shake,' Joel said.

'What's that?'

'That whatever happened to Kelly caught up with her too. That she isn't a survivor anymore.' Joel let the silence grow. He rubbed at his face, pulling at the bags under his eyes like it might breathe new life into his skin. 'We're not getting any closer tonight either way. You look like you're done.'

'Unless you tell me otherwise?'

'Go home. It's late. We'll have another long day tomorrow, no doubt.'

'Are you heading home too?' she said.

'No. I was thinking that sofa was looking a little inviting, to be honest. By the time I'm done here it will hardly be worth it.'

'Your wife might not agree.'

'She's stopped texting me. She must have gone to sleep.'

DS Rose grinned. 'That might not be why she's stopped texting you.'

'Even more reason to stay here.'

'And do what?'

'Probably nothing productive. I was going to have a look on local, see if I can find anything similar to what we've got. Maybe some of what we saw out at that phone box appears in a historical assault, or a burglary or stalking case. I want to contact the central analysts too, so they can put the same enquiries out to other forces. Oh, and pull all the licenced shotgun holders in five square miles. Who knows, maybe this was road rage with a local!' Joel found a chuckle from somewhere. 'If only it was that simple.'

'All stuff that Eileen can be tasked with first thing. Rest would probably be more productive.' DS Rose stretched her arms wide.

'You might be right. But Eileen's picking back up with the social media first thing. She's checking all of Kelly's online contacts against the image we have of our bloodied girl in red.'

'She's the key.'

'She is . . . Shit!' Joel suddenly sat straighter.

'What is it?'

'I meant to task out the anniversary walk. That needs doing.'

'You mean tomorrow morning?'

'She was picked up from Lenham at 6.34, so in about seven hours.' Joel cursed again; it was aimed at himself. An anniversary walk was common in investigations and for good reason – it could be very effective. It was a simple walk along a route at the same time of day as a crime or incident had occurred. In this case a woman had got off a bus at a busy bus station just after 7 a.m. It was a commuter bus. The people getting off it or in that area at that time the morning after would likely be some of the same people as had done so the day before. They would remember the girl, no doubt about that, and someone might have seen something of interest.

DS Rose offered a tired smile. 'I can cover that. I'll go see the night duty patrol skipper on my way out to see if they can spare someone to help me. There's always a few that are keen on easy overtime. It's a walkabout and names taken for anyone on the bus. CCTV showed twelve people getting off. Nothing I can't handle. Means you can still go stick your oar in with the PolSA.'

Joel smiled. 'I just like things done right.'

'I know that. Which doesn't always have to mean *done by you*.'

'Go get some sleep. You're grouchy when you're tired,' Joel said, then reacted to his mobile phone, which burst into life beside him. He read the screen. 'Talking of grouchy,' he said, rolling his eyes at DS Rose who had already stood up to start packing away.

'The wife?' she said.

'Almost,' he replied, then spoke enthusiastically into the phone. 'Superintendent Debbie Marsden, to what do I owe this pleasure so late in the day?' He grinned and waved goodbye to his sergeant.

'Why are you answering like that, Joel? Is there someone else there?'

'At this time of night, ma'am? Of course not. I'm the only one stupid enough to still be here.'

'Not the only one it would seem. I'm still in my office and, after the conversation I just had, I thought it only right that I call you straightaway. I'm glad to hear you're still at work. It means I don't have to feel bad for calling this late.'

'Sounds ominous. What *do* you have to feel bad about then?'

'Actually, this is a good thing. For you and me both. You're getting a DCI.'

Joel took a moment. He didn't feel like this was the right time to offer that he had already met someone claiming to be his new DCI earlier that day.

'OK,' he said.

'That's it?' Marsden said. '"OK"?'

'Well, yeah, I mean we've talked about it and I know how

the rank structure works. I always knew something was going to come between us.'

'Very good, Joel. I think it's a good choice. Someone you can really benefit from.'

'Someone I know?'

'A man by the name of Jim Kemp. And you may not?'

'I don't,' Joel said. Which wasn't really a lie. Yes, they'd met, but he still knew nothing about him.

'He's done most of his career in Essex. He was the firearms lead for them when he came over to us to do a counter terrorism role when Kent and Essex Counter Terrorism merged. Now he's adding the Serious Crime Investigation Team to his portfolio. I mean he's still a seasoned detective, just his SIO roles were leading major terrorism investigations. I've heard nothing but good things.'

'So he's got us as well as all his CT stuff?'

'For now. We will be expanding, Joel, we're going to have to. Major Crime will be centralised and this team will be at the forefront. The existing area teams can do all the kicking and screaming they want, but this is happening.'

'And all this time I've been telling them how we're no threat to their setup, that we're just here to take some of the workload. They haven't believed me from day one, but I believed it because it was what I was told!'

'Did you?' Marsden said.

'Not for a moment.' Joel couldn't contain his chuckle any longer.

'And do you care, Joel?' Her voice was starting to break into laughter too.

'Couldn't give a shit, ma'am. Fuck 'em!'

'Yes . . .' Any laughter was instantly lost from her voice. 'That sort of reaction is part of the reason I wanted to call you immediately and give you a bit of a heads-up. This last few months . . . I know it's been tough, I know you may have formed an opinion or two, maybe even a bit of an us-against-them attitude, but I don't want that to be the first thing DCI Kemp gets to see. Not straightaway at least. You can swear at me anytime you want but I want you two to hit it off. I don't want him thinking you're some sort of uncontrollable pitbull that PSD have backed into a corner.'

'I see,' Joel said.

'What does that mean?'

'It means I understand. I've been keeping my head down just recently, like you told me to.'

'I also told you I would get you an investigation, did I not? How was it being back on active service today? The murder out in Lenham, I see your name as the SIO?'

'That was you then?' Joel said, trying to hide the humour in his voice. 'How did you get that one to us?'

'I told you we only get the best jobs, the highest profile, that's what my CHIT team is for.'

'We really need to change that name, ma'am. Major Crime have already changed one letter.'

There was a pause. 'Very good, Joel. I'll speak to DCI Kemp about when he will be coming over to meet you and the team.'

'You're the boss.'

'I am. And now you have a new one I will be taking some annual leave. I'm off from tomorrow for a couple of days, I know it's a bit sudden but something came up. I may not be around when you do meet Jim Kemp. So, like I said, no foul language, no . . . Just don't fuck this up, Joel.'

Day 2

Chapter 11

'I'm sorry . . . You know that, right?'

Lucy Rose rolled her eyes in an exaggerated movement under the muted lighting of the communal hall and outside the door of Flat 18. 'You said.'

'I didn't know who else to call.' Lisa Hopkiss shook her head while looking sad and it wobbled her jowls. Lisa's frame was wrapped tight in a lilac dressing gown, the cord round her middle tied in a small bow that peeked beneath her interlocked hands. They were stood out in the hall of a block of flats well known to Lucy – and to any police officers who had worked the area for any length of time. Called Phoenix Court, it was originally the Phoenix Hotel, built as a large, cost-effective square box in order to offer cheap hotel rooms to the holiday-makers drawn to the famous Margate coastline. But the steady decline in that demand had seen it bought up by the council as a cost-efficient way to house some of their more 'demanding' tenants. Far from its sunny and bright beginnings, it was now a place for the forsaken, the last place on offer. It was rammed full of petty thieves, drug addicts, prison releases and people with mental health issues who really needed a more settled or secure environment but had somehow fallen between the cracks. Rock bottom; the place where sorrows came to be drowned.

'There is no one else,' Lucy said. She had brought her key. At the time of getting it cut she had questioned why she was bothering. This was the first time she had known the door to be locked – most of the time it was swinging open. There was nothing inside worth stealing; even the occupant had no value to anyone. And yet when the call had come at 2 a.m., Lucy still couldn't find the strength to say no.

'DAD?' she called out from where she had pushed the door open but stayed on the threshold. The interior was dark. She could see far enough into the hallway to make out closed doors. The living room was at the end; there was no door to that, just a block of darkness. It wasn't the lack of light that was holding her from moving forward, but the smell that had rolled out like an uppercut the moment the door had been pushed in. It was damp, putrid. Stale air mixed with body odour, detritus and tobacco smoke. Every time she pushed that door in, the smell was the same. And every time she braced herself for when it wasn't, for when it was the unmistakable stench of putrefied flesh, for when her father's liver had finally pickled to the point of no return and he had died alone, to rot until the stench could leak out into the corridor and begin a process that would inevitably end with Lucy standing over him.

'DAD!' She bellowed louder this time. It was gone 3 a.m. but she had no concerns about disturbing the other residents – whoever was playing Duran Duran at full volume on the floor above was winning that battle. She stepped in and found a switch, snatching her hand back to her side the moment the dull yellow light revealed filthy walls.

She heard a groan. It was from down the hall, from the living room. No surprise there. This tiny little flat had somehow been manipulated to contain two bedrooms, but both were stacked from floor to ceiling with rubbish. There had been a clearing in one of them for a mattress once, a place for her dad to sleep, but even that had become consumed by discarded clothing, bags and boxes – none of them his. Now the living room was his bedsit. The sofa a Swiss army knife of modern living, the do-it-all tool for the down-and-out. A place to sit, to sleep, to inject, to drink and smoke. And no doubt to die.

'Dad, Jesus!' He was laid out on the floor and on his front. Lisa worked the light switch this time and again it revealed a sight that made Lucy snatch her hand back: a dried puddle of vomit, arcing out from her father's mouth like a comic-book speech bubble. The smell hit her now, like it had been waiting for the light so all of her senses could be assaulted at once. She had been crouching but now stood up. There was another groan, and his arms appeared from under him, flailing and knocking bottles that clanged together as he lifted his face towards the light source.

'What the *fuck!*' he managed.

'Dad, it's me,' Lucy said.

'What the fuck are you doing here? I didn't call you here, I don't WANT you here!' Anger always came first. It always had. Before any conversation could happen she would always have to wait out the anger. It was why he had no friends left, why he was so despised by the police. He was an angry little man. No one else waited him out, to see what was behind what first presented. And why would they?

She made eye contact with Lisa then stepped past her, pushing open the door to the bathroom. The bath ran along the right wall. There were more clothes, more bags, a new-looking rucksack of the type a hiker might use, still stuffed full of something. Her dad was no hiker – but he was a thief. An opportunist – and because of his health, the opportunities were becoming fewer and fewer. Stealing bags was just one of his MOs, mainly from parks or public transport, anywhere he could sit down and wait. They were what cluttered his bedrooms, piled up high enough to block the natural light; a lot of them were unopened because he had been so out of it that he would open the door and just throw them in. His whole attitude towards other people that walked this planet with him summed up in a single action. He took what he could when he could and from whoever he could – to then discard it in a forgotten room.

The piles of bags represented the times when he didn't get caught, but his arrests ran into the hundreds and theft was only one reason.

'I got a call. Lisa was worried about you. She heard a big bang and then you didn't respond,' Lucy called out.

'Lisa's a fat, nosey bitch!' He had rolled onto his back, his eyes fixed on the ceiling where a guitar solo seeped through. 'That fucking dog!' he yelled, then pushed himself to his feet, a little unsteady at first, and Lucy got to see what condition he was in. He'd lost more weight somehow and his clothes hung off him as if he were a scarecrow made of a cross of sticks. His shirt fell open, revealing that his chest was covered by an ugly bruise that ran up the whole of the right side. Lucy had spent the last ten years amazed that he was still alive and standing, but death itself finally seemed to have him in a choke-hold.

'Lisa's worried about you. You're not looking after yourself.'

The fact that Lisa was right there didn't seem to register. He set off, walking so unsteadily that he bumped into the door surround as he stomped out of his own front door. Lucy didn't have the energy to go after him. There was no point – he would be back. Instead she turned her attention to emptying the bath of clutter. Lisa still hung in the doorway, her eyes swollen with grief.

'He doesn't mean it. You know what he's like. He gets embarrassed and lashes out, when it's not you, it's me,' Lucy said to her.

'I don't know why I bother. I just . . . I don't like seeing anyone like this. Not anyone.'

'I know that. You're a good person, Lisa. It's always the good people he goes for. I'm sorry, and he will be too when he realises what you do for him.' Lisa nodded, her lips now pursed together. She stepped out of the way as Lucy moved a handful of bags and winter jackets from the bath to throw them into the bedroom across the corridor. She was quick to close the door before any of the stacks fell towards her. 'I don't suppose you have any soap? Anything he can use . . .' Lucy was looking around but there was nothing. Not even a toothbrush. She used to buy him toiletries, regularly, but had soon worked out there was very little point.

Lisa suddenly brightened. She snapped her fingers and spun away. Her flat was almost directly opposite and she was back in under a minute.

'"Relaxing Meadow".' Lucy read the name of the bubble-bath as she took it, and as her eyes met Lisa's they both burst out laughing. The hot taps gurgled, spat and hesitated; the first run was rusty red in colour.

'How long since he's run these taps?' Lucy was talking to herself. Lisa answered.

'I guess he's not a big fan of the bath.'

'Well, there's no alcohol content, is there?' Lucy said.

'Alcohol? What now?' Her dad was back. He swaggered into view, his shirt still open, dried vomit still caught in the hair on his belly. He was swigging from a can of strong lager too and Lucy noticed that the music had stopped above.

'I'm running you a bath,' Lucy said. 'Where did you get that from?'

'The Black Dog. Turns out he was having a bit of a party and didn't think to ask me up. If I ain't invited I don't want to hear the fucking music, do I? I took a beer for the road. He didn't have a problem with that.'

Black Dog. Another name familiar to the police. Lucy didn't work this area but she had people who kept her up to date with what her dad was up to and even she knew that Black Dog was a man by the name of Malcolm Arnold. A talented professional once, by all accounts, but serious bouts of depression and other mental health issues had seen him lose all control of his life. As part of his early battles with depression, Malcolm had referred to it as a 'black dog' visiting, referencing Winston Churchill, who had coined the phrase. Unfortunately the nickname had stuck around, unlike any hope he had of a return to his former life.

'Lisa got you some soap, Dad. Have you got any clean clothes?'

'What do you mean?' Her dad lifted his hands up like a toddler who's just spilt their juice down their front. 'These are clean, ain't they?'

'You've been sick on yourself. You need a bath.'

He mumbled a curse then balanced his beer on the edge of the bath. He tugged at the buttons of his jeans then plunged them to his ankles. He wasn't wearing any underwear.

'Jesus, Dad!' Lucy said. She spun away. Lisa was bright red.

'I'll let you . . . I'll leave you to it . . . I'm glad you're OK!' Lisa stuttered. She was already crossing the corridor to her own flat. Lucy bade her good night, lingering to take a deep breath before she turned back towards her dad.

He was in the bath, his modesty now concealed under a mound of bright, white, scented bubbles that seemed out of place in the filthy surroundings. His hair was slicked back, two streams of dirty water appearing to run from his temples and meet under his chin and drip.

'When was the last time you had a bath, Dad?' Lucy said.

He ran a hand through his hair. 'I don't know, love, if you want the truth. And you lot, you always want the truth. Nothing but the truth, ain't it?' He smiled. It was laden with mischief. He couldn't smile any other way.

'That's right, we do.'

'How's it going, on the force, like? You nicked anyone recently?'

'We got a murderer in, last job out.'

'A murderer!' His eyes lit up. 'That's a proper criminal, that is! My girl, out there nicking murderers. You threw the book at him, I hope? Gave him a lifetime locked up?'

'I don't think he'll be coming back out. One of his victims was just a kid.'

'A kid!' Her dad's face hardened. 'Tough life behind that door, a lot tougher for the nonces. They'll tear a man like that apart. Good riddance. I'm proud of you, my Lucy, you know that?'

'I do,' she said, thinking better of pointing out her dad's error.

'That means something too. I remember my old man, I never was able to make him proud. Worked the mines his whole life, no job I could ever do was gonna be as hard or as honest as that. I stopped trying in the end. Look where that got me.'

'You said.' He told the same story every time.

'I messed up. I should have worked it out when you came along, there you were, all wrapped up and beautiful, like. I should have said to myself that there was someone to make proud, someone who really mattered. Finding your old dad like this, running him a bath like he's not capable.' He tutted, his head shaking. 'Not what any man wants,' he said. Lucy listened. Just like she always did. She was out of things to say in reply, and she didn't like wasting her breath. 'I'm getting out of this place.' He made eye contact with her, intensity in his gaze like he was reading her for a reaction.

'Moving?' she said, her tone carrying her surprise.

'Moving. I been onto the council and they can do it. My quack started it off. They listen when you got a doctor doing the talking.'

'You go to the doctor?' Lucy's surprise was stronger still. Her dad smiled.

'I need to start looking out for myself. This place, I don't want it to be it, to be the last of me. There's enough chemicals and the demon drink between these walls to kill a million men. I need to get away from it, I need to do something different. You know I ain't nicked a bag for three weeks?'

'I try not to think about that, to be honest. I certainly try not to listen when you talk about it.'

He laughed. *The bastard actually laughed*. 'Nightmare, eh? Having a dad like me. That's what this was all about, you know – tonight, I mean. I've been on the wagon, you see.' He had his can of beer back in his hand again now, his eyes locked on it as he swung it in front of his face. 'Tonight I fell off it.'

'You've stopped drinking before, Dad. We both know that.'

'I have and always because other people were telling me to, telling me it would keep me out of prison or it would stop the women in my life walking out of it again. So I tried, I gave it a good try a couple of times. But it was never gonna work while it was for the wrong reasons.'

'And this time is different?'

Her dad shrugged. 'This time it makes me feel like shit. It might have always done, to be honest, but some days I can barely get up off the floor. I'm an old man, an old man made older by this shit, and with nothing to show but a room full of someone else's stuff and hands that shake. I might be too old for much to change but if I kick the booze then who knows. It also means . . .' He faded out. He shook his head slightly and crushed his can in its middle, the contents spewing out to show it had been far from finished. He threw it down in disgust.

'Also means what?' Lucy prompted. Her dad stayed staring at the crumpled can.

'I can be a dad. I know you don't need it, I know you might not even want it, but you came to see me, to talk to me when you lost your girl, so maybe it's not too late to be something to you.' He moved his focus back to Lucy. 'When you're here I'm not just a pisshead bloke with a room full of other people's stuff, I'm a dad. A dad that can talk to his daughter about her life, a bloke who can listen and try and make sense of it all. You're the only thing I've got to show for my life and I'm proud as punch. Somehow you turned out all right.'

'Just all right!' Lucy said, swallowing a sudden emotion as she did. Her dad always had a way of catching her out. It was probably a lifetime of seeking his approval, his love, that meant that just a snippet of it could have such an impact.

'How have you been, since . . . well, since we talked? I know you took it hard. I could see she was the girl for you, you got that twinkle when you talked about her. That's what happens: when life takes something away it does it like a sticking plaster, rips it right off your skin.'

'I'm fine, Dad, it's getting easier.' They'd talked it out a couple of times now, the couple of times he had managed something close to sobriety. It had helped too. Lucy had been loath to admit it at the time but the truth was that she didn't have anyone else to talk to. She'd spent her life avoiding having close friends and personal relationships, another hangover from a childhood that had taught her that getting close to people meant it hurt a whole lot more when they let you down.

She didn't want to talk again, not in that place or at that time. The silence was awkward enough that her dad must have worked that out.

'And what is this!' He suddenly reached forward, his filthy fingernails wrapping round a pink bottle. 'Relaxing *fucking* Meadow!' he said then howled with laughter. And Lucy did too.

The disturbed sleep, the trip all the way down to Margate at 2 a.m., the repugnant smell, her disgust at the state of her own father, the anger and abuse she had to wait out – every time she told herself she was stupid, that she wouldn't do it anymore.

But she needed moments like this and not just for the laughter. Her dad was someone she could tell anything, someone who wouldn't judge – couldn't judge. She needed him; they needed each other. It was an uncomfortable realisation, and even more uncomfortable was how she suddenly found herself daring to hope that he would stick to this latest pledge of sobriety. Maybe he had found the right reason to be better.

Maybe they could both be better together.

Chapter 12

'I KNOW YOU CAN HEAR ME!' Alan Lewis's voice bounced back off the walls of his solid white prison with such ferocity that it seemed like it was all bouncing back, like none of it was getting out. The door was ajar at the end, and a thick chain hung on the outside. He couldn't see it now but when the wind had been stronger it had swung enough to be visible and to thud against the door. The door must be tied open so as not to move. Last night the wind had been enough for the branches of the trees to clack together. Tonight was back to calm, lighter too. The moon was out and had been visible for a short time earlier, but all he could see of it now was its silvery shimmer.

He was in the back of a lorry trailer, sat at the opposite end to the door, his back against the cold, white wall. A thick chain, fed through two crude holes, one either side of him, was pulled tight to hold him in place. The floor was filthy, an even layer of dust and dirt. The walls were scarred with black smudges where loads had shifted or been dragged against the walls in transit. There was a refrigeration unit above him. It was stainless steel, the fan blades pointing down and unmoving behind a mesh, the cobweb that hung from it thickened by dust. It must have transported perishable goods when it was in use. The fridge was a giveaway but even without that, the smell of rancid food hung in the air.

Now the only other thing in the trailer was something that looked like a sandpit in a kids' play area. It was large, the plastic sides tall enough to hide most of what was inside. When the sun was just right he had seen a thick shadow that revealed it to be nearly full.

'IF YOU CAN HEAR ME, TELL ME YOU CAN!' he bellowed again, his windpipe and chest burning with the exertion. 'WE DON'T HAVE TO DIE HERE! WHAT HE SAID, ABOUT US BEING AGAINST EACH OTHER. THAT'S ONLY TRUE IF WE LET IT BE TRUE.' Still nothing. Alan's head fell forward but his shoulders stayed in place, held firmly by the chain. He had felt pain at first, in his chest, shoulders and sides, then his buttocks where he had sat on them, unmoving for hours on end. Now it was all just numb. The numbness had spread to his legs and feet.

He had been convinced he was alone at first. He had been told he was, but it had felt like it too, like he was in the middle of nowhere. But last night, when the wind had been just right, he had heard something: the sound of someone sobbing, then crying out in anguish. The clacking branches and constantly shushing leaves had made it difficult to be sure and when he had shouted back there had been no answer. He started doubting his own mind. But he had heard it again, a voice, a shout back; he *knew* he had.

'WHEN HE LETS US GO, HE WANTS US PITTED AGAINST EACH OTHER. BUT WE DON'T HAVE TO. WE CAN BE A TEAM.' Alan's chest burned worse than ever. He was exhausted. The lack of sleep, his hunger and his attempts to move against his constraints had seen to that. The thought of another human being had given him a lift, almost brought hope back inside this four-walled prison, hope that there might be a way out that wasn't the horror that had been described.

He peered up at the diagram etched into the white wall. He had been told it was the directions he needed – a map – but to him it looked like the diagram from the top of the manual gearstick in his car. There were eleven numbers written out above it, the format consistent with a mobile phone number. He had his instructions. Follow the map, call the number; be first.

And if I don't make it there first? he had dared to ask.

The answer had taken his breath away. And now he couldn't shake it from his mind. He moved his legs, trying to work some of the numbness away. When the time came, when that bell chimed, he would need to be ready.

Chapter 13

Lucy Rose was almost glad to step out of the warm interior of her car into a freshness that was only present at that time of day. It was just after 5 a.m. The heaters had been a bad idea, creating a warm, cosy environment, dangerous for someone who had barely managed an hour's sleep the night before. She had made it home just in time for a quick shower and change before heading back out to work, having declined her dad's offer of his facilities to wash.

On the drive that morning she had daydreamed about falling asleep at the wheel and how she could probably snatch at least fifteen minutes' sleep before anyone arrived to drag her car out of one of the comfortable-looking ditches she had passed. Her journey was without incident, however, and she reached for her sunglasses in the hope it would cover the exhaustion that had etched itself into the skin beneath her eyes.

Lucy pulled her fleece top a little closer. She always felt the cold more when she was tired. The phone box was fifty metres ahead; the inner cordon was the only one left and was still marked out by a clumsy square of police tape. The police car parked just beyond it had a layer of condensation on the outside and misted windows on the inside. The door popped as she approached.

'Morning!' The greeting was forced-cheery, verging on panicked. The officer emerged holding a flask that he had to put on the roof, and as he turned to do so he seemed to tangle some of his kit in his seatbelt and almost had to get back in to free himself. DS Rose waited him out with her hands held up.

'Hey, no need to get out. I'm DS Lucy Rose, just doing the anniversary walk to the bus stop.'

'Ah!' The officer visibly relaxed. He seemed to be wearing uniform that was too large and was still pulling his coat tails out of the vehicle. 'We've been asked to talk to anyone we see, just to ask if they saw anything of what went on.'

'And have they?'

'You're the first person I've seen, Sarge . . .' Suddenly he looked embarrassed, like it was his fault a key witness hadn't strolled past at this time of the morning.

'No surprise. The search team will be out soon enough and you should be able to get off home.'

The walk to the bus stop was over two miles with only one obvious route. The search team would cover the same ground in a line search formation but that didn't stop her eyes following the ground in the faint hope of finding something that might add to the story. There was nothing, not a single person either, until she stepped out onto what a rural village might refer to as their main road and saw figures hunched under a bus shelter in the distance. Lucy had cropped images of the people from the CCTV and she took them out of her pocket to scan them again.

There were two people waiting. The elderly woman was in the lead, standing almost by the edge of the kerb so as to secure her seat, despite the fact the bus would almost certainly arrive empty, since this was only its second stop. The woman was instantly delighted to have someone to talk to but useless as a witness. Lucy recognised her as the same woman who had been on the bus the day before, but she was quick to explain how she 'kept herself to herself' and didn't take much notice of the other passengers. She did say there was a girl who 'looked a mess' but she couldn't remember anything more and she certainly didn't speak to her. She had a trolley with her. Lucy eyed it closely then made a call, leaving a message on Sandra Allum's mobile phone. It was far too early for her to be in work but the call was still returned within a minute.

'Lucy Rose, you called me,' Sandra said in that matter-of-fact way that had become familiar.

'I did. Expecting you to call me back at a more appropriate hour to tell me off for asking a stupid question.'

'I've made a career out of answering stupid questions. I'm getting quite good at it by now. I've also made a career of calling back Major Crime when they call first thing in the morning. It normally means trouble see, the sort of trouble that will lead to a sixteen-hour shift if you put it off.'

'We're not Major Crime, you know that.'

'Ah, that's right. You and Inspector Norris are just playing at it. There will come a time when we all have to accept that as you're investigating murders, you're Major Crime. Maybe I'm just ahead of the curve.'

'Maybe.'

'What can I do for you?'

'Answer a stupid question,' Lucy said.

'Of course, go on?'

'I'm waiting for a bus, the same bus that a woman got on at this time yesterday morning. She's elderly and she has one of those tartan trolleys that seem to be popular.'

'I know the sort.'

'Yesterday, someone helped her lift it on. That someone I really need to identify.'

'So you want me to ridicule you for thinking that prints might last that long for identification purposes?'

'I'm not sure I want you to ridicule me. I wasn't going to call, only . . .'

'Belt and braces. Very Major Crime, that attitude. Where are you headed?'

'Headed?'

'Where can I have someone meet you with a bowl of powder?'

'Maidstone bus station, eventually. So this wasn't such a stupid question?' Lucy suddenly had to keep a lid on her excitement, knowing that a CSI's method of managing expectations was to quash any signs of hope.

'I make no promises. Another thing I've made a career out of. We're talking a plastic or metal handle, I would imagine, good for prints but also good for being rubbed back off again. It's not likely but—'

'Actually, our Jane Doe took hold of the bottom. I'm looking at it now; there's a toughened bit of black plastic where I reckon she grabbed it.'

'Jane Doe? I thought we got a name for the victim in the telephone box?'

'We did. This is the survivor.'

'I see. You know Jane Doe is the name we give the unnamed dead, right? It doesn't suit a survivor. Unless you're thinking that she walked away from the first incident to get caught up in a second?'

'That's one theory. She hasn't come forward, why would that be?' Lucy was thinking out loud.

'I really can't think of any other reason,' Sandra admitted. 'Let's just hope there is one, that Jane Doe doesn't end up sticking.'

Lucy thanked her colleague and ended the call as the bus pulled up. She watched the elderly woman get on. Today she didn't need any help. The driver's name tag read 'Henry' and DS Rose was sure to thank him for his statement the day before. Henry spent the next seven stops pointing out the people that were on the bus the previous morning and DS Rose approached each of them, giving the same opening spiel about a 'serious incident' and an 'injured young woman' while stopping short of giving any more details, so she would know a genuine witness. One man stood out. Today he carried a leather satchel rather than the oversized holdall he'd had the day before but DS Rose recognised him as the man who had talked to their survivor when she had stepped off the bus.

He was happy to talk. He said he had been concerned about her and that the big bag had contained a squash racket and his kit for a game after work. The hoody was for coming home in but he had offered it to her and she had accepted. He also offered to call someone for her or to give her the use of his phone but she said she had already called the police, that it was nothing to worry about and she was OK. She also refused his offer to walk her home, explaining that it 'wasn't far'. DS Rose took it all down, along with his details for any follow-up. She would run him through their systems later to see if there was anything of interest but DS Rose had a proven nose for criminals and liars and she wasn't getting either vibe from him. He seemed more like a genuine guy who had tried to help someone out in trouble. When no one else had.

By the time they had arrived at the Chequers Bus Station she had spoken to everyone. Two early-turn officers in uniform were there to greet her. They were chatting with a slim young woman with a neat ponytail down her back and *CSI* sewn into her polo shirt on the front. Commuters were arriving on any number of buses, their numbers swelling all the time to just about cover the walkway on the left side, and DS Rose set the detectives off talking to as many of them as they could. She stayed with the CSI officer, who walked them to a quieter area on the opposite pavement, where she opened a solid-looking Peli-case. DS Rose had managed to convince the elderly lady to walk over with her but her expression was now one of horror.

'And I'm not in any trouble?' she asked.

'No! Goodness, no. It's like I told you, we're trying to find a young lady who might need our help and I think she might have touched your trolley.'

'When did you say that was, love?' The elderly woman squinted at DS Rose, doubt clear in her expression.

'Yesterday morning.'

'Yester . . . Oh no, no, you won't be getting anything off there then. I walked it all round the town yesterday, stopped for a coffee, did my food shop in Markses, and all the while there was quite a breeze, almost had me over a couple of times. There'll be nothing left.'

The CSI officer chimed in while Lucy did her best to hide her smirk.

'Wind's generally OK, it's water that's the enemy. If it had been raining all day we might not even have bothered, but as it stands . . .' This side of the station was noticeably darker; most of the lighting was over the waiting area on the other side, so the blue-tinged light of the specialist torch she was running over the bag stood out all the more. 'We might have got lucky.'

'Lucky?' Lucy said and her colleague leant back a little, inviting Lucy to see what she was referring to. The exposed prints were clear against the black plastic.

'Lucky. We've got mainly partials on the bottom but that one on the side.' She pointed at one mark in particular. Even Lucy could make out swirls and ridges in the light. 'That one will be a full thumb.'

'Will be?'

'Yep. I'll send the image back and the software will tidy it up and confirm. I've seen much worse that have still worked for comparison in ID cases.'

'Great . . . What sort of timescale?'

The young woman smiled. 'Always the first question. Sandra said it was urgent so I'm sending it to her and she's going to endorse it. You should get a response same day.'

'Should?' Lucy pushed her a little.

‘Should. Best case, we’ll be back in touch with a name in a few hours. Worst case, it will take a few days and it won’t match anything on our system. A good print is a good start, but it’s nothing more than that.’

Lucy got the impression of a well-rehearsed script. Certainly this wasn’t the first time her CSI colleague had been careful to set the expectations of a detective.

The elderly woman continued to look appalled as photos were taken of her bag and then Lucy got a signed account to confirm her presence on that bus the day before and the movement of the trolley since then: belt and braces. Lucy would check the CCTV again. She knew she had seen the young woman lift it on the bus, but with the pictures of the prints and their location she could now match them up.

But first, Lucy took the short walk to McDonald’s. She was sure to buy a coffee before asking for the manager. She preferred not to have to turn down the inevitably offered free one, instead paying her way and then introducing herself as a police officer on enquiries. The bus driver had given the young woman some money for breakfast and this was just about the only place open at that time. The manager explained how he wasn’t in the previous day but he was able to work the CCTV. A group of men in matching hi-vis vests and pit boots and a male police officer in uniform were pretty much the only patrons around the time. Lucy made a note to find out who the officer was that had been in there to buy a breakfast muffin – more belt and braces. Surely she would know about it already if an officer had spotted anything like her missing girl.

When she came out of McDonald’s she took a moment to scan for council cameras. She thought she could see one in the distance and a couple of shops looked like they had something covering the entrances to their stores. But they were only going to be of use if she had walked round the main shopping areas of King Street or Gabriel’s Hill or some of the streets leading off them – and she hadn't. Lucy felt certain of that now. These areas contained people, even at this time in the morning. Someone would have noticed a girl in obvious distress. And they would have had an opportunity to make her safe.

But that hadn't happened. This young woman had walked off into another area of Maidstone and no one had called. And now DS Rose had to consider that the opportunity to make her safe might already have passed them by.

Chapter 14

Nicola Jones's tears were already flowing as she strode up the path to her mother's house. Any moment now her mother would surely open the door to her, her arms out wide to sweep her up in an embrace, and the world and its worries would be filtered, even just for a moment. Because that's what a mother's hug could do.

But the door remained closed and there was no response when she knocked. The tears quickly gave way to anger.

'Mum!' she shouted at the door then stepped back to take in the windows. Both the ground floor and the upstairs had curtains pulled. She hadn't answered her phone last night – Nicola had called the moment the police had left – nor this morning, first thing. Nicola turned to where her husband scowled in confusion and shrugged. She shouldn't have let him talk her out of coming here last night when her mother hadn't answered the phone. She always answered. But Stuart hadn't wanted her driving in that state when he would have to stay home with their children.

Nicola had been forced to agree. She'd continued calling but stopped short of getting in the car until that morning, leaving as soon as she'd been able to get a neighbour to take the kids. No way her mother was out, not for this long. She didn't go out at the best of times.

'MUM!' This time she bellowed at the top of her voice and she hammered her fists as hard as she could, making her hands sting. She stared back down the garden path, her eyes resting on the roof of her mother's car that was poking up from behind the hedge.

'Can I help you?' A man had appeared to call out over a low fence, her mother's neighbour.

'Billy, have you seen my mum?' she said.

'Seen her? I was with her just last night. When . . . when she received some bad news.'

'Tell me about it. The police came to me too. She's in there, she must be.'

'She left already. I'm not sure where.'

'Left? It's not even eight. Where can she go at this time in the morning?'

Billy shrugged. 'I don't know. She took a taxi. Maybe she was going back to speak to the police . . . They were here a while to talk to her yesterday – about your sister. I'm so sorry.'

'She's not answering her phone,' Nicola said. She could feel the tears pushing their way back. She was still just as angry. 'She's still got me, we need to be together.'

'Of course. Maybe she was going to see you, to your house?' Billy offered. 'Have you thought of that?'

Nicola thought about it now. She couldn't think where else her mother would go at this time of the day. Her only trips out were to the supermarket when she couldn't get a delivery of groceries arranged or for regular social engagements – the last thing she would be attending at a time like this. She knew her mother didn't like driving so the taxi was no surprise. Nicola hurried back along the path. 'I should have left you there,' she said to her husband, 'she's probably sat outside our house right now!' Her shoes caught as she stopped and spun, a thought suddenly occurring to her. 'Billy, could you take my number and give me a call if she makes it back? Or tell her to call me straightaway? Would that be OK?'

'Sure.' Billy took his own phone out from his pocket to record the number. 'No problem.' His face was heavy with wrinkles that were accentuated when he smiled. It was a kind face, however, like it was a lifetime of smiles that had condemned him to those wrinkles in the first place. He said again how sorry he was. Nicola was already striding back to her car. She needed to get moving. She couldn't bear to think of her mum sitting outside her house, all on her own, desperate to see her daughter.

Her husband spun the wheels on the loose gravel of the country lane as they moved away.

Billy watched and waited. It took a while for them to be out of sight – the joys of living in a valley. Them he hammered on his neighbour's door.

'They've gone, Margaret, for GOD'S SAKE, IT'S JUST US!' He was back to waiting, this time while standing at her door, his left ear and left hand flattened against it. When there was no answer he pushed off it to bark his frustration. 'I don't like LYING!' he roared.

'I'm sorry.' Billy had started to walk away but Margaret's voice stopped him dead. It was muffled and weak, and there was a scuffing sound that told him she was close against the door. He imagined her using it to hold herself up. 'I just can't talk to her, not right now, OK. Not her, not anyone. Not right now.'

Billy stared at the door a little longer, his mind running with replies, with options and worries, but right then none of them seemed to matter. Her message couldn't be clearer.

She wanted to be left alone.

Chapter 15

'Shannon Hendry.' Sandra Allum almost sang the name through the speakers of Lucy Rose's car.

'Is that a name I should know?' DS Rose said, caught out a little as she tried to negotiate a busy roundabout on Maidstone's one-way system.

'It's the name you wanted to know. We got a full print lifted from your old lady's bag. Shannon Hendry was once arrested for theft from an employee. Her prints were taken before it was found to be a load of old shit. She probably shouldn't have been arrested in the first place from what I could see. We got lucky.'

'The prints from the bag? I thought it was going to take days. That was an hour ago!'

'Two actually. When the image came through I saw the quality was good enough for a quick search so I called the fingerprint bureau myself. I told them it was life and death and narrowed their search to Maidstone and Medway . . . *Et voila*!' Sandra was still singing. Lucy didn't think she had ever heard her so cheery.

'That's fantastic.' Seems cheeriness could be contagious. This could be a huge moment.

'I am, aren't I? Where are you?'

'Just leaving Maidstone town centre. I need to check back in with the boss. He's going to be delighted.'

'*Leaving* Maidstone town centre? So you're not far from her address then?'

'You have an address?' Lucy took her eyes off the road to glance at her phone's display.

'I have a tongue in my head and an office full of CID just down the corridor who are terrified of me, so yeah, I have an address! Oh, and a full intel picture and a mugshot. She's moved since she was arrested, it would seem. Someone did a check for me on Voter's and she popped up. Lives with someone by the name of Jacob Barnes. I would guess at boyfriend but you never know these days. I can't tell you much more about him.'

'That's really fantastic.'

'I know I am. I've just pinged it to your email. It will be ready by the time you pick your boss up. You can take the credit by all means but I'll be seeing him later to put him right.'

Lucy laughed. 'I don't need the credit. I might not need Joel either. I assume this Shannon Hendry still hasn't made contact with the police – for any reason?'

'She hasn't. CID ran her details. No calls from her, none from her address, from Jacob Barnes, and none from any numbers linked to her.'

'They were very thorough.'

'They were. When I say they are scared of me, I mean terrified. I find it's even more effective than being owed favours. And less work.'

Lucy was now only half-listening. A junction came into view on her left, signposted as a cul-de-sac, and it seemed to prompt a decision. She swung into it. She would open the email right now and see what she had. She knew Maidstone relatively well; certainly she knew the areas where she would need to be accompanied for a door knock. She could at least get an eye on the address, maybe call the boss in from there.

'Well, I for one am glad that they're so terrified. Thanks for this. I've pulled over to have a look now.'

'You're welcome. Be careful now, nothing too hasty. The one thing I know about coppers is that they always work better in twos.'

'I'll bear that in mind.'

Lucy ended the call to open her email application. The attachment was quick to download. The address right at the top.

'James Street?' she said. She typed it into Google Maps then zoomed out to take in the area. It was just behind Maidstone prison. Less than half a mile from the bus station, which would make it walkable even with bare feet. It wasn't a bad area of the city either.

She would just go take a look.

'There's a wet for you there, Guvnor.'

Joel hungrily swept up the tin cup from the dusty floor of the Police Incident Van. He thanked the uniform officer who had made it and turned away to gulp at the tea inside. It was searing hot and it slopped out over the sides as he pushed it away from his lips.

'Don't be wasting it though!' the man who had made the tea now called after it.

'Hotter than I thought. What did you use to boil the kettle, the sun itself?' Joel tried to hide his embarrassment behind a joke.

The man patted a sealed urn. 'The old faithful. She never lets us down.'

Joel continued his walk away. More officers were returning for their tea break and he felt a sudden tug of nostalgia, a yearning to be back with his old TSG team, tipping out on an all-day – or all-night – search, where the most important member of the team was always the one who had control of the 'wets kit'. No police work ever got done without the support of boiling urns and cheap teabags.

In his previous life, he would be the one briefing his search pairs, and already with a feeling that the whole thing was a lost cause. A tick-box exercise by an SIO looking to avoid criticism at some major case review further down the line. Only now he knew first-hand that it was nothing of the sort. He knew the odds of finding anything were slim, but he had still started out with hope burning a little brighter. They were now a few hours into the search and already it was starting to fade.

He was tired. The search team that had arrived consisted of seven officers and a sergeant: nowhere near enough. Another team were promised for later in the day, but even after agreeing to come in earlier they wouldn't be starting until midday, by which time they would only have eight hours of light left to assist the team who were already on site. Joel had stuck around with the intention of helping out with the first square mile but had ended up flitting around the areas on the map he had seen as most likely to be where those girls had come from. Their phone-box victim was dirty, but it wasn't just mud. He didn't need the CSI report to know that the layer of filth contained animal faeces and it had been present in her hair, on her legs and hands and under her fingernails. To Joel, that was someone who had been in close proximity with animals for a period of time, not someone walking through a field or stile. There must have been a source of water too. The filth would have been wet when it had been applied for it to stick – and it hadn't rained for days.

Surely this meant a farm building. An outbuilding perhaps, a barn or a pen, but something that was primarily used to shelter animals. It was the only thing that made sense. So convinced was he that he had been moving between any buildings he could find in their search area to try and pick out anything obvious.

But an evidential search needs to be methodical. It is planned as such: areas are entered, searched properly and then ticked off as done. Something he knew better than anyone. It wasn't until the PolSA had sent Joel back to the Incident Vehicle that he had stopped to think just how much of a pain in the arse he was being.

The PolSA appeared now: PS Maxine Jones. Joel hung back while she stripped off her load vest and belt to ditch them on the grass. Her black T-shirt was damp enough from sweat to cling to an athletic body. She undid her zip and was pulling at the clothing when she made eye contact with Joel.

'You got a cup of tea then. There are biscuits in there somewhere too but you do have to ask Scotty nicely. He only gives them out to people he likes.' Her cheeks were flushed with exertion and heat, her fringe swept across her forehead and stuck down by her perspiration. She still had a smile on her face, but it looked a little strained.

'I'm not sure I deserve your biscuits. I was just thinking how pissed off I would be to have a Guvnor like me turn up to my search.' She didn't reply, just held her smile until it disappeared behind her own tin cup. Joel continued. 'I'm sorry. I don't mean to be a pain. It's just . . . This is all we have. I can't stop thinking that somewhere out here there might be something I need. And when it gets dark I lose control of the area. Maybe someone comes back and the opportunity is gone for ever.'

'You were TSG too, right? Some of the lads said they worked with your old team before,' Maxine said.

'I was.'

'A bit of a legend by all accounts. More than a decade leading a team like this. I'm only a couple of months in but already I can see it's quite the job.'

'Legend!' Joel laughed. 'On a team like I had, the *legend*

was the one who had moved on from using crayons. We got the job done though. I had a good bunch.'

'I have the same. And yeah, you're a pain in the arse but don't worry about it. We get the easy job, turning up for the search, I mean. You know how these go for us, we use a map, start at the scene to pick out our reference points, divvy it up into sectors then send the troops in, ticking off areas as we go. The occasional cup of tea to keep them going. I've thought about it myself.' She gestured towards Joel. 'The detective role, I mean. Like today, if we do find something we'll hand it over and off we go. I've often thought that maybe I want more than that. I like to see things through. But the flipside to that is the pressure. If we *don't* find anything out here then we still get to roll onto the next job and without a second thought. I guess that's the difference, that's the pressure that comes with doing what you do.'

'Bang on.'

'If there is something out there then we will find it. But from the briefing I got, the victim was found at first light by a dog walker. When we were at the scene earlier, that street with the phone box is the only one I've seen where you might be able to guarantee a dog walker. She was always going to be found – and early. You talk about your man slipping back when we're gone to clear anything up he mighta left behind, but I don't think so. I think he already got his house in order before he left her there. If it were me, I wouldn't want to have to come anywhere near this place again.'

Joel watched as, this time, her whole face was concealed by a tin cup knocked right back. 'You're right,' he said.

She shook out the remnants and started back towards the van. 'So don't beat yourself up, that's all I'm saying. If we don't find anything out here it's because this bastard was sure to take it with him.'

* * *

'Are you sure you don't want me to try and call Inspector Norris again?' DS Rose could hear Eileen Holmans clucking down the phone line. She was not a woman who was comfortable with going off-script.

'It's OK, I'll try him again if there's anything to tell him. This might be nothing at all.' Lucy hoped she sounded convincing and tutted as her pen pushed through the paper again. She was leaning on a wall, finishing writing down the key points from her conversation with Eileen. She had hesitated before calling her, knowing that she would instantly want to update Joel with a hit on fingerprints – the potential was very significant. But there was something off about this whole thing, about a potential survivor fleeing a scene and not reporting her ordeal to the police. Lucy could only think of two reasons – that she was still under an element of control and terrified that the killer would know if she attempted contact with the police; or she was the killer herself. And Lucy still couldn't believe the latter.

'I tell you what,' Lucy said, 'I'll call you back in twenty minutes. If I don't, you can get hold of Joel and tell him what I'm up to.'

'Twenty minutes,' Eileen said in a tone that suggested she had fifteen at best.

Lucy ended the call to take in the building in front of her. She took a moment to coach herself too. Joel was a little rough round the edges – brash even – and his muscular build and over-enthusiasm were not what she needed here. The girl she had seen on the CCTV had looked fragile. Dirty, bruised and scared and no doubt with a good reason to avoid the police. Lucy had a far better chance of speaking to her while she was on her own.

The communal door was heavy, the corridor behind almost empty, so the sound of her footsteps bounced back at her off the painted brick. She counted up to the third floor.

'Door number twenty-two,' she muttered just as it came

into sight. But she stopped when she got to it, frozen to the spot. The door was open; there was the sound of something heavy falling over, a scraping, then cussing.

Lucy took out her Pava spray to hold it in one hand. With the other she pushed the door. And that was about the time she considered her mistake in not calling Joel.

Chapter 16

Lucy could hear two voices, both male, both out of sight at the other end of the flat. A long corridor would lead her down to them.

'Hello! Police!' Lucy called out, holding by the front door, not wanting to move past any of the closed internal doors in case anyone came out of them to block her exit. The only response was silence. Then she heard the mutterings of a conversation. Then footsteps towards her. Lucy now took out her asp and jerked it towards the ceiling; the steel sprang out to lock into a solid weapon. She rested the hitting end on her shoulder and adjusted her stance so she was ready to strike.

'Is everything OK?' A man appeared: thirtyish, broad, two-day old stubble and a slick haircut. He wore jeans and a T-shirt. His cheeks were flushed like someone who might have just shifted something heavy, and there was a plaster on his finger that was too small and was leaking blood from both ends. The left side of his neck was catching sunlight from a window she couldn't see – it highlighted the tattoo rising from his collar to behind his ear.

'Who are you?' Lucy said.

He looked nervous. His eyes darted left, and a slight lift of his shoulders told her he was communicating with someone else who was out of her sight. 'I'm Andy . . . I own the place, I don't live here, mind. What's going on? Why are the police here?'

'I'm looking for someone. Shannon. Is she here?'

'Shannon!' Suddenly he grinned like he was off the hook. 'You and me both, love! No, she ain't here. She drops the keys in to the agent yesterday and then she's gone. One day's notice. She owes me a month's rent, she can't just ditch like that.'

'Agent?'

'Letting agent.'

'What was the noise? You were shifting something?' Lucy still had her asp raised to rest on her shoulder but her grip was looser.

'Shifting? Yeah, a sofa. Shannon, she left a message with the keys, said she had taken what she needed and I could do what I wanted with the rest. What I want is to get rid of it. It's a big old heavy thing with sharp bits where you don't expect no sharp bits.' He waggled his bloody finger at her to back up his point. 'I don't want it here. I don't rent my places furnished, more trouble than it's worth. She's left me missing a month's rent, no time to put it up for new tenants, and sofa to move. So if you find her, let me know where, would you?'

Lucy let the asp drop so it was by her side, suddenly a little embarrassed to have racked it in the first place. 'No forwarding address?'

'Nope. I got the impression the agent might know a bit more but they can't tell me nothing. I'm just the guy out of pocket. I tell you, the rental market's a bit of a bastard. The whole system's geared up for the tenants, there ain't much helping me out.'

'Which agent?'

'Freedom Property Services. Little place off the High Street. Tell 'em Andy Watson sent ya. I'm all for helping you lot out.'

'When there's a month's rent outstanding?' Lucy said.

'Exactly.'

'Did she leave anything behind that gives a clue where she went?'

'No. All she left was a water-stained bathroom and a mess. She's not getting her deposit back, I tell you that much. I said to Coops here that she left in a hurry. Seems I was right. On the run from you lot then, is she?'

'Coops' slunk into view at the mention of his name. He was a little younger and much scrawnier than his companion, also wearing jeans and a T-shirt but with a belt that appeared to be wrapped round him twice. He looked untidy overall, his eyes darting over and around Lucy, rather than settling on eye contact.

'Nothing like that. I just want to talk to her. Can I have a look around? I just want to see if there's anything of use.'

'Be my guest!' Andy grinned. 'Just put that stick away, would you? Brings back bad memories!'

Chapter 17

Joel pushed himself away from the computer monitor with force enough to make it wobble. If was also enough to disturb the sensors in the ceiling and the white office lights erupted like a camera flash. Joel slammed his eyes shut. He needed to stop. He had promised himself a cup of coffee and a break at 10 p.m., which was now just over two hours ago, a promise that was part of making sure he was alert enough to drive home. Now, for the second night in a row, he was past the point where his wife was messaging him. He knew he was pushing his luck.

The messages had started just after 4 p.m. – asking when he might be home so she could let the girls know. Then asking what time she should aim to make dinner for. Then his phone had rung, but it hadn't been his wife; it was his two children trying to operate a video call while fighting to be in front of the camera. *When are you coming home, Daddy? Are you ever coming home, Daddy?* Joel had laughed – *of course I'm coming home!* But the direct questioning style of children had forced him to admit that he wasn't sure when. Joel suspected they had been coached by their mother when they had made him promise that he would be there when they got up in the morning. He didn't mind, of course. Any police officer with a family will attest that the mundane elements of family life are the first things you start to miss.

And now it was gone midnight and he had already made a nest on the sofa at the back of the office. He would have that coffee, then maybe put a brief plan together for the next day before a few hours' rest. He could still sneak home in time to have the breakfast going before anyone woke up. Then it would be a shower and change and straight back.

His phone erupted to skitter and buzz across the work surface until it chinked into his empty mug – making a mockery of the *silent* setting. He lifted it to his ear without checking the screen. It could only be his wife.

'Hey, I lost track of the time a bit—'

'Joel?' The voice caught him out. It took him a beat to place it: DCI Jim Kemp. And there was humour, even in that one word.

'Boss.' The word fell from Joel in a sigh.

'You seem delighted to hear from me. I think I preferred the fear in your voice when you thought I was your wife.'

'Six in the morning and now midnight. You're not a man with a strong belief in office hours, are you, boss?'

'It seems we share those beliefs. Are you still in your office?'

'Yes, but—'

'I'll be right up,' Kemp said and the call was cut. Joel swore into an empty office. He stretched as he got to his feet and headed for the tea-making area that was just across the floor. He spun a cup, grimacing that someone had put it back still dirty. He would give that one to the Chief Inspector. The kettle was just starting to rattle and billow its excitement when DCI Kemp walked in.

'Casual,' Joel said, referencing the fact that his DCI was wearing a hooded top over tracksuit bottoms. 'Did you come back in just to speak to me?'

'Well, it is true that I don't like these sorts of conversations over the phone, but no, don't start thinking you're special.

I'm living on site at the moment. I'm staying in the student digs at the training school. I figured I would use them for a week or two until I found somewhere to live but I'm not sure how I'm supposed to make time to look.'

'Sorry to hear that,' Joel said, 'I won't ask how you're sleeping.'

'Longer than you, I would suggest. I'm surprised to see you still here.'

'I could have been at home in bed, woken by your call,' Joel said.

'Fine. I spoke to security, who told me you hadn't swiped out yet. I can't say he was surprised. Seems you have a bit of a reputation of making this place your home.'

'Is that what you wanted to talk to me about? I assume that's what you meant by *these sorts of conversations*?' Joel used the excuse of finishing making the drinks to turn away.

'Well, firstly, I was hoping to get an update on your case.'

'Did you not get my summary?'

'I read your email.'

'I put everything on there, boss, I'm not sure what else you need to know.' Joel stopped his movements to wait for the reply.

'I just assumed there must be something else I don't know about, seeing as you're still at work?'

'What do you mean?' Joel was suddenly guarded. Kemp's tone had a marked change.

'The Super's worried about you. Which means I get to be worried about you too.'

'Well, you don't need to be. There's always a lot to do early doors, this is a murder investigation.'

There was a brief pause like Kemp was considering what he had said but that wasn't the case. Kemp's entire reason for calling was about to be revealed. 'This job we all do has a thing: totting up. It's this black cloud that follows you around, quietly getting bigger until one day you realise you can't see out of it. Debbie's worried about the impact from your last case. About everything. She thinks you have a tendency to be hard on yourself. Add in the fact that some of our esteemed colleagues have been piling on the pressure a little and we're both worried that your black cloud might have got bigger.'

Joel turned back into the room to face Kemp. He handed him the soiled mug he had filled. 'What is this, some sort of intervention? A month ago I might've understood.'

'I wasn't here a month ago.'

'Debbie Marsden was.'

'She was. We've only met a few times really but I have the impression of someone who doesn't do the *feelings* bit too well. I don't think she would be comfortable at all in this situation.'

'I certainly couldn't imagine her in a tracksuit,' Joel said, trying to defuse an atmosphere that had suddenly become tense.

'You know what I mean. I think I'm her way of making sure you're OK. You were the first task she gave me.'

'I'm flattered. And I'm fine.'

'Sometimes you can't know you're struggling until it's got a good hold of you.'

'I would know, I've learnt a bit about myself. I'm not struggling now, this is different. This time I'm just angry,' Joel said.

'I understand that, but you are going to have to let that anger go. Maybe get rid of it on the punchbag. Being angry at PSD is never going to end well.'

'I don't mean PSD. I'm angry at me, at trying so hard to be something I'm not. I won't do that again.' Joel was using his tone to make it clear he was done with this conversation.

'OK then.' The DCI's response was a half-smile laden with mischief. 'Go home to your wife, Joel. Tonight, now. And again tomorrow night and the night after that. Dead victims stay dead and exhausted detectives don't catch their killers. You don't have to stay at work until a case is solved.'

'I know that.'

'You don't have to do it all, either.'

'I know that too,' Joel snapped, stopping himself before he carried on with something career-threatening.

'Lucy Rose might disagree.' Kemp put his teacup back down on the table and stood up like he was leaving.

'You spoke to Lucy?' Joel had meant to sound less bothered.

'I'm trying to get round everyone. She's a massive asset if she's handled right.'

'And I'm not – handling her right, I mean?' Joel was now studying his boss closely for his reaction.

'She has her own struggles too, away from work. Talk to her sometime. Managing people isn't just making sure they're doing their job, it's making sure they're OK to do it. You were good at it when you were the skipper on the TSG, they all still adore you.'

'You spoke to . . . Of course you did, you're speaking to everyone.' Joel groaned and pulled a chair out to slump into. The DCI's grin had grown wider.

'I like to know as much as I can about the people that work for me. You did too, once. Oh, and those cups need a rinse.'

Joel watched his boss leave, his exit taking him right past where the sofa was laid out ready to be slept on. Kemp was right, about some things at least. He should go home to sleep and wake up next to his wife after being bundled by his children.

'The world's greatest alarm clock,' he said out loud to the empty office.

Day 3

Chapter 18

This time Alan was sure. He edged back, sitting straighter where he had slumped as far as the chain had allowed him. *There had been a voice!* He was just drifting off, and at first he had thought that it was part of a dream, but it had come again after he had snapped back awake; he was sure of it.

Outside was daylight. The sun low enough to be visible, its rays pushing through the open door of the trailer to turn the side of the sandpit translucent. He had been staring at it earlier, from the moment he had been left alone. The man controlling this nightmare had been here, still dressed like some demented mechanic in overalls, rubber boots and a leather hood that covered his head completely. He'd given Alan a drink, the first since he had been chained up, then played another recorded message, the same distorted voice from a small speaker that didn't tell him anything new – just that this would all be over soon. Alan had questions and he'd started to speak but instantly a bread roll was forcefully pushed into his mouth, where it broke off, most of it falling to roll down his front and onto the filthy floor. Alan watched as the man took a step to the side and his thick-soled rubber boots came down on the rest of his dinner.

The pit! The recording had said, then been stopped while the figure rather unnecessarily took the time to point it out. The man was taking obvious pleasure in dragging this bit out. His overalls were baggy enough to hide his shape and size. He seemed tall, though it was hard to judge when sitting on the floor. Even the size of his hands was distorted as they were pushed into large rubber gloves. He made another dramatic movement to continue the recording: *The pit has tools, weapons, things you will need. You will need to search for them, but you will not have long. There will be five chimes, each one will allow you to move another metre. After the fifth chime you will go. And so will he.*

That was it. Alan already knew that he could expect a race against someone evenly matched – whatever that meant. The race was to a phone, and the directions to that phone were etched into the side of his lorry prison, as was the number he needed to memorise and call. When the line connected he needed to say a single sentence: *I had to win.*

That was it.

Then he would be free to go, his family would be safe and this whole nightmare would be over.

Still he had questions. *Why him? How does he know so much about his family? Who was he running against? Why make them race? How does he know this will really be over?* Alan had tried to ask again but the reaction was similar; the figure had stooped to pick up the flattened bread roll before stuffing it back into Alan's mouth. It was too far in to spit out and anyway, he was starving, his strength suffering as a result. So he chewed and swallowed. Bits of grit were painful against his teeth, crunching in his ears. By the time he had forced it down, the man was out of sight and he was alone again.

Except he wasn't. Because now someone nearby was shouting.

'HELLO!' Alan shouted back.

'I think you were right!' Alan was holding his breath to be

sure he would hear; the words were still faint, almost out of range for a conversation. *'We need to work together,'* the voice continued. The silence after was longer this time, like Alan was meant to respond.

'OK!' Alan called out, some of the strength lacking in his voice where he felt a surge of emotion that almost overwhelmed him. 'OK!' he shouted again, louder.

'We can both come out of this OK. Find what you can and let's get this bastard! Do you know where we are?'

'No!' Alan shouted back.

'We need to work out where we are, that's the first thing. I'm Bradley. We're going to be OK.'

'Bradley . . .' Alan repeated, this time just talking out loud to himself, his voice now breaking down completely. 'I'm not alone . . .' He sniffed and peered out of the open door to focus on the only part of the outside world he could see: a square of green grass and the shape of a distant tree. He had spent the last few days yearning to be out there, to be walking through that grass, out under those trees. It could happen. The man in the hood and overalls had outlined a horror race, powered by terror and violence. But if they worked together, if they didn't play his game, then they could both win, they could both walk away from this. 'ALAN!' he bellowed back, his voice stronger. 'MY NAME IS ALAN!' His last word was sobbed, the relief flowing out of him.

'Alan . . . Are you chained up?'

'YES!'

'With a sandpit like a long jump?'

'YES!' He was right, that was exactly what it was like. They'd had one at his secondary school.

'OK. So we're the same. Keep your chin up. No more talking now, he could come back. He told me we're going to be released. Then he wants us to follow his instructions. But we don't have to! Do you agree?'

'YES!' Alan bellowed back, and then he broke down

completely. He could feel the thick chain through the numbness in his shoulders as he sobbed, digging into him, tightening as he gulped in air. But he didn't care. He wasn't alone anymore and he wasn't going to have to fight for his survival either.

Fighting didn't suit him, it never had.

Chapter 19

'I'm not going away! PLEASE! I'm not going away!' Nicola meant it too, despite her stinging hands. It was Wednesday and still she hadn't seen her mother since she had first been told about their family tragedy on Monday evening. She had even called the police to tell them that her mother might be missing but they weren't interested. They had phoned her back at least, but only to say they had been able to speak to a neighbour who had confirmed that she was still coming and going. They had also told her that they had a record of her receiving bad news at around the time Nicola had last spoken to her.

No shit!

When Nicola had cut the call her frustration had bubbled over to the point where her phone had been flung the length of her kitchen. The evening she'd been told the news about her sister was murky at best; she had been all over the place and so it was no surprise that she had lost the phone number for the two officers who had broken the news. They would just tell her the same anyway, that her mother needed some space and time.

But Nicola needed her mother.

'OK!' Her mother's voice and Nicola snatched onto it. The instant relief was soon forced aside by a tidal wave of anger.

'You're in there! SERIOUSLY.' She lashed out at the door again, this time with a closed fist against the solid wood.

'OK, OK!' the voice said again. The door made unlocking noises. Nicola reached out to rest her hand on it. She was bleeding from her knuckle. The door pulled open and all that anger in Nicola dissipated just as quickly as it had come.

'Jesus, Mum! You look terrible . . .'

'Thanks.' Her voice had an instant rasp; talking at all looked like it had been an effort. Behind her was only shadow. Nicola had seen that the front windows were blocked by curtains but all the others must be too. 'You'd better come in.'

Nicola moved quickly, so that she caught her mother still holding the door as she swept her up in a tight hug. 'Jesus, Mum . . . you don't have to do this alone. None of us do.'

'She's not alone,' said a male voice. Nicola had scrunched her eyes tightly shut to inhale the familiar scent of her mother's hair. Now she opened them to an outline in the gloom. 'Hello again.'

'I gave you my number.' Nicola let her mum go to spit her words at Billy. Her anger, it seemed, was still just below the surface. 'So you could call the moment you saw my mother.'

'I know you did,' Billy replied.

'I told him not to, Nic. He was only doing what I asked.'

'He had no right. You had no right. What the hell is going on?'

Her mother sighed. Nicola followed her through to the kitchen. It was just as she had remembered – impossibly neat, maybe even more so than usual. Nicola tugged open the fridge. The light was harsh in the gloom. It shone down on two plated meals covered in clingfilm.

'Are you eating?' Nicola said.

'I made her those and brought them round. I have told her she needs her strength . . .' There seemed to be a tiredness to Billy too, exasperation also clear. Nicola knew how stubborn her mother could be.

'Thanks,' she said, her anger contained back under the surface. 'So what's going on here? No food, no daylight . . . This is no way to live, Mum.'

'Live!' her mother snapped, standing straighter where she had slouched against the work surface. 'What makes you think I want to live!'

'You still have me, you know that, right? Me and your grandkids. I know you're struggling but you're hardly alone. Unless you choose to be.'

Her mother huffed. She moved too, pushing past Nicola to make for her living room. Nicola fixed Billy with a questioning look and he just shrugged and said, 'I'll put the kettle on.'

The gloom in the living room seemed thicker still; the curtains weren't just pulled closed, the ends were tucked firmly behind the radiator to hold them tight. Nicola knew the view that was the other side of those curtains, out over the valley where the sun was now rising: beautiful, the whole reason her mother had fallen for the place so hard, and yet here it was, blocked out.

'What's going on, Mum? This isn't like you, you don't just give up. I know this is . . . this is terrible, this is massive. I know it's knocked you for six because it's done the exact same thing to me, but we need each other. More than ever.'

'You don't understand,' her mother sighed. Her face was scrunched up like every single movement was hurting. She lifted a shaking hand to cover her eyes.

'Then make me,' Nicola pleaded.

'You can't understand.' She whipped the hand away with a flourish then moved over to her chair and hovered over it unsteadily.

'I'm not stupid, Mother, don't treat me like it. I know Kelly was your favourite, I always said you would be lost without her, but I was joking! I didn't realise it was the truth. That I mattered so *fucking* little to you.'

'Don't you come here with that foul mouth!' Her mother

was shrill, the fragility in her voice gone in an instant. She had flopped into her chair but she grabbed at the arms now like she was ready to pull herself out of it for a fist fight.

'Maybe I shouldn't come here at all. Is that what you want?'

'No!'

'Then what is it you want? What the hell is the matter with you? My sister was murdered, stabbed to death on some country lane out there, and all you can do is sit in your chair with your curtains closed. Where's the woman I know who wouldn't rest until she had answers? Don't you want answers?'

'You can't understand!' Her mother was shrieking now; it wasn't anger, desperation more like, and maybe for the questions to stop. It only made Nicola more angry. Her next words were through gritted teeth.

'You said that. And you're right, because I'm done trying. I'm going to go back to my family now, *my* kids, *my* husband, and I'm going to try and piece my life back together. You can stay here and rot in your own self-pity for all I care.' Nicola made it as far as the hallway, passing Billy as he emerged from the kitchen to see what the shouting was about.

'I don't need answers!' Her mother's voice was louder, back to being shrill, and it pursued Nicola down the hall, catching her up as she held the front door open, stopping her dead.

'What?' she called back. The silence that followed was punctured by movement. Nicola's eyes were struggling to adjust where the light had changed again. The outline of her mother appeared at the end of the hall.

'I knew she was gone, OK, missing. I knew someone had her . . .'

'What are you talking about?'

'Kelly's strong . . . fit, a fighter. I thought she would be OK.' Her breathing was heavier, faster too. Billy appeared behind her to fuss.

'Now come on, Margaret, let's get you sat back down,' he said.

She shook him off, but suddenly bent double and groaned like she was in pain. She quickly reached out for him and he helped her to the floor.

'MUM!' Nicola pushed away from the door to cover the ground back to her mother. She was struggling to breathe, her head shaking. Billy pushed an inhaler towards her and she grasped it and took three long drags, each making a whistling sound. Finally her breathing seemed more natural, a little more under control. She looked up, her eyes catching in the light leaking in from the kitchen as she stared at Nicola.

'I knew someone had Kelly and I didn't say a word to anyone. Now she's dead . . . This is all my fault!'

Chapter 20

It was like a cattle bell, and the sound was enough to shake Alan from a sort of sleep. It had become a familiar state over the last couple of days: his anxiety had been keeping him awake but there were periods when his exhaustion forced his eyes to shut for a few minutes at a time. Normally it was just until the door fidgeted in the breeze or a bird dropped something to skitter across the roof. The sound of a bell was certainly a new one.

The next sensation was the cold breeze that piled in through the open door to sweep over him. His bare legs were covered in goosebumps; the shorts and T-shirt that he had been forced to change into had no thermal quality at all. His bare feet were cold to the point of numbness. He folded his hands across his chest, desperate for some warmth. His fingertips brushed across the thick chain and with it, the realisation swept back over him as the fog of sleep cleared.

The bell had rung!

The instructions flooded back. The bell sound was the signal he had been waiting for; it was where it all started. There would be five bells, ten seconds between them, the final bell marking the beginning of the race. His eyes jerked to the map scratched into the trailer's side and the number scrawled beneath it.

The second bell sound was like a jab to his side.

The chain suddenly had some give. It clunked and scraped as panic took over and he lunged forward. The thick links caught and banged through the holes punctured in the walls behind. His legs were numb, from his buttocks to his feet. He had to get moving. He managed to roll onto his side, grabbing and clawing at the dusty floor to pull himself to his hands and knees. He started crawling, faster than his numb limbs would allow him, and toppled forward to graze his face. The chain came with him, digging into his shoulders, but suddenly he could shrug it off. The sound of it hitting the hollow floor reverberated around the trailer. It took all of his strength to get back to his knees. He knew that 'Bradley' would be in the same situation, that he would be waiting for him, and now, together, they could get to safety. He clung to that, using it as the strength he needed to propel himself forward.

There was another restraint. He hadn't noticed it before. It was much smaller, thinner too, a piece of wire wrapped around his middle to tighten if he went too far. He wasn't free just yet.

'My mum safe . . . A hot bath.' He was leaning so far forward he disturbed the dust with his breath as he spoke. 'A hot meal . . .' He used the reminder of his rewards for getting through this to fuel him as he pushed off the floor, dragging his knees up to take his weight. Then he managed to set one foot down to raise himself to an unsteady standing position. 'I just need to get this done . . .'

The third bell. It came with a sudden release of the tension in the wire round his waist, tension that he was using to help him get to his feet, and he stumbled forwards. The edge of the sandpit came at him and he had to jump to prevent him from tripping; his bare toes caught on the side and he crashed to his knees. The restraint had him tight again. Every sound of that bell was getting him closer to the door, to the sunlight and shaking trees beyond. Through his fog of panic and desperation he remembered the recorded instructions, how he needed to search for tools and weapons.

His eyes dropped to the sand. It had a pattern over the top like it had been raked flat. The pit was larger than he could have realised from where he had been sitting. He dug his hand in. The sand was coarse – builder's sand, not the soft sort that kids might play with. It was damp too, enough to clump together, to feel cold and heavy.

He forced his hands under the surface, numb to the pain in his toes and knees and now the discomfort of the sand scraping against open wounds on his hands and under his nails. He needed to search. He needed to find something that would help them. He and Bradley were working together now, but he had no idea what else to expect from the man who had held them prisoner – what they might need to be working against.

The fourth bell loosened the restraint again. He was leaning forward so that it had been restricting his breathing but he'd barely noticed, the realisation only coming when the pressure was eased. He moved forward again, his hands clawing and scooping with increased aggression at the damp sand. He threw clumps out of the pit to his left. He stopped as his fingers bumped against something. He had to dig around it, until he could reveal enough to get a grip, to lift it out. *A baseball bat!* It looked brand new – brushing off a layer of sand revealed polished wood underneath. He threw it towards the door where it thumped and rolled towards the daylight.

The fifth bell.

He froze. He should be free. He pulled at the wire around his waist, the last restraint. It was limp. He kept pulling, his hands moving faster and faster as the wire trailed through a small hole between the two larger ones in the back wall. It was a loop, the tension now gone, and the more he pulled through, the looser it got until it fell to rest on the sand by his knees. He struggled to his feet and stepped over it.

He was free!

He moved towards the door. The baseball bat would do for now. They could come back in and search some more if they needed anything else. Alan yearned to step out into that sunshine; he wanted that grass under his bare feet, that sunlight to drench his face.

He picked the bat up and hesitated at the door. Bradley was already out – it had to be him. There was a man of a similar age, but with a thicker build, standing in a pair of tight blue shorts and a blue vest. Alan was wearing the same but in a vivid green. Bradley looked a little unsteady on his feet, swaying and blinking in equal measure; he too would be experiencing numbness in his limbs. His face and arms looked every bit as filthy as Alan's own. Bradley stood in the middle of a patch of yellowed grass shaped like a large rectangle, like a lorry trailer had recently been moved away. Six others remained in situ, parked up in a crescent formation to follow the corner of a field. A lorry cab was visible now too, but face down, its hydraulics hanging out like its throat had been ripped out. In the far distance the grass of the field ran into the grey of concrete with a clear track to take them there. From the directions scratched on the wall, Alan knew that he was supposed to follow that path, that the phone was somewhere near its end. The number he needed to dial was still etched in his mind. Alan couldn't see anyone else, there was no sign of their captor, and his relief mingled with the sunlight to form an overall feeling of hope.

Bradley was carrying something too. It caught the light when he lifted his arms like he was stretching them out. His blinking was becoming more controlled. Alan stepped forward, his muscles stiff and the soles of his feet hurting on the perforated steel of the step. But the grass was instantly soft and gratifying.

'Are you OK?' Bradley called over. Alan's legs and arms felt like they were awash with pins and needles. His first few steps were deliberate, like he was learning to walk again. They were towards Bradley.

'Yeah. Not used these in a while.' Alan didn't recognise him. He wasn't someone he had seen before, but he had been told he wouldn't. Now he was a little closer he could see the item in his hand; it was a crowbar. It looked heavy. He was using it like a crutch holding him up. He looked tired, his face turned to the sun, his expression a half-smile.

'There's a phone at the end of the track, the directions up on the wall in there, I think I can remember them,' Bradley said.

'I had the same.'

'We should assume he's up there though. We need to be ready. I searched it pretty good in there, are you sure there's nothing you missed?' Bradley gestured to the trailer Alan had just stepped out of.

'I found this and got out, to be honest,' Alan said.

'So there might be something else of use? Makes sense to have a look while we can.' Despite his words, Bradley stayed still. Alan looked back over at the step he had just jumped down. He didn't want to climb back in there; it was the last place he wanted to be.

'I'm not getting back in there, not ever! I can do enough damage with this, I promise you that. No matter what this piece of shit has waiting for us. He's not expecting two.'

Bradley rubbed a clump of sand from his arms. He didn't look convinced. 'I'll have a quick look,' he said. His walk was stiff too when he started out. Alan followed him, using the opportunity to stretch his legs some more. He lingered at the door, peering up as Bradley scrabbled into what had been his prison for at least twenty-four hours. He wondered if their captor was indeed waiting for them and they would have the opportunity to use what they had found. He turned back to the sun, closing his eyes to the warmth and moving a few steps towards it.

It was a mistake.

The first blow was across the back of Alan's legs. The pain was instant, flashing across the front of his knees and down his shins. The next sensation was the grass against his palms. He shouted out in pain, twisting immediately to face the threat. Bradley was standing over him, the steel crowbar raised overhead, his eyes wide and fixed on Alan. There was barely time to react. Alan threw a hand upwards to meet the swinging crowbar. It wasn't enough to stop it completely but the curled end was deflected enough to thud into the ground beside Alan's head. The pain increased, then he was aware of a cold sensation spreading down his forearm. He still had his arm raised. Bradley seemed fixed on it but was taking a couple of steps back, shock now clear on his face.

Spots of warm moisture dropped onto Alan's cheek. Most of the pain in his arm was gone. It looked wrong too. He could see his hand – *it was hanging down towards him!*

'You broke my arm! Jesus! What's the matter with it?' It was worse than broken. A shocking white stick was exposed to stick out at the wrist, and the falling moisture was blood, the drips now coming faster. The whole of his right arm was useless and it flapped to lie back on his stomach. 'What DID YOU DO?' Alan shrieked. He tried to push away with his feet, to scoot backwards and away, but his right knee shot with pain and he didn't move. Bradley seemed to shake himself out of his shocked stupor. He still stood over him. He threw the steel bar down to thud on the floor. 'Bradley! You said we could work together. We *can* work together! We don't need to fight. You said that! You *said!*' Bradley still looked shocked at what he had done, enough for a flash of hope that he would stick to his word after all, that he had realised that they didn't need to be hurting each other.

But Bradley was holding something else in his hand now.

The sun was strong enough to make it difficult for Alan to see. But Bradley stepped closer, close enough for Alan to make it out. It was a large pair of scissors.

'No . . . NO! We do this together! That's what you said!'

'I'm sorry . . .' Bradley said, his voice now the one with the shake. 'Please . . . I'm sorry . . . I have a family . . . kids. It can only be one of us.' He opened the scissors up, gripping them so they locked open with a blade exposed. 'Please don't fight me . . . Don't make this worse.' Alan threw both his arms up this time. His right hand flapped, shedding more blood over his face as the sun was blocked out by a figure bending towards him.

It was useless. Alan was utterly defenceless.

Chapter 21

The scenery was vivid. Everything was glowing white hot where the sun beat down from its highest point to pool in the basin of the valley. There seemed to be no shadow, no contrast of light and dark, just a brightness from everywhere that forced Joel to squint painfully. Margaret Marshall's home had the same vivid glow and the moment Joel stepped out of the pool car it seemed the ancient bricks were reflecting the heat too. The front door was already pulled open, a figure standing in it and waiting. Joel wasn't sure if that was a good sign or not.

'Nicola. Nice to see you again,' Joel said as he walked up the path. 'How is your mother?'

'She should be in hospital but she's refusing to go. She had another panic attack. She's a lot calmer now. They wouldn't send an ambulance; they said they don't send them out for things like this.'

'OK, well, how about we have a look. They'll always send someone if they get a police request.' Joel walked through to the living room as he had done before. Billy, her neighbour, was there, although he appeared to be doing his best to merge with the back of the room, while Margaret was sat in the same high-backed sofa with elaborate wooden arms that she had spent most of their last visit in. Her head was bent forward, her eyes fixed to the floor. Nicola stayed leaning on the doorframe, blocking the way into the kitchen. The room had a tangible atmosphere.

'What's going on here? You didn't just call us all the way out here for us to put pressure on the ambulance service, I hope? My colleague said you wanted to talk to us.' Joel directed this last part towards the seated Margaret. She didn't react at first, then her head lifted gently. She gave him a fleeting glance before turning to her daughter, who had her arms crossed.

'Tell them, Mum,' Nicola said.

'Mrs Marshall?' Joel prompted.

'You'd better sit down, Inspector. You see, I wasn't quite honest with you the last time you were here. I didn't quite tell you the whole picture.'

Billy shuffled, maybe trying to push himself further back into wall. Nicola huffed and fidgeted. Joel fought his temptation to say *out with it!* giving her space to continue in her own time. 'You have to understand, you have to know that I'm scared, I'm so scared . . .' The words ran out to be replaced by sobs. This was not the strong, defiant, slightly grumpy woman that Joel had seen the first time round.

'Then you seem to have invited the right people round, Mrs Marshall. I help scared people for a living.' This was meant as a prompt, but it was gentle, subtle, in keeping with the fragility in front of him.

'He said . . . He said if I called the police, if I spoke to *anyone,* he would come back! He would come back for everyone else. But maybe it's OK that it's you, you could just be following up . . . I'm not scared for me, you understand, I don't care about me, it's everything else. This man . . . He said he could wipe out my entire family!'

Joel took a seat on the edge of the longer sofa and leant towards Margaret, who seemed to be lost within herself. He waited until she started speaking again.

'He knows everything,' she said quietly, 'and before you ask, I don't know who *he* is! Or even what he looked like. He was wearing overalls, something over his head too, but it was a glimpse at best. I don't know how he found me here either, or how he knows so much. I was out the back, watering some plants just before bed. There's not been much rain about just recently and the sun had been so strong that day. You could still feel the heat coming up from the ground, even though it was dark. I knew someone was there. All at once I knew. I thought . . .' She turned to take in Billy. He had moved forward a little, away from the wall at least. 'I thought it was you, Billy!' She forced a chuckle. Billy took it as permission to move closer. He squatted down by her knee, taking her hand in his.

'As soon as I turned round he grabbed me. Hard! Round my throat, both hands. I couldn't breathe and I just remember thinking that this was it! That I was going to die. I was pushed to the ground but on my front. There was weight on my back and my face was crushed against my own stone patio. He was too strong for me. I remember that I couldn't catch my breath for ages. I thought he had done something to me, permanent damage.' She faded out again, then turned towards her daughter, still standing in the doorway. 'I'm so sorry.'

'Just tell them what he said, what he made you do,' Nicola said and Margaret fixed back on Joel, who was studying her bare neck, where he could make out faint bruising. She'd been wearing a neck-scarf the first time they had visited that would have concealed it.

'He didn't say much.' Margaret was shaking her head as she continued her account. 'It wasn't talking either, he had a recorded message that he played on a phone. But even that was all distorted, it was like someone growling. It was awful . . .'

'What did it say?' Joel was still keeping his prompts gentle.

'He let me know that he had my daughter, my Kelly,

Inspector. He said that he was going to force her to fight for her life, to fight someone else. He said that she would need to run a race and she would need to be first. And if she was then she would survive the night. And if she didn't . . .' Her face creased up into a ball of stress and sadness.

'It's OK, take your time,' Joel said.

'He threatened me, made it quite clear that if I spoke to the police, if I spoke to anyone, then it wouldn't just be Kelly, he said it would be the whole family. He knew Nicola's name, her husband's name, my *grandchildren!*' She visibly shuddered then shook her head, prompting a tear to run over her bottom lip and drop. 'I begged him to leave me alone, to leave my family alone, but he just kept telling me that she would have to run, that she would have to win and that I had to make sure the police didn't go looking for her. I agreed. There was nothing else I could do!'

'What happened then, Margaret?' Joel prompted again.

'He took my phone. He made me unlock it and then he took it and he put something on it, so he would know if I called anyone, if I told anyone anything. He knew so much: when I go out, who with, about Billy . . . How could he know so much?'

'So he gave you your phone back?' Joel continued.

'He left it along with another one. Some cheap thing. He told me to keep it on. He told me that someone would call it first thing Monday morning. That it would either be Kelly if she won, or . . .' She fell apart. It had been just under the surface the whole time but now she was lost completely. Joel told her it was OK, and DS Rose moved closer, taking hold of her hand as Billy took the opportunity to stand up and back away, his wrinkles arranged into a mask of deep shock.

DS Rose gently rubbed the back of Margaret's hand. They both waited out her tears.

'Or it would ring. It would be a stranger and they would

tell me that they were sorry but they had to win. That's what they would say and I would know that my Kelly was . . . that she was gone.'

'And is that what happened?' Joel said.

There were no more words. Only tears. But amidst it all, as Margaret Marshall fell apart in front of them, there was a distinct nod. Confirmation of the hellish call she had taken in the early hours of Monday morning to be told that her daughter had lost the race.

Joel backed away. Nicola and Billy joined the scene of misery and suddenly Joel felt the need to be outside in the fresh air. He headed for the back door and stepped out among the potted plants on the patio that Margaret had described as her landing place when she was attacked. He felt like his head was spinning, like all the colours were blurring into one. The garden was a small flat patch of grass cut into the valley that sloped upwards beyond it. The three gardens were separated by hip-high fencing, and beyond, thick scrubland was quick to take over from the manicured perfection of Margaret's garden. It would be easy enough to get undetected access to any of these properties on foot. He walked out onto the grass, stopping only when he was out of the sharp shadow cast by the roof.

'You OK?' DS Rose appeared. She had taken a few minutes to follow him out. The sun that had been sweltering to the point of oppressive was now a comfort round his shoulders.

'Not really,' Joel said. 'I'm just trying to imagine.'

'It's probably best you don't.'

'What they were wearing, those girls, it didn't make sense as a dress but it does if you think of it as colours: two different women, two different sides, maybe? Is that what this was, two young women pitted against each other – and for what? Entertainment?'

'From what we just heard, that would make sense. As much as any of this can make sense.'

'You gave the details of the survivor to Eileen, right?' Joel snapped, despite knowing she had.

'I did. She's finding out anything she can. I specifically tasked her to look for any link between Shannon Hendry and Kelly Marshall.'

'This is why she didn't come forward, this Shannon. She's too scared. She must have had the same instructions – or someone else in her family got it and now they're all keeping their heads down.'

'That doesn't mean they're safe,' DS Rose said.

'It doesn't but we need to make sure Margaret and Nicola are safe first. I need to make some calls. We should assume this man is still monitoring the family here, which means we have to consider there might be a knock-on effect for this other girl.' With new intent, Joel lifted his eyes to the shivering grass that sloped upwards. There were trees and strips of scorched hedgerow that were easily thick enough for concealment. Someone could be watching right now. The thought, as unlikely as it might be, made the hair on the back of his neck stand up.

'He does seem keen to keep control. Margaret said a little bit more in there. She said that she was given a strict time when she should report her daughter missing, that's why there was some delay with her suspicions in the morning and the report that came later in the day. She had a good few hours when she knew Kelly was dead and just had to sit on it.' DS Rose rubbed at the shocked expression on her face, but it didn't serve to remove it.

'She's been through hell. Does beg the question though, if you have that much control over someone, why make them report it at all?' Joel's eyes had been flitting to every movement of grass or tree branch. They now rested on his sergeant.

DS Rose seemed to take a moment to think. 'She's going to be reported at some point. Maybe our killer preferred to have control over when that would be – and he wanted it to be by someone who was already in fear of him.'

'Do you think there's something she's still not telling us?'

'I didn't get that impression, but it can't hurt to ask again.' DS Rose shrugged as she gave her tired reply.

Joel was feeling it too. The tension that had kept him upright left all at once and he half-turned to lean forward, both his palms flat against the wooden top of the dividing fence to take his weight. 'So we have a killer who's thought this out, who's intelligent enough to remove two people from the street without us getting a sniff, who exerts considerable control over close family members and seems to be able to keep one step ahead. We also have to assume that he's watching our survivor too, that he knows where she is even if we don't.' Joel's head was swirling; it suddenly felt heavier and drooped forward.

'He might be watching us too, if we're saying he's controlling where we are and when he would have opportunity,' DS Rose said.

'I'll have Elaine see if there's a convoy report opportunity, but I don't think there will be. There isn't much else we can do other than be aware of it as a possibility.' A convoy report was a basic police tool. There were a number of ANPR cameras around the county; he would ask Eileen to perform a search for all the cameras Joel and other colleagues might have hit as part of this investigation; then she would flag the next fifty cars to see if one or more had also followed them through a camera at any other point. It was a long shot. Joel wasn't even sure he had been anywhere near a camera since this whole thing had started, and it was even less likely that he should have been through two – they didn't tend to cover rural areas.

'And our survivor's moved. Maybe she's smart enough to hide herself.' DS Rose lacked conviction and Joel felt it too. When he lifted his head back up it was to peer over into Billy's garden. It was almost as neat, but different in style – simpler. It was mostly lawn with just a small patch of grey flint that had a steel structure rising up out of it like it was partly buried beneath the ground. It was engraved, the letters large enough to see from where he stood: *KISMET.* Joel had grandparents who had used that as their house name so he knew it was Turkish for 'fate'. His grandfather had been a strong believer in fate, in a life all laid out in front of you where everything happens for a reason. Joel found himself wrestling with that thought, with the idea that what had happened to Kelly Marshall and her family could have any reason to it at all.

'People can't hide,' he said, turning back to face DS Rose. 'I've worked with witness protection before. The things they do to make someone disappear – and still they get found. Smart phones, social media . . . The whole world is built around letting everyone else know where you are. We need to find her.'

'We always did,' DS Rose said.

'We need to find her *now!*' Joel snapped. Until we do I'll need to sort something up here, the whole family need to be under our protection . . .' His voice faded. A phone was ringing to interrupt him; it was DS Rose's and she pulled it from her pocket to greet Eileen. Her face contorted into frustration, like Eileen was taking her time to make her point on the other end. But he could tell the moment it came: DS Rose's face changed, her eyes flicked up to meet Joel's and her expression was delight.

'We might know where our survivor is!' DS Rose said.

Chapter 22

'We need to think this through.' DS Rose spoke out. They were back in Maidstone but away from the glass-fronted modern shopping outlets of the town centre and in what looked like a more 'traditional' High Street a little further out: a line of flat-fronted brick and stone buildings, their doorways opening onto grey-slabbed pavements. A butcher's canopy, the spinning red and white lure of a barber shop and the bold, empty promises of a betting shop added the only colour.

Joel had pulled them over onto double yellow lines while traffic streamed past on both sides. The pavements were busy with pedestrians too but no one stood out as paying any attention to them. That might change very soon, however, as Joel checked his mirror to take note of a tall man with a stiff walk and a green-rimmed hat working his way towards them.

'There's a bloody parking attendant behind us. I need to put this thing somewhere – we can't stay here for long,' he said. Eileen had provided DS Rose with an address; the door number was 124A but the visible numbers ran out when the shopfronts began. Joel had pulled them over suddenly when he spotted an address along the top of the betting-shop window, only to realise that he had pulled them up almost directly outside. It was another reason not to loiter.

‘I’ll get out and keep eyes on while you find somewhere to park.’ DS Rose gestured out her side of the car. ‘There’s a café just behind us. I should be able to get a view of the address, enough to see any comings or goings at least. Let’s talk in there, work out what we’re going to do.’

‘Good idea,’ Joel said. They had passed a car park not too far back, and the walk back would give him the chance to check in with Eileen and make sure there had been a response to his flurry of hurried calls on the way over. The longest conversation had been with DCI Jim Kemp – their first as part of a live job – and Joel had been further encouraged by his new boss. Kemp’s reaction had been to listen, then respond with what force policy stated should happen, then ask what Joel actually wanted to do. The Marshall family was the first order of business and Joel was actually very happy to follow force policy here. There was a serious threat to them all and Witness Protection was the only thing that would give him the piece of mind he needed to continue. He knew it was a big move – expensive, difficult, resource-intensive, and it often made it more difficult to keep the support of the witness in any court proceedings – but Joel still pushed for it. Kemp was happy to listen and agreed when Joel said it was him learning from his mistakes, that PSD had stated a number of times that Witness Protection should have been a consideration in the fallout from his last case. Joel still didn’t care about PSD and their criticism but he did care about Margaret Marshall and her family and was quite happy to use the words of Professional Standards to justify a course of action here.

Of course Margaret had refused the very idea of any sort of protection, but Joel had reiterated the danger, then told her he couldn’t guarantee her safety, or the safety or her grandchildren, until they had caught and contained the threat. Her daughter had added to the pressure on her mother – to Joel’s surprise – when she had agreed to take part, even after being made aware that it meant getting out of their family home to be relocated. It also meant not going to work, her kids not going to school; it meant disappearing from clubs, gyms and even close friends. Witness Protection was not something you could sugar-coat. Joel had a line he always used for those facing Witness Protection: *It will be harder than you think, worse than you think, but better than being dead.* Nicola had countered, insisting that it was only temporary and they could go back home when the police had caught her sister's killer. She was right, of course, and at that moment the pressure to do so quickly had increased tenfold.

Now however, they had someone else to make safe. DS Rose stepped out into the din of a bustling High Street. Joel took one last look at the flat above the betting shop, then at the approaching parking attendant and pulled away.

The café was ideal. Lucy couldn't quite get next to the window, but close enough to see out across the road and to the bare windows of flat 124A. Now she had time to take in the details she was concerned that it might not be in use at all. The windows were devoid of nets, curtains or blinds, but also, on a steaming hot day, they were sealed shut. From the moment Eileen had been tasked she had gone to work, calling round all the letting agents to see if anyone had helped out a couple presenting as needing somewhere instantly, and with Shannon Hendry as one of those to be named on the lease. Eileen also had a list of hotels and B&Bs to go through but a letting agent had called her back with some good news. As Joel had said – people don't disappear easily. The agent told the story of a couple who had come to them with savings that were not enough to cover the deposit and references that were eighteen months old, but she'd felt for them. They seemed nice – desperate too, with their belongings bundled in sacks at their feet. She'd smoothed it over with the owner and got them in the only place she had at short notice.

But now DS Rose was wondering if they'd changed their mind.

Beneath the sealed windows a door popped open. It was right on the edge of the betting shop and painted in the same colour so it blended in. The view across was obstructed by constant cars and people but the woman's shape and the way she held herself convinced DS Rose it was her. She could see flashes of slim legs covered in tight-fitting jeans and a thick top with hood up that looked odd in the heat. When the figure leant forward to check right and left, she also got a glimpse of a ponytail with a red tinge. DS Rose stood up at her table, waiting for the woman over the street to move before she did. The woman picked something up first, pacing away in the same movement. Now she held a Bag for Life, bright yellow to catch in the sun. It looked full too, heavy enough to affect her stance. She walked left to right, across the front of the betting shop, her head now down, her pace as fast as she could manage. Lucy left the café and crossed the road. It was easy enough to merge with the busy foot traffic. The woman was now in front of her and was having to hold the bag unnaturally across her front to stop it bashing the other pedestrians. It was slowing her down and Lucy had to adjust her stride accordingly. The woman's destination wasn't far; she veered left, did a little dance with someone coming the other way and then stepped off the street and into a launderette. Lucy continued past. The frontage was all window. Perfect for her to see her target move in and drop her bag on a plastic chair and to see there was one other person. The woman dropped her hood to show her profile – final confirmation that it was the same woman captured on the bus CCTV. She had found Shannon Hendry.

Lucy kept walking. She had seen a charity shop when they had driven in that shouldn't be far. It was six more shop fronts until she stepped into Cancer Research. Immediately on her left were a stack of jumpers. She swept them up and took them to the till. The elderly woman didn't dither and Lucy was back out with four jumpers swinging in a bag in less than a minute.

Shannon Hendry was still in the launderette, now sat beside an empty bag with the machine in front of her spinning. She held a magazine slightly too high to look natural and jerked to face the door when Lucy pushed it open. Lucy was careful not to make eye contact. There was still one other person, an older man sat towards the back, but he was readying his own bag like his time was coming to an end.

Lucy sat right beside Shannon. There were plenty of other chairs. She put her pile of freshly folded jumpers in the next washing machine along and closed the door. Then she pretended to scroll through her phone. The man at the back now stretched, coughed until he needed to steady himself, then emptied his machine. It was another few minutes before he left. They were alone.

It was Shannon who spoke first. 'You have to put money in there. For it to work, I mean,' she said.

'I didn't bring any change,' Lucy said.

'If you're asking then I'm a bit short at the moment, like brassic.'

'Actually, I was hoping you wouldn't notice, Shannon.'

Shannon still had the magazine lifted, and had slid down a little in her seat too. But the use of her name straightened her up, eyes flared wide. She shifted to the edge of her seat, maybe considering bolting.

'My name is Detective Sergeant Lucy Rose . . . Lucy, just call me Lucy. Stay calm and we can talk. That's all I'm here for.'

'Police!' Shannon hissed, her eyes now moving away from Lucy and towards the street through the window.

'I was careful. I didn't come knocking on your door. I didn't call the number I have for you, I know he monitors the phones. I know a lot more than that too. I know how to keep you and Jacob safe. But you have to talk to me.'

'Police?' she said again, but this time there was doubt in her voice.

'I'm a detective sergeant from a serious crime squad . . .' Lucy stopped herself. Shannon was starting to breathe faster and harder, she was glazing over too, her whole body shaking and fidgeting. This was all too much for her; she needed a moment. Lucy waited until she had her breathing better under control. Then she said, 'This isn't just about you, other people are suffering after what happened.'

'You're going to arrest me!' she said. 'You don't understand. You can't . . . You don't understand what he'll do! You can't, you CAN'T!' she shrieked, rising to her feet as she did. Her whole body now in flight mode. Lucy had seen it building and she was ready. She threw herself forward, her momentum enough to take Shannon to the floor. She tried to control the fall but heard Shannon's head thud against the tiles. She groaned and the grip she had on Lucy's arm immediately slackened. When she breathed out it was like a long sigh, and her eyes rolled back in her head.

'Shit!' Lucy said. She lifted her phone. She had a missed call from *Insp Norris*. She pressed to call him back.

Chapter 23

'Did you get him? Is Jacob here too?' was Shannon Hendry's instant reply to the formal caution read out to her in interview room three at Medway Police Station.

'He wasn't there, at the flat,' DS Rose replied. Joel had stayed standing at the back of the room, allowing his colleague to take the seat opposite their prisoner the moment it was vacated by the Force Medical Officer who had been required to clear her as fit for interview.

'He was! I left him there!' Shannon whined then threw her hands down to slap on the table top, her head quick to follow. Afetr a few seconds and a couple of shakes of her shoulders, she raised her face back up to show fresh tears smearing her mascara. 'He saw you coming, you idiot! There's stairs at the back, a way out. You don't get anything out of me, not a word, not until you find him!'

'We're looking for him, of course we are,' DS Rose said. She was leaning on the table too. It was one of the few items in the room that could be called furniture: the solid chairs they sat on, a short bench against the wall on the other side, even more uncomfortable than the chairs – and so reserved for the solicitors – and an aluminium-framed trolley, dented and scuffed where it had been pulled from room to room, carrying the recording equipment. The machine on top whirred and hissed in Joel's ear as it committed everything to a spinning DVD. In a digital age with cloud storage it felt totally archaic but change always seemed to be slow when it was funded by the public purse.

'Well, you're not looking hard enough!'

'And you talking to us, telling us what you know, telling us why you're so scared, why you're so worried about what might happen to Jacob . . . Do you think that helps us find him? Or do you think that makes it far less likely that we will?'

'I don't know, I don't care.' She lifted her head again, her focus flitting from the seated sergeant and beyond to where Joel still leant against the back wall. 'Just *find* him!'

Shannon's head dropped back onto her arms. She was wearing a long-sleeved T-shirt but the movement had dragged a little of the sleeve up on the forearm that now supported her head. Joel could see some reddening, which seemed to get angrier the higher it went. DS Rose must have seen it too.

'How did you hurt your arm, Shannon?' she said, her tone warm, encouraging rather than accusatory.

'Why am I under arrest?' Shannon snapped back to sit up. Her red hair was messed up enough to stand out at the sides and she had to push the fringe out of her eyes. She rubbed her face at the same time, removing the tears but further smudging the mascara.

'Because a young woman is dead. Because I believe you were the last person to see her alive. Because you gave me no choice.'

'No choice?'

'You tried to run. Put yourself in my shoes, Shannon, how would that look to you? And then you refused any swabs out there in the cell.'

'And you threatened to force me!'

'But I didn't.' DS Rose's tone was suddenly firmer. 'I could have you held down, one officer on every limb. I could have you stripped to your underwear, your skin swabbed and photographed, hair combed and your nails clipped. And it would be horrific for you. But I didn't, and I will be criticised for *not* doing that, but I know you can help us far more than an evidential swab might. But you have to talk to us. I want to find whoever it was that did that to your arm.' DS Rose leant forward, forcing eye contact from Shannon. 'But that other girl, we did swab her hands, we did strip her, clip her nails and comb her hair, and we did it without worrying about any upset or discomfort. Because *dead* women don't care, Shannon. And right now, the only theory we have is that you *killed* her.'

Shannon took those last three words like three slaps to the face. 'I didn't kill anyone!'

'What happened, Shannon?' The silence was as instant as it was oppressive. DS Rose leant forward, as still as a statue. Joel was still too, meeting Shannon's stare when she looked over at him for help. Shannon quickly buckled.

'I didn't kill anyone . . . I just ran, OK. And that would have been me if I hadn't . . .'

DS Rose still didn't move or react at all. Shannon lifted her eyes to meet hers, like she was waiting for her to speak, before she continued. 'I don't know anything about him, OK. I know what you're going to want to know, but he made sure that if I was ever here, sat in front of you, that I wouldn't be able to tell you anything. He wore big overalls, big gloves, big boots – a sort of hood over his head. It's like when you see a scarecrow, just clothes wrapped around sticks, no shape. And a weird voice. I can't help you anymore, not with anything.'

'You said "he",' DS Rose said.

'He, yeah. It was a man, I'm sure of that. From how he sounded and his size, he was tall and wide.'

'What do you mean by a weird voice?'

'Weird like distorted. And it might not have been his voice

even – he played it on a phone. It was a recorded message and he wouldn't answer any questions. I think about it now and I didn't hear him actually say a word. But it was a bloke, I know it was.'

'So he was a tall, well-built man who used a mobile phone recording. So you do know some things that can help us. What else do you know?'

'I don't *know* anything, I told you that. I was terrified!'

'From the start, Shannon. Tell us what happened.'

'It's not me . . .' Her lips suddenly trembled. 'It's not me I'm worried about. I've done what I needed to do. It's Jacob. He said he would hurt him, he knew everything about him, about his family too . . . And now . . . I've seen what he's capable of, he told me what would happen and it was exactly how it played out. You need to find him, you need to find Jacob! You can't be sat here!'

'Tell me about that day, Shannon. That day when you got on the bus in a dirty red dress, when a lad gave you his hoody because you looked *beaten up* – those were his words. When you were barefoot and when you had run away from a dead girl dressed just the same. Tell me about that day, from the moment you woke up.'

There was another pause.

'I didn't wake. I didn't really sleep. I . . . I was tied up. I was in a stable, I think, or a pigpen. That's what it looked like to me. There was straw and it smelt terrible. The walls were concrete and it was a thin room, long and thin. There was a door in front of me, but I was tied to the back wall by a wire that came through the wall. It was only thin, but so strong. When I got out of the pen I was in a much bigger barn. The roof was much higher than the walls, if that makes sense?'

'It does.'

'I was there overnight. It was cold. I was made to change into that dress. It was really uncomfortable, really stiff, and he called it my *colours*. He passed it under the door and I had to pass my clothes back out. And then he told me the rules.' She faded out, her lip trembling more. 'Could I have some water please?' she managed. DS Rose sat back. Joel was already moving to the door. He heard DS Rose explain to the numerous microphones hidden in the walls that he was leaving to get her a water and noting the time. The kitchen was close, and he was only out of the room for a few seconds. Shannon's hand shook when she took the paper cup from him. He put another down in front of his DS. This time he took a seat next to his sergeant.

'What were these rules?'

'It was a race,' Shannon blurted. 'But everything was at stake. He told me there was someone else nearby getting the same instructions. I thought he meant another barn at the time but she was just over the way. He told me she was evenly matched, seemed to take pride in that and how it had all been thought out. There was a phone box nearby and the first one there had to call a number and then they got to go home. I was told it would all start with a bell. That was how I would know it was time. He said there would be five bells in total, ten seconds between each one, and the last one would start the race. Every time a bell rang I was able to move a bit further away from that back wall. He said I needed to search the floor, under the straw and the pigshit for anything I could use.' She paused, her shaking hand lifted to her mouth. 'He promised that it would be over, that I could get back on with my life. With Jacob. But only if I got there first.'

'But you didn't believe him?'

'I did.'

'So why did you move? I went to your old place. You left it in a hurry.'

'We just didn't feel safe there. He knew so much about me. He knew that I lived there, he knew all about Jacob, even telling me about Jacob's mother and his little brother. I just couldn't be there anymore. But I did believe him, he's done with me. I did what he wanted. Otherwise why would he let me go when he . . . when he did that to the other girl? I was right there!'

'What did he do, Shannon?'

She was shaking her head even before the question; it looked like it was part of fending off the tears. Her eyes glazed like she was locked inside her mind with the memory. 'She made a mistake. She took a wrong turn. She was faster than me, faster out, faster to get going . . . My legs were stiff to start with, I couldn't get them to work right. But she went straight on and that gave me a chance. She made it back though, and when I got to the phone she was right with me. I managed to wrap something round the door frame, a leather belt I'd found, it gave me a few seconds to make that call. She knew what that meant, just like I did. I saw it in her eyes. The moment I spoke into that phone she stopped, everything stopped . . . Then he was there. I don't know where he came from, he might have been there all along. I was so focused on getting that call made, on keeping her out. She begged him and he didn't even say a word, just hit her with something. Then there was a huge bang and she *screamed!* She was hurt real bad. He *shot* her! Jesus Christ . . . He shot her right in front of me!'

DS Rose gave her a minute but this time she did prompt. 'What happened then?'

'He came right up to me. He had a gun in his hand. It looked like the sort you shoot at birds with but shorter. I thought that was it, I thought that was when I died. But he talked to me – he did talk to me! I remember now. It was quiet, almost a whisper and he told me to go, he told me never to talk to anyone about this. Then . . . do you know what he said?' A thick tear chased down a well-worn track to rest on her lip. She blew it away. 'He told me *well done!* Well done . . . Like I wanted to be there, like I should be proud that some other poor girl was dead because of what I had done. I just remember trying to get that belt off the door. I didn't think I was going to be able to, I thought I was trapped again, but it did come loose. He was back out in the road and I just ran. I could hear screams – she was still alive, she was *begging*. I knew she was going to die and I still ran away. What sort of a person does that make me?'

'There was nothing you could have done.' DS Rose sounded like she was talking out of a tightened throat.

'I could have got help. I was stood in a phone box. I could have dialled 999, he wouldn't have even known. I didn't even have to talk, I could have just left the phone off the hook and you lot would have known where it was. I've thought about that since but . . . at the time . . . I just wasn't thinking about anything.'

'It wouldn't have changed the outcome, Shannon. And you can help now.'

'She's dead!'

'She is. There's nothing we can do about that, but we have a second chance. You do. The chance to help us find the man that killed her and put you through that ordeal. You said he spoke, what did he sound like?'

'It was like a growl, like real deep even though it was quiet. That's all I remember.'

'Any accent, anything distinctive?'

Shannon shook her head firmly. 'No! I don't know, I wasn't taking much notice. He'd just shot that girl and she was crying. I just wanted to run away. I still do . . .' Shannon shifted her watery eyes to meet Joel's. 'Please don't make me talk about him, he told me what would happen if I talked about him.'

It was DS Rose who cut back in. 'You already are. And I think that's because you know it's the right thing to do. Because what you just described to me is pure evil, isn't it? And the one thing I know about evil is that it doesn't just stop. Evil goes again. He might have already identified another young woman to tie up in a place like that. She'll be just as terrified as you were. But you can help.' Another silence. This time DS Rose looked over at Joel like he had permission to break it.

'Where's the dress, Shannon? We need to have a look at it.'

'I left it in the bin outside my old place. I didn't want to keep it, I didn't want to be anywhere near it.'

Joel suppressed his disappointment. He would send someone to look for it but he wasn't convinced they would get anything from it anyway. Their offender was forensically aware and he had let her leave in it. 'Was it an area you know? We need to find where you were being held.' This was far more important as a line of enquiry. Shannon suddenly looked panicked again.

'I have no idea where I was. There were directions scratched into the wall above the door. The phone number too . . . 07652 995559. I'm sure that's it. I stared at it just about the whole time I was there, but I was still getting it wrong . . .'

Joel made brief eye contact with DS Rose. She wrote the number down but he was sure they both knew already that it would be the number for the burner left with Margaret Marshall.

'How did you get there, to be in that pen in the first place?' Joel said.

'I was grabbed. I didn't know what was going on. I feel so stupid. I thought I was meeting my mum. I got a text message from her saying that she wanted to do some shopping and she asked me to meet her at the Fremlin Walk car park in Maidstone.'

'The multi-storey?' Joel said.

'Yeah. I tried calling her when I got there and she texted me, saying she was in the car park and had something for me. I was stupid. I walked up the stairs. Some guy was coming the other way but I didn't pay him any attention. The next thing I know I was looking up at the ceiling. I remember the steps digging into my back . . . Not much else.'

'Do you remember anything about him at all? This guy?'

'He had a hood up, I think, but I never actually looked at him anyway.'

'When was this?'

'Sunday. Late for shopping, I thought, like around 4 p.m. Next thing I know I was in some filthy pen being told to change my clothes. I've never been so freaked out. And scared. So scared . . .'

'Have you spoken to your mum since then?'

'I had a missed call from a number I didn't know. It was from my mum giving me her new number because she'd lost her phone. She was out shopping Sunday but with a friend. I called her back. She had no idea.'

'You talked to her about what happened?'

'Of course I didn't! She would have frogmarched me down here to talk to you that very minute. I made small talk, pretended like I was fine when she asked. It was so hard not being able to tell her.'

Joel took a moment. This was different. Kelly Marshall's mother had been involved to prevent her calling the police, but Shannon's mother wasn't even aware. 'Jacob didn't report you missing?'

'He was threatened too. He was roughed up a little, then shown pictures of his mum and his little brother. She remarried, his brother's nine years old, and this piece of shit was describing exactly what he would do to him if Jacob did anything but wait.'

'Wait?' Joel prompted.

'For me. Or for a phone call. As it happened, he got me.'

'Was he told any details about the phone call?' Joel said.

'I guess it would have been the same as the one I made. I guess that other girl had a different number, and she would have got through to Jacob. When Jacob was roughed up, he was given a phone, some cheap thing. If that had rung, it would mean . . .' She took another moment. Considering what she had been through, she was holding it together well. Her account certainly confirmed her as the survivor they had been labelling her from the start, but Joel now thought this was a better description of her than they could have realised. 'You have to find him . . . Jacob. He's everything to me and he's so angry. If this guy . . . You can't fight him, I've seen that, you have to do what I did, you have to run.'

'You said you had directions to the phone box.' DS Rose came back with the question to get Shannon back on track.

'Hardly. Like a jagged line scratched into the concrete. He called it a map but it weren't no map.'

DS Rose leant in again, this time reaching out, her hand resting gently on top of Shannon's. 'Do you still remember it? Do you still know those directions?'

'I want to forget, but I can't.'

'If we took you there, to that phone box, could you take us to where you were held? Do it in reverse?'

Shannon's eyes suddenly opened as wide as they could. She looked like she was struggling for breath. 'I can't! I can't go back there! You can't make me do that, can you?'

There was a light tap at the door and Shannon eyed it nervously. Joel pulled the door open to be met by an apologetic-looking jailer who mumbled some words in his ear. Joel nodded and sat back down.

'Shannon, we've got Jacob. He went out looking for you and ended up at the local police station, in quite a state apparently. He's being brought here. He obviously decided that coming to us was the best thing, that no matter what that man said, we're your best bet.'

DS Rose took over with the appeal. 'You need to help us. That's how we can keep you safe, that's how you get back to walking a few paces to a launderette without having to put your hood up.' DS Rose gazed directly into Shannon's eyes.

'Take us there,' she continued. 'I'll be with you every step. And then you and Jacob get to be somewhere safe together.'

Shannon's lips trembled like words were close but kept being discarded. Finally she nodded, as a single tear rolled down her cheek.

Chapter 24

The moment the tarmac ran out under the convoy of police cars, and chunks of stone and grit flicked and crunched under the wheels, Shannon Hendry's whole demeanour changed. She had been true to her word, bringing them right to a place that would forever be a part of her nightmares. She had surprised Joel so far; he hadn't known how she might react to the phone box where her guided route had started, but she had insisted on getting out, then stared it down with a look on her face that made Joel think of a gunslinger in a Western, waiting to turn away and take their ten paces. It was a clear refusal to be frightened, but everything changed the moment the jet-black throat of a distant barn appeared. This was the end of her instructions. They had arrived with not a single wrong turn, a route perfectly executed, which, considering she was guiding them backwards through a route she had sprinted in a panic, was mightily impressive.

The track sloped down to the barn. Joel pulled over as per the briefing, signalling out of the window for the firearms team to sweep past in their matching Land Rovers and take the lead. A third marked car fell in behind Joel as the patrol that would take Shannon away the moment they didn't need her anymore. That moment was now.

'How are you doing?' Joel peered into his mirror. Shannon was on the left of the rear bench, DS Rose on the right. She turned to monitor their passenger. Shannon lifted her eyes to meet his, the movement awkward, the eyes swollen, damp and starting to redden, something that stood out against a skin pallor that was suddenly washed out. She looked paler even than when they had sat her under the unflattering lights of the custody block.

'I want to go home.' Her words seemed to slip out without moving her mask of horror. Joel nodded at his colleague. The transfer was seamless, Shannon allowing herself to be led from one police car to another like she was in a trance. Then the marked car pulled alongside them while turning around, so that Joel could look across. Shannon was in the back again, this time on her own with the two uniforms in the front. She was still staring ahead but she had lost all focus, and although she was facing the barn Joel was pretty sure she wasn't seeing it, not in real time at least. The images she was seeing were from a few days earlier, when she been forced to run away from this place.

When her life had depended on it.

Joel's old TSG team were there too, but hanging back for this part. Their choice of vehicle was a Sprinter van and their role was the search. Joel was delighted to see them – not just because they were old mates, but because he knew the job was about to be done properly, just as soon as firearms had made it safe. The barn was a hundred metres away and the four armed officers were already out of the cars, which had been pulled across so as to provide maximum cover from anything fired from the barn. There was only silence. The tension in the car increased as every moment passed without an update coming back out of the shadow that consumed the barn's large open front. Joel turned his radio up but only succeeded in making it hiss louder.

'*Clear!*' The increased volume made them both jump. Joel

gave a nervous chuckle, then started the car and moved forward. He parked untidily and was first out, the heavy-booted search team crunching close behind as they all made for the darkness, crossing paths with the four armed officers coming out the other way.

'All yours, boss,' one of them said. Joel could only acknowledge with a nod, his throat suddenly tight, his mind heavy with the realisation that this was it. The horrors they had seen and heard over the last few days: *they had all started here.*

The temperature change was instant. The draft whipping through the barn were almost cold for Joel in his short-sleeved shirt and trousers. He certainly wouldn't want to be dressed in just a single layer of cloth for a stay overnight. The breeze carried the distinct smell of a farmyard.

'Boss!' The voice came from the left side, from someone stood on the threshold of one of the pens. There were eight, all identical, divided by scuffed walls and mirrored directly opposite by eight more. His colleague had called out from the fourth pen down. Joel joined him, DS Rose too. They all hung by the door. The floor was concrete with a thick covering of straw. It didn't look fresh. It looked disturbed too, uneven where it appeared that clumps had been pulled up. The smell was stronger here. Joel stepped in, relieved, as always, that his CSI resource had been held up and couldn't be here to restrict his movements. His eyes lifted to the concrete lintel above the door. He saw the numbers first, bolder, scratched deeper and matching the phone number they knew. The lines next to it that made up the 'map' were more faint. This had been Shannon Hendry's holding pen.

'Jesus,' DS Rose said. She was looking towards the far end, to where a loop of wire was visible lying on top of the straw. There was something else too. Joel strained but couldn't make it out. It was directly in the middle of the loop, standing up. He stepped closer, squatting over it, careful not to touch it. 'What hell is that?'

'Looks like a figurine of some sort.' Joel fought the urge to pick it up so he could inspect it more closely. It looked plastic and about the size of a thumb. He carefully pulled away a clump of straw concealing the bottom half.

'It's her!' DS Rose gasped. Joel could see it now. The figurine was of a young woman in a running stance. It was mostly light grey but some parts had been crudely painted. The figurine wore a tattered dress that trailed behind her and was coloured red while the hair was a lighter orange. The painting was clumsy, the colours uneven and ran into each other. But the intent was clear. It was supposed to be Shannon.

Joel stood up. 'She said the other girl came out opposite, didn't she?' He was already heading for the door to cross the floor. He found the pen, not quite opposite but a little further along, closer to the open front of the barn. But it had the same scratched map and a slightly different number on the concrete lintel; the same loop of wire too. The figure left standing in its middle had subtle differences: the dress was painted white, the hair blonde to match Kelly Marshall's. But there was additional detail. The face, which had been the base colour of grey in the pen opposite, was scrawled over in black to make two rings around the eyes that continued to drip down the cheeks. Joel looked up at DS Rose.

'This one is crying,' he said.

Chapter 25

'Eileen, what do you have for me?' Joel walked back into his office at Headquarters, which, despite its shortcomings, was still far better than squatting at a canteen table with a laptop as he had found himself doing when down at Medway nick, between interviewing Shannon Hendry. DS Rose was with him too, she made for her own desk.

Shannon herself was now safe – or at least safer. She had refused any further police intervention as part of her release, and she and Jacob would take their chances staying with one of her uncles. She seemed to think that the fact he hadn't been mentioned by the monster who had abducted her meant that she would be safe there. Joel wasn't convinced. If her attacker wanted to find her again, Joel was pretty sure he could, but he also had a strong feeling that Shannon Hendry was finished with. She had been allowed to walk away, after all.

They had still made sure that both Shannon and Jacob had a remote alarm that was linked directly to the Force Control Room and Joel had personally filled out the 'Operational Info' tab on PNC against the address she was going to, so all calls – silent included – from that address or any numbers linked to her would get an immediate blue light response. Other than advice on staying off social media and avoiding anything she had habitually been doing before, it was the best he could do.

Eileen harumphed before she replied. 'A message from an angry wife – yours, I'm afraid. She said she tried you first. You remember I told you how she has a number for me that she uses when you ignore her?'

'I wasn't ignoring her—'

'Save it. I'm definitely not the one after an explanation. Apparently you were supposed to call your brother back . . . Clive, is it? Seems my transition from Intelligence Analyst to PA is now complete, sir.' Eileen was doing that thing again, holding him in a gaze over the top of her glasses whilst scolding. She also looked a little flustered, which is a strange look for a woman sat at a work desk in slippers with frilly clumps of wool on top.

'Thank you, Eileen. Just be sure to remind me of all the times you've gone above and beyond in your performance review discussions.'

'Don't you worry about that, Mr Norris, I have them all written down.'

'I'm sure you do . . . and Eileen, why won't you call me Joel?' He sighed this sentence as part of slumping into his seat.

'I joined a disciplined organisation with a rank structure. The moment one of those is forgotten the whole thing falls apart.'

Joel didn't have the strength to argue and even if he did, now certainly wasn't the time. 'So now we have a killer mocking us, pissing about with little figurines. There can be no doubt that was left for us to find, so then, any ideas?'

Eileen still fixed him over her glasses. 'I will let the bad language go. I can see you're upset. And besides, you might be on to something but, rather than mocking us, our offender could actually be playing a game.'

'What do you mean?' Joel sat up straighter and dug his heels in to move his chair over to his Analyst. Once CSI had arrived he'd requested they send pictures of the figurine to Eileen as one of their first actions, knowing that she would accept the challenge of finding out everything she could about it. She wasn't about to disappoint.

'The figurine you found is stamped on the bottom with "*AR*", which references Arch Rival Games. They're a strategy board game company. The figurine is part of a game called *Escape!*'

'*Escape!*?' Joel cut in, forcing a tut of frustration from the seated woman. Eileen angled her screen towards him. The image in the centre was the very same running woman figurine but this one was grey all over where it hadn't been painted.

'An adult strategy board game. I must confess, I didn't realise there was such a thing. From what I can see, it would appear the rules of play echo our crime scenes.'

'Go on?' Joel prompted when Eileen seemed to pause for effect.

'Four zones, two players in each that are pitted against each other. The aim of this game is to get out of your zone and to a point on the board first. It's a straight race. There's a little more to it than that, of course. I printed the full rules in case you wanted a little bedtime reading.'

Joel spun to the printer, where he could see a stack of papers that was still being added to. 'Summary?'

'How did I know you were going to say that . . . Players each have one of these figurines that sit on the gameboard. You roll the dice, your score determines what actions you can take. That includes searching for tools or for weapons or you can move. The tools and weapons are in two stacks of cards and are random so some are better than others.' Eileen paused for effect. 'Anyone want to hazard a guess at what is available?'

'A pitchfork,' DS Rose had moved closer too, Eileen clicked her fingers.

'That's one of the weapons. Also, the painting element is a key part of it too. There seems to be a whole community around *Escape!* that live on social media. There are a number of different figurines available to buy and all come in a flat grey colour but with the option to purchase paint sets. People like to share their own creations. You get issued plastic weapons too and again, people paint those, some of them in quite extraordinary detail. The game is just the beginning of it all really.'

'Where are you running to?' Joel said. 'What's the end point?'

Eileen's smile was a little smug. 'Very good, Mr Norris, it's a phone box, although they have gone a little US and called it a payphone.'

'Is there a list of all the weapons?' Joel said.

'All the possible weapons, all the possible tools, but some are different depending on what zone you are in.'

'Zone?' Joel said.

'The board is made up of four zones. It just so happens that "abandoned farm" is one. Choose that zone and the list of weapons includes a pitchfork and a shotgun.' Eileen again gazed at him over her glasses, awaiting his next instruction.

'Any mention of a belt?' Joel said.

'Leather scarecrow's belt, in the tool list.'

'Of course it is.' Joel got to his feet. It helped him think. 'Can you call the skipper out at the farm in Lenham and give them the full list of weapons and tools for the game – not just the farmyard zone, or whatever the hell it's called. Anything they find on that list needs to be photographed in situ and then a forensic seizure.'

'Will do,' Eileen said.

'Are we saying our killer is playing this game out live?' DS Rose spoke now, doing nothing to hide the incredulity in her tone.

'It has to be a working theory, doesn't it? We need a copy of this game,' Joel said.

Eileen came back in. 'I'm a step ahead of you. Facebook

has a marketplace; you can filter it by distance. There are quite a few bits related to that game changing hands but there's at least one full game for sale less than ten miles away. I've messaged to reserve it. I figured you could pick it up in the morning.'

Joel was shaking his head. 'I'll go now. We need to understand it, every part of it. The only way to do that is to play the damned thing.'

'Tonight?' Eileen's voice rose an octave in either surprise or delight.

'Now. This changes things, doesn't it?'

'Changes what?' DS Rose said.

'Everything. Up to this point we were investigating a murder, one murder, one survivor. But if it's a game with four zones and what was it . . . two players in each?'

'Up to eight people . . .' Eileen breathed, seemingly catching up with what Joel was getting at.

'So what is this, round one? We have to work to that for sure.'

'Jesus,' DS Rose breathed.

'So tonight then. I'll go get this game, maybe pick up a pizza on the way back. I could play it myself but I think we all need to know what we might be up against.'

'Well, actually . . .' Eileen began, and both officers fixed on her. 'I do have plans this evening, sir. There's a crossword that simply won't do itself . . . I'll have to call my neighbour, get my cat fed, and I can catch up on my soaps . . .' Her excitement was increasing. Joel thought it was the realisation kicking in that she was being asked to stay late to play her part in working a murder investigation and preventing more lives lost, but then she said: 'And I do *love* a boardgame!'

Joel shook his head then aimed a questioning look at his sergeant. 'Of course,' she responded instantly, 'I like Hawaiian.'

Eileen was back working her screen, the clicks on her mouse seeming firmer and faster as she moved back to Facebook's marketplace page. Joel moved to peer over her shoulder. She brought up the profile of the seller. A number of *Escape!*-related items were shown. One stood out. Another figurine, but different. It looked larger than the runner – wider certainly and in this case expertly painted, right down to tiny poppers on the navy blue overalls and a lighter shade of blue on the turnups over black rubber boots. The face was covered by a yellow hood that flared out to meet the shoulders, with a rectangle on the front to look like safety goggles stitched into it. In its right hand it held a lit welding torch, in the other a bronzed cattle bell.

'What the hell is that?' Joel said.

'That is The Captor.' Eileen's reply was instant.

'What does he do?'

'He's the main character, the one you have to defeat.'

'How do you defeat him?'

Eileen stopped her clicking to peer over the top of those damned glasses. 'You stay alive.'

Chapter 26

Bradley was aware of the voices, shrill, slightly panicked – familiar. His two children in the back, talking to him.

'What!' he bellowed and instantly felt bad. It wasn't their fault he was distracted, that his anxiety was such that he was having to focus to breathe at all, his grip on the steering wheel so tight that his hands were flushed white, while he squinted out at a quickly sinking sun, desperate to find his way before dark.

It wasn't their fault that an old-style Land Rover Defender was right up his chuff either. It must be a local, someone far more used to these roads and heading home for dinner. There was nowhere to pull over and he didn't want to speed up in case he missed a landmark. He was hopelessly lost.

'Where are we going, Daddy?' Bradley didn't know. Not really. He had hurriedly booked somewhere, a holiday cottage, the first one he had found that looked remote. But his reasons were nothing to do with taking a family break. It had been a reaction after what he had done, what he had been forced to do. He had killed a man. It hadn't been easy either, not like the movies might have you believe. His victim was barely a man, a baby-face with soft skin, but he had fought hard, even when his arm had snapped under the blow of a baseball bat. Even when Bradley had stabbed him in the neck he had still lashed out, still twisted under the blade like he might get away. None of it had been what he might have expected; it wasn't soft, there weren't the sudden wide eyes and a few seconds of clutching at his neck before his victim went limp – nothing like it. There was gristle, spurting blood, hands getting in the way as he tried to push the scissor blade deeper. The blood was thick and slippery; he had even resorted to a sawing motion. In the end he had pulled the blade away and just started stabbing, striking the hands and fingers that were in the way first so he could get to the neck. But the pain didn't seem to register; the hands didn't move. There was so much fight. Bradley had even started to wonder if you *could* kill a man with a pair of scissors.

But you can.

The resistance seemed to leave all at once. The man's hands finally fell out of the way and he had continued stabbing at the mess that was revealed. Soon the skin of his neck was nothing but jagged tears of flesh, open wounds flushing white for an instant before erupting in deep red. The more he stabbed the less the blood. The first good blows had been like popping a balloon; the last one barely did anything at all. The man died in his arms.

Alan.

He wished now that he hadn't asked for his name. Maybe it would be easier to dismiss a nameless victim – or at least to shake him from his mind just long enough to follow directions.

He glanced at his mirror to glimpse his children, the very reason he had reacted the way he had. He couldn't lose them. They couldn't lose him. They had barely started being a family.

'I told you, a fun place in the woods. That's all.'

'But I have school, Daddy. Am I still going to school?'

'No, Tommy, you're not going to school, OK, mate? I've

spoken to them, you don't have to. Your teacher's fine with it. Your brother's nursery the same.'

'Where's Mummy?'

'She'll be there too, OK? She just had some things to sort at work. Oh FOR GOD'S SAKE!' Bradley roared. The Defender was now flashing its lights, snaking across the road to fill each mirror in turn. There was a passing place just ahead under a canopy of trees. He slowed, pulling over to let the local past, and looked into his side mirror, his fist already raised in a *wanker* gesture against the driver's window. Then Bradley quickly snatched it back.

It had pulled out to go round, but it didn't look like it had pulled out enough. Sure enough, the Defender hit, its nearside front pushing into his rear quarter panel. It was slow moving, and his car leant away from the impact as it scraped up the side. He heard an engine surge as the scraping got closer; it seemed to turn harder into the side, now reaching the driver's-side door. He leant away. The plastic housing under the window popped out, the wing mirror was dragged from its housing to hang down and thump against the side on a wire as the Defender continued past. Then it veered over to block the way, the brake lights dim through a layer of mud.

Bradley swore. He pushed his door open but was able to control his rage enough to turn back and take in the faces in the back. 'Everyone OK?' he said and got hurried nods in reply.

He spun away, stepping round his door to take in the fresh scrapes and dents. The wing mirror bounced against the door once more as he slammed it shut. The front wing had damage too. The sight of his car, those terrified eyes in the back, it all fuelled his rage as he strode towards the Defender. Its reverse lights flickered like the driver had put it in neutral while the engine still ticked over.

'NOT LIKE I DIDN'T GIVE YOU PLENTY OF ROOM!' he bellowed towards the car, approaching from the side where he could see the windows were smoked almost black but the driver's window was down. There was no reaction, which only served to make him angrier. He made it to the driver's window. 'WHAT THE FUCK IS WRONG WITH—'

He stopped dead.

The yellow hood was the first thing he saw, then the blue overalls. Then his eyes dropped to the weapon held in a loose grip on his lap. He recognised it from when it had been pushed into his face at the start of his nightmare just a few days earlier.

'You cheated.' That same growled voice – he'd only used it for a few words, most of the time he'd communicated through a tinny recording. 'You remember what I told you? It would be your children first.' The door opened. Rubber boots dropped to the floor and Bradley found himself stepping backwards.

'No!' Bradley threw his hands up, side-stepping to block the man's way back to his car and his children in it. 'Listen to me, *listen* to me! I didn't cheat, I didn't know that was cheating. You said the first one there and I . . . I was first!'

The man stepped in, close enough for the scent of the leather hood to flood Bradley's nostrils. The barrel of the blunted shotgun dug him in the chest. 'You don't take the life. I take the life. Everyone plays their role. Yours was to run.'

'I didn't know! You said first one to the phone, a race, I knew that. You didn't say I couldn't hurt anyone else. You think I *wanted* to? I had to make it, I had to be the winner, I've got two kids . . . Come on, you know that. I just did what I could! Please!'

'You will play again.'

'What . . .? No! No, come on, I did what you asked, that was all—'

'You will play again or you will all die here. Now. Kids first.' The man took a side-step like he might be going round him.

‘OK! OK, I’ll do it again. I’ll play by the rules, by your rules, OK? I’ll do that. Just don’t hurt them.’ The man stopped in his tracks. He seemed to hesitate; at least, he stayed still. When he did move again it was towards the back of his own car. The boot door was large and hinged on the side. Bradley had to step back so he could open it.

‘Get in.’

‘I can’t! My boys are in—’

‘Get in!’

‘I’m not leaving my boys!’ Bradley stood still. The man with the hood moved to the side of the Defender. He pulled open the back door this time, leaning in for just a moment. There was another voice now, a muffled scream then a whimper. ‘Jesus, Julie!’ His wife stumbled to stay upright as she was wrenched from the car. Her hands were bound, her mouth gagged tight with material that looked like a torn-up towel. The man threw a pair of scissors at her feet. Bradley recognised them instantly. He could still see the red staining on the blade. He had first seen them when he had pulled them out of that sandpit.

‘Get IN!’ The growl had a higher pitch when it was louder. His wife glanced around and saw their car. Their oldest boy had got out to stand beside it, his eyes filled with fear and confusion. Julie was shaking her head vigorously, the gag starting to come away as she did. The man raised his shotgun again, this time resting it against the side of Julie’s head to stop her movement. She stared over at Bradley, her eyes pleading, her chest heaving.

Bradley stepped up into the boot, talking to her as he went. ‘Don’t worry! I’ll sort this—’ The boot door slammed into his hip. He felt another shove where it hadn’t closed, and this time the blow pushed him off balance and he rolled onto his side. He heard the front door pull open and slam shut, and felt it too – then the movement of someone getting into the car.

‘Just do as he says!’ His wife’s voice, her words screamed. She must have been free of the gag, maybe using those scissors

that had been dropped onto the floor, still stained with the blood of the man he had killed. She shouted something else too, but he couldn't make it out over the sound of the engine revving. He made it back onto his knees only for a sudden surge forward to send him sprawling again, his head banging against something solid. He curled into a foetal position, doing the best he could to protect himself as he hurtled away from his family, already muttering his promises that he would do whatever it took to get back to them.

Chapter 27

The pizzas were barely touched. When Joel had picked them up the scent was full of promise as it flooded the car for the short journey back to the nick, but for all of them it seemed, their appetite diminished with every item unpacked from the box labelled *Escape!*

The tagline on the front of the box was the first thing to grab Joel's attention. Under the game's title was a strapline: *You Have To Win*. It was written across the midriff of the character that seemed to be central to the whole thing: The Captor. He was shown as a cartoonish welder in blue overalls, his face concealed behind a leather hood. 'Cartoonish' was a good way to describe the tone overall. The set Eileen had secured for them was part painted, which meant the plastic pitchfork was finished with blood droplets, as was the glass hammer. Everything seemed to be covered in gore of some sort: all part of the fun.

But it didn't seem funny now.

They played a condensed version of the game, just using the Abandoned Farm as its backdrop. You could fit all of the zones together, four squares to form an area large enough to challenge the dimensions of most dining-room tables, but they didn't have the time to play out the full thing. Joel just wanted an idea of what they might be up against and the *Decrepit Fort, Abandoned Lorry Park* and *Abandon Ship!* zones stayed in the box.

The game was essentially a dice game in which you took turns to throw five at a time, needing one of them to be a six to get out of your chains and start your *Escape!* Once out, your score across the dice determined your options and you could use this score to search for tools or weapons or to move towards the final goal of the payphone. At times your path could cross with your opponent's or, if the circumstances were right, The Captor could catch you up – hence the need for weapons to repel a threat, and tools to gain access to the phone box at the end. The tools and weapons were in two piles of playing cards, both face-down so you couldn't know what you might get next. The backs of the cards displayed the cartoonish welder and his blowtorch staring out with *Escape!* written across him.

If Joel could have forgotten for a minute the fact that two young women had been forced to play this out as part of a terrifying reality, then he might have been able to see the game's appeal and how it could be a fun way to spend an evening. But it was far from it. Cards were turned over, more and more grisly-looking weapon options were revealed, and all the time The Captor was in close pursuit.

The game ended for Joel when Eileen overturned the *Death Card*. A simple skull and crossbones image that had them scampering for the rule book and accepting that its reveal meant that all of them had to lose a life. Joel didn't have another one to lose as he'd already been damaged from an attack by The Captor that had left him wounded.

He couldn't say he appreciated the irony.

Day 4

Chapter 28

The images of cartoon weapons dripping with blood were no doubt part of the reason that Joel slept so poorly. He woke up with a start, his bedside clock telling him it was just after 5 a.m., but his mind clicked in, seemingly unconcerned about his lack of sleep and forcing him to abandon any attempts to get any more.

He crept downstairs to hunt for his running shoes. If he had to be awake, he might as well try and make something positive out of it.

He ran into the sunrise for as long as he could, his eyes half closed, enjoying the sensation on his face. Too soon it was snuffed out by tall trees that lined most of a loop that touched the outskirts of the medieval city of Canterbury before bringing him back to the rural setting of Elham and his home in the centre of the village.

His wife was there to witness him stumbling back through his front door. She sat halfway up the stairs, wearing a dressing gown wrapped tight.

'I was hoping not to wake you.'

'You didn't,' she said.

'Are you going back to bed? It's early.'

'It's gone six, it won't be long before the kids start making their demands,' she said with a shrug.

'Is it? I went a little further. I can sort the kids out this morning if you want another half hour. I'll bring a tea up.'

'That's OK. But I'll still take that tea.' She smiled and stood up, pulling her gown at the hem to straighten it. He walked through to the kitchen to fill the kettle and Michelle moved to lean on the counter opposite him. 'I'm sorry, I know I was supposed to be making the kids' dinner last night, to be making you dinner—'

'We don't care about dinner, you can't cook for shit, Joel. We just want you here spending time with us. That's all.'

'I know. I'm sorry.'

'It's partly my fault. I guess I got used to seeing you for regular hours. I'm happy for you, I know you wanted a good job to do, to be working again and I know if you're late off it will be for something important.' There was a smile but the eyes above it were questioning.

'We were playing boardgames,' Joel said, deliberately not saying anymore.

'You missed time with your family to play a boardgame with your workmates?' He was going to need to explain himself.

'There's an strategy boardgame for adults, it's called *Escape!* You have to roll a dice, make moves, get tools and weapons, and the aim of the game is to stay alive from some evil captor character. This killer that we're looking for might be playing it for real – and I know how that sounds – but he has two people up against each other, forcing them to search for whatever they can use, then making them run for their lives. Literally. The person who makes it first is cut loose to find their way home, barefoot, lost and half-starved. The person who loses the race . . .'

'What?' Michelle said, disbelief now thick in her voice.

'Game over,' Joel said. 'And now we think it might happen all over again if we can't stop it.'

'Jesus, Joel, what the hell is wrong with people?'

'The old TSG days, I saw a lot of violence, dealt with a

lot of violence. Pub fights, gang fights, stabbings over drugs . . . There was always a reason that someone was a victim.' Joel shook his head. 'If you're being stabbed by a drug dealer you're probably a rival dealer, or an enforcer, or just *part* of that world. I can almost accept someone getting hurt because they made some wrong life choices, because they went after the easy money. But this girl, she could have been someone this sicko just walked past in the street – wrong place, wrong time – totally random. I can't get past that. I think about our girls, I think about keeping them safe, bringing them up right so they stay the hell away from drug dealers or any world where violence is normal. But how do I keep them away from someone like this?'

Michelle stepped in to take hold of his shoulders. 'You find him and you put him away. That's what you do, that's your job now. Think how important that is. Those drug dealers you talk about, you used to tell me how you would arrest one and two others would pop up somewhere else in the same town – *whack-a-mole*, right? This guy, he has to be seriously unwell, he has to be unique. Stop him and no one takes his place and our girls are safe, the whole world's a safer place.'

'That's what's keeping me up at night – it doesn't feel like we're getting any closer. What if this is just the start? What if we don't get him in time to stop it happening again?'

'You're no good to anyone this shattered – and you do look shattered! Why don't you get a few hours now, work a later day? Even a couple will make you feel so much better.' She tutted, her gaze dropping to search for the vibrating phone that had now come between them. It was in Joel's pocket – his work phone. Who the hell would be calling him at this time in the morning? He pulled the phone from his pocket. The number was one that had called him often enough for him to give it a label: **Force Cntrl Rm.**

'Hello?' Joel said, holding eye contact with his wife.

'Inspector Norris?' A female voice, nasal and matter-of-fact;

she was a supervisor at the FCR and apologised for disturbing him at this hour. They were words she clearly didn't mean. Then she got onto the reason for the call. Joel's face must have changed as he listened. His wife reacted by shuffling from one foot to another, her face expectant when he thanked the woman for her call and ended it. He didn't mean it either.

'What's up?' Michelle said immediately.

Joel pulled his cheeks down with both hands, his exhaustion now a wave that threatened to consume him.

'We didn't stop him in time. Seems like he's played another round.'

Chapter 29

'So this will be the *abandoned lorry park*,' Joel said from the passenger seat as they entered Sandwich Industrial Estate. It was actually on the edge of the town, closer to the border with Ramsgate than to Sandwich's medieval centre, and fifty minutes from where Joel had picked up DS Rose from Maidstone Headquarters – even with the activation of the blue lights concealed in the grill and use of a siren when needed. In total it was almost two hours since Joel had received the call.

The marked cars of the local patrols who had first responded were still on scene. The industrial estate backed onto the River Stour. The summary that Joel had been given reported that the man who called the police ran a boat repair shop in one of the units. Apparently he had been confused to find the unit next to his crudely broken open. He'd investigated and found signs of a disturbance and the phone off the hook. A police dog handler had turned up expecting to trace the steps of a fleeing burglar, but instead his spaniel had located a dead body described as having its neck 'hacked to pieces'. The grim discovery was some way from the phone, across a bridge that led to a temporary lorry park that could also be accessed via the A256. This was where DS Rose had brought them.

The phone records from the empty unit had been hurriedly applied for by the Force Control Room and they had already confirmed a call had been made that lasted seven minutes. If Shannon Hendry's account was correct then Joel could be sure it wasn't a seven-minute conversation, more likely a single sentence and then a phone left to dangle off the hook. Again the number dialled out led to an untraceable mobile phone. These similarities were why it had been linked to Kelly Marshall's murder so quickly – and why the scene was now waiting for Joel to take over.

There were some differences, however: timing, for one. The call had been made the previous morning, so twenty-four hours had passed. Kelly Marshall had been left in a public phone box, her quick discovery inevitable, but this was the quietest part of a half-full industrial estate. Joel was already interested to see what other differences there might be.

He wasn't to be disappointed.

They stepped out of the car. The sun was still low in the sky but packed no less of a punch from where it hung over an untidy row of lorry trailers. Their open ends were towards him, the A256 a dull roar beyond thick trees. All of the trailers had at least one of their doors tied back. Joel knew this was something the drivers did to show that they had nothing on board worth causing damage to get to, although it seemed a little unnecessary here as would-be thieves couldn't see the trailers from the road and the field they were parked in had been hard for the police to find, even with directions. Joel reflected that you could work on the site daily and still not know of the trailers parked in a field at the back. He made a mental note to find out who did.

'Sir . . .' An officer in uniform approached. She was wearing Sergeant chevrons on her shoulder but the Velcro name-tag on her stab vest said different: *PC Angela DAWES, Neighbourhood.*

'Angela, nice to meet you, what do we have?'

'Just what you can see. We haven't moved anything or searched anything. The dog handler did track the area but that was a negative . . .' She stopped and took in a breath. 'Sorry! I'm just acting for a few shifts. My sergeant's on a course and this is the first time I've been asked to cover.'

'And look what happens.' Joel laughed and Acting Sergeant Angela Dawes seemed to lose some of the tension in her body.

'We got a call. One of the blokes who runs a unit here saw the padlock had been snipped on the next one over and the shutter was up. They all look out for each other round here. He went in and saw the phone was hanging off. We did some work and the phone was used to call a mobile number at 0545 hours yesterday morning. There was blood too – not much, a few spots out on the concrete and then inside the unit. We thought a burglar had caught himself on the way in, but then . . .' She gestured towards the last lorry on the left. It took a couple of seconds for Joel to see what he was meant to. There was a pile of something lying in the shadow of a trailer, almost directly under the metal steps. The door to the trailer was tied open. It took another moment for his brain to start making out details, like a hand with splayed fingers on the upturned hip and one bare foot lying on top of the other with the sole towards him.

'The handler who found the body – I assume he's still on?' Joel said.

'Yes, but he was heading back in to get his statement done.'

'OK, I'll just take contact details so he knows who I am.'

The sergeant nodded. 'No problem.'

'Right then, I'd better take a look.'

'Do you mind if I . . .' The sergeant stayed where she was. 'It's just . . . What with being here a day or so, it looks like an animal has had a little nibble and . . .'

Joel smiled back at her. 'I'll only call you over if I need you,' he said. 'If you could direct our CSI friends when they arrive, that would be great.' Her relief was clear.

They had actually passed a marked CSI van on the way, but Joel knew they were processing the unit first. The spots of blood described would already be deteriorating and Joel would make the most of assessing the victim before anyone was here to tell him what he couldn't touch. A different CSI resource would be attending the body, they would need to treat each scene separately until they could be officially linked. After all, who was to say that the unit wasn't the target for a clumsy burglar and the body up here wasn't totally unrelated? As unlikely as that was, Joel could picture the smug defence solicitor rocking on their heels in delight and delivering a grand speech about how *likely or unlikely has no place in a court of law – nor does coincidence. A conviction has to be done on cold facts, facts that are proved by the police beyond reasonable doubt or they are not proved at all*! A single CSI working both scenes would provide an excuse for an argument about how forensic evidence linking the two was simply transferred by police personnel. And Joel would rather not enter into an argument he wasn't going to win.

At least there was no doubt that their victim had been murdered.

Joel was drawn first to the angry and numerous lacerations to the throat. The victim was male, early to mid-twenties. His position on his side meant that he had a bony hip exposed from under a green T-shirt to match with his green shorts. The hand that he had seen from a distance, the one trailing along the side of his body, had come to rest in an unnatural position against an arm that was clearly broken. The washed-out pallor of the forearm was interrupted by a raised bump, coloured red, black and yellow, around the break. The blood that was left in the body had settled, giving the impression of a man lying on a layer of purple. The bite marks the patrol sergeant had referred to were around the open wound to his arm and on one of his exposed hamstrings and looked red raw. Joel reckoned it could have looked worse – the first thing to go was often the eyes.

'So we can assume we're looking at the green runner,' Joel said to DS Rose. She nodded slightly, the shock clear on her face. Joel looked away from the body to the lorry trailer looming above. The floor was just below eye level, and he could see an obstruction among the shadows at the back. It looked like a wide box with low sides, lying in the centre. 'Do you have a torch?' he called out to Sergeant Dawes. He met her on her way back and took it from her. She was quick to move away. The rubber of Joel's gloves caught and snapped on the door as he hauled himself up the steps and into the trailer. The first sensation was cold. A breeze was being sucked through, suggesting an opening at both ends. Sure enough, Joel could see daylight through three small holes at the far end. 'It's a sandpit!' Joel's voice bounced around to mingle with the sound of his footsteps as he moved forward.

'A sandpit?' There was surprise in DS Rose's voice too. Of all the things to be transported in the back of a lorry, this didn't seem the most likely. 'Boxed up?'

'No. Laid out. And full of sand?' Joel ran the torchlight over it. It was long, four metres at least and over a metre wide. The sand nearest to him was smoothed out, the surface pattern suggesting it had been raked. The far end was a mess, like it had been disturbed in a hurry. There was sand outside it too that had been damp enough to clump together, evidently a handful at a time. He was careful not to disturb anything with his feet as he walked round. He studied the holes in the wall and found a wire trailing through one of them. He followed it with his torch light, away from the wall, along the floor and back into the pit. Just as in Shannon Hendry's pen, the end formed a large loop and in its centre something was dug into the sand with just a tip sticking out to catch the light. Joel was careful as he pushed the sand away to reveal a little more.

'Another player piece,' Joel said, and then he was aware of the trailer floor vibrating as DS Rose climbed up the steps. 'Green shorts and T-shirt and a painted black tear. All the same.' Joel was on his haunches, his feet still outside the pit. He traced the wire back towards the bright spot of sunlight. 'The pit is for the victim to search. Any tools or weapons would have been hidden in here. There's nowhere else. It's the whole reason it's here.'

'There's a baseball bat under the trailer, and there's blood and sand on it. I left it in situ,' DS Rose said.

Joel sighed. 'OK then. That could explain the injury to the arm.'

'It would, but the neck . . . It's a right mess. I don't think it was a knife, not a sharp one at least.'

'What else was there?' Joel said.

'You mean in the game? Scissors would be my bet.'

'Scissors!' Joel said. 'That wouldn't be easy.'

'It doesn't look like it was. Or quick.'

'This is different. If what we learned from Shannon Hendry is true then she followed the rules closely and someone else did the killing part. This looks like a fight from the moment of release. Our victim's arm is a defensive wound. The scissors wouldn't be an ideal choice and the wounds are not from someone skilled. And we're a long way from the phone here.'

'Do you think the rules changed for these two?'

'Not necessarily. We played the game out – you can meet an opponent at points.'

'Or maybe someone didn't fancy their chances in a straight-out race,' DS Rose said. She stood straighter, her gaze back towards where the wire restraint poked through into the trailer. 'Can you imagine what went on in here? What someone has to go through to hack at a stranger's neck the moment they're released from this place? They must have been *so* scared . . .'

'We don't know this was two strangers.'

'Even if they did know each other, hated each other, I

couldn't do that to my worst enemy, could you?' DS Rose was looking back towards the slab of sunshine at the rear of the trailer. Joel had been taking the scene in as an investigator, trying to piece together what had happened; now he considered what she had said, what it might take to reach that point, where the only option left was stabbing another human being in the neck until they were dead. He flushed with anger, aware that this could have been the perfect show for their killer.

'Either way, we have another survivor. That's another person who might have something that helps us stop this madness,' Joel managed eventually. He peered back at the wall and the map diagram and phone number that was drawn in thick marker, rather than dug out like the previous scene. 'Something else we learned from Shannon though – they may not be easy to find.'

Chapter 30

The door of his cell was ripped open and blinding sunlight poured in. Bradley stayed still, squinting out. Waiting. When the man appeared he was still wearing the hood and overalls. As a dark silhouette it made him look tall and wide, the hood flaring out to meet his shoulders.

'This time will be different.' The growled voice was even more disconcerting in that he couldn't see where it was coming from, just that it was somewhere inside that black shadow – like a demon barking its orders.

'I said I was sorry, OK, I didn't know, I was just mak—'

'Your opponent will be better prepared. You will remain restrained, just like before, but this time your opponent will be free and they will be coming for you. The race ends here.'

'Please, ple—' All at once, the shadow moved forward. Bradley didn't see what struck him but it was hard. He felt his nose give and heard the crunch, as the back of his head slammed into the solid stone behind him. The dizziness added to his confusion, blurring his eyes and making it more difficult to see his attacker.

Then the voice said, 'The closer they get, the more freedom you will have. This time there will be no searching. This is all you have.' He pointed to the wall. To a pistol that hung on it. It looked odd, with an extended handle and a metal arm that reached out from the back. He'd seen one before at an airsoft event so he knew it was a pistol that fired as an automatic. Then it had been spitting little pellets of plastic, but this one looked far more lethal. It was hooked over two pieces of steel protruding from the thick stone wall, pointing away so it faced the solid door at head height. The whole building was solid. He had been able to look it over as they had walked towards it, to see that it was an old fort, long since abandoned. He didn't recognise this one but he had played in something just like it as a kid. Then he had lived on the Sussex coast, where Martello Towers and any number of hidden pillbox forts were sunk into the South Downs. This one was larger, a different shape too – long and slim. The central door was accessed down a steep slope, and the whole building was out of view until you were up close. To his left, the room he was in quickly shrank down to a corridor filled with shadow.

Wrapped around his waist was the familiar feeling of unrelenting wire that fed into the wall behind, holding him tight against it. Bradley had questions; he wanted clarity about the weapon on the wall, about who was coming. But his face still stung from the last time he had spoken out of turn. The hooded man spoke again.

'Your competitor has the exact same weapon. Because of your cheating it is they who will have the advantage of being unrestrained. But if they come straight for you, if they are hasty, they will lose their advantage. And then you will have your chance.'

'What do you mean?' The figure had stepped back but he jerked forward again and Bradley slammed his eyes shut in preparation for the blow. It never came. When he opened them, the hood was again close enough for him to smell the leather and for him to make out the shape of an eye socket through the glass panel.

'There are trigger points. If they are hasty, if they are not measured, they will trip them all. Each one will get you closer to your weapon.'

'And if they don't? If they don't trip these points?'

'Then they will come through that door, with a weapon just like that and you will be sat here, just like this. And your end will be quick and easy.'

The hooded man stood back up, kicking Bradley's bare foot with his big boots as he turned away. He made it to the door then stopped where his form had merged back into a silhouette. He seemed to hesitate, then both hands came up together, lifting the hood away. He shook his head and his fingers ran through hair that was long enough to reach his shoulders. Then he turned round. Bradley squinted. The features were familiar, but then the voice came without the growl and just like that, a name and the memories came with it.

'Some extra incentive for you, Brad. You come through this and you get to tell everyone who the big bad man was. Good to see you again after all these years.' The door slammed shut and snuffed out the light. Bradley shouted in vain after him.

There were no real words, just the din of anger, hurt and confusion.

Chapter 31

CSI arrived in plenty of time to spoil Joel's initial assessments of the scene and it became apparent very quickly that he was wasting his time watching other people work. His new role had him working with his forensic colleagues more than ever and he already knew of their dislike of any conversation that started with the word 'Theoretically'. Joel gave up trying the third time he was met with the sentence 'It will all be in the report' and left them to it. They hadn't been back in the car long when Eileen called to give them an ideal opportunity to make better use of their time: a man by the name of Peter Marshall had made contact with the police. He wanted to talk to the officer responsible for finding the man who had killed his daughter.

It was another fifty-minute drive to the west of the county before they pulled up at a semi-detached place that looked typical of estates built in great numbers in the 1990s. The windows, front door and garage door were all brown to blend with roof tiles on show where the roof slanted as far down as the ground floor on one side, and that were also part of an overhang that ran most of the width of the house. The impression was of a builder trying to make the shape look interesting overall, something that might have been more effective were all the houses not virtually identical in design.

They stepped under the cover of the overhang to knock on the door. It was answered almost immediately by a woman wearing jeans and a jumper, with brown hair tied up like it was just keeping it out of the way. Her initial expression had been expectant but was quick to change to one of upset and shock. Joel had seen the same transition any number of times; the arrival of the police always brought with it an increased sense of reality.

Joel did introductions. The woman seemed to struggle with her own name, managing just her first – *Jessica* – then stepped back and gestured to their right, through to a medium-sized kitchen with a door out to the small rear lawn. The man sitting in the kitchen didn't move from where he had his back to them. He sat up straight, his arms trailing along the knotted wood of a characterful table, shock clear from his bearing even before Joel had seen his face.

'You must be Mr Marshall,' Joel said and he pulled out the bench opposite to sit down at the same level. DS Rose opted to stay standing behind him. 'I'm very sorry for the circumstances that bring us together. My name is Inspector Joel Norris and this is DS Lucy Rose. We're investigating the murder of Kelly Marshall and I am what is called the Senior Investigating Officer. That means I am your point of contact.' Joel took a card out of his pocket and placed it in the centre of the table. Peter Marshall fixed on it, his bottom lip gripped tight in his teeth, nodding slightly. 'You called our control room this morning, early hours. You said you'd just found out about your daughter. Do you mind me asking how?' Joel was trying to keep his tone flat, neutral. Peter answered quietly, wringing his hands and seeming to struggle for his first word.

'I . . . I work nights . . . They're building a whole new television production site. Studios. A lot of it's done, a lot of specialist equipment in there already so they've got security twenty-four-seven. This is my week of nights.' His eyes fidgeted from side to side like was struggling to focus. Joel deliberately didn't reply. Jessica – whom Joel assumed to be his partner – jumped in to prompt.

'But how did you find out, Pete?' She stood at his left. 'I don't think they're asking why you were up at that time of the day!' The sentence finished with a nervous chuckle and Peter lifted watery eyes to her. 'You need to answer their questions. You need to tell them what happened and then the police can tell you a bit more of what's going on.' She looked away from him now to fix on Joel. 'He's not himself. This is all a bit of a shock, as you can imagine. I had no idea – he came home a little early but that's not unusual. Then I was wittering on at him about my day at work and he just came out with it. We didn't know what to do, so I said he needed to call you, to speak to the officer investigating all this.' She moved back to focus on Peter. 'Who told you about your daughter? That's what he asked.'

Peter scowled and Joel waited. He'd seen shock in just about all of its forms; he'd certainly seen it like this before. The way Peter Marshall was presenting was almost like a drunk. He was struggling to think, struggling to get his thoughts in some sort of order, and that turmoil would only have been worsened by the arrival of the police. He finally managed a word.

'Margaret.' His focus snapped back as he said it, and he shook his head to clear the last of the confusion. 'Margaret Marshall. She's my ex-wife. She turned up at work in the early hours and said she wanted to tell me something. She said I should know. She said she wouldn't have a conversation about it, just that I should know. Then she told me that our Kelly was dead. She said that she was murdered. *Murdered!*' He seemed to take a moment to consider this. 'She gave me a name to ask for, Joel Norris, then she just left. I couldn't stop her leaving. So I called the police. I needed answers, I need to know what's going on. I asked for you . . .' He managed eye contact for the first time.

'And here I am,' Joel said, then leant forward so that his elbows squeaked on the polished surface. 'I'm sorry I didn't get to you in time to tell you myself but we didn't have an address for you. Margaret and Nicola did mention that you'd moved recently—'

'More than a year!' It was Jessica who answered. She tutted, then seemed to check herself. 'Sorry.'

'I haven't seen them since we moved. I think the girls have cut me off for now, but I always thought . . . I always thought we would make it up, that *I* would make it up to them.' Peter's eyes glazed, his attention slipping back into the turmoil of his mind. Joel needed to keep him thinking straight.

'Why would Margaret come to you so late, and at work?'

'She was upset. She said she couldn't sleep and it was on her list of things to do. I was working security when we were together, always for the same agency, so she would know people who could tell her where I was, and when. I was surprised to see her but not that she had found me.' Peter's focus was back with a new intensity, and he stared at Joel. 'What happened? Just tell me that.'

Joel didn't hesitate. 'Kelly was found at sunrise on Monday in a rural location six miles from her home address. She had a gunshot wound to the leg and stab wounds to her chest and abdomen.' He took a moment for Peter Marshall to react, but there was nothing. He was back to bowing his head, his breathing even and measured. Jessica moved to sit next to him, took his hand and gripped it tightly. 'It's very early in our investigation so I can't tell you much more than that, but of course I will keep you informed of developments as they happen—'

'Who?' Peter said. The word almost sounded like a cough, like he'd needed to dig it out from deep in his chest.

'Who?' Joel repeated back. 'What do you mean, Mr Marshall?'

'Who did this?'

Joel glanced momentarily at his sergeant. 'Like I said, it's very early. We have a lot of enquiries that are ongoing and still a lot to do. This is a huge operation, something we are taking very seriously and I can assure you that we are doing everything we—'

'So you don't know who did it.' There was sudden strength – and volume – in Peter Marshall's voice.

'No,' Joel replied, then came a silence that he was happy to let grow. 'But talking to you is part of finding out—'

'You think I would harm my own *daughter?*' Anger now, evident in the hissed final word.

'I didn't say that, Mr Marshall.' Joel's tone was still measured and neutral, despite Pete staring at him, his lips curling into a snarl. Jessica moved her thumb in an attempt to massage his hand, to calm him down perhaps. He threw it off. 'Why would you assume we were here to treat you as a suspect?' Joel continued.

'You asked me how I knew, that was the first thing you said to me. I've seen cop shows on the telly, the dad always gets the treatment, always gets suspected. I wouldn't hurt my little girl, not a hair on her head. Do you understand what I am saying?'

'I do. Mr Marshall, you called us. At three o'clock this morning. And you asked for me to provide you with some answers. Do *you* understand that's why I am here?'

'But you don't have any answers.'

'I don't intend for this to be the only time we speak. Major investigations start with far more questions than answers. Whoever *did* harm your daughter does not want us to know their identity . . .' Joel paused and leant further forward, his elbows squeaking again, upping the tension between him and Peter Marshall. 'So evidence might be hidden or attempts made to destroy it and lies might be told. But we will get them. This person will have made a mistake. Maybe he underestimated my CSI colleagues – or maybe he underestimated me.'

'*He?*' Pete spat.

'Statistically speaking,' Joel replied, moving back a little, 'the nature of the crime, the fact the victim is a young female tells me we're likely to be looking for a man. Not that I'm making any assumptions.'

'The nature? Did he . . .' Peter's voice changed again, the strength and the anger that were propping it up suddenly gone.

'There's no suggestion at this stage of any sexual element in the attack, if that was your question.' Joel had known exactly what Peter had meant and the other man's shoulders lost their tension, his whole body suddenly seeming to hang off his frame.

'When did you see her last, Mr Marshall?' Joel was deliberate in changing his tone to something a little warmer. He had tested him enough for now. Peter pushed himself back and rubbed his face, digging his palms into his eyes sockets like he was trying to get some life back into them.

'Like I said, I haven't seen my girls for over a year. We talked a little on the phone – messages only though – just before last Christmas, about meeting up for a coffee or something. I wanted to see them both together. Nicky agreed but Kelly . . . She hasn't really engaged with me since . . . I know what she's like, stubborn like her mother!' A flash of a smile, gone even quicker than it came. 'She said no. I thought by now she might be talking to me, or at least saving my phone number. I was going to make more of an effort, I know it's down to me to do that. Those girls have been through a lot because of me.'

'Because you split up with their mother?'

'Yes . . . They took it hard. They all took it hard.'

'People split up, it happens,' the inspector said and Peter's first response was to scoop up Jessica's hand again.

'It does. But I had a family, a home and children and . . . Well, I guess when you announce to that family that you aren't happy, that you haven't been happy for a long time, their reaction is never going to be a good one. Of course they took their mother's side; they were right to, I know that. I just hoped that we could make something out of this mess in time.'

Joel noticed the grip Jessica had on his hand tightened when he said *mess*.

'And Kelly has never talked to you about anything that might be relevant? Anyone who might have caused her concern in the past, any stalking incidents, fallouts, ex-boyfriends—'

'We didn't talk,' Pete snapped to cut Joel off, then started again, his words soaked in melancholy. 'We didn't talk, even before I split with her mother. I mean we did, but not about that sort of thing. And now Kelly won't even return a message. I've got messages to her through Nic, but only if I beg and I never get anything back to say she's got it. So no, I can't help you, I'm afraid . . .' He took a moment. 'I always thought they would forgive me, the kids at least. I fell out of love with their mother, that can happen . . . And I fell in love with another, that can happen too and I am so glad it did.' He raised Jessica's hand, closing his eyes firmly as he kissed it. 'But now Kelly . . .'

Joel made eye contact with DS Rose again. It was time to go. He announced his intention by tapping his card, still laid out where he had left it. 'I know this is all very raw. I'll keep you informed, of course I will. In the meantime, if anything comes to mind that we might need to know then please call me.' Peter didn't react, even when Joel stood up.

'Let me show you out.' Jessica took her hand away from Peter and stood up. Joel paused at the front door, speaking deliberately quietly as he took her full name and a contact number, explaining that he might make contact with her rather than Peter direct if they needed to come back for anything.

'That would make sense, he's not . . . I don't know how

he's going to be,' Jessica replied, then she turned to peer into the kitchen, taking in her partner's form where he still sat facing away from them. Joel glanced back too. The sun made a sharp-edged square of light on the polished tile floor. Peter's seat was in the part the light couldn't touch.

'He'll be fine with people like you around him. All you can do is be here for him,' Joel said.

'I might be going into work later this afternoon . . .' She tutted at herself. Joel's surprise must have been clear from his expression. 'Pete doesn't want me here, not all the time. I know how he deals with things and it's generally on his own. I had some appointments I couldn't cancel anyway. People don't pick up their phone anymore, it would seem.'

'What is it you do?' Joel said.

'I'm a relationship counsellor actually.' The title seemed to sit a little uncomfortably with her. 'And yes, I do know the irony of my situation with Pete in there . . .'

Joel waved her away. 'I'm not here to judge,' he said. 'Peter said it himself, these things can happen. I'm only interested in finding the person who could take the life of a young woman. That's not something I can understand so easily.' Joel's intention was to make Jessica follow the same thought: might Peter Marshall be that sort of man? He watched her carefully but got nothing.

'I know . . . I can't believe all this, with Kelly, I mean. I know you see it on the news but you just never think it's going to happen to someone you know. It's so awful.'

'Did you ever meet?' Joel's question was as casual as he could make it.

'With Kelly, you mean? No. I don't think that would have worked at all.'

'She didn't like you?' Joel chanced.

'Like I just said, she didn't know me, but she was never going to like anyone that got with her dad. Not in these circumstances. I respected that.' Her eyes suddenly flared wide,

'I liked her well enough! At least, I never wanted her to come to any harm . . . I didn't even know the girl—'

Joel waved her away. 'I wasn't getting at that,' he lied. He lingered for another moment, peering again at the man sitting in a shadow that seemed to be thickening around him.

Chapter 32

Joel swept back into the office already feeling like he needed to make up for time lost. There was a lot to do and he felt like it should start in the incident room. This was a loose name for it. Having secured a permanent space to work, he had then asked the estates team to create a separate room within it that he could use as the incident room – just like any professional murder investigation team. What they had come up with was a sound-deadened area made out of padded dividers on creaking metal feet. It was 'make-do', a phrase that already seemed to be dogging his detective career.

Eileen Holmans was already in this incident *area*, DS Rose a few steps behind him. Eileen knew the emphasis Joel placed on having everything up and visible to all and had made good use of the sound-deadening material, which was at least drawing-pin friendly. There was a whiteboard too, rattling on its splayed legs as Eileen ran a marker pen over its surface. The drawing pins held up images and information sheets, the scenes kept apart by using a different corner for each one.

'What happens if we run out of corners?' Joel said. Eileen took a moment to finish what she was writing, then turned smoothly on one heel, like she was still in her teaching pomp and addressing a class of noisy students who had just filed in.

'You will just need to stop this madness before that happens, won't you?' she said, falling short of adding *boy!* to the end of her sentence to really give that school vibe. She continued, 'The photographs from the scene this morning have all come through. I assume you have a story to tell me that goes with them?'

'Well, you are in charge, Eileen!' Joel got his usual glare-over-the-glasses as a prompt. 'We have another victim. The similarities are very clear as you will have seen. The clothes he was wearing, the figurine, the map and phone number on the wall . . .'

Eileen thoughtfully chewed the end of the pen she was holding. 'So are we saying serial killer here?'

'No.' Joel was a little caught out, the surprise clear in his voice. 'This wouldn't fit with that and we don't really want to use that phrase either. This isn't a Netflix series, we need to be toning the drama down if we can.'

'Not yet anyway,' DS Rose said to cut Joel down a little.

'OK, so "not yet" is still "no, we are not using that phrase,"' Joel said.

'We need to be prepared for the press to call him that. We're already getting questions coming in. There's a sniff of two separate murders but with the same offender. When are we going to put something official out in the media?' DS Rose had mentioned a press release early on for Joel to dismiss it. Now she crossed her arms like this time she would not be so easily dismissed.

'I didn't want to, not yet. If we're right and he's following *Escape!* even loosely then there is a known structure that should give us an advantage. We know from Shannon Hendry that survivors are told they cannot speak to the police. If we reveal that someone has, then it may put others at risk. It may mean that there can't *be* a survivor next time.'

'Next time? We might get something from a media appeal that stops there being a next time,' DS Rose retorted.

'We might,' Joel conceded, 'but his choice of locations, the times of day – we can't expect witnesses, all we would be doing is putting people in danger by showing our hand. There's nothing to be gained from that.'

'People are already in danger,' replied DS Rose. 'We have another person dead today, maybe more than one – we don't know if there was a survivor who came out of the back of one of those lorry trailers. Kelly Marshall was left in a public place, her mother was even *told* to call the police, while Shannon was cut loose to take the bus home—'

Joel raised his hand just as his sergeant was getting into full flow. 'OK, OK, I take your point.'

'Do you? Our killer knows the police are involved because he means for us to be. We think this is quite literally a game so we should assume our puppetmaster is very happy for the police to have a part in it too.'

Puppetmaster. The phrase hit Joel hard because it was right. It forced the realisation that, to this point, they had all been doing exactly what they were supposed to.

'OK then,' he said, 'get something together for the press. The boss will need to sign it off but we don't need any mention of potential links to a strategy game, just places, times and if anyone saw anything. And let's put a big emphasis on how we can protect anyone that comes forward.'

'I'll include the usual request for private CCTV and dash-cams to be checked in the area too – if they captured someone on foot anywhere near either scene then we will need to have a look.'

'What about The Captor?' Eileen cut across the two riffing detectives.

'What about him?' DS Rose replied.

'We know from poor little Shannon that he is dressing up as the role.' Eileen stepped out of the area, and when she returned she was holding up the game box with the cartoony image of the overalled Captor. 'Do you think someone might have seen this?'

Joel didn't. Not for a moment – and he knew the mentality of people well enough to predict that if he released it as a description of a killer there would be a craze of dressing up as The Captor by the end of the press conference. Sightings would be reported everywhere and the whole thing would become a big joke, something to mock the police and their investigation with.

'I don't think we put that description out. It might be misleading. He's not playing dress-up, he's killing people. I don't want the message to have something that specific as a focal point. We want to hear from people who saw something out of the ordinary, something that didn't feel right. If we can identify people that were in the right areas at the right time then maybe they will tell us about a man they saw in overalls and a yellow hood and we will know to take them seriously.' Joel was interrupted as two detectives who had been sent out on tasks bundled back in. DC Leonard Trott was in the lead, his forehead beaded with sweat, his dark eyes flicking between the three of them, the uncertainty clear. DC Mary Cumberland was just behind him. She had permanently flushed cheeks and curly red hair that was cut short but never enough to look as if it was under control.

'Boss.' Leonard spoke after a rushed glance between the two.

'How did it go?' Joel said. They had been tasked with going out to the manufacturer of *Escape!*

'It's their most popular game,' Leonard said. 'She said they can't just give out details of people that have bought it. She wanted us to follow data protection protocols. There's a form—'

'I know there's a form . . .' Joel stopped himself to take a breath. He wasn't angry at them, he was still reeling a little from the expression that DS Rose had used: *puppet-master*. They didn't have time for forms. 'I know there's a process, but this is a murder investigation and it's very possible that someone on their database as having purchased that game is killing people for his own entertainment.'

'I said that, but she didn't agree. She said that was just an opinion, that we didn't have any proof of that. She also said that they've sold, like, millions of those games all over the world and what are we going to do, knock on the door of every name?' Leonard snorted a laugh. It was unwise and it hung in the air to thicken the silence that followed. Joel was aware that the room was waiting for his reaction. He could feel his anger rising. DS Rose was the one to break it.

'It's a fair point. That might be nothing more than a waste of time, a lot of time too.'

'It's a place to start though.' Joel rounded on her. 'What else do we have right now?' His anger was spilling over, giving enough force to each word that his sergeant actually took a step back.

'And we know data protection exists,' DS Rose said. 'Those customers have rights and that company won't want you knocking on doors and pointing fingers at them. A company like that trades on its reputation.'

'Reputation?' Joel could feel heat rising through him now. He thrust out a finger at the padded dividers. 'Look at these photos. Look at what he's doing. We're worried about reputations?'

'We're nearer than we were.' DS Rose's tone was as calm as she could manage, designed no doubt to appease his rising anger. It didn't work.

'I'll go ask them myself,' Joel said and DC Trott's eyes flashed wider. DC Cumberland was already hanging back but a sidestep moved her behind her colleague. Joel was careful to take a breath and come back calmer. 'If nothing else I might learn a bit more about the game as a whole. There's this whole community around it, maybe there's something relevant in there.'

'And maybe there isn't.' DS Rose was done with calm. 'Arch Rival Games might make *Escape!* but they've also created this whole scene of painting, swapping and selling on social media, eBay and who knows where else. These games are changing hands all the time and if our killer has any sense, he would have picked up a set from somewhere untraceable. And he has to have some intelligence to be able to do what he's done so far.'

Another silence, just long enough for Joel to know she was right and he had been acting desperate – he *was* desperate. Those game pieces are relevant, central even; of course a killer would be careful about how they were obtained.

'I'll go back and see the company,' Joel said, 'and not because you didn't do a proper job . . . I can authorise a data protection waiver. We should be doing this properly anyway. I do want a better understanding of this game, of the community around it, even if it does turn out to be a waste of time.' Joel stopped short of saying that he could do with a drive too. He needed to get away from here, away from the images of the dead and the sorrow in their eyes. It might clear his head at least.

'Did you talk about AR Games as a whole? Ask if there was any reason why they might be targeted over the other strategy game makers?' DS Rose's tone was calm again.

'We didn't!' DC Trott's panic seemed to peak and Joel responded.

'I'll cover that too. Don't worry about it.' He thought better than to point out that this information was surely a basic requirement. 'If you can work on the press release for now, I'll take my drive and try to come back in a better mood.' Joel spoke directly to DS Rose, but it was meant as a sort of apology to the whole room. He hadn't meant to get angry.

His team were doing their best – they all were. But still that one word wouldn't leave him.

Puppetmaster.

And it was about to become truer than ever.

Chapter 33

AR Games had a frontage that suggested they rated themselves highly. The website labelled this address as their Head Office but there was no suggestion of any other offices. The 'head office' was small, a borrowed space on the edge of a brick unit dominated by a kitchen company. Perhaps to overcompensate, the AR GAMES sign was large enough to look silly and the choice of gold lettering, raised above the surface of the wall on silver metal pipework in a sort of 3D effect, only added to the silliness.

The gold-on-silver theme continued in the tiny foyer, as did the lack of spatial awareness. Another oversized prop was enough to stop Joel dead, looming in to fill his periphery, and he turned to where he was being sized up by a life-size version of the figurine he now knew as The Captor. The blue overalls emblazoned with the *AR* logo were probably Joel's size; the arms were coated in fake blood and a plastic flame was stuck to the end of the welding torch held in one of the hands. There was a full-size cattle bell in the other. The Captor was crowned with the yellow leather hood and the screen over the eyes was mirrored so Joel could take in his own scowl. Meeting The Captor had done nothing to improve his mood.

'He works security!' A voice dragged Joel's attention away

to rest on a middle-aged woman whose smug expression suggested that most people who entered were stopped in their tracks by the game's main character. No doubt they all got the same joke too.

'I'm sure he's very effective,' Joel replied.

'We don't get many people arguing with him. You wouldn't, would you?'

There was only a raised plinth for her to stand behind with a doorbell button and a sign to *ring for attention* peeling at the corners under dirty tape. The pane of glass behind her was mirrored on this side: one-way, Joel guessed, so she would know when it was time to pop her head out and deliver the 'He works security' line. She still looked delighted with it. She might be in her forties but her hair was direct from the eighties and, with shoulder pads prominent in her blouse, Joel saw a passing resemblance to George Michael in his Wham! days.

'No, I suppose I would just do what he says. Why a welder?' Joel said. The woman's expression changed. Joel had clearly stepped outside the standard small-talk of the reception desk. She even looked a little panicked.

'Welders are scary, aren't they? That's a pretty nasty thing to point at someone, wouldn't you say?'

'I would. Just that welding makes me think of fixing something. Would a weapon not be more suitable?'

'He is The Captor. I suppose the creatives imagined him to be making cages. How can I help you?' Joel's questioning had sucked all humour from the room and Joel lifted his warrant card to complete the change in dynamic. The woman, who had been leaning forward, straightened.

'Oh. We had a visit from the police already. I assumed they had what they needed?'

'Not at all. I'm Detective Inspector Norris, the Senior Investigating Officer, which means that this is my case. Did my colleagues explain to you the seriousness of this matter?'

Joel left the question hanging, watching as the woman seemed to struggle to find a suitable expression.

'I . . . I didn't speak . . . I mean, I just showed them through to Alison. . . . She's the boss here, she spoke to them.'

'And is Alison still here?'

'She . . . Yes!'

'Could I have a chat with her?'

'I . . . Hang on.' She was gone before Joel could reply and with the speed of someone desperate to get out of there. The door hadn't fully shut before she pushed it open again. 'She's just taking her lunch, unfortunately. Would you be able to come back a little later?'

'No, that's OK. I don't mind!' Joel moved forward. For a second she held her ground but then thought better of it, stepping aside for Joel to squeeze his large frame past her. The back office was small, enough for a desk, an electric heater and a battered-looking sofa. Another door led out to the rest of the unit's ground floor, which was a big open space, the back wall consisting of a double-garage-sized door. The floor was painted in scuffed grey and littered with pallets of stacked boxes of games still sealed in clear plastic as well as trays of figurines. Joel couldn't see *Escape!* among them. On the right side was a flight of bare wooden steps leading up to a timber-framed room that sat on exposed steel slats, its windows bleeding light. He took the steps two at a time and saw a flurry of movement through the window as someone met him at the door.

'I said I was busy!' The woman who appeared wore a sharp suit jacket and skirt, with shoes to match an overall theme of pale blue. Her white shirt was unbuttoned enough for Joel to note her flushed chest and neck.

'Actually, she said you were taking lunch. I figured that's different to busy and, seeing as we're investigating murder, I thought I might count as important enough to sit with you. I'm not someone who gets sensitive about people talking with their mouth full. Maybe you've got a packet of biscuits in there to go with the cup of tea? That way we can be two people talking at each other with their mouths full.' The woman stared at him. She had dark features: dark hair straightened to within an inch of its life, dark eyes from under a sharp fringe that were effective portals when it came to expressing her anger, and a tanned tone to the skin around them.

'Tea?' she spat, her tone angry enough to suggest she was beyond being able to say anything more.

'White, no sugar,' Joel replied.

The woman spun away, her control impressive considering the height of her heels, and reentered her office. 'There's nothing more I can tell you,' she said. But Joel took the fact that she left the door open as an invitation.

She sat down. On the wall above her was a certificate that bore her name, Alison Reynolds, in gold lettering, with a shiny seal in the top right that made it look all the more genuine. Joel noted that the gold theme had continued from outside in. The lettering that explained what the award was for was far smaller but he could make out that it was something to do with the completion of a business course. If it was a course on how to look the part in the boardroom then Joel reckoned she would have aced it. The leather of her chair squeaked a little as she sat back to take him in from behind her desk.

'Nice office,' Joel said.

'I'm very rarely here. I work from home most of the time.'

'So I'm lucky to catch you?' Joel said.

'*You* were lucky, yes.'

'And you, not so much?'

'I'm a very busy woman, officer, and already much of my time has been spent assisting the police with their enquiries. I feel I have done enough for one day. Do you not talk to each other?'

'Inspector,' Joel corrected her. 'I'm the SIO, the Senior—'

'Investigating Officer, yes, I got that from Helen,' Alison snapped.

'Excellent. So she would also have told you how I am investigating the brutal murder of two people and how this company is a part of that investigation?'

'I would hardly say we are a part of your investigation, offi . . . inspector. Language like that will have me asking you to leave until I've spoken to my solicitor. She's an absolute pitbull – not my description, by the way; that came from the last person to cross me. Do I need to be calling her out?'

Joel couldn't help himself. The Captor was here again. This time a smaller version – around ten inches tall and made of bronze, standing on a marble base like a trophy. The plaque underneath stated: *Escape – One Million Units Sold.* He plucked it off the shelf.

'And who are you, Alison? In all this, I mean.' Joel gestured with The Captor to take in the whole room.

'Who am I?' Her chest flushed a deeper red.

'Regional manager? Area manager? I've never really worked the private sector so I always struggle with the titles you lot give yourselves . . .'

'I own this company, Mr?'

'Joel Norris.'

'Inspector Norris . . .' She made a show of writing it down. Joel leant over her.

'Two Rs, one S,' he said.

'This is my company. That may come as a shock to you, that women own companies too.'

'Not at all. The women are always in charge, even the ones that aren't. My sergeant – Lucy Rose – the next rank down according to the structure, but we both know she's in charge. And then there's Eileen. A civilian worker with a penchant for comfy footwear who is technically on the bottom rung but no one's told her that, and as for my wife—'

'Is there something I can do for you?' Alison asked, cutting him off.

'One of your customers has taken this game of yours, the *one-million-selling* game, and decided to play it for real. Two people are dead so far. We both know the body count can get much higher in your game so I'm sure you understand the reason why my colleagues were requesting access to the records of the people that have purchased it.'

'It's a board game. A bit of fun, sold for entertainment purposes. And it's closer to two million sales now.'

'Two million!' Joel whistled. 'Maybe a tasteless, oversized gold trophy for that milestone then?' Joel said, sliding The Captor back onto its shelf. '"A bit of fun", a cash cow, call it what you want, but someone on a list that you have access to murdered two people and we can only assume more deaths are on the cards. The way those people died . . . You know your game, I'm sure I don't have to fill in too many details for you. Earlier today you refused to help, I wanted to come here myself and ask you why?'

'I did no such thing, I helped all that I could. Your colleagues could not assure me that someone on my list is responsible, not for certain. That your twisted killer didn't just buy one of the many sets that change hands on the second-hand market every single day – assuming this person has a set at all. Are you here to tell me that you now know more?'

'Knowing for certain is exactly what I am trying to do and exactly what you are hampering. Why would you do that?'

'There's a bigger picture here. Of course I'm appalled that our product might be associated with something as horrific as one person taking the life of another, but data protection states—'

'Data protection!' Joel spat the words out as a laugh. 'You think data protection is important enough to use as a reason not to help us?'

'Like I said, I did help. I answered all the questions I could,

I gave my phone number for anymore. I even offered a complimentary version of *Escape!* to further assist, despite the fact we are running low. So, like I said to your colleagues – who seemed to have a much better attitude – I will do what I can, but I will not break the law. I would think police officers, of all things, would understand that.'

Joel took a moment, his eyes again scouting the shelving while he bit back his first reaction to being called a 'thing'. There were more awards, certificates and framed pictures. He skimmed rather than taking in the detail.

'Why a welder?' Joel said. There were two chairs on the left side, standing by the window that looked down to the stacked games on the ground floor. He pulled one over, positioning it so close to the desk that his knees bumped it when he sat opposite Alison.

'Welder?' Alison said, momentarily caught out. 'You mean our lead character? Why not?'

'I said to Helen downstairs that it didn't seem like the most obvious choice, you know, for a kidnapper and a murderer.'

'I bow to your expertise, Inspector. Actually, the person who set the company up was a former welder. He made a career out of it until he was made redundant. I guess it was a nod to his roots.'

'*His* roots. That wasn't you, then?'

'No. Do I strike you as a welder?'

'Come now, you were quick to suggest I was being misogynistic when I questioned your role here earlier. Sure you could have been a welder.'

'I don't remember saying I thought you were misogynistic.'

'I'm a good detective, as it turns out. That means I can sometimes see when people stop short of saying what they mean, or say one thing and mean something entirely different. Like when you said you were happy to help us.'

'You're not getting that list. This is beginning to feel a little oppressive. I can't be bullied, Inspector Norris. The welder found that out to his cost.' She snapped her lips shut, like suddenly she had said too much. Joel seized on it.

'Did he now? Is that why you happen to know a bulldog of a solicitor?'

'The business world is a competitive one, sink or swim. This company would have sunk. And now we are thriving.'

'BTE Games,' Joel said, pushing away from the desk and getting to his feet. He took a closer look at the framed picture he had only glanced at before. It was of five people, taken at the front of the building they now stood in. A ribbon was being cut over the door. The sign showed 'BTE Games' and was smaller and definitely classier. Its shine suggested it was brand-new. The smiles and enthusiasm looked brand-new too, at least in the three adults at the centre. The two children standing like sullen bookends looked around nine or ten. 'The same company?'

'Technically, no. But the foundation for AR Games.'

'You look a little . . . different.'

'You mean younger. It was fifteen years ago. I was brought in to head up the manufacturing and distribution side of things at that time. We were expanding, hence the new office.'

'AR Games, that's Arch Rivals, right? So what was the genius behind BTE?'

'Beat the enemy,' she said, with an expression like the words left a bad taste. 'Like any of this is relevant.'

Joel grinned. He was wasting her time; he was wasting his own too, time that could be much better spent elsewhere, but he was hoping she didn't pick up on that. If he wasted enough of it she might cave, give him what he wanted just to get rid of him. Or at least start to play ball.

'I can see why you changed it. That's not quite so catchy.'

'No. The previous owner, our welder, he wanted to use his initials and then found something that loosely fitted. The whole thing was a bit of a vanity project for him. The first sign of someone in business for the wrong reasons.'

'What happened to him?'

'I saw the potential in this company right from the start. I was able to become an investor and then, when that money ran out, we went public. He was running the company into the ground and he wanted to use the money we raised from the flotation to change direction when we needed to do the exact opposite. We needed to focus back on our core business.'

'You mean *Escape!*?'

'It's always been our biggest seller. But I had the idea of keeping a relationship with customers once they had bought the game. We added expansion packs, different boards, special editions, and, most effective of all, we took to providing the figures in their base colour. Previously they had been supplied coloured, but this change meant our production costs were lower and the customers could paint them any way they wanted. We sold them paint packs too, of course, and with the growth of social media we were able to create a whole community. This was all within twelve months of selling that exact vision to our shareholders. It was an almost instant success.' She practically beamed with pride.

'You pushed him out?' Joel was suddenly more interested. This sounded like the beginning of a story of a disgruntled employee, someone who might want to bring negative attention to a company that he had started but that had discarded him.

'I did no such thing. He was wise enough to take a very generous severance package and step away. He had his chance. After presenting us with a proposed new boardgame that was basically his previous creation only on boats and with a cheesier title, he then came at us with a vision that involved opening branded escape rooms across the country – and with the idea of his son leading this expansion. It was whimsical at best and with the investment needed, it was a ridiculous risk. Yet he was cap in hand, asking for *more* from the very people who had already put capital down and were right to expect a return. He would have ruined us all, including himself.'

'Recently?' Joel said.

She shrugged. 'Four years now.'

'Do you ever hear from him?'

'I have nothing to do with the man. The severance was just that.'

'I'd like to talk to him. Do you have any contact details?' Joel took out his pocket book and readied a pen.

'Just a name and that photo. He's the one with the scissors. I took that picture down a few times but, whatever I think of the man, that was the start of it all.'

'So, B.T.E.,' Joel said. 'I won't get very far just with his initials.'

'You won't,' Alison agreed, her tone perhaps softening a little. Then she gave the name in full. And just like that, the meeting was over.

Chapter 34

'Billy Terrance Easton!' Joel took at ill-advised run up at a speed bump on the way out of the estate and it almost knocked the air out of him. In the pause that followed, Eileen tutted on the other end of the phone. At his request, she had put him on speaker in the office so DS Rose could listen in.

'Was there something you wanted?' Eileen said.

'All you can find on that name.'

'Should I know who that is?' Eileen's monotone was maddening at the best of times.

'Our first victim. We spoke to her mother. Billy Easton was there at the time. He lives right next door. He owned the company that make the *Escape!* game but he left, on bad terms by all accounts.' Joel glanced over at the framed picture he had tossed on the passenger seat. Billy Easton was on the left of the three adults, holding an oversized pair of scissors, and his grin was by far the broadest. Joel could see it was Margaret's neighbour now but he had needed to be told. In the fifteen years since that photo had taken, Billy's skin had contrived to conceal his identity under deep wrinkles.

'So we now think he's involved?' Eileen's voice was still very matter-of-fact.

'We need to talk to him, that's for sure. I've just tried getting hold of the officers looking after Margaret Marshall but Witness Protection never pick up, they always call back. I'm hoping it will be soon.'

'Do you think she's in danger?' DS Rose's voice now filled the cabin. 'Or more danger at least?'

'She shouldn't be. Witness Protection know their apples. They were the ones who insisted that Billy couldn't have any contact details for her. The only way Margaret will be found is if she slips up and makes contact with him.'

'And you think she might do that?'

'He'll be keeping an eye on her house, you can be sure of that. I bet she even left him a key. She's going to want to know it's all OK. I'm heading out there now anyway. Lucy, can you meet me there and bring a patrol? Anyone you can get. You're closer than me, find a suitable RV point away from that valley. I don't want to spook Easton if he's there.'

'I take it this is an arrest?' Lucy asked.

Arrest had been Joel's first reaction but the question forced him to consider his options again. He did so out loud. 'We have the company link and we know he has good access to our first victim via Margaret, enough to find out whatever he needed. And he's skilled, a welder by trade who was talking about making escape rooms, so a wire restraint would be easy enough . . .'

'There's more than enough, boss,' DS Rose cut across to end any doubt. 'We're a long way past reasonable suspicion and these questions need to be asked under caution, plus it gives us a power to search.'

'I agree. Let me know when you're somewhere suitable. And Lucy . . . Make sure you wait for me to get there.'

Joel cut the call, trying to work his phone into its holder on the dash while also negotiating his way onto the busy A282 that would take him back to the M25. He managed to bring up *WP Jones*, the saved details of the officer who was his contact in Witness Protection. He pressed to call and got the same nasal request to leave a message as before. Joel was moving slowly in lane one and abandoned the call. All three lanes flared with brake lights as he activated the grille lights and sirens.

DS Rose leant forward to rub her hands as they moved down one side of the valley. She hadn't bothered to put her seatbelt on since leaving her car when they had met up in a Woodland Trust car park half a mile back. Joel checked his mirror; a marked police car was close behind, its bonnet livery bright enough to be uncomfortable to look at.

'He had a silver car, a Land Rover. I can't see it,' DS Rose said. Joel was also leaning a little to get the best view. He remembered the car too, and that it was parked round the side so they might not see it until they were closer. It was an old Defender model. He swore a little when they pulled up outside and it wasn't there.

The houses had long front gardens penned in by stone walls. As Margaret's home was the middle one, she had to park her car directly out front. She had a blue Nissan Note, an 06 plate. It was still parked where he had last seen it. Leaving the car at the home address, where it was expected to be seen, would have been part of the witness protection element.

Joel pulled up as close as he could get. DS Rose was first out. The marked car skewed off to the left, as had been discussed, and the occupants were fast out, jogging to a point where they would have a view of the rear. Joel and DS Rose made straight for Billy Easton's front door, but Joel already knew it was pointless. The whole look and feel was of somewhere shut up for the day.

'I took a phone number from him.' DS Rose must have felt the same. She spoke as he hammered on the door. 'I could call and ask him where he is. Tell him we need to meet to talk about something Margaret needs.'

'He might see through that.'

'He might, but it's plausible and he's been pretty brazen so far.'

'Give it a go,' Joel said. It must have been answered on the first ring. The conversation was short, DS Rose was suitably casual and some agreement was made.

'He'll be a couple of hours or so. I said we would meet him here.'

'Did he say where he was?'

'No and I couldn't think of a reason to ask.'

'No problem, we can ask him in interview when he turns up in a few hours' time.'

'Why say it like that? You don't think he'll come?' DS Rose said.

'I don't know . . .' Joel took a moment. He took a step back to gaze at the first-floor windows. 'There's no reason for him not to, I suppose. The one thing I do know is that I'm hungry and I make it lunchtime. Let's head to civilisation and get something greasy.'

'Sounds good to me.'

Rusthall came up on phone searches as the closest place to offer a selection of takeaway food. The 'something greasy' they chose was a bag of chips to keep it simple. Joel sent the marked unit to pick it up for them all as he didn't want to leave. It wouldn't have mattered. Billy Easton was almost bang on the two hours he had suggested. After the food drop-off, Joel had positioned the marked car back outside the valley so they could call it in when Easton approached. There was only one way in, one way out, so they also followed Billy's Land Rover to block any chance of it spinning around and making off. There was no such attempt and there was nothing about his body language that suggested this was a man looking to run.

His greeting was sullen. He was wearing jeans over hiking boots and a polo shirt stitched with a Chelsea FC badge, and his wispy hair was even more unkempt than normal. He fussed and fidgeted on the back seat, taking out a carrier bag that he then hung on his right arm. The bag was open enough to display a car magazine and a fleece. Billy held out his arms, his palms up and together – like he was making it nice and easy to cuff him.

Joel exchanged a quick glance with his DS. 'Were you expecting us by any chance, Billy?'

'I thought you might come back for a chat, son,' Billy replied.

Joel wasted no more time. 'Billy Easton, you're under arrest for the murder of Kelly Marshall. You do not have to say anything, but it may harm your defence if you do not mention something which you later rely on in court. Anything you do say may be used in evidence. Do you understand?'

'I understand, son.'

DS Rose took up his offer and handcuffed him. Joel took the bag from him, pushed the fleece aside and revealed a toothbrush, some roll-on deodorant, a tobacco pouch and folded underwear. 'What's this? An overnight bag?' Joel said. 'You're not expecting a short stay, then?'

'I think we might have a lot to discuss.'

'Did Margaret leave you a key?'

'Yellow fob, hanging with all the others in the kitchen.' Billy was still monotone and Joel was finding it hard to read his reaction. He didn't know what he was expecting, but a packed bag and grudging acceptance hadn't been it.

Joel called the uniform officers back. They patted Billy down, removed his phone and a set of keys and sat him on the wall. Joel hopped over it to get to Margaret's door. The key with the yellow fob gave him access and he did a complete walk-through of her home. He wasn't sure what he was looking for – nothing specific – he just wanted to be sure there were no nasty surprises, since the witness protection people hadn't come back to him yet. Joel still found it difficult to believe that Billy meant his neighbour any harm. He was pretty sure Billy was infatuated with the woman, and with no sign of any malice. This made his decision to harm her daughter even more difficult to understand but Joel believed answers were coming. Billy seemed like he was ready to talk, and right now there was nothing more important to this investigation.

Joel handled the logistics. Two officers would always transport a prisoner and he wanted to be one of them, in case Billy was chatty on the way back. Joel had a uniform colleague drive him and Billy back in the marked car. DS Rose would stay with the other to start a search of Billy's home. Joel had already called up for a search team and, on their arrival, DS Rose would hand over the scene and head back in their pool car. She had made him promise not to start any questioning until she was back, but it was unlikely anyway. The custody process for a murder suspect was long and laborious. There would be a full forensic strategy; CSI would attend to seize his clothes, scrape his nails, comb his hair and all manner of other very necessary processes that were needed to assist with a conviction. Then there would be the delays around legal representation. If Billy didn't have his own solicitor they would use whichever duty solicitor was on call for that day, with no guarantee that they weren't already involved with another job. They would have to wait their turn and he knew that any delay at this point was going to be painful.

Joel just wanted answers.

The trip back to custody was in near silence. Joel had asked generic questions about Billy's comfort, whether he was taking medication, his mental health – all things he would be asked again in custody, but with some prior knowledge Joel might be able to save time in the long run. Billy gave one-word answers that revealed nothing obvious to hold them up. The custody sergeant documented their arrival at 4.07 p.m.

On the way, Joel had also taken a call from Witness

Protection. It wasn't ideal – he could hardly talk freely – but he had managed to get what he needed. The Marshall family were all accounted for. He also got assurance that WP Jones's next call would be to DS Rose, who was already briefed to talk more about the man sat next to him in the car. Joel wanted a reaction from Margaret, to see if there was anything else she might now consider relevant if she was forced to think of Billy as a suspect, rather than a friendly neighbour.

Billy showed no obvious change in his demeanour on his arrival at Medway Police Station. Since Joel was away from his home station, he would once again need to try and steal some desk space somewhere. He logged onto his email system in the back office of custody and would stay here until he was kicked out. The system was still booting up when someone tried to get his attention with a directed cough.

'Sir?'

He turned to a young jailer with a large build that was all belly, his flushed cheeks suggesting it was an effort to cart it around all day.

'Let me guess – he's changed his mind and wants a solicitor?' Joel said. Billy had refused legal representation at the custody desk, something that Joel hadn't accepted at first, reiterating the seriousness of his situation.

But it wasn't that at all.

'No, sir. The prisoner . . . I've been helping with the forensic seizures and he's been asking the time a lot. When I just told him, he said that I needed to get you. He said that there's another game just about to start. He said it's different. He said they will tear each other apart but there's still time to stop it.'

Chapter 35

Interview room three, Medway Police Station. The same hard seats bolted to the floor, the same cracked white table with plastic cups of water, the same undertone of stale air.

But the atmosphere was very different.

This time it wasn't a terrified Shannon Hendry sat in front of Joel, arrested for something he was already sure she hadn't done, her arrest a means to get her talking and keep her safe. This time it was Billy Easton, the man seemingly responsible for Shannon's nightmare. A two-time murderer who had callously plotted the death of his neighbour's daughter and wrapped it all up in the guise of some sort of game. And now he had given up another location. Another 'game' was about to start; two more people were tied up and terrified, waiting for their starter's orders.

Joel gripped his police radio. The recording equipment lay silent, and both men were silent too. Joel should be firing questions at his prisoner by now, and in this very room, but the moment the jailer had repeated Billy's words back to him it had become apparent that the opportunity for questions was some way off. Joel's reaction had been to drag Billy back to the custody desk, explaining to the sergeant that there wasn't time to go through the formal elements of an interview, that Billy had some new information he was offering to share and it was time critical so the custody desk would have to do. It was just about the only area that was constantly recorded, both audio and visual, so Joel had rushed out another caution to remind Billy of his rights, reminded him that he could still have a solicitor present, silently prayed that he didn't want one, then asked him if he had any reply to the caution. That was when Billy had told them about this 'new game' in more detail. He talked about Burgoyne Heights in Dover. About more victims waiting for their signal to start, about how he was getting better so it was now fully automated and it didn't matter that he wasn't there. This was going to happen. He also said that his prisoners would both be armed the moment they were freed and it was very likely that one or both were going to be hurt.

Joel had so many questions but he couldn't launch into them. Not there, in that setting, with those cameras on him. Billy seemed to be changing, evolving his methods, and Joel was desperate to probe why with questions. But he couldn't. All he could do was clarify where they needed to go, repeat his understanding that two people were being held captive and about to become an imminent danger to each other, and then ask what he needed to know to keep the responding officers safe. Anything else would constitute an interview and would be deemed unlawful, any answers instantly inadmissible – or, worse, deemed a breach of process.

What Joel most wanted to ask was *why?* Still Billy's motivation was lost on him. There was no real expression on Billy's face that might give a clue, no joy, no satisfaction or any attempt to boast about how clever he had been, no explanation or justification for any of it. Rather than describing the horror of two people tied up and waiting to fight each other to their death, Billy Easton might as well have been reading the shipping forecast.

Joel had relayed all that he knew to DS Rose and cursed

his luck that he couldn't be part of the police reaction. Instead, he had moved his prisoner into an interview room and posted a jailer at the door until one of his DCs could come down to ensure there were always two to witness anything said. And then they had just sat in silence, waiting for an update on the radio from either DS Rose or the Firearms Sergeant now tasked with leading the response.

Waiting for something to change.

Billy Easton slumped on one of the polished wooden chairs, his weathered face lowered. Joel couldn't tell if he was looking at someone resigned to what was happening to him, or sad about it. Nothing about his reaction had seemed right. Before Billy was in the frame, Joel had imagined their offender as a gloating, swaggering beast of a man, delighting in mocking the police, leaving clues for them to chase while admiring his own cleverness. That was how Joel had imagined he would catch him: his arrogance and desire to gloat would be his undoing. But Billy Easton was none of those things.

The radio update made Joel flinch. The volume was down low but in the thick silence of that room it was like a firecracker suddenly released. The update was from DS Rose: they had arrived at the location. Joel got up. He needed to listen to this next bit closely and away from the seated prisoner. Billy called after him, urgency in his voice for the first time.

'If they've arrived there's something you need to know.' Joel spun back to see Billy removing something from down the front of his trousers. 'The only place they didn't search,' he said like he was offering some sort of explanation. Then there was a flash of something white in his hand and he slid it across the table top. 'I reckon by now you might know what this means.'

Joel had moved back towards him, ready to deal with whatever he had concealed. Billy hadn't been subject to a strip-search; a forensic seizure meant changing all of his outer clothing anyway, and there wasn't time for Joel to wish he had insisted. Instinctively he grabbed Billy by the wrists while his eyes chased after the object on the table. It was a playing card. It had fallen face down but the back was instantly familiar: a cartoonish torso of a welder, a bell in one hand, a lighted welding gun in the other, with *Escape!* written over his midriff. Joel turned it over to reveal a skull and crossbones symbol drawn in thick black.

The death card.

Everyone loses a life.

Chapter 36

Bradley coughed to clear his throat and felt the familiar sensation of a wire tightening its grip around his waist. The sensation was there with every movement; even when he turned his head he could feel a pull on his torso or a pinch of his skin. Just like when he was secured in that lorry trailer. And that wasn't the only sensation that was familiar; the constant knot of anxiety was back too, only this time it was worse, because he knew more of what to expect, and he knew only too well the price of failure.

Sat in the back of that trailer he had told himself that it was all a trick, designed to mess with his head. He'd even thought it was one of his mates in that ill-fitting outfit, mates who would know the relevance to him of choosing to dress as a character most of the world knew as The Captor. But any doubt was gone when that recorded message had played out in full and made the link to that game clearer. He knew *Escape!* He knew it well. And at that point he had known that he was part of a game being played out live.

Even before the message had gone on to tell him what losing meant, he had been able to skip ahead in his mind to the weapons he had seen as small plastic pieces in the game box. Turning a card to claim a baseball bat and a pair of scissors for use in a final showdown was fun at a kitchen table, surrounded by your mates, with cartoon figures and cartoon violence. But pulling a cold, heavy baseball bat from coarse sand, hurriedly stuffing a pair of blunt scissors in your waistband and then peering over at a younger, smaller lad whose trust you have earned, knowing those were your tools to take his life, was a million miles from *fun*. This was Bradley's worst nightmare – and it wasn't done yet. He couldn't imagine who might want to put him through anything like this, or why.

And yet, when The Captor had pulled that hood away from his head, everything had made sense.

Bradley didn't know how long it had been since he had been left alone. The sun had been bright, shining directly through the doorway, when the door had last slammed shut, and its light still flared as a strip along the bottom. The previous evening he had watched the light slowly die to be replaced by whispering shadows and a then a faint slash of moonlight standing out from the thick darkness around him. Already, he thought, the light was getting weaker. He hadn't expected another night to pass, but he hadn't been given any idea of timescales either.

His limbs had gone numb through the lack of movement and the cold. His mind was racing ahead again, running over and over with worst-case scenarios, always leading to the same result: not seeing his children again. He couldn't have that, he *wouldn't* have that.

He knew a little more about himself now; he knew he could be a killer when it was necessary. Not a skilled killer, but determined. His mind still conjured images of hacking at a neck with blunt scissors until the thing had stopped moving. It *was* a thing too – Bradley was desperate to think of it like that, not as a human being, not as a man, not as a father, perhaps, like he was. But Alan was a name that wouldn't leave him, a name that resonated in his mind. He might as well have been shouting it with every blow at the man's neck.

And that name was still there now – as the wire dug into his midriff, and his legs and arms grew numb with the cold and his throat was coated with dust from the interior of this stubborn stone fort with its solid wooden door. He stared at the door now, knowing that another *someone* was coming. He would be ready again; he would win again. Someone was going to have to die.

It couldn't be him.

Lucy's hand had a slight shake as she gripped the phone tight in her palm. The digital image of roads and fields flexed around a big blue arrow that stayed central as they turned. Their destination appeared briefly as a pulsing dot for her while she held her breath, then it slipped off the screen where they had to drive past to find a way into the large open area of woods and grass.

'Three minutes,' she said, her throat tight enough for the tension to wring out her voice.

Sergeant Tristan Hughes was driving their marked 4x4. He had tried to make small talk, telling her how just an hour earlier he had been taking a slow walk around the Bluewater Shopping Centre, his assault rifle across his front, sidearm strapped to his leg, trying to override the intimidation of visible weaponry with smiles and nods at the shoppers. It was a default foot patrol site and he was always delighted to be called away from it. His pleasure increased when Lucy explained what she had: a location given up by an arrested man for two kidnap victims who were believed to have access to an assortment of weapons, and had both been instructed to fight each other to the death if necessary. And a very short window in time to get there.

Sergeant Hughes had insisted on picking her up. There were two vehicles, four armed officers in total, and they would lead the search. During the blue-light run from the motorway services where they had met, Lucy had spent much of the time on Google Earth, trying to work out what challenges the site might offer. Sergeant Hughes needed far more information than she could provide and he had soon stopped asking. The basics were simple enough: the location was Burgoyne Heights, Dover, and there looked to be only one vehicular access point. There had once been a series of forts and pillboxes built for use in World War Two, and the specific location Billy Easton had provided was a single building out on its own in the hills above Dover's Connaught Park. The aerial shot from Google Earth gave enough of a glimpse through the trees to show a doglegged layout to the building, and a photo found on an Urban Adventure website showed a door in the centre as the only way in. That tallied with what Joel had been told. He had also been told that their victims were somewhere inside.

The moment they arrived at the site for real the terrain changed, the smoothness of the roads giving way to rutted fields and clumps of grass that bucked and rolled the 4x4 until Lucy's phone was unreadable. It didn't matter anyway, not now. The red spot marking their destination was directly ahead. She could see a mound of earth with a path worn enough to give a glimpse of something grey, flat-sided and solid. No doubt the local kids played their war games here.

The cars weren't going to be able to get much further. The last two hundred metres would be on foot. Sergeant Hughes' door was opened before he even killed the engine. He was quick to remind her to stay where she was until she was called forward; they would clear it first. There was no room for argument and Sergeant Hughes moved straight on to barking orders at his three armed colleagues. They listened as they kitted up, slipping balaclavas and ballistic helmets onto their heads. Their black gloves were the final items. Then they each lifted an assault rifle as their primary weapon and started out in formation, pacing directly towards the worn path.

Chapter 37

They started off at a quick jog. Lucy had been told to stay in the car but the moment they set off she stepped out, leaning on the open car door, watching as the team fanned out in front of her, their rifles all honed on the same point. The ground had a gentle slope and Lucy stepped up into the 4x4 to get higher, her hand resting on its roof as she stood out of the open door. She could now see the top half of the fort – and the central door. She had no doubt the trenches would have been much larger when they were dug; this whole building would have been invisible until you were almost touching its sides. Mature trees had probably added another layer of concealment but now it was surrounded by thick, weathered stumps, probably representing action taken by a council that was paranoid about children falling from the trees and being held responsible. The part of the door she could see looked newer than its surroundings and her first thought was that this too would was a council action – an attempt to keep the kids out. But perhaps it was put in far more recently; perhaps Billy Easton had needed a more solid door? There were fence posts that looked recent, too. Lucy stepped back down onto the springy earth and noted that they stood out on their own, sunk into the ground two at a time, maybe ten metres apart and in five rows between here and the fort door, like airport landing lights. She didn't know what they could be for. They were too far apart for panels and besides, why just two at a time?

The firearms team passed through the first of the posts. The jangling sound of a bell was almost instant. Lucy's phone, still on the passenger seat, burst into life at the same time. She could see Joel's name lit up. It added to her confusion so she ignored it, cutting Joel out of her mind to focus back on that sound. A bell? That meant something in all this, she knew it but couldn't put her finger on it immediately. The team were still moving away from her, and their approach had slowed a little to a quick walk, their rifles still levelled; they would soon be through the second row of fence posts. The bell sound was instant the moment they did.

And suddenly Lucy knew exactly what it meant.

The feeling at the sound of the first bell was a knot of anxiety that Bradley had to firmly swallow back down before he vomited it up. He lurched forward in the gloom, the wire suddenly slack enough to let him. The door, as solid as it looked, was still bleeding sunlight at the bottom and he fixed on it. His legs were still numb, his hands too, and they flooded with pins and needles, so that he had to scrabble in the dirt to get onto his side and then pull himself up using the side wall. His legs wobbled, his knees threatening to give out at any moment. He managed a step forward, and the movement seemed to force a hacked cough from his dry throat. The pins and needles burned hot, but his feeling was coming back overall and he was able to take another step before the wire caught his middle again. He stood still, his breathing shallow and fast, the adrenaline visible as white spots that flashed and sparked in his eyes in time with the beating in his chest. He shook his head and tried to focus on his breathing. The automatic pistol was still where it had been left, still hooked to the wall. Still out of reach. But he was two steps closer.

The firearms team had thick balaclavas and earpieces for Lucy to try and penetrate as she sprinted forward, bellowing with all her might. But the team were passing through the third set of posts before she even made the first, and a flash of red light caught her eye, projected by a silver metal button pushed into the wood, as another bell sound rang out into the woodland setting.

'Sensors!' she bawled. 'Movement sensors!' But the team were already coming together, their focus bearing down on the door. And the two posts either side of it.

The movement wasn't smooth; the wire around Bradley's waist had a sudden give and he was too anxious, pushing against it too firmly, and as he stepped forward he stumbled. He raised his arms, despite knowing that he was still too far away to reach the weapon.

This was different to before: the bells were coming faster, their timing erratic; this wasn't a ten-second pattern like the first time. If that meant someone was approaching, they were coming quickly, in a hurry to kill him, to get this over with, throwing away their advantage just like he had been told might happen.

He was ready.

Another jangle of the bell. The wire gave again with the same clunking sound and his feet dragged forward, kicking up the dirt. The light round the door flickered and changed where there was movement behind it, and someone was shouting. It sounded distant but his ears beat with his own pulse and that, with the thickness of the wooden door, made the words indiscernible.

He reached out. The fingertips of his right hand could now brush the butt of the gun. Pushing forward with all he had meant he could get enough pressure on it just to push it away an inch before it fell back onto the metal pins. One more step and he would have it.

The light round the door changed again; now the sun was blocked completely, like there was something immediately on the other side. It was some*one*; the sound of footsteps merged with the sound of a jangling bell.

The fifth one.

The wire fell slack, his feet moved forward, his right hand took hold of the smooth wood of the butt and his left wrapped round the barrel to yank it off the wall. Daylight exploded in his face to force his eyes shut, his right hand scrabbled for the trigger and all he could do was point the explosion of automatic fire in the direction of the light.

Chapter 38

Lucy skidded, her knees locking in front of her on the loose dirt. Then she was aware she was falling. The gunfire had started the moment the door had been wrenched open, and the first two officers had gone down in front of her, the second pair throwing themselves either side of the door, leaving a gap for her to stare straight through.

At an automatic weapon still flaring from the shadow.

She didn't know if she had been knocked down. There was no pain. Not at first.

The firing ran out quickly, though the weapon still tutted with mechanical clicks. For a moment that was the only sound. But only for a moment. The two officers who had split in front of her now swung back into the doorway, their own weapons raised, and, with their colleagues at their feet, they returned fire. Lucy still had a perfect view of the man who had moved forward enough for the daylight to touch him, enough that she saw his reaction as the weapons were levelled, his eyes wide as he took in the masked police officers and their assault rifles. He threw his hands out, the spent weapon falling to the ground as the first rounds struck and pushed him backwards. The forces at work were invisible; it was as if the shadow he had come from had reached out to reclaim him. The officers followed him in, their movements now looking jerky as their muzzle flashes added a strobe effect to the horror.

This time there was no silence when the weapons stopped. The shouts were immediate, *Medic!* One of the officers reappeared from the gloom to kneel by his colleague, his hand lifted to operate his radio, his voice a shaken babble that Lucy couldn't work out. Her ears whooshed and shushed. The sun was behind her, the sensation warm on her back the only thing to break through her numbness. She turned to it.

The view from here was beautiful. To her right the ground sloped away sharply to the green and brown patchwork of Connaught Park below. The terrain was mainly long, wild grass that shook and danced in a warm breeze. She focused on a tree in the near distance, its trunk and branches thick and strong, the leaves the brightest green she had ever seen. The sight was enough to pull her to her feet, fixing on branches that moved to beckon her over. It was a struggle at first, but she got up. She could still hear muffled shouts and calls but she was protected from them by the warm breeze in her ears acting like a filter to the panic. The sun and that beautiful tree were leading her away, stopping her from turning back, protecting her.

One foot in front of other, that was all she had to do. With every step the leaves were becoming more vivid, the breeze like a friend that had her by the hand, the warmth of the sun mingling with the warmth of the bright, red blood that ran down to drip from her fingertips.

Chapter 39

The marked cars were abandoned in such a way as to block the entrance, their lights still flickering, some with their engines running, and Joel was forced to do the same with his car. He ran around and between the obstruction to emerge out of the treeline. The chaos at the entrance was a theme that continued over to his right, while straight ahead was an elevated view of Connaught Park and much of Dover. It was the two ambulances that grabbed his attention, both with their back to him, both with doors wide open. His pace quickened.

'Who are you?' A officer in hi-vis seemed to emerge from the long grass to challenge Joel as he got closer. She was flushed red, her hat tucked under an arm that held a blaring radio. She turned it down.

'Inspector Joel Norris.' He lifted his lanyard, and her body sagged in relief. 'DS Rose,' he said, 'where is she?'

'I don't know.'

'Casualties?' Joel snapped.

'I don't know! I just got here, I should be over there!' She pointed the way he had just come. Suddenly it made sense to him; she was supposed to be watching the entrance, holding the scene, making sure no one came in who wasn't supposed to, but she had got sucked in. Chaos had a way of doing that.

Joel left her, running past the empty ambulances and down a short, steep slope where a squat building had been dug into the hilltop. Two firearms officers were sat on a tree stump to the right of the entrance. The officer who was closer had his head bent, his face pale. Sweat ran unchecked down his face to gather at his chin. His weapons, ballistic vest, balaclava, helmet, gloves and load vest littered the grass in front of him like he had ripped them from his body. The middle finger on his right hand was clamped by an oximeter, its digital display flickering in time with a racing pulse.

'DS Rose?' Joel snapped and the officer lifted his head in slow motion. The eyes took their time to settle on him, but there was no focus. The finger with the oximeter lifted to point back, almost the way Joel had come. Joel spun to follow its direction. There was a figure, some distance away, far enough that Joel couldn't be sure. He ran straight for it.

'Decrepit Fort,' Joel said, stopping short, several metres from where DS Rose was sat on a thick tree root that appeared for a metre before plunging back into the earth. Another root supported her feet. 'The third zone,' Joel said. She was facing away, towards the sun and that view of the town. Her right forearm was coated in a thick layer of blood. It didn't look like she had even noticed it.

'One left then,' DS Rose said, her tone flat

'They're saying everyone's OK,' Joel said, gesturing with the radio he had gripped in his right hand.

'Not everyone,' she said, still with no emotion.

'No . . . not everyone.'

'Blank rounds,' DS Rose said.

'Blank rounds?' Joel repeated. He didn't know what else to say.

'He was always going to die. That man. He knew someone was coming for him, he was trying to defend himself. I saw it. I saw how he looked . . . He was terrified, Joel.'

'That's what happens when you get someone from the Force

Control Room giving out updates. They say things like "everyone's OK". But of course they're not. I've just seen the firearms skipper over there with a thousand-yard stare, and his mate didn't even look up. Some cop who was supposed to be standing at the entrance was stood out in the middle of a field instead, just trying to work out which way's up. No one's OK, and that's exactly what I would expect.'

'He never stood a chance.'

'He didn't. Back at custody . . . Easton waited until you were here then he pulled a card from his pants. It was the death card. You remember we played it last night, it's part of *Escape!*?'

'Death card?' She shook her head. Joel didn't know if she couldn't remember or just didn't care.

'Yeah, there's only one card like that, hidden among the tools. If someone pulls that one out, everyone in the zone in play loses a life. It was too late to warn you. This was always an ambush but I thought . . . I was *supposed* to think you were all in danger . . .' Joel stumbled to a finish.

'Dead, you mean.' DS Rose finally turned away from the sun. Her skin pallor was also a clear shade of shocked white. Her eyes were ringed by a redness that almost matched her bloody arm. She worked her jaw with a grimace like it was painful.

'Did anyone look you over? There are paramedics—'

'I'm fine but you were supposed to think I was dead, that we all were. He's fucking with us, showing us how clever he is. What else did he say?'

'There's blood,' Joel said and pointed.

'A nick on my elbow when I fell over. Trust me, it could have been worse. What else did he say?' she repeated.

'I haven't spoken to him yet. There wasn't the chance. The DCI called me on the way and we agreed to bed Easton down. I've asked for him to get the ball rolling on an extension in custody. All this . . .' Joel gestured back towards the gaggle of officers by the stone fort. 'We can't speak to him until we know what went on here.'

'We murdered that man, on his behalf. And after we all thought we were dead – that's what happened.' There was life in her tone now, anger. Joel was delighted to hear it. He wanted emotion from her, something. 'He had sensors on posts, infrared to ring his bell. We were getting closer and the man he'd tied up in that miserable building knew it, he knew every step we were taking. God knows what he thought was coming for him, Joel. Death itself, judging by how he reacted when we opened that door. And he was right.'

'He was.'

'I couldn't stop them. I knew, I just knew. When those bells started going off . . . just like Shannon said . . . I knew we were here to take part in his game . . . and we played our roles perfectly for him.'

'We all were.'

'But you didn't see it. I got to see it, I got to be here.'

'I'm sorry, Lucy. I can't imagine what that was like. I know how police shootings work, this is a PSD scene, or at the very least someone a lot more important than me will deal with it and they won't miss a thing. We don't need to be here, in all honesty. No one wants us here. Let me drive you home. We can get something to eat and we can talk it out.'

DS Rose shook her head. 'Home sounds good, but I want to be on my own.' She lifted those puffy eyes to meet Joel's. 'No offence.'

'None taken. Let's get you home then.'

'My statement . . . they'll need it.'

'They will and they can wait. You can tell them that was an order from me.'

'He has to pay for this, for what he's done. I saw it, Joel . . . I don't want to write that statement, I don't want to write what happened because I can't do it justice, no one can.'

'Billy Easton will pay, you have my word on that. That's

another reason to bed him down, to start this again in the morning. Let him stew, let him worry about what we've found and what we know. It's his turn to be trapped behind a door and to be scared of what's coming.'

Chapter 40

The headlights swept through Peter Marshall's estate, leading the way home like glowing rails, the steering wheel just something to hold him upright. The lights led him right to his drive, shortening, then brightening against the brown gloss of his garage. Peter Marshall stepped out into a breeze that rushed him, shuffling his shirt tails and moving through his hair before dying away to nothing just as quick as it had come on. The forecasters had been talking of a windstorm that could arrive the next night but with a trajectory that was unpredictable. The last update had suggested it wouldn't make it this far inland but they were wrong, it was coming. All his senses told him something was building.

He winced as his front door creaked open, then consoled himself that he needn't worry; Jessica was a heavy sleeper. He'd lost count of the number of times he had given up on sleep and gone downstairs to listen to some music under headphones or even take a walk around the block, and all without her even stirring. He had never really slept well, a reason perhaps he had gravitated towards a job working nights.

When he pushed the door shut, the darkness thickened. He made it to the kitchen and tipped the blinds to give him enough light to work with. The combination of the warm orange of the streetlights and the silvery hue of the moon gave his home patches of shadow and softened edges. When he selected a kettle to make tea it was the cast-iron one he had bought specially for his insomnia, allowing him to boil a kettle in near silence on the top of the hob rather than use its hissing, popping electric counterpart. The blue flame added more light, enough to reveal a dirty coffee cup on the side, directly above where the dishwasher was concealed in the units. Jessica was two things consistently: impeccably tidy and a creature of habit. She would only leave something like that out on the work surface as a reminder that the dishwasher needed emptying after its cycle. He'd never known her to go to bed before doing it – even when she'd had a few glasses of wine.

He pulled it open now. The white light from inside was instant and harsh enough to force him to narrow his eyes. The washer was full, the contents clean but cold as the cycle had long since finished. There were what looked like bowls and smaller plates from breakfast and lunch. Another thing he knew about Jessica: she always ate proper meals. His eyes moved to the oven where the digital display was flashing a notification that the timer was up. When he pulled it open another harsh light erupted, this time shining down on a baked pasta dish that had cooked and then been left untouched. It was also stone cold.

Peter closed it again and shut off the gas under the kettle. Now as he moved through the house he was turning on lights. He lit the landing before starting out on the stairs. He lit the bedroom too – their bedroom – the room where she should be sleeping, where right now she should wake to blink at the light and demand what the hell was going on. But she wasn't there. No one was there. The bed was still made, the silly number of cushions – a constant in-joke – still arranged like something from a home decor magazine.

His hand shot to his pocket. His phone display woke with no notifications of missed calls, no text messages – no explanations. He pulled up Jessica's contact and pressed to call. A second or two of holding his breath and then she answered. Only it wasn't live, it was Jessica's recorded voicemail, cheery yet professional. He suddenly thought of her car. The last time he had seen her had been through the window, leaving in her car to cover some afternoon appointments at work.

He moved back out of their bedroom and down the stairs to the hall where he inspected the wooden unit with a bowl where she would dump her car keys the moment she came through the door. The keys were missing. He hadn't seen the car outside but she often parked it in the garage. He broke into an almost jog to check back into the kitchen and in his haste he bumped his nose into the back door as his hands fumbled over the lock. He walked down a short path to a side door to the garage. He could already see it was empty before the light gave its audible flicker then stayed on to illuminate a clear patch of grey concrete.

'Jessica?' His voice met with another rush of wind. This time he was side-on and it took hold of his trouser leg like it was carrying out a rough search of his pockets.

He moved back into his house, back to the hall, where he had noticed something out of place but never focused on it. He did now. It was a small plastic figure, like a running woman stood on a wide base, next to the bowl for keys. He picked it up now, studying it closer. It looked like it had been painted and without any skill. The brown hair ran into the green of the dress while a white zip detail running down the back looked like it had been painted when the rest was still wet.

A white zip?

Peter knew that dress.

He was back on the stairs, this time taking them two at a time, the figurine gripped tight in his left hand. His bedroom was still lit. Jessica's wardrobes lined the far wall. He tore the doors open.

The dress wasn't there.

He knew it wouldn't be, but he had so wanted to be wrong. That was the dress she had been wearing when she had gone back into work – the last time he had seen her.

The figurine was of Jessica.

Something was very wrong.

Chapter 41

Lucy Rose had hoped that the transition from day to night would bring with it some relief. As a child, when her dad came back in one of his moods she would hide in a wardrobe or under her bed with a blanket over her head and the darkness would make her feel safe, like it was impenetrable, like she couldn't be hurt by what she couldn't see. Most kids grew up fearing the darkness and the imagined horrors it concealed. Lucy Rose had grown up fearing the light, because nothing was more terrifying than a horror you knew to be true.

It had worked for her too. Her dad had shouted and yelled, he had smashed windows and doors and landed blows on others, but nothing beyond the sounds had penetrated her darkness.

Today, the bright light of the day had shown her a helpless man shot dead and it was that image that still lingered while she watched the darkness slowly consume the distant buildings first, then close in to take the grounds of her home. The window was just about floor to ceiling; she lived in a townhouse in layout but not in style. It was the smallest home in the development of an old chapel that sat just off the High Street in a large village called Tenterden near Ashford. It was an affluent area, the property prices high enough to push it a long way down on her list of places to think of living, but something had told her to take the showing here, at this place. And she had never looked back. Where she had been standing for the last couple of hours was the reason. A mezzanine level that, at the time of the showing, had been nothing but a blank layer of carpet that the selling agent had used as part of his sales patter, conjuring images of movie nights in front of a huge television, soft furnishings to point at that view, or a modern office space. Two years later it was still a blank layer of carpet. She had tried chairs and cushions but always ended up standing, leaning against the window's deep stone surround, the glass cool against her shoulder, soft carpet under her bare feet and the view stretching away from her. It was perfect. Her happy place.

But today it was nothing of the sort.

Her mind replayed the day's events over and over, the lingering image of a man facing down death, knowing what was coming, bleeding fear from every pore before the bullets could strike him to tear out his blood for real. That would be enough on its own, but it had forced Lucy to go back over the death of Hannah Ribbons, their previous case. The victim in this instance had been a young woman Lucy knew well, chained up to be shot in cold blood. Hannah would have seen it coming too; she would have bled fear, she would have had that same final moment consumed by panic and helplessness.

Lucy might even have been Hannah's final thought. In that same situation, Lucy was certain Hannah would have been hers.

Lucy needed to move. She felt like she needed to talk to someone who had some idea what she was going through, who might be able to move her on, or at least help get rid of the feeling that a part of her was still back at Burgoyne Heights with a bleeding elbow and a dry mouth gaping open to capture a warm breeze. Someone who knew what it was like when the world revealed its ugly side.

There was only one place she could think of to go.

Phoenix Court, Margate, was doing its best to fend off the darkness. Every window seemed to be lit; some had curtains, but none that fitted. Stepping through the communal door came with the familiar musk of unwashed human bodies, damp earth and stale cigarette smoke – all carried by the overriding funk of cannabis.

Her dad's flat was on the ground floor, towards the end of the long corridor that stretched out in front of her with a gentle curvature to hide his front door from where she entered the building. She walked it. The sound of beating music again accompanying her steps, only this time it was getting louder as she got closer until it was apparent that her dad's flat was the source.

The door was wide open and a long male body was jammed sideways in it, his foot up to leave dusty treadmarks on the face of the door. The man wore cargo shorts and pit boots that had a layer of baked-on concrete. He gripped a can of strong lager, the hand similarly layered, the fingertips a solid grey that thinned by the time it reached the wrist to give the impression of a man slowly turning to stone. He greeted her with a smile that had a focal point – his two front teeth, stained a deep orange to stand out from the off-yellow that made up the rest. His long hair was twisted into rough, dusty dreads. Lucy had long since stopped trying to work out the age of men who had spent their lives abusing one substance or another. His long, thick arms were strong and lean but the bags around his eyes and the creased skin on his neck indicated someone north of forty.

There was movement from the other side of the corridor. The door to the flat opposite opened and Lisa Hopkiss peered out.

'It's been like that for a hour now,' she said. She was in the same dressing gown as the last time they had met, her expression the same exasperation too. Lucy didn't have time for it; she wasn't there to appease her dad's neighbours. She considered turning around at that point and heading back home.

She should have.

'You're a pretty one, ain't ya!' The man at the door grinned up at her. He'd trapped one of his dreads in his teeth to suck on.

'Get out of my way,' Lucy said in reply. His smile held. She looked beyond him, and the thick cigarette smoke that hung in the air suddenly shifted as a woman stumbled out of the bathroom door on the left, pulling up a pair of ill-fitting jeans round her scrawny waist. Her dead eyes momentarily took in the figures at the front door then she turned away, walking back into the living room. A man followed her out. He pulled a cigarette from between his lips and threw it to the floor, his next step crushing it into what was left of the carpet.

'Working the door, ain't I! There's a list.' The voice drifted up in the smoke, and it took a few seconds for Lucy to decipher it. Her ears were still ringing from being close to gunshots, but, rather than the gentle shushing when she had been in her silent apartment, it was now an angry beat where it mingled with the music to pound in her head. Her whole body flushed with anger. Her dad had lied. He'd told her how he wanted to get away from this building, away from the people in it, so he could be something to her and yet here they were as invited guests, stubbing out their cigarettes, filling his doorway and doing whatever they wanted in his bathroom.

And she'd believed him.

That was what made her angry. That was what beat in her head. She'd learned not to believe him some time ago; he must have caught her in a moment of weakness. Of course he had, he thrived on the weak, on the vulnerable. She thought she had seen something different about him, a new intensity. But there was nothing different at all.

'Get out of my way,' she said again. The doorstop started to answer but her patience was gone. She swung her foot. It was reactive, a flick out, a toe-poke in the nose that knocked the back of his head off the doorframe. It had the desired effect. The man swore loudly and brought his legs down so Lucy could step over him. He called out after her, menace in his words, and she heard him scrabbling like he might be getting up as she walked the corridor and into the living room. The stereo was on her right. She reached down for it, pulling the plug clean from the wall, and the force dragged the unit off the stool, sending CD cases and unopened mail onto the floor. The floor was where she found her dad too.

He was laid out, his trousers down enough to show underwear worn into numerous holes where the material met with the band, and he was shirtless. His head was moving like it was being operated by someone with a remote, clumsily and jerkily. She had seen it a million times. The one thing Lucy knew well was the sight of her father drunk.

'What the fuck happened to my MUSIC!' he bawled. His hand reached out to rummage through the fallen cases for the remote. He found it, lifted it to where the stereo had once been and frowned when the buttons did nothing.

'Dad,' Lucy said. His head jerked towards her. At the same time she was grabbed from behind. The voice that had hissed at her through those orange-stained front teeth spoke again.

'"Dad"?' it said. 'This your fucking girl, Walt?'

'Take your fucking hands off me or I break them into little pieces,' Lucy hissed, her arm tense in his grip. She was fighting herself not to lash out. He laughed, letting her go.

'Got spirit *and* looks, your girl!'

'She ain't no girl of mine, coming here, turning off the music. What sort of a *cunt* does that!' Her dad's head dropped in stages. He caught it each time before it hit the floor. His eyes had given up the search for her, but his right hand still reached up from the floor, still clicking at the remote to start the music up again.

She had never wanted a dad. At least she had never wanted *her* dad. She had seen what he did, the damage he caused everywhere he went, the hurt and the pain that followed him around, and most of her life had been about trying to avoid it. But right now, for once in her life, a few days after they had shared laughter right here, in this flat, she had needed something that only he could offer. She had needed a parent.

But she had wasted her time. She should have stayed at home and suffered on her own; that was the life she knew.

'Get up, Dad,' she said, her voice low, her tone flat. 'Get up now.' She kicked out, more lightly than she had at the doorman, more a nudge with her foot. It prompted another volley of profanities. 'Get UP!' The power in her voice was enough that it broke, the last word a shrill screech that bent her double and forced phlegm from her lips.

'She's crazy, man, this party's done!' A woman's voice drifted past as it left. Her date from the toilet went with her. The doorstop said something similar but with more profanities, most of them at her, some of them at the pathetic excuse for a man laying at her feet. Then he left too.

'What the fuck do you want from me, girl?' her father said. He'd discarded the remote and was now rummaging for his can of beer. He lifted it to his lips. Lucy lashed out to send it flying into a frothy mess under a dilapidated TV cabinet. His eyes followed it for a moment, but then they turned to her, his other hand now reaching for an empty spirit bottle. And that was when she saw it: a look he had always reserved for her mother. It was unmistakeable. He was becoming the man she had needed the darkness to protect her from, his aggression now directed towards her, and she knew exactly what was coming next.

He was fast, powered now by rage. But she was faster. She

kicked out again, this time more strongly, catching him in the midriff, hard enough that he bent around her foot and she could feel his chest retching and shuddering for breath against her shin. She stepped forward, forcing him onto his back, one foot either side of his gaunt body. He had never looked more pathetic. He flailed at her with his left hand; he had scooped up the spirit bottle to hold it by the neck but she knocked it out of his grip easily and his hand fell back down. There was a rasp in his throat from being winded, and he muttered more profanities when he could manage them. He peered up at her, no longer with evil intent; his eyes were pools of nothingness. He was beaten and it had been simple.

It made her more angry.

With the first blow she struck him hard on the cheek with an open-hand slap. She followed it up by dropping to sit on his chest, trapping his arms. There was no fight, no nothing, though she gave him a moment to show it. She yearned for him to fight back; taking a hit might make her feel something, at least. She swung again, this time with a closed fist that split his nose open. Still nothing. His head rolled from side to side like he was clearing his daze. She lashed out again, but this time with no pause, no waiting to see what he did in reply. She was lost, lost to her rage, lost to the first thirty years of her life, lost to the injustice of the world and its manipulation of her. The bottle appeared in her hand. The noise was sickening as she brought it down as hard as she could muster. The second time sounded worse than the first. When she lifted it for a third time, someone else's scream penetrated the fug of rage.

She turned to Lisa Hopkiss, who was covering her mouth, her eyes locked on the unmoving figure Lucy sat on. The bottle slipped from Lucy's hand to thud onto the floor and she pushed off his chest to stand up. The movement forced a breath out of him, and his nose and throat rattled as he sucked air in. She took a moment to take in his pathetic form, his eyes twitching behind half-closed eyelids, his breathing coming in long gasps, blood trickling from a gash under his eye and from both nostrils. The realisation was just as sudden as her anger had been: *She'd beaten her own father unconscious!* Tears of rage were already blurring her vision, but now the tears were for a different reason and they fell thicker. She had to wipe them away as she leant back over him to push his head back and open his throat so he wouldn't swallow his tongue. The rattling sound was gone.

She looked over at Lisa, a blur at the door, her hand still covering her mouth while her eyes bulged like they were taking up half her face.

'Get him an ambulance . . .' Lucy whispered. It hurt her to speak. Lisa didn't respond or even move, and Lucy had to push past her to get back out into the corridor. There was loud music again, coming from the floor above. The same beat as before. The same people must have found somewhere else to party.

Only now they were providing the soundtrack for her exit.

Day 5

Chapter 42

'You found us then!' Squatting on the edge of a canteen table on the top floor of Medway Police Station had been a temporary solution for a short interview with Shannon Hendry – and not a very good one. Billy Easton's stay in custody and the work required around it were expected to be far more intense and Joel had needed a complete relocation of his team. DS Rose had obviously got directions to the only space available in the whole building.

'Nice place,' DS Rose said, taking a moment to look round what was a very small office.

'I know! I didn't think this building had any available cupboards, but they managed to clear one out for us.' The estates team seemed to have taken Joel's request for somewhere temporary to work a murder investigation as a challenge to find somewhere as far away from the naturally lit and calming centre of the building as was possible. They were at the end of a corridor that became more foreboding the further you walked down it. The office itself had a tiny window, like they'd used up their quota of glass everywhere else. There was no obvious way of opening it either. The room was stuffy and oppressive and yet Joel had felt instantly more at home. This was more like what police stations should feel like. 'I wasn't expecting you in,' he continued. He watched DS Rose closely for her reaction. He hadn't spoken to her since she had refused his lift home after the shooting. He'd stopped himself calling overnight, opting to send a message instead. DS Rose had replied, but it had been curt and given no real clue to her state of mind. No more than he might have expected but it hadn't stopped him worrying. She looked tired, exhausted even, and Joel wondered if she had slept at all.

Eileen had been busy, and the largest wall was already covered in pictures, names – even key statements. There was an area free where Eileen had started putting up what they had from yesterday's shooting, only for Joel to stop her, unaware what version of DS Rose might appear and what impact colour photos might have.

'Really?' DS Rose replied.

'No, not really,' Joel said and his sergeant flashed a tired smile. 'How did you sleep?' Joel chanced.

'I didn't,' she said. Joel gave her room to elaborate and she continued, 'You need to know something. There was a disturbance at my dad's place overnight. The police came round to see me because I was named as being there. I suppose I should be the one to tell you.' There was a chair for her next to Eileen. She took it.

'Did you want me to . . .' Eileen pointed at the exit with a look that suggested she was really rather keen to take it.

'You can stay, there's nothing you can't hear,' DS Rose said.

'Is he OK?' Joel said.

'He took a bit of a beating.' DS Rose wrapped her left hand around the knuckles on her right where they were rested on her lap.

'What happened?'

'I hit him. His neighbour called it in. She saw what happened,' DS Rose said in a matter-of-fact manner that added to Joel's confusion. There must be more to come, like how it was self-defence and she had no choice.

'What happened?' Joel prompted.

'I got angry and I hit him.'

'And yet here you are,' Joel said. 'Is that the version you gave to the cops that came out?'

'They turned up to tell me how they had to come out because I was named and how they knew it was all a misunderstanding.' She shrugged. 'My dad had already told them it was nothing to do with me. He didn't tell them who it was, he just said there was a lot of people at his place drinking and he wasn't even sure. If you knew my dad . . . well, you'd believe it too. The neighbour that called it in said she'd made a mistake too . . . She said I was there but I'd left before there was any trouble.'

'But now I know better,' Joel said.

DS Rose shrugged. 'You do. I had no intention of coming in here and lying to you.'

'But you lied to them, to the cops that came out to you.'

'I didn't have to. They had a version already sorted in their minds. I think they'd just come out to tell me what that was. I only had to confirm that I was there earlier in the evening and my dad was hammered so I left. That's all true. Then they told me which hospital he had been taken to.'

'You hospitalised him?'

'Fractured eye socket and concussion. Some bruising too, nothing serious.'

'Nothing serious!' Joel breathed back at her. 'Jesus, Lucy, the position you put me in! The position you put us both in.'

Eileen held up her hands. 'I didn't hear a thing, fortunately. Any conversation you have in private is just that, it's not for me to interfere.'

'You're my team, this is my team and this is all I have, OK?' Lucy took in both of her seated colleagues, and seemed to rush a breath in too. 'I didn't want to come in here and lie. I don't make a habit of this sort of thing, I just . . . I needed someone, last night, after . . . after what happened,

I just wanted to talk it out and that useless sack of . . . He was too drunk to even sit up, let alone be of any use and listen to his daughter. That's the bare minimum, isn't it? Just sit and listen.'

'You coulda called—' Joel started.

'You? You've got your wife and kids and I know you haven't been there much. The last thing you needed was me calling, taking over your evening with more work stuff.'

'You're not work stuff.'

'I am . . .' She seemed to catch another breath, then jerked straighter in her chair. 'Talking of which, we need to get working, right? What did I miss when I went home?'

Joel sighed. He didn't reply straightaway, just stared at his sergeant, trying to work out what the hell he should do with her. 'We don't have the time for this, for you, for whatever the hell you did last night.'

'I agree.'

'That doesn't mean it's over. If someone asks me what I know, then I will tell them.'

'You should, too,' DS Rose said. 'I told you, I won't lie to you and I don't expect you to lie for me either.'

Joel needed to move on. 'You missed a lot. Eileen worked all of yesterday afternoon on Billy Easton and we've got some things that we need to put to him. DC Trott and I were here 'til late prepping for the interview that needs to happen first thing. Easton's PACE clock started at just gone 4 p.m. yesterday and we've done nothing with him yet so we're already up against it.'

'I thought you were getting an extension?' DS Rose said.

Joel shook his head, not just as an answer, but in disbelief as he checked the clock, which showed it was just gone 7 a.m. They had already lost fifteen hours. 'We can't rely on it. Debbie Marsden's on leave, which means that we need another superintendent to authorise it, and can you guess who's covering the region as acting superintendent in her absence?'

'Go on.'

'Mark Hall,' Joel said, 'and I think you were present when he made it quite clear what he thought of me.' Mark Hall was the DCI for Major Crime day-to-day and the same man who had been called in to take over Joel's last job when it was clear it was starting to spiral. Joel had resisted, played a little dirty even to get the job done without him. Mark Hall had made his contempt quite clear in a memorable debrief and any number of times since. He would not be looking to do them any favours.

'He can think what he likes, he still has to have a good reason not to extend it,' DS Rose said.

'He might have that. Just the fact that we've had Easton in custody for more than half his time and we haven't actually interviewed him yet will be enough. For all we know he might give a full and frank admission straight off the bat, in which case we won't need an extension at all. I can't argue with that.'

'We won't need an admission to get a charge,' DS Rose said. 'I don't care what he says, we know what he did and he'll answer for it one way or another.'

'There are gaps in the evidence, Lucy. We're a little way short of what we need for a charge.' Joel held his hand up as DS Rose suddenly flushed in anger. 'I know, I know, but you missed the updates from yesterday. Eileen here will bring you fully up to date while we go and interview.'

'You're not taking me to interview?' DS Rose snapped.

'No. Like I said, DC Trott and I prepped last night. I wasn't sure you would be in at all today and there isn't time to bring you up to speed. You don't have to be here, you know, if you would rather be at home.'

'But I am here. And I want to be in there with Easton.'

Joel was shaking his head. 'You're too close to this, to what happened yesterday, it wouldn't be right to put you down there. And the fact that you're not up to speed makes this an easy decision.'

'Wouldn't be right? I can't think of anyone better.'

'Really? After what you just told me? You think you're ready to go and conduct an interview?' Joel could feel his hackles rising.

'More ready than I've ever been.'

'And what happens if last night's *incident* does come back to bite us on the arse? A violent assault the night before you interview a murder suspect? It wouldn't take much of a defence solicitor to drag us both over the coals for that one, and then to question your involvement a few hours later.'

'That's why I told you about it. There's nothing in it. A crime report was generated because it's an automatic process, but it was closed at source, nothing to report. I'm not even a named suspect.'

'But there's a CAD? From when the neighbour called it in and said that she'd just seen some bloke bottled by someone she knows as *Lucy Rose*? You keep reminding me how you're the real detective here, so tell me now, would we have to disclose that as part of this investigation? Would it have to be submitted as unused material for this case?'

DS Rose shrugged. 'Technically we might, but even then it would be part of a legal argument that the judge would throw out as irrelevant.'

'The judge might not. And it's an argument we can avoid so we should. It's already taking up our time, right here, right now.'

'A defence solicitor could do far more damage by focusing on you and Leonard as the interview team. He's a few months out of his probation, not yet accredited. They'll pick up on that and then they'll take great delight in picking holes in your procedure.'

'I won't leave any holes.'

'You will. There's always holes. The difference is that they won't be looking so hard if they see a DI and a DS on the top of the ROVI. Take Leonard Trott and you're asking for trouble.'

Joel's immediate reaction died before it made his lips. She was right. The ROVI, or Record Of Video Interview, was basically the whole interview typed out in words. A laborious waste of time but solicitors liked things in writing; it meant they could underline, highlight, and have something to waft in the face of the officers in the box as part of a challenge. The very start of the ROVI always included details on who was conducting the interview. It was an official document and they would have to list Leonard as *PC* Leonard Trott, which would reveal him as not yet being an accredited detective. Defence solicitors don't miss details like that and it offered a very easy opportunity to undermine the validity of the whole investigation. Leonard Trott might not thank Joel either, when he was dragged into the box at court and asked to list his relevant experience. Joel could picture the glee on the solicitor's face. *So, under two years' experience in policing as a whole, and a matter of just a few weeks as part of an investigative role,* PC *Trott. And, pray tell, what was your role prior to joining the police? Just in case that could be deemed relevant for someone who carried out such a pivotal part in an investigation where my client could be facing the rest of his natural life in prison?*

And Leonard Trott would do what he was trained to do: he would answer simply, one word whenever possible and always the truth: *Carphone Warehouse.*

Joel sighed, then sighed again. DS Rose took the opportunity to force her point home. 'I'm going down there. I can be your scribe. No doubt that was the role you had for Leonard anyway. It doesn't matter what I missed yesterday, I can bring something to that interview.'

'What?'

'I was there, Joel. I was right there, when . . . I saw what he did, what he set up to happen, and we fell for it. All of us. I want to tell him that, I want to tell him what that was like.'

‘You’ll do no such thing. If we’ve got to that point, it’s not going well.’

‘Fine then, I’ll just sit quiet and do the writing.’

Joel had been played. He couldn’t help but smile. ‘I might still tell him you were there. It does matter, it will sharpen him up, he’ll know that he will need to think a little more before he lies.’

‘How can he lie? After what happened yesterday, after what he told us?’ DS Rose said.

‘Eileen will have a full update ready for you when we come back up, but we made some progress yesterday and one thing we did find out is that he may well have been lying to us all along.’

Chapter 43

'Still no solicitor, Billy?' This was the first thing Joel said, having covered his handwritten list of formal requirements.

'I told you, I don't need a solicitor.' Billy's reply was tired. He leaked exhaustion from every pore, his skin seemed to hang heavy on his frame, and every word appeared to take physical effort. The custody sergeant had updated that he didn't seem to have slept at all; most of his night had been spent pacing his cell.

'I would argue that someone arrested for murder *always* needs a solicitor,' Joel countered.

'I'm not here to argue.' Billy sat back. Yesterday he had struck Joel as a man going through the motions, a robot following instructions with no anger or sadness. Today there was an aura of annoyance, impatience perhaps. He seemed keen to get on with it, ready to give his answers. That suited Joel, of course – he wanted answers quickly too – but he also wanted the truth, and for that he reckoned he might need to make Billy sweat a little.

'What are you here to do, Billy?' Joel said.

'Answer your questions.'

DS Rose was unmoving next to Joel. The bolted chairs were

slightly staggered so when she sat straight he couldn't quite see her in his periphery. She was sat straight now.

'Did you murder Kelly Marshall?' Joel asked.

'No.' Billy glanced up to deliver it straight into the camera pointing down at them all.

Joel stood up. He had put a large box file on the table and he opened it now to take out a picture frame, the one he had taken from the 'Head Office' of AR Games. He put it face down on the table. The box was supposed to be a visual representation of everything they knew and Joel made sure to struggle with its bulk a little as he put it back on the floor. Billy didn't need to know that most of it was a stack of blank sheets. Billy's eyes stayed on the picture anyway. Joel turned it over.

'Who are these people, Billy?'

'One of them is me, would you believe?' he said his wrinkles breaking out in a smile. Again his answer was quick, quick enough for Joel to know this was a picture he had seen before.

'I would. I can see it now.' With both versions of Billy Easton in the room it was far easier, but he could still forgive himself for missing it the first time. Billy must have had a difficult fifteen years.

'And who is this?' Joel pointed at an older, smartly dressed man with a gut that surely made his suit jacket impossible to button up.

'Colin McGowan. One of the originals. A very clever man who knew how to cast plastic on a mass scale with minimum cost. He retired shortly after but he was good enough to leave us with his methods.'

'And this?' Joel pointed out the woman standing between the two men. She had hold of the ribbon that was in the jaws of Billy's scissors.

'That is Alison Reynolds.'

'And how do you know Alison Reynolds?' Joel was watching

closely for reactions; he was still getting very little. He wouldn't expect anything yet. People were always comfortable when they were answering with the truth.

'We worked together. She was responsible for the manufacturing and distribution process at that time,' Billy said.

'And now?'

'She runs it, the whole shebang as far as I know,' he said. Now he was trying not to react, but the words were tinged with bitterness.

'And how do you feel about that?'

'What does this have to do with anything? I know how this works, I can pick and choose what questions I answer. I don't want to answer questions about Alison. I've actually got a lot to tell you, stuff you actually need to hear.'

'About what?' Joel said.

'About that girl that died, Kelly, Margaret's daughter.'

'The girl you killed?'

'I didn't kill her, I told you that already.'

'Do you know who did?' Joel said.

'The other girl, the girl who was with her. That's the whole idea of this.' He gestured like that was enough, like he had given his explanation and they should all just move on. For a moment, Joel believed Billy thought it was OK to force someone to murder another, as long as you weren't the one doing the murdering.

'Why would she do that?'

'To save her own skin,' Billy snapped.

'What was her name?'

'I don't know, it never mattered.'

'What would have happened to that girl if she hadn't killed Kelly Marshall?'

'She would have been hurt herself, maybe even dead. I thought you would have worked this out already. I'm not blaming her. In that situation I would have done the same thing.'

'So who are you blaming? Who made her kill that girl?'

Billy's wrinkles lined up into another smile but it was different somehow. He ran his hand through his wispy white hair. 'I know what you're getting at, I know what you want me to say. You're right, OK. I put these girls in a situation where they had no real choice but to hurt each other.'

'Why?' Joel said. It was the key question, the one part of this he hadn't really understood from the start.

'Does that really matter? I'm holding my hands up, I'm the reason that girl is dead.'

'There was another, similar incident.'

'The lorry park, out at Sandwich? I did that too, OK, all me. And yesterday, well, you already know that was me so this is really rather simple for you, isn't it?'

'What did you do?' It was DS Rose that cut in now.

'What do you mean?'

'Yesterday. What happened exactly?' Her words were thick with emotion and Joel flicked a glance in warning. He couldn't have emotion from their side. Not yet.

'You tell me – that's how this works, isn't it? You tell me what happened and I tell you if I did it or not.'

'That isn't how it works, not at all,' DS Rose hissed back. She leant forward, well into Joel's periphery now, her intensity forcing Billy to sit back. 'Tell me what happened yesterday.'

'No comment,' Billy said.

'No comment!' Joel even laughed a little, 'I assume you got that from the television programmes, did you? The ones about police interviews?'

'I know I can say that, I don't have to answer your questions.'

'But you've been so clever, Billy, don't you want to tell us about that?'

'Clever how?'

'You tell us, your chance to shine. Yesterday, that setup was all automated. A man shot dead at the end of it all. It was clever. How did you do that?'

'No comment.'

'Revenge,' Joel continued, leaving a slight gap for impact, 'that's what this was about, isn't it? So why don't you indulge us?' Billy didn't reply. Joel left a longer silence this time. 'A solicitor may well have advised you to say, "No comment." That's something they do a lot, particularly in a serious investigation like this. But you didn't want a solicitor and I couldn't for the life of me work out why. You've never been in trouble before, you don't know how any of this works and you're facing a very serious charge – why wouldn't you want someone on your side?' Joel paused, giving Billy another chance to speak, but he said nothing. 'But then I considered what a solicitor actually *is*. A solicitor is someone who will ask the same questions I am, only you can't say, "No comment" to them, can you? When they take you off to a little room here, just you and them before this recorded bit, they want the truth and, trust me on this one, they're better at spotting liars than we are.'

'I'm not lying.'

'Shannon Hendry, the girl who survived – that's her name, by the way. How did you get her there? To that place?'

'No comment.'

'What place *was* it?'

'A farm, outside Lenham, near Maidstone. Near a giant chalk cross painted into a hillside.' Billy leant forward himself now, giving off both anger and smugness. His nostrils flared with each breath, his eyes locked. Joel waited him out, waited until he was the first to move backwards and the back of the chair squeaked where his custody top was too small and had ridden up.

'I remember basic interview training,' Joel said. He turned aside and directed his words now at DS Rose. 'We had a scenario in which someone was lying to us. He gave this whole account where he was just being evasive and vague, but every now and then he would give us a load of detail about something, far more than we had asked for, far more than we had needed.' He turned back to face Billy. 'Do you know what it means when someone does that?' Billy didn't reply. 'It means they're lying. Lying is difficult and details provide us with bits we can check so we will *know* it's a lie. So amongst a big lie there will be details that are true and a person sat in your seat will focus on them, give every detail they have, because they think that if they give as much of the truth as they can then it will hide the fact that it's all a lie overall.'

'I'm not lying.'

'So Shannon Hendry killed Kelly Marshall?'

'Yes.'

'And you forced them into a scenario where that would happen, using the confines of an adult boardgame.'

'Yes. *Escape!* The game *I* designed. *From scratch*.'

'You abducted Shannon Hendry without even knowing her name?'

'Yes, it was random. I just needed someone evenly matched to Kelly. I knew Kelly from Margaret . . .' He seemed to fade out. Joel knew that Margaret was a weakness to exploit, but it could wait.

'Were you there? When Kelly died?'

'I was there to make sure they went through with it.'

'Did you get something out of watching those girls fight for their lives? Did you masturbate about it at the time? Maybe after? Maybe last night in your cell you had a little tug—'

'No! I'm not some sicko.'

'But that's exactly what you are. You must know that, right? What do you think people will call you? What do you think Margaret Marshall will say about you when I go and talk to her later today and I tell her that the man responsible for *murdering* her daughter was good ol' Billy Easton?'

'I don't know! I don't know what she will say.'

'I think I do. I think when it's all calmed down, when she's past the initial feeling of utter betrayal, I think she will want to know *why*. Wouldn't you? So should I tell her my masturbation theory, or—'

'Alison Reynolds!' Billy blurted and pushed the picture away from him so it skidded across the table towards Joel. 'Alison Reynolds,' he said again but more quietly. 'I was trying to ruin her. I thought the police would go public with links to their game. That woman ruined me. She ruined everything.'

'What game?' Joel was instant with his question.

'*Escape!*, like I just said!'

'Go on,' Joel said.

'It's the core of that business, the only way they really make any money, and it was mine, it still *is* mine. I thought that seeing as how I created it, I could destroy it too with bad publicity.'

'A sicko forcing young women to play an adult strategy game for real, to fight to the death using the implements from that game, maybe even a little dress-up as part of it? Are you serious?' Joel said. 'If we had put that information out, what do you think would have happened to their sales? I bet I know.'

'I guess I didn't think it through . . .' he mumbled.

'But you did. You've had years to think it through and what we saw yesterday wasn't thrown together overnight.'

Billy shrugged. 'I guess I thought about some bits more than others.'

'So revenge against Alison Reynolds was your motivation? Why didn't you just pitch Alison against someone else, make her play the game you say she stole? Wouldn't that be more fitting?'

'There's nothing more important to her than money. That's all she cares about.'

'More than her life?'

'No comment.'

'How did Shannon Hendry kill Kelly Marshall?' Joel's change of direction was instant.

'I . . . No comment!'

'You don't know, do you?' Joel said.

'Stabbed! She stabbed her!'

'With what?'

'That doesn't matter. I'm right, aren't I?'

'What happened to the weapon? To whatever she used?'

'She must have taken it with her!' Billy flapped his arms.

'On a public bus and in broad daylight?'

'Ditched it then!'

'We didn't find it and we would have. She didn't have it, not at any point, did she?'

'I didn't kill her!'

'The lorry park, who died?'

'What?'

'White male, found dead at an industrial estate in Sandwich, you said you were responsible for it, for putting him there. So who is it?'

'I don't know.'

'Where did you abduct him from?'

'No comment!'

'Was there someone else at Sandwich too? The winner? Who was that?'

'No comment!'

'Yesterday, who died?' Another change of direction. Joel was restricting Billy's time to think.

'What?'

'Another poor bastard, trussed up in the same way as the others but manipulated to fire on armed police. Another male. Was that someone else you plucked off the street at random or do you have a name for this one?'

'I . . . Random, OK, they all were except Kelly Marshall!'

'How did you get him there?'

'No comment! I don't have to answer—'

'What did you leave for us to find? After they were gone?'

'What?'

'Where you kept Shannon, where you kept Kelly, those lorry trailers, where we found that poor sod yesterday . . . Something was left for us in every place, something we were meant to find. What did you leave?'

'No comment.'

'You don't know, do you? It's the details, see, this is why this is all falling apart. But not just that, you're disgusted, Billy, I can see it. And not with yourself, with what you're hearing.'

'Ridicul—'

'Margaret Marshall said she was grabbed at home, threatened, held close and held tight. Why didn't she know it was you?'

Billy paused. He seemed to be flailing. 'I used a recording. You heard her talk about it.'

'I did, and so did you. Tell me something she didn't tell me when you were stood behind her.'

'About what?'

'Make me believe that was you. Tell me what you did to ensure she didn't know it was you.'

'I was rougher with her, threw her about a bit, my face was hidden . . . I even looked taller. She wouldn't have thought it was me for a moment.'

'Why?'

'To get to Kelly.'

'Why Kelly?'

'She . . . I wanted . . . I had intentions towards Margaret. I made those intentions clear and Margaret rebuffed me. She must have mentioned it to her daughter, to Kelly, because Kelly spoke to me about it too.'

'Intentions towards Margaret that were rebuffed? What is this, Victorian England? Tell us what happened.'

'That's it. You understand what I mean, surely?'

'You wanted Margaret for sex and her daughter told you to leave her alone? And she deserved to die for that?'

'No . . . Yes . . . Look, there's more to life. It was companionship, that was the main thing, but yes, OK, I find her physically attractive.'

'Rebuffed. What did Margaret say?'

'She told me to fuck off, Inspector.'

'We're not in Victorian England anymore, are we? And Kelly? What did she add to this?'

'She was angry. Seems her mother had moved to that location to be away from *creeps like me*. I think that was how she put it. It was a little unfair but I think it was a bit of a reaction to Margaret's previous relationship. I'm a good man, I could have been good for her.'

'And because she wouldn't let you demonstrate just how good you are, you killed her daughter?'

'I . . .' Billy ran his fingers through his hair, 'I had the idea for the *Escape!* thing before I knew who would be playing. Then Kelly just sort of . . . volunteered herself.'

'Because she called you a creep?'

'It was nothing more than an idea until she said those words, a fantasy that ruined Alison, and then she treated me like that, like dirt, like she already knew who I was. Just like Alison did.' Billy sat back, his expression that of someone who might have just made a good point.

'Do you think that Kelly Marshall's death was her own fault?'

'She wouldn't have died if she had kept her thoughts to herself. Her mother had given her answer. We were still friends. The situation was dealt with by two adults.'

Joel took a moment, letting the silence thicken, waiting until it was uncomfortable. 'Investigating murders is a recent thing for me. I'm still getting to grips with it, to be honest, and the one part that still eludes me, might always elude me, is the motivation. What is it that can matter so much to one person that they would take the life of another? I don't think for one minute that Shannon Hendry took Kelly Marshall's life, but if she had, that might be the first motivation I could understand:

kill or be killed, a fight for survival. I have seen revenge before, a far stronger case than what you're claiming, and do you know what I learned from that? Revenge is a cold, empty feeling that only gets colder and more empty the further down the line you get.' Joel paused again.

'Is there a question you would like me to answer in there?' Billy said, finally.

'You had nothing to do with the death of Kelly Marshall, Billy, did you?'

'What? I did, I just told you that!'

'Who died yesterday? Who was the man who was shot twelve times by armed police because he fired first?' Joel changed direction again.

'I . . . I don't know! Some random guy, I told you that already!' Billy's brow now had a layer of sweat that gleamed in the harsh white lighting. Joel didn't answer, leaving Billy the opportunity to elaborate. He didn't.

'The weapon he had yesterday, where did you get it from?'

'No comment.'

'Describe it at least.'

'No comment.'

'Come on, if someone's selling lethal weapons on my streets I need to know about that.'

'No comment. I know the rules, you don't talk about things like that.'

'Why haven't you asked me about the police? I said he fired first. Were dead police officers part of your plan?'

'Dead!' His eyes flared wide; the shock was genuine. 'I didn't mean . . . I'm sorry about that, OK, you have to believe that.'

'They're not dead, Billy. They should be. But that weapon was loaded with blanks, something you don't seem to know. That poor bastard was convinced that the devil himself was coming for him and all he had to fight for his life was dud ammo. What sort of a person would do that?'

'I . . . No comment.'

'Are you that sort of a person?'

'I . . . Yes. I told you that already.'

'So you did that to some stranger? Someone you can't even name? It comes back to motivation, doesn't it? Why would you do that?' Billy had no answer. Joel thumped his finger down on the picture that was still lying on the table. 'Who is this person?' he said. There were two children, one on each side. Joel's finger was above the child on the left.

'That . . . That's Robert . . . My son,' Billy said.

'And this?' Joel thumped his finger down above the other child, the one on the right, almost outside the picture area. From the boy's expression, he was the most unwilling participant.

'That's Alison's son. The boys used to spend a lot of time together back then. Not so much anymore, I don't think.'

'You see,' Joel leant in as close as he could to where the sweat had gathered enough to trickle down the side of Billy Easton's face, 'that's more detail than you needed, so we know that bit was true. And what's his name?'

'Brad . . . Bradley Reynolds,' Billy said.

'Bradley Reynolds,' Joel said. 'Yes it is. And yesterday, Bradley Reynolds was shot twelve times by armed police. He was the man you just told me you didn't know, the man *you* want me to believe was chosen at random.'

Chapter 44

Joel stopped the interview there. Billy was floundering, his struggle clear in his expression, in his body language and in the sweat that was clumping his fly-away hair into thick strands. Joel had the confirmation he needed: Billy didn't know enough to be responsible. The final demonstration had been the strongest: his genuine shock when Bradley Reynolds was named as the final victim.

Now Joel wanted him to stew on that reaction a little more.

Billy Easton was covering for someone and, back in his cell with only his thoughts for company, he would soon work out that the police already knew who that was. Joel's parting words had prompted a flicker of fear: 'We'll just be a couple of hours, Billy,' he had said before slamming the cell door hard – because that noise has a real finality to it.

'A couple of hours?' DS Rose waited until they were out of custody completely.

'Twenty minutes, more like, but I like the idea of him facing up to hours alone.'

'That didn't exactly go as I expected. What's going on, Joel? What *did* I miss?' DS Rose said.

'A fair bit. Luckily for you, Eileen was tasked with bringing you up to speed so there should be a full PowerPoint by now.'

Sure enough, when they pushed through the door into their temporary office, Eileen stood up to greet them. She stepped out from behind her desk to wring her hands, the cardigan she had admitted knitting herself flapping against a stiff skirt whose pattern matched her slippers, and stared over the top of her glasses. 'Did he roll over? That's the term we use, isn't it?'

Joel couldn't help but laugh a little. 'Not yet, but like I said to you, policing is just like being a schoolteacher: we're giving him a minute to think about what he's done.'

The look over those glasses intensified. 'I do wonder if a situation is ever so serious that joviality is not your first reaction, Inspector Norris.'

'Policing, Eileen, is not a career you can survive by taking it seriously. Now, have you been able to get a briefing together for our bare-knuckle fighter here?'

'Right then . . .' Eileen unfurled a pointer, a recent online purchase that she now carried in her pocket at all times. The end made a nice *thwack!* when it came into contact with the photos pinned to the walls, a sound she seemed to enjoy a little too much. Its first resting place was on a picture cropped from a social media site. It was of a young lad, mid-twenties, but boyish in his looks. 'Alan Lewis,' she said. 'Our body from Sandwich. He was identified yesterday while you two were sat out in the sunshine eating a bag of chips and I was continuing with the real police work.' Eileen allowed herself the beginnings of a smile before continuing. 'His mother called in to report him missing, but her role seems to have been quite different. For a start, she never received a phone call.'

'She didn't have the burner?'

'No. Uniform attended in the first instance and they have determined that no family members appear to have been notified of his abduction. Lewis is an only child, lives at home with his mother and is known to stay out for a couple of days at friends' houses. She only called when he missed something with his mates and they called her.'

'So there wasn't any worry about him being reported missing before he could play his role,' DS Rose said.

'But that call went somewhere?' Joel mused.

'There are some other differences too,' Eileen cut back in. 'I was tasked with liaising with PSD, who are still holding this as a scene. You wanted me to be sure no one else was present in order to ensure Bradley Reynolds' death. It is still early but it would appear it was fully remote.'

'What does that mean?' DS Rose said. Eileen's eyes met Joel's like she was checking for permission. He nodded and she continued.

'Mr Reynolds' movements were controlled by an electromagnet. "Crude but simple" is how they describe it. They found an adapted door lock hooked up to a car battery. We use these locks all of the time. Every day when you enter the main door you press a card against a sensor and the door unlocks long enough for you to gain entry. Rather than a door, think of that same mechanism holding a length of wire. When the switch was flicked it allowed some cable through, enough for a couple of steps before it locked again. It just had to be under tension or it might not have moved at all before it locked again.'

'Under tension . . .' DS Rose uttered. It wasn't something she needed more explanation of but Eileen offered it anyway.

'Mr Reynolds would have needed to be pushing against it. There's evidence that the weapon he fired was on show and out of his reach. He would have been—'

'I think we get it, Eileen,' Joel cut in.

'Of course.' She took a moment to clear her throat. 'Anyway, rather than the card we use, the switch was a movement sensor like the sort you get on a security light. Five actually. Each one gave him a further length of wire. But . . .' Again Eileen stopped to check with Joel. This time he reacted with a slight shake of the head.

'But what?' DS Rose said.

'That's all that matters. It was set up to work remotely and left for us to find. We're not looking for anyone else,' Joel said.

'And I'm not some kid you need to protect. What else?'

Eileen stared over at Joel for permission. 'Go ahead,' he said.

'PSD said it was designed so the wire didn't come off the reel,' Eileen stuttered.

'Didn't come off the reel? What does that mean?' DS Rose said.

'This is different too,' Joel cut in to answer. 'At the farmyard and the lorry trailers we only found the wire that was left, we didn't know what the other end was attached to. The loops were designed to be tight under tension but could be slackened when the tension was lost. Bradley was different.'

'Different?'

'Bradley was never going to be free,' Joel said. 'The length and the design were such that he was always going to end up as far as that doorway and no further. It was an extra layer of assurance.'

'That he would be shot to pieces . . .' DS Rose said.

'That he wouldn't escape,' Joel confirmed.

'And the figurine?'

Eileen answered this one. 'There was one left but it was out of the way, over to one side. It could have been put there at any time.'

'Crying?' DS Rose said.

Eileen again flickered to fix on Joel but she answered this one without permission. 'Yes.'

'So it was put there when he was still alive, before he was even trussed up in that fort?' DS Rose breathed.

'He was supposed to die.' Joel confirmed what they all knew.

'How specialist is this? The ability to set this up, I mean?' DS Rose seemed keen to move on.

‘Not very for someone who’s a bit handy,’ Joel said.

‘Mr Norris said you might go out to Alan’s family a little later, but the night-duty DC was sent back to take a statement and that contains everything you should need at this stage.’

‘I don’t think Alan Lewis needs much focus. I think he was just someone chosen as reasonably similar, who has no relevance to our killer, like Shannon,’ Joel added before Eileen continued.

‘We did more work around Billy Easton and there are still questions to ask of him that Mr Norris said he would cover in the second part of the interview. Assuming that’s still the case, you might be interested . . .’ Eileen paused for confirmation from Joel, then continued. ‘ANPR checks on his car show irregular trips down the M20, A20, coastbound. The last camera is just outside of Folkestone, capturing traffic as it heads for the Eurotunnel link, or Dover’s ferry port. He makes the trip at least a couple of times a week and is the only movement from his Land Rover vehicle that is caught on ANPR. It might not be relevant but an explanation will be needed.’

Joel nodded again. Eileen thwacked her pointer down on the mugshot of another young man. He was a year younger than Alan Lewis, but you would guess him older from his photo. It was another cropped from a social media site and showed him with short but scruffy hair over a pockmarked forehead and cheeks. His expression was stern, none of the smiling, fooling about or pouting that are commonly found in pictures of this type. His online presence as a whole seemed to be very serious in its nature.

‘Robert Easton,’ Eileen announced. Her pointer flicked to a piece of paper text underneath. ‘Known PNC and on local. Robert is the son of our friend Billy Easton, but that is just the beginning of his story. With our attention on the Easton family last night, we were able to build a picture of a very unhappy family. Billy Easton was married to Joy Easton, now

Joy Harper, having gone back to her maiden name following their divorce. Robert Easton, it seems, played his part in that relationship falling apart. There is enough to suggest he was a . . . difficult child. Well known to police for violence as a juvenile with much of that directed towards his mother. She is listed as a victim of assault times seven, theft, fraud, arson . . . and one incident is listed as a sexual assault, although it was more a very firm grip on a very intimate part. And all with Robert Easton as the named offender. Four years ago it would appear she had enough and left. We don't know where she is.'

'We know we need to find that out,' Joel interrupted. 'We need a welfare check and some background.'

'So we now think that Robert is our man?' DS Rose said. 'I get that he seems more capable, but—'

She stopped when Eileen lifted her pointer to thwack it back down on the same piece of paper to continue.

'Robert Easton's full name is Robert Tristan Easton, but no one calls him Robert, he's *Bobby*. B.T.E. Billy set up the game business with a view to handing it on to his only child and, from Robert's online activity dating back to when his dad was running that company, that was something he was very, very keen to do. But when his mother wanted a divorce, she claimed half of the business, which meant Billy had to look for an investor. At that point, Alison Reynolds became that investor. And so started a process where Billy Easton was to go on and lose his stake altogether. AR Games rose from those ashes and BTE – Beat The Enemy – Games, aka Bobby Tristan Easton, was wiped from the face of the Earth along with all his hopes and dreams of his own business.'

'You might be enjoying this a little too much,' Joel said, but was again hushed by the raised pointer. Eileen was quick to thwack it back down, this time on the desk in front of her and a blank piece of paper.

'The plot thickens with a counsellor, the counsellor who

treated Bobby Easton's mother and father when they were making an effort to save their marriage. We know about her because she made a report to the police with concerns about this family while they were in her therapy. DC Trott and DC Cumberland are out to speak to her this morning for her side of the story, but I know you wanted to cover this with Easton today, Inspector?'

'I do—' Joel said, then stopped as the pointer was lifted so quick it made a whipping sound.

'As I said, our counsellor had contact with the police at the time of their sessions. Unfortunately, these records are not accessible at this time as they fall under child protection and are hidden on the local system. The requests are in for that information to be released so we will see what went on, but from my phone call to that department, they suggested that something must have been said in one of those sessions that had concerned the counsellor enough for her to report it to the police. Of further interest, standard practice demands that said counsellor gain consent from the couple in order to involve the police. At the very least she *must* tell them that she is reporting an incident.'

'So it was something about Robert, perhaps?' DS Rose said.

'About Robert, about Billy, a final nail in the coffin for their relationship; who knows? What we do know is that our marriage counsellor's boyfriend has recently been given some terrible news.' Eileen's pointer finally lifted from the paper on the desk. It wasn't blank, just turned down. She fixed on DS Rose as she turned it over to reveal a professional-looking shot of a smiling fifty-something woman in a stylish suit jacket and skirt.

'Jessica Harrington?' DS Rose read out the name written beneath the picture of an instantly familiar face. 'We met her yesterday.'

'Jessica Harrington is our counsellor. Her boyfriend is Kelly Marshall's father, Margaret Marshall's ex-husband. And yesterday's victim was Bradley Reynolds, Alison Reynolds's son, the man who is now on the board at AR Games and in line to take on the business as a majority shareholder. Or at least, he would have been.'

'So you have an angry young man with a propensity to violence, his dreams dashed, who lashes out at the person who replaced him?' DS Rose said, like she was trying to organise her thoughts but didn't seem convinced. 'It's circumstantial though, and a bit of a tall story. The link with Kelly Marshall still isn't clear to me either, unless I've missed something?' DS Rose was looking at Joel now.

'You haven't and you're right. Bradley Reynolds makes sense, but there must be a stronger reason for Kelly Marshall, something we don't know yet. That's why the interview is so important. We fully expected Billy Easton was going to take the blame, part one was just demonstrating that he doesn't know enough of what's gone on to be responsible. He will know he's failed to convince us, so now we can talk about who *was* responsible.'

'Robert Easton,' DS Rose said, now a little more enthusiastic.

Joel picked up the account. 'Those crime reports Eileen mentioned, where his son was accused of assaulting his mother; guess what Billy Easton's reaction was?'

'To take the blame,' DS Rose said.

'Absolutely. It's in the log of a few of them. He never went far enough to get arrested in his son's stead, but it shows a propensity to cover for him.'

'And we think he finally did something serious enough for his dad to do it properly,' DS Rose said.

'There's more, something that has to be relevant.' Eileen was holding her pointer up again and both detectives centred on it like it was a wand. 'When Robert Easton's dreams of running his own company died, he had to go out and get himself a proper job. He had a few, but the most relevant was as an estate agent. He was involved in selling a large farmhouse that was developed into three separate terraced houses. One was kept as a holiday let by the owner – and gets the occasional weekend guest. The other two, however, went up for sale. Robert Easton sold one of those plots to his dad, but he also sold next door.'

'To Margaret Marshall,' DS Rose said. 'Which did he sell first?' she blurted and Eileen broke into a smile before pushing her pointer down to a stub.

'Sharp as a tack as ever, Sergeant Rose. Mrs Marshall's sale closed first. He moved his dad in next door a short time later.'

DS Rose had the same expression on her face that Joel reckoned he had when they'd discovered this last night. It meant something; he'd known it then and he knew it now. Moving his dad next door to Margaret Marshall gave Robert access. It gave him an excuse to go up there, it gave him anecdotal information; maybe he even formed a relationship himself with Margaret and Kelly Marshall. He had already sent a request to Witness Protection for contact with Margaret to ask that very question. They knew Kelly Marshall had been targeted, they knew a little more about how, now Joel just had to work out why. The desk phone was ringing, the only noise in an office frozen in time. Eileen reacted to it first.

'That will be DCs Trott and Cumberland. I gave this number out. They may have something to add.' She pressed a button and barked at the phone, 'Eileen Holmans.'

'Eileen, is the boss still in interview?' This time DC Cumberland was the spokesperson and she sounded stressed.

'Stood with me right now. You are on speaker phone,' Eileen replied.

'Boss?' Cumberland said, like she wanted to be sure.

'Go ahead, what have you got?'

'It's not good. We tipped out to Jessica Harrington. Her fella's here but she isn't. He called her in last night.'

'Called her in?' Joel said.

'Missing,' Cumberland said and Joel immediately exchanged

glances with the two women in the office. No one said anything. Cumberland continued, 'Peter Marshall works nights. He said Jessica went to work yesterday afternoon and wasn't back before he left to cover his night shift at around 6.30 p.m., which didn't ring any alarm bells. But when he got into work they'd already arranged cover; they weren't expecting him back after the news about his daughter. He stayed for a few hours drinking tea with his mate and then he came home. Jessica Harrington still hadn't made it back.'

Eileen jerked away to disturb a screensaver. 'There'll be a CAD if he called it in,' she said and the answer came from down the phone.

'Uniform attended in the early hours and took a misper-one. Joel rubbed at his face. A misper-one was a standard form filled out by first attending officers in all instances. It meant they would have carried out some basic actions too.

'Did they get anything on the search of the home address?' Joel said, referring to one of them.

'They did, boss. Peter Marshall gave it up.'

'Go on?' Joel prompted.

'A running figurine, made of plastic and painted like a dress Jessica Harrington wore to work the last time she went. The news doesn't get any better either, boss. I'm looking at the figurine as we speak, sir. It's crying.'

Chapter 45

Joel was ready, waiting and clutching the custody record when the duty solicitor arrived. He introduced himself as Tom Lovelock and held out a card that Joel snatched from him. Lovelock was a younger man than most in his role and his rabbit-in-headlights stare deepened when Joel dragged him off to a separate room, skipping any pleasantries or formalities to launch straight into his story. Joel gave full disclosure, reeling off everything he knew like he was scared to forget it, the pace and tone all part of getting across how serious this situation was for them all, but particularly for his client. Joel did hold back the latest development, the fact that another potential victim was missing and that he had just directed all resources towards Alison Reynolds to find out why she now seemed unable to pick up her phone.

The pressure of two missing women piled on top of his murder investigation might be crushing if Joel took the time to sit and think about it, but there was no time. He had made the call to bring a solicitor in, whether Billy Easton wanted one or not. Easton's situation was very clear and very dire. He had just confessed to multiple murders and, even if Joel didn't believe him, he was still facing a lengthy prison sentence for perverting the course of justice or even conspiracy to murder. Billy Easton now needed to talk about what was really going on or his situation was only going to get worse. A legal adviser should recognise that and advise him accordingly, but it was still a gamble.

Tom Lovelock listened to Joel's hurried disclosure then, understandably, took a moment to let it all sink in. He adjusted his tie, sniffed and almost started to speak a couple of times. He had the standard department-store suit, with trousers that were just a little too long and bunched up over cheap shoes. Joel reckoned him to be in his mid-twenties, at the beginning of a career in law where cutting his teeth in the dungeons might seem like a good starting point for his CV. He wouldn't stay long – they never did: a role at CPS or at one of the law firms would have far more appeal – and then he would invest in a better suit. No one wore anything decent to a custody block. The surfaces down there had been covered by every bodily substance imaginable at some point – and fairly regularly. Even the scheduled deep cleans could do nothing to remove the unique smell, or dispel the thickness of the unmoving air, which seemed to leave a layer on everyone that visited, like standing too close to a bonfire.

Lovelock's final delaying tactic was to pick up the custody record that Joel had discarded on the table. His eyes roamed over it quickly, like he was looking for something.

'This states he's refused legal advice.' This was on the front sheet; he then flicked through the handwritten notes that detailed the prisoner's treatment and movements. 'Nothing on here to say he's changed his mind either.'

'He hasn't.'

'And yet here we are?' Lovelock said, his confusion adding to his uncertainty.

'The prisoner has been happy to talk to us, but he's not telling us the truth, I'm sure of that. The man's digging himself a hole in there. This is the point where he either climbs back out or he pulls the earth down on top of him.'

'Nice analogy.' His uncertainty dropped away; smugness had found a way to push through. 'And you care about him, do you? You don't want him to incriminate himself so you've called me out.'

'I don't care about a charge for obstruction, for assisting an offender or perverting the course of justice. I do care about getting the right person under arrest for murder, I want *that* person in here answering these questions and I don't want to waste any more of my time.' Joel was hoping Lovelock was buying this. He had to come across as the right amount of desperate, he had to have Easton believing that they already knew enough about his son for any attempt to take the blame to be useless, but he also needed him to believe that it was in his interest to help, that he could stop his son getting into any more trouble and also avoid prison for himself. Joel had been hoping for one of the more experienced solicitors to come in, one who knew the game a little better. He would have to take what he was given and hope, but Lovelock's reply was to offer no comfort.

'And you seem to think my presence here can move this investigation on? The best thing for my client right now might be to keep his mouth shut.'

'He said enough this morning for me to charge him right now. He handed something to me in here, on the cameras, that was part of a plot to take a young man's life—'

'That's not quite—' Lovelock cut across Joel, who immediately cut back.

'If he shuts up now I will charge him and I will remand him to prison on the grounds that I suspect him to be a co-conspirator. I will also make it very clear that the advice for him to stop talking left me no choice. But if he talks, if he opts to tell me the truth from now on, then he might be able to fall into the category of witness. And witnesses don't go to prison.'

'Are you suggesting a deal?' Lovelock said.

'Absolutely not,' Joel said, instantly. 'I'm suggesting he might have a chance to be something other than an offender.'

The solicitor stepped back. Joel had moved forwards, though not consciously, and that had upped the intensity. The solicitor took a moment to look Joel up and down. 'I haven't seen you before. You don't look like the detectives I normally deal with.'

'I'm nothing like them,' Joel said. 'Thirty minutes, Tom. Then I'll be back down and we can either work together to get the best for your client or I will screw him into the ground until there's nothing left. I'll let you work out which one might be my preference.' Joel stepped back in to loom closer than ever and Lovelock, to his credit, held his ground. But Joel was pretty certain he actually gulped. 'Thirty minutes to work your magic.'

The office was a whirl of activity when Joel returned. Both Eileen and DS Rose were on calls, Eileen leaning over her desk phone while his sergeant had her mobile pressed to her ear. Both conversations looked intense – only one was wearing carpet slippers. It was Eileen that finished first to give her update.

'Alison Reynolds is missing too,' she said, straight off the bat. Deep down Joel had known this already. He had dared to hope she had slept in or forgotten to charge her phone. But her abduction always seemed far more likely. He couldn't think of a more perfect opponent for Jessica Harrington.

Evenly matched.

The thought made him shudder.

'How do we know that?'

'I spoke to a woman who works with her. Alison was expected in the office today and never arrived. She lives alone so there's no one expecting her at home but I sent a patrol. They forced entry and they found a plastic figurine on her kitchen table.'

'OK,' Joel said.

'It was crying, just like the others.'

Joel rubbed at his face, trying to suppress the idea that it meant they were dead already. That didn't make sense to him. Joel had seen both women the previous day, Alison being the last in the early afternoon. The previous murders had involved an overnight stay at least. No doubt the killer enjoyed the process of telling them the rules and what was at stake and then letting them sit and contemplate. It was part of the experience, part of the torture. Joel couldn't see why there would be any deviation for the two women who seemed to be central to this whole thing.

'I've updated the DCI with the fact that we haven't been able to locate Jessica or Alison as yet,' Eileen continued, 'and he's authorised both to go on as high-risk mispers. He said we need to stay focused on Easton and the misper investigations fall into Major Crime's remit. They resisted at first.'

'Of course they did!' Joel huffed.

'With good reason. They've got their hands full with their own murder enquiry. A homeless gentleman was found dead in Sittingbourne on Tuesday, suspicious circumstances it would seem, so they're making no promises about what they can spare. They took all the details and when I gave them Jessica Harrington's place of work . . . Guess what?'

Joel really couldn't. 'They knew it?' He shrugged.

'They've got people in that area already doing CCTV reviews and knocking on doors. Their homeless gentleman was found less than half a mile away so there might be a way to combine the two enquiries. DC Trott and Cumberland are working their disappearance too. They've already put the requests in with banks and mobile phone companies for both women.'

'Fine,' Joel said. These were standard actions for people reported missing: checking in with banks and mobile phone companies for any activity. They made sense in standard cases but this was far from being one. They would be a waste of time. Tracking phones and assessing access to bank accounts were not going to find these two women; finding the man responsible for their abduction was the only way. 'What about Robert Easton? Are we any closer to finding where he might be?'

'No . . .' Eileen's expression was almost apologetic. 'Nothing from the usual checks so I went after the mother. I figure if anyone knows where her son is . . .'

'And?'

Eileen sighed to give him an immediate answer. 'Witness Protection didn't move them, they just gave advice on how best to disappear. This is worst-case scenario, unfortunately. If Witness Protection *had* relocated her we would know where. Instead, they just told her to stay off social media, probably to change her name, to rent accommodation, et cetera . . . The fact I can't find a trace of her anywhere suggests she took that advice to heart.'

'Registered vehicles, insurance databases, voters, PNC, local intel, Home Office, benefits payment, utilities companies . . .' Joel reeled off everything he knew Eileen would have checked already. She shook her head vigorously.

'Every one checked or requested. The thing is . . . they're on one or more of those databases, they have to be, but if they have changed their name legally—'

'There's a process, you have to apply to change your name. It's recorded somewhere!' Joel knew he was leaking his desperation, but he also knew how thorough Eileen was. Sure enough, she had an answer for him.

'Change your name by deed poll and it's voluntary as to whether you register it. Most people don't. I've checked the database where they might show up and of course they don't.'

'I've got Major Crime,' DS Rose cut in, changing the angle of her phone so she wasn't talking into the handset.

'Go on.' Joel spun to her.

'They've found both cars. Uniform have Jessica's car pulled up on a country lane near her home. Looks like it's been pulled over in a hurry – half parked in a hedge, they said, and with some damage to the offside wing. It's on the route she normally takes to work and her phone's visible on the passenger seat. Alison's car is parked on the industrial estate where she works. They think it's been moved, but not far.'

'Anything relevant? Signs of disturbance, keys, anything that tells us *anything*?' Joel said.

'No.' DS Rose never said more than necessary, but this time her brevity grated on him.

'So we've lost both women without trace and Robert Easton could be anywhere in the country, calling himself anything he wants?'

'We have his dad,' DS Rose said. 'We know he's had contact with him recently.'

'We do,' Joel said, 'and that's all we have.'

Chapter 46

On his way back down to the custody block Joel had a moment of clarity, and barked down his phone to send his two detectives back to Jessica's place of work. Jessica's work was her link to the Easton family, to Robert; maybe in the records or the minds of her colleagues there was something that could help. In case Billy Easton refused.

'He'll talk,' DS Rose said, noting Joel's pause for breath on the threshold to the custody block.

'That might not be enough on its own. I don't like the idea of relying on him solely to make progress. Those women . . .' Joel faded out for DS Rose to prompt him.

'Those women are all that matter right now.'

'They're meant to die, Lucy. That's one thing we do know.'

'Then we'd better get this right.'

Billy Easton glared at them as they came in. Joel hadn't known what reaction he might get, or even if he would get a second interview at all. Prisoners don't have to come out of their cell if they don't want to and Joel knew he was taking a risk bringing in a solicitor when Billy had insisted it wasn't something he wanted. But surely a man left to stew in his current situation would at least listen to a legal expert, to someone on his side. The problem would come if the solicitor's advice was silence.

Lovelock didn't make eye contact. Instead, he pulled at his shirt, lifting it away from his chest in a flapping movement. Each room was individually air-conditioned and Joel had been sure to turn it off the moment he had closed the door for the solicitor–prisoner consultation. The sweat patches visible on Lovelock's nylon shirt confirmed it had been effective at ensuring an uncomfortable meeting – but hadn't been so effective in keeping it short, and another precious hour had slipped by. Now both looked agitated. He had hoped for impatient, for two people desperate to say what the police needed so this could all be over.

Billy was still in his custody tracksuit and would be feeling the heat worse than any of them. Neither man complained about the heat, but both reached for the water the moment it was placed in front of them.

Joel sat down, DS Rose next to him. This time there was no box file, no props or pictures. Nothing. He rattled back through the formalities, everyone was introduced, their roles made clear and time announced as 12.20 p.m. for the continuation of the interview.

'What do you want to tell me?' Joel fixed on Billy Easton and waited. It was a risky opening; there was an easy answer to it. The two men opposite exchanged glances, then Billy Easton cleared his throat and leant forward onto his elbows.

'Two days ago I spoke to my son, Bob . . . sorry, *Robert* Easton. He was very distressed. We don't talk very much anymore so I was very surprised to see him, but I love him like any father loves their son. He told me that things had got out of control, that he didn't know what to do and that he needed my help.'

'OK,' Joel prompted.

'I think you already know about Robert. He has had some

police interaction in the past, not recently – as far as I am aware at least. I haven't really seen him for a couple of years, not since he arranged the purchase of my home. He's an estate agent, you see, at least he was.'

'What did he want to talk about?'

Billy leant forward to break eye contact and hover just a few inches above the table surface. His voice had a different resonance as he talked into it. 'He wanted to talk to me about how he had orchestrated something where a young woman had been hurt. I know that young woman was Kelly Marshall. He told me how he had used my game *Escape!* as an outline. He gave a few details, but not many. I was very angry. I simply do not know what is wrong with that boy.' His head was shaking and he lifted it a little, enough that Joel could see eyes that had lost all focus. 'I told him that and we argued. I think he was upset, I think he actually thought I would be delighted with what he was doing. He even said he was doing it for both of us!'

'Doing what?' Joel said.

'He also told me that he had something else planned that was similar,' Billy continued like he hadn't heard Joel's question. He took a moment to swallow a couple of times. 'I begged him not to go through with it, not to cause anyone else any suffering. I begged him to tell me the full details. I said we could sort it out, whatever he had done I could help. I told him that he needed to go to the police, that I would go with him and we would sort this whole mess out. That was when he told me that the girl he had hurt was Kelly. He said that if I went to the police, he would harm Margaret too.'

'And you believed him?'

Billy's focus was back in an instant to settle on Joel. 'Absolutely,' he said with sincerity.

'Because he's been violent before?'

Billy's wrinkled face shook 'That boy's violence, that boy's anger . . . It's ruined my life, Inspector, it's ruined all of our lives. And just when I thought I was free of it . . .'

'What happened, Billy?' Joel said, his tone now warm enough to be encouraging.

Billy's face contorted into a pained smile. 'You really did leave me to rot in there for a couple of hours, didn't you? I thought it was part of some tactic, I thought you would be back in ten minutes. It gave me time to think . . . He's not a bad lad, you understand?'

'Kelly Marshall, Shannon Hendry, Alan Lewis, Bradley Reynolds . . . Four victims, three of them dead and one survivor who will never be the same again. So no, I'm not sure I do understand.'

'I know how it sounds. I thought about those young people too, I thought about their families, about how they all have dads too.'

'Families for sure, all waiting for answers, waiting to find out why they were targeted. Did Robert tell you that?'

'He was upset, he was all over the place and difficult to understand. I know about Kelly Marshall . . . It was Margaret really, that's who Bobby was interested in. Me and Bobby's mother are divorced. Thirty-three years of marriage, we were trying all sorts of things to save it but *divorce* . . .' Billy was shaking his head. 'I never thought that would be us, not for one moment of our time together. The day she told me was like a slap in the face. Bobby was there with me. She came home, had a cab she left running out the front.' Billy fixed back on Joel now, and a flash of emotion that seemed to be a mixture of anger and sadness accompanied his next words. 'She just popped in to tell me it was over!' He flickered an incredulous grin. 'She said she was sorry, said she couldn't do it anymore and that she would pop back for her stuff. Just like that.' He took another moment, massaging the loose skin around his eyes. 'Less than a minute. She'd sent me a message to say she was on her way home, just like she always did when she was out. I made us both a cup of tea but she must have got held up, because hers went cold. When I saw her pull up I reheated it, stuck it in the microwave . . . It's strange what you remember, isn't it?'

'At significant moments we tend to remember every detail,' Joel said, resisting the urge to tell him to get on with it.

'She came in, told me she wasn't staying, that it was all over and she was gone again just as the tea finished. Fifty seconds. That was the first thing Robert said. He would have heard every word from where he was standing in the kitchen watching that cup spin. I don't think he could move. Fifty seconds to ruin everything, he said.'

'That must have been difficult for you both.'

'More difficult than you might think. Me and Robert's mother loved each other, we always have, but Bob – Robert . . . He was difficult. He was so horrible to her, I didn't blame her for looking for a way out. We tried everything. We had a few relationship counselling sessions but it was a waste of time. It was when we were speaking to the counsellor that we realised we were actually fine as a couple, strong even. All our problems revolved around Robert . . . We were very honest, we had a long chat about him, maybe for the first time, and our conclusion was the most upsetting moment of my life. We couldn't be together, my wife of thirty years and I – we both agreed . . . and all because of our son! Can you imagine that?'

'No,' Joel said, 'I don't think I can imagine how hard that must have been.'

'We couldn't say that to him. We skirted around the subject and talked about him getting counselling, just some sort of anger management conversation. Something that might help him have a better control of his world. It wasn't just at home that there were problems, he was losing jobs, girlfriends . . . friends in general. But he resisted everything. In the end, Joy said that maybe he could come along to one of our counselling sessions. I guess she thought that we could all sit and talk about what was going on at home and maybe our son would come to the same realisation we had.'

'And did that happen?'

'He was in there for less than five minutes, sat and sulked with his hood up the whole time. Then he got angry. I knew he would, I don't know what we were thinking. He ended up getting abusive towards the counsellor, he called her a slut, accused her of flashing her legs at me, at him . . . It was nonsense, he was just lashing out. Then he stormed out. Me and his mother stayed and we ended up having the most honest conversation we've ever had. I don't think the counsellor even said a word! But that was when we agreed . . .' Billy's head dipped again. The room fell silent. Joel left it as long as he could.

'What did you agree?'

There was new intensity in his stare as he snapped up to lock onto the inspector. 'That the threat to his mother was getting bigger, that Bobby could even . . .'

'Even what?' Joel pushed him.

'He's made threats, serious threats to his mother, stuff we didn't tell the police, *couldn't* tell the police, but . . .'

'How bad?'

'Joy said he was going to seriously hurt her . . . maybe even . . . She said it was the way he looked at her as much as what he said. I didn't believe her at first, maybe I just didn't want to, but I couldn't ignore it. Deep down I knew she was right.'

'You think Billy is capable of murder?'

'Please don't make me say that.'

'But that's what you mean, and that's what your wife was scared of?'

Billy's head moved from side to side, his lips bumping together like he was trying to find the right answer, despite the whole room knowing what it was all along. Finally he gave it. 'Our son was going to hurt his mother, badly, maybe enough for murder . . . Jesus, that's a word isn't it!' His smile was glassy; the magnitude of what he was saying suddenly laid bare.

'So what did you do?'

'We came up with an action plan there and then. Then, when we walked out of that office, Robert was sat in the waiting area, smiling with a milkshake. But it wasn't a normal smile, you know . . . It was empty. It was like he knew.'

'About what you had discussed?'

'About what we had agreed. We were going to live apart. That was what we had come up with. It wasn't supposed to be a divorce, it wasn't even a split. I was going to sell off a chunk of the company and we would use that to get Joy relocated, set up somewhere else. It was all going to be done in secret and as a temporary measure. We thought Robert would have to mature at some point and get his own life, where his mother wasn't the focus. We couldn't have told him, he would never have understood. He would just have seen what it meant for the company and . . . he would have blamed her and we might never have got her safe. I still think now that if he knew where to find her . . .'

'He doesn't know where she is?'

'There was a system already in place. The counsellor told us about it. you'll know more about it than me. She said that the nature of her job means that she might hear things that concern her in a session – I'm talking husbands beating on wives generally – but in this case she heard about how our son posed a real threat to his mother. She told us there was a council led scheme, in conjunction with the police, that was designed to get people stuck in abusive relationships safe. It meant that Joy could go into a refuge for a little while, just until I could free up the money from the business to get her somewhere more permanent. The refuge could be anywhere, normally well out of the area, out of the county, and even I didn't know where it was. It also meant other things, like a personal alarm linked to police monitoring. She would be safe, that was all that mattered. It was a big decision, but actually we didn't have a choice by that time.'

'So your marriage counsellor hid Robert's mother.'

'And the police helped, according to our son at least. The truth is that we just happened to have the conversation in her office and she just happened to have a system in place that could help us. Anyway, we went ahead. It only took a few phone calls. It wasn't a standard case but that didn't seem to matter. But Robert doesn't see big pictures, he doesn't listen and he never accepts the consequences for his own actions. He blamed the counselling sessions for his mum walking out, for the divorce that cost me the business.'

'Who was the counsellor?' Joel said. He might have known already but he needed Billy to say it.

'Jessica someone . . . I forget the surname now. I shouldn't really, she was a big part of our life for a short time. She might have saved Joy's life.' Another glassy smile but laced with something, shock still, Joel thought.

'So where did the divorce come from?'

The intensity was stronger than ever from Billy now, the shock gone and his anger clear. 'Joy. She said she needed a clean break, she liked the idea of being somewhere that even I wouldn't know, and that could only happen with divorce. I was gobsmacked, but then she told me why and you know what? She was right.' He leant forward to stare right into Joel. 'Do you know why she couldn't have me knowing where she was living?'

Joel thought he did. He sighed as he spoke. 'Because your son is capable of getting information out of you. And he would do it any way he could.'

'We're terrified of him. Of our own son. He grew up listening to me talking about BTE Games, about how it was going to be all his one day, and he took that as read, like it was his birthright.'

'And he's looking for someone to blame for taking that away from him.'

'He's always been so angry. I don't know why, that's just how he's wired. When his mum left . . . You can't imagine, he was so much worse. He blamed her for running off with half the company, he saw that I had to raise money with an investor, then a flotation. Then I lost the company completely when Bobby was already acting like the company was his. He was twenty years old with big ideas of expanding out to escape rooms and suddenly he lost the only future he had ever considered.'

'Escape rooms were his idea?' Joel said.

'It was his main focus, to be honest. He had been pushing me to invest in escape rooms for a couple of years but it was something I knew nothing about, something none of us at BTE knew anything about. It was departing from our core business and I knew it would be suicide for my career . . . and that's why I championed it to the board. I wanted to be forced out. Then it wouldn't look like it was my fault. I thought once the business was gone . . .' Billy was back to massaging his eyes. 'How can I be saying this about my own son . . . I thought there would be no ties, no reason for Robert to still have anything to do with me. I gave him some of what I got for the company and I told him to go on his own, to do what he wanted to do.'

'And did he?'

'He did. He pursued the escape rooms idea, pitching himself as a competitor to BTE. I didn't even bother telling him that it might not be the right move. My son believes himself to be quite the strategist, he's grown up playing strategy games and he sees the business world a bit like that, a game to win. Alison renamed the company at that point as AR Games. She'll tell you it means Arch Rivals and maybe that's the truth but it's also her initials where it used to be his. He saw that as Alison rubbing his face in it. She had no idea, of course. I could see it in her eyes when I was up there giving an awful pitch to push the idea of escape rooms . . . She thought I'd lost my mind! I built that company from scratch, my life's work, and I was glad to be out of it all. Robert's venture died a death just like I knew it would. There's money to be made, but you need a big investment from the off, more than I could give him. When he worked that out for himself it just made him angrier – at his mother and the police, at me, at Jessica, at Arch Rival Games and Alison Reynolds . . . Everything has always been someone else's fault. He did a few jobs after that. When he was working as an estate agent I actually thought he might have turned a corner.'

'How so?'

'I'd talked about wanting to move. We'd sold the family home to free up some cash for Joy so I was renting a place until the company paid me off. I wanted to buy somewhere. Somewhere quiet, away from everything really. I told him that and he turned up with the details of my house. I loved it, even as a picture. He bent over backwards to get me in there. I know he was on commission, but it was still out of character.'

'Why do you think he did that now?'

'Margaret Marshall. He was obsessed with her. Just like he was obsessed with the marriage counsellor – fixated even. You see, he found out that this Jessica was a homewrecker herself. That was what he called her anyway. I think he had been watching her, and for a while. The fact the man she's involved with left a whole family to be with her bothered him. I mean I don't care, it's no skin off my nose, these things happen, but Robert seemed to take it personal. Margaret Marshall knew about the affair towards the end and she tried to rescue it for their kids.'

'And he saw parallels with your situation?' Joel said.

'I think he did. I think he saw Margaret Marshall being prepared to do whatever she could for the sake of her children while his own mother ran away from him for no reason. He also saw a woman who was giving advice to his parents while she herself was tearing another family apart. He was beside himself.'

'So he *killed* Margaret's daughter?' Joel probed. This bit still didn't make sense.

'Jessica's step-daughter too, don't forget. He wanted to ruin her life. He wanted her relationship to fall apart. He can't understand why other people can't see her for what she is so he made this her fault, her fault that Kelly Marshall was targeted, her fault that the Marshall family has been ripped apart. At least that was how he saw it and he thought the world would see it the same.'

'That's some twisted logic.' Joel was thinking out loud rather than asking a question. Billy answered it anyway.

'I told you he doesn't think like the rest of us. There's something . . . *different* about him. But this all comes from somewhere far simpler: Joy isn't around. He can't take out his anger on his mother but it has to go somewhere.'

'And Bradley, that was just simple jealousy?'

'Alison's poor lad . . .' Billy said, while nodding. 'They were friends for a while when they were kids, late teens even, but never really close. My Bobby's bolshy, too much for most, so they went their own ways. Then Bradley's mother took over the company, renamed it AR to send her message, and I guess he saw Bradley as next in line to get everything he had been promised.'

'Did you know his intentions towards Bradley?'

Billy's head was shaking before the question was even finished. 'When you said his name . . . it was like a ton of bricks. Good kid. I heard he got married, kids . . . Jesus.'

'And Shannon? Shannon Hendry?'

Billy's head-shaking had continued but now there was a snort to accompany it. 'Wrong place, wrong time. He watched her for a while. He said he went along to a running club to find someone. I think she stood out to him as being fast.'

'He knew she would win.' Joel was thinking out loud again.

'Maybe, but I don't think that mattered. Even if Kelly had been the one to survive, her life would have been tough after that. For her whole family. I guess he would still have got what he wanted.'

'He was right.' Joel's mind ran with images of the last time he'd seen Shannon Hendry. She was a frightened, anxious shell of a woman who in just a few days had uprooted her home and her whole life to run from an invisible threat. Kelly might have been the lucky one, but the word *lucky* was barely applicable.

'And Alan Lewis?'

Billy's head was still shaking. 'I can't help you with that one. I would guess another person in the wrong place, but he's never mentioned that name.'

'Is there another survivor out there? From when Bradley was killed? That one seems different, like Robert changed what he was doing.'

The sound of a chuckle fell from Billy's mouth but there was no warmth of humour behind it. When he locked back onto Joel his eyes looked glassy, almost like a drunk's, and he took a moment to focus. 'I don't think so but I don't know for sure.'

'You gave me a card that warned me of Bradley's death. We both know that's the Death Card in your game. You must have known what that meant.'

'I didn't! I mean, of course I know what it means in the game, but I didn't know in this context.'

'But you still delivered it for him,' Joel said.

'Robert told me to. He said I might get arrested, he told me to have the card on me so you would find it. The moment I saw it I asked if there were more people in danger and he said that there would be if the police dared arrest his dad. Then he asked for my phone, he did something and said that he could track it and if he saw me go to a police station then he had something set up at Burgoyne Heights that was ready to go. Something about two people tearing each other apart and how it would be the fault of the police.'

'And you didn't tell me this when you gave me that card?'

'I didn't know what it meant. How could I?' Billy shook his

head, his face twitching like he might break down again. 'I wasn't going to show you at all, that's why I hid it. I thought you might see it as a threat and if you ever found my boy you might . . . Well, it might show him up as a bigger threat than he is.'

'But you did show me. At the same moment my officers arrived where Bradley was being held.'

'That's *why* I showed you! I knew there was danger, for you, for whoever was there, for everyone. I just wanted you to be careful, to know everything there was to know before you acted, and I panicked. I can see now that it was too late . . .'

'What else did he say? Is there anything else you've kept from us, anything else he's said or asked you to do?'

'He said the game's changed. He's changed the strategy, he said he was keeping it *fresh* and he had a big grin like he was so proud. I think he thought I would be too. *Escape!* is my game. It was like he was expecting me to be impressed that he was putting his own stamp on it.'

'Changed? What does that mean?'

'This whole thing was about the people he took at first . . . but now—'

'By "took" you mean kidnapped?' Joel couldn't help but cut in.

'I do,' Billy said, shaking his head more vehemently than ever.

'But now, what?' Joel said.

'Now he sees it as playing against you, against the police.'

'So we're his target now?'

'I don't think so. He said he had been giving the police chances to stop him all the way through. I think . . . Those people that got hurt, I know how he thinks, you had a chance to stop it, it's your fault they died, and finding the card on me was supposed to be part of that.'

'Why involve the police at all?'

'You would always be involved, wouldn't you? When people get hurt, I mean. And he hates the police, I know that. Not just because he thinks you had something to do with moving his mother away but before, when you used to come to the house, he always said that the police never listened to him because he was a boy. His words were always dismissed. I think this is his way of being impossible to ignore.'

Joel sat back. It was starting to make a little more sense. They had known the link to a game early on, but the changes in the crime scenes, in the methods used, had seemed odd. And now they didn't. DS Rose had been right in what she had said in her shocked state just after Bradley Reynolds had been shot dead; the police *were* there to play their role in a game – and, for Robert at least, they had done it perfectly.

'Where is he, Billy?' DS Rose cut in. 'Where is Robert?'

'I don't know.' Billy's answer was quick enough to suggest it had been ready to go. It would have been the one question he knew was coming. 'I don't know anything about him. I guess I never really have.'

'When did you see him last?' she continued.

'Two days ago. He's been borrowing my car . . . I thought about that, when I was sat in that cell. I thought about what might have happened in that car, what he might have been using it for. I didn't ask him. You don't ask Bobby what he's doing.'

'Did Robert ask you to take the blame? Maybe more threats if you didn't?'

Billy shook his head. This time his fight against breaking down was more obvious. 'I don't know why I did that and I knew it wouldn't work anyway. He . . . he did say something else to me, OK, he said there's more.'

'More? What does that mean?' Joel said.

'I don't know any details but he said it was tonight. You left me in that cell and I had some time to think and I realised that I was wasting my time taking the blame. If I could have got you to believe me I would have stayed here and then something would happen and you would know it wasn't me. It would all have been for nothing.'

'What is this something else, Billy? You have to help us, you have to tell us what you know, for your sake, for Robert's sake too. We can stop this getting any worse for him.'

'I don't know, OK, I know you're going to want to know all about it. All he said was there's a storm coming. He said it was on the news and I've seen it myself but I knew he meant something else, like something bad was going to happen. I was horrified, I begged him to tell me what he meant but I could see he was enjoying himself, enjoying my reaction. He's lost, Inspector, he's lost to me. I really don't recognise him anymore.'

'What did he say *exactly?*' Joel pushed.

'That was it, there's a storm coming and that it's the fifth day . . . I guess this all started five days ago, did it?' Joel looked away from him to lock eyes with DS Rose. Billy Easton continued. 'He's still my boy, you know? He's still my little boy and I've seen some good in him, I really have. It's the anger . . . It festers in him, it changes who he is.'

'He doesn't plan on getting away with it, does he?' Joel held his breath for an answer he already knew. Those wanting to get away with their crimes had to show some restraint and so far Robert Easton had shown very little. Billy's answer started with a shake of the head.

'That's the thing that bothers me the most – he knows it's coming, he knows the police will catch up with him eventually and he's not bothered by that. I think this is how he wins, this is how he proves his point to the people that wronged him. He can't see past this, he can't see a future, so he can't see he has anything to lose . . .' Billy raised his hands to cover his face. It didn't stop the sobs from escaping.

'I think maybe we could all do with a break,' Lovelock cut in. Joel had forgotten he was there; it was like the solicitor had unmerged himself from the grey walls. His words seemed tight with tension.

'Fine,' Joel said. 'But we'll be back. I need you to think

about where he might be, Billy. We need to find him, for everyone's sake, including his. Do you have any way of contacting him?'

Billy unburied his face to reply. 'No. He hasn't had a phone for a while that I'm aware of.'

'And his mother, do you have any way of finding her?'

'No. Not for a long time now. She said she was disappearing, I thought it was temporary, like I said, but she meant every word. It's been *years,* Inspector. I've lost her and now I'm losing my son . . . Everything I've ever cared about.'

'Do you think he will come to you?'

'I don't know what he will do anymore. My own son and I don't know him at all.'

'If he does come to you, you need to tell us, Billy. We need to pick him up.'

Billy stood up, his movement sudden enough to make Joel jump. Billy walked to the corner of the room. DS Rose had also jerked to her feet and Joel lightly touched her arm to hold her back. Billy stopped so he was facing away from them. 'I will,' he said. 'He has to be stopped. He doesn't belong out there, I know that, I think I've known that a while. And then maybe me and Joy . . . Just to be able to speak to her again! Just to know where she is, that she's OK . . .'

Joel ended the recording. He put his card down on the table and waited for a knowing nod from Tom Lovelock. He would pass the details over and Billy Easton would help them find his son – and then the two missing women could be found in time.

In a perfect world.

Chapter 47

The screen on Joel's mobile phone carried two pieces of key information as he checked it on the way out of custody. The first was the time – 1 p.m. – while the second was confirmation in the form of a text message that DCI Kemp had arrived. Joel had tasked Eileen with getting him over; he had the beginnings of an idea that would need the DCI's endorsement, and the interview he had just left had reinforced it as the only option they had.

Joel bundled through the door to his temporary office – his movements were always clumsy when he was tired – and the DCI stood up to greet him.

'How did it go?' Kemp said instantly.

'Better than it could have gone, not as good as I hoped.'

'What does that mean?'

'It confirmed that we're looking for the son. Billy helped us understand why but he didn't help with where.'

'Is he holding that back? We still have options if he wants to play that game. He's committed offences, we could go for a charge and remand for conspiracy to murder—'

'I don't think heavy-handed is our way forward here,' Joel said to cut him short.

'Oh?'

'We need to let Billy Easton go,' Joel said, 'as soon as possible. As soon as we can arrange the necessary surveillance.'

'Surveillance? You think this Robert will go looking for his dad?'

'Robert Easton told his dad that he had something planned, something that happens tonight. We have to assume that involves our two missing women and we have to assume it's bad news for them. The impression I got from that interview is that Robert somehow believes that what he's doing is for his dad, as much as it is for him. I think he's going to want to involve him.'

'Surveillance is resource-intensive, Joel, time-intensive too. You and your whole team would be needed to support a surveillance team, assuming we could even get one. What you're describing is all eggs in one basket and that's not how I like to run an investigation.'

'Jesus, boss, me neither but I don't see any other option. We do still have Major Crime looking for the women so there are other avenues being explor—'

'Major Crime have their own murder to investigate. They've kicked back, argued that this is no longer a misper search, it's part of your murder investigation, and I'm inclined to agree.'

'This is how we find them. Billy Easton met with his son as recently as a few days ago. The son borrowed his car and talked to him about what he was up to. If tonight is his finale then I think he'll make contact with him at some point.'

'We've seized Billy's phone, his car too,' Kemp said.

'Exactly. So the only way he can speak to his old man is in person, turning up at the house.'

'That's not quite true, Joel. He probably has a landline, or a laptop for an internet call.'

'I know that. I think there's a way to push Robert to go and see his dad. We put surveillance on the house and then pick him up when he does. Robert might be the only person who knows where those women are.'

'*Push* a killer? I'm not sure I like the sound of that.'

'Press release. There's a lot of press interest around this job already, and they can smell there's more to it. All we have to do is put out a release that we've arrested a sixty-three-year-old man from Tunbridge Wells in connection with the murder of Kelly Marshall and he's been released pending further enquiries. Robert will see that and he will want to know what went on.'

'He's scared of him, Joel, terrified, you could see that. Billy thinks his son could hurt him and we know he's capable of it,' DS Rose cut in. Kemp reacted with a questioning look.

'It's a risk, but it will work, it will draw him out and it will give us a chance to get hold of him.'

'There's nothing stopping him killing those women first, then getting in touch with his dad to gloat, to show him what he's done,' Kemp said.

'I know that.' Joel huffed out his frustration. 'Billy told us that his son has something planned for tonight. That means we still have time to get Billy out of here and to get word to the press, to force Robert Easton's hand. If we do that he will make a mistake and stick his head up.'

'He might not, Joel.'

'He might not, but it's like you said, all eggs in one basket.'

Chapter 48

The movement of the ocean was unrelenting. It had swept in to fill the space three times already, lifting Jessica Harrington up each time as it did. The anchored wooden pallet she was chained to did not keep her entirely above the water and her neck ached from having to lift her head to gasp for breath. The constant waves that rolled in were pushing her to the back of the cave where the ceiling was lowest, and it was now scratching and scraping at her face. The constant movement of water over time had found weakness where it could, eroding the soft chalk of the cave wall and ceiling so only the stronger rock was left exposed, pointing downwards like stone daggers.

Her fingers bled, and she had lost two nails from constantly fighting to drag herself back to where the ceiling was high enough to create a pocket of air. The water level had been at its highest point for long enough now, and the tide might even have turned already, but it would be some time before she was dropped back to the gravelly sand and given any rest.

The waves that rolled in to slap against the back wall then fizz an enthusiastic retreat all around her were becoming noticeably bigger, their movement harsher. The wind that Jessica had heard whistling and whispering its threats over the rocks at low tide was starting to live up to its billing, growing in strength. There was a storm coming, she knew that; this was just the start. The Met Office had said as much on the news, but she hadn't been paying attention at the time and couldn't remember much about it.

The pallet lurched on the biggest wave yet, ripping her hands away to drive her towards the back of the cave. The sound of splintering wood was inevitable. It wasn't the first time it had happened but it was no less terrifying. She could only watch as bits of the only thing keeping her above the water line broke off to be sucked back out into the angry mass of ocean.

She reached back up for the ceiling, her hand wrapping around the sharp stone, ignoring the pain as she dragged herself backwards once again, the exertion forcing the air from her nose. Her mouth was gagged by a sopping, salty rag tied tight enough to hurt. Her eyes burned, her mouth burned, her arms burned.

But she was still fighting.

Chapter 49

When DCI Kemp came back through the door his face and neck were flushed. He had left the office to make some calls after announcing that if he had to negotiate with people who might free up a surveillance resource, he didn't want to do so in front of a live audience.

'How did it go?' Joel was back on him immediately.

'Seems you can't just summon up a surveillance team. They're deployed, north Kent on a county lines job with the Met.'

'You can't pull them?' Joel said. County lines were a web of drug dealers based in the capital. It was a big priority for the force – and rightly so – but it was ongoing, had been for years, and at that moment his job was surely higher up in the priority stakes.

'No, and you can be sure I tried. There's an Initial Surveillance Course at Headquarters that finishes at four and there was some suggestion that they could help, but I'm not holding out too much hope.'

'Initial Course?'

'Yeah, cops new to surveillance but most of the way through their three-month course.'

'And what, they can't help?' Joel was doing his best not to

explode. This was serious, life or death, how could someone else not see that?

'I spoke to the guy leading the course. He's got twenty years of experience in surveillance behind him and he wasn't keen. He said it was destined to fail with what he had but he would talk to his students and one of the other trainers. It's not the sort of thing I have any sway over, I can't order a team out to do a job they're not signed off for yet.'

'We don't have time for them to have a cosy chat. I need to go and get Billy Easton out of here. I'll get a uniform to drop him home so we have him housed. Have you still got a direct number to this surveillance trainer?'

The DCI took a scribbled phone number out of his pocket. 'You think you might have more luck?'

'I did a foot surveillance course. I know that's nothing like full surveillance, but we took part in a live job as part of our training. I know it can be done and I'm going to suggest they do the same here.'

'He'll know that too and he definitely didn't offer it up. What if he still says no? You need a plan B.'

'Then I'll head over to Headquarters and ask him face to face. I'll be a lot more difficult to turn down when I'm choking him out.'

'That's some plan B.'

Joel had taken the number to start typing it into his phone. 'And the press release?' he said.

'With the Press Office. It should be out on the force social media channels already. The nationals monitor that so they'll pick it up straightaway. It will be everywhere by the time Easton leaves the building.'

'That makes surveillance more important than ever,' DS Rose said, her discomfort about putting Billy at harm's risk still obvious.

'This will work out. It has to,' Joel said. But if he was trying to reassure DS Rose, his boss or himself, he failed on all counts.

Chapter 50

'OK, so it would appear that common sense has prevailed!' Tom Lovelock looked to be back in his comfort zone. His demeanour was closer to Joel's limited experience of defence solicitors: self-assured and well aware that the legal framework of an early investigation was massively stacked in their client's favour. Billy Easton, by contrast, looked exhausted, fragile and beaten. A night in a custody cell could do that to a first-timer.

'We got to this point as quickly as we could,' Joel replied with a shrug. 'We had a lot to try and work out, I'm sure you understand.'

'Every hour is like five hours when you're sat in one of those cells, I can tell you that much. I'm too old for those mattresses.' Billy's voice was breathy and feeling sorry for itself. His wallet, watch, belt and an open envelope were tipped out onto the custody desk in front of him. The bag he had brought was secured with a plastic tag through the handles, and the car magazine, which he hadn't been allowed last night, was still poking out of the top. 'So what happens now, Inspector?' Billy said.

'Get yourself home, catch up with any sleep you might have lost and, like we discussed back in there, if Robert makes contact with you, call me straightaway. Any time of day.'

'And if he doesn't, will you need to speak to me again?' Billy replied, but it was Tom Lovelock who jumped in to provide the answer.

'Not without contacting me first, Billy, and you don't have to respond. DI Norris may want to speak to you as a witness as some point, and should that happen' – Lovelock thrust his card towards Billy – 'I would recommend you insist it happens here, with me present. Remember, I only care about your interests, the inspector here only cares about convicting prisoners. At least I think that's what he meant by *crushing into the carpet*.'

Joel held back on explaining how solicitors get paid per consultation and how Lovelock was very much pushing his own interests. Instead, all Joel could muster was 'until we meet again then', directed towards both men, then he nodded to a response officer who had been loitering in the background. 'My colleague here is going to run you home. I imagine a taxi fare would be quite steep from here and I don't see the need to make you wait at a bus stop in one of our tracksuits and a pair of plimsolls.'

Billy peered down at his feet. 'There's really no need. Call me a taxi if you like, but I'm sure your colleague here has more important things to do.'

'I insist,' Joel said, ignoring the ever-increasing smugness of Tom Lovelock, who took the opportunity to speak again.

'Come now, no need to be out of pocket. They don't give many people a ride home. This is as close as you will get to an apology for your twenty-odd hours of incarceration for no good reason.'

'My boy . . .' Billy said, appearing to study Joel closely, 'when you find him, you will let me know, won't you? And go easy, OK, he's not such a bad lad.'

Joel repeated his earlier request. 'Get him to call me, Billy.

You'll be doing him a favour in the long run. Or you can call me direct. This needs to stop, all of it.' Billy had no more answers. Instead, he turned for the custody exit. Joel waited for the door to shut before lifting his phone to his ear.

'Billy Easton has left the building.'

Chapter 51

Jessica gripped the pallet and felt the underside scrape against the sodden sand as the water continued to recede. Her fingers ached, indeed her whole body did, and she knew she was just about done, that she wouldn't survive another high tide. The weight of the chains and padlock on her stomach and torso that had given her a sense of doom were now a comfort to her – like a weighted blanket. When the time came, they would take her to the bottom and they would hold her there. The frothing, chaotic violence of the surface would still play out above her, but she would be in the depths, laid out on the seabed, away from it all. And for her, this would all be over.

She had been submerged and battered, lifted and scraped against the teeth of the stone beast, fighting to survive each time, and now she was close to the ocean placing her gently back on its floor, a heap of sodden exhaustion.

But it was a cycle, and it would start all over again.

Time and tide wait for no man. This was a phrase that had been bouncing around in her mind over and over. A Chaucer quote, recalled from her English studies all that time ago. Forgotten for most of her life, but it had made a return with middle age, with seeing her kids grow to adults themselves and even start their own families. It was true, of course. There are very few certainties in life but, from the moment we are born, we are running out of time. Perhaps it was this understanding that allowed her to think so calmly and clearly. Her energy levels, a gathering wind and a marked change in the ocean's mood had forced the realisation that her time left was now extremely short.

This would be how she died.

The next high tide would arrive when the night was at its blackest, agitated by that strengthening wind to consume her. And she would let it. The fight had only caused her pain, panic and utter desperation. There was nothing left now, nothing left to fear, nothing left to fight.

The pallet bumped and scraped on the sand as the sea retreated from the mouth of the cave, and she lay still. The salt burned on her skin and blurred her eyes until the entrance was just a bright white blob, visible when she arched her head back. She watched a wave roll back in, the water flicking up to force a shiver. Most of her skin was exposed; she was only wearing a coarse dress and underwear.

With the water gone, the breeze seemed louder, surrounding her with whispers laden with menace, spoken from the pockets of shadow in the ceiling. The message was clear.

This would be where she died.

She wiped at her eyes with her hand. It made no difference; if anything her vision was made worse by the grit that dripped from her forearm. She had given up trying to pull the gag away. It was too tight, too painful. And it didn't matter anyway. Not anymore.

There was movement on the other side of the cave from the other woman laid out on an identical-looking sodden pallet. She lifted her leg to bend it at the knee, her head lolling in Jessica's direction. Her dress was also black. Jessica could see it only as a block of blurred colour, contrasting with the white smear that was her gag.

She had survived this far too.

Jessica felt sorry for her. She wished she could talk to her and tell her not to fight, to succumb to her exhaustion, to stop the pain and let it happen.

Death was going to be merciful to them both.

Chapter 52

Joel peered in through the open passenger door of a red Ford Focus being driven by DS Rose. They were still in the yard of Medway Police Station. The door rocked in a breeze that was strengthening.

'We have three cars, two of them from the initial course and one other the surveillance team could spare. And us, of course. It's better than I had hoped.'

'And you didn't have to get anyone in a choke-hold,' DS Rose said.

'No, I made him aware of a few more of the details and he seemed a little more keen to be involved. We got lucky. Let's hope that holds out.'

DS Rose had already driven to the speed-gate at the back of the police station, a piece of furniture that was surely named by someone with a sense of humour. As they both watched it crawl open, right to left, in front of them, Joel continued, 'We're meeting the surveillance lot nearby. They need to give us an encrypted set. They were very keen to tell me that we just need it to *observe*.'

DS Rose managed a nervous chuckle. 'I bet they were.'

Surveillance teams used different radios from standard police resources. They had a higher encryption that the surveillance team would say was to add a layer of assurance that the target couldn't listen in. But the real reason was to ensure those 'standard' police resources were not monitoring what they were up to. Coppers were nosey; it was part of the job, part of their makeup, and most wouldn't be able to help getting involved in something that sounded 'juicy' on air. So surveillance didn't give their radios out lightly.

Sure enough, the greeting from the makeshift surveillance team was businesslike to the point of cold. Their support included a caveat: if there was no movement by nightfall they would be standing down. A reasonable instruction from a team cobbled together out of volunteers nearing the end of their shift; Joel wasn't about to argue. It was nearly 3 p.m. Easton would arrive home in an hour or so. It was fully dark around 9 p.m.

It didn't feel like a big window of opportunity.

Chapter 53

'Subject has been returned to his home address. He still wears the custody issue navy tracksuit. There are no vehicles assigned to the property. A blue Nissan Note is assigned to next door and I can confirm the registration matches with the one provided. No other vehicles present. Subject states he will be having an early night.'

The update was from the uniform colleague Joel had borrowed to drop Billy home. He had managed to drag the journey out to an hour and ten minutes, enough time for the surveillance team to get into their positions. The broadcast had come over on the standard radio set, and Joel had to swap to the encrypted set to hear the instant chatter in response, each car confirming its readiness.

Joel thanked his colleague and confirmed that he was clear to come away. They were in position too; DS Rose had parked them up the A228, Paddock Wood, an arterial road that put them in reasonable striking distance of Billy's address. She had turned the engine off. It was just twenty minutes before she would need to turn it back on again.

'Standby, standby, standby.' The pause that followed was maddening. *'Blue Nissan Note vehicle passes me on Harold Road, general direction of Rusthall village. One male occupant. Unable to confirm ID.'*

'Margaret Marshall's car!' Joel said. 'Billy's moving.' It had been part of Joel's briefing that Billy was known to have had access to this car previously – Margaret herself had told them that – and that it was his only option for transport. He straightened up. DS Rose had been on her phone but it was now abandoned in a cubby to bump and scrape with the movement of the car. The Nissan Note's general direction was towards them. The three cars that made up the surveillance team now called in their positions, trying to plot ahead as best they could. Two sightings came in one after the other. The way Billy was driving was helping; the Nissan Note was sticking to the legal limit. One of the cars was quick to report that they had fallen in behind it.

Then the radio fell silent.

Joel held his hand over his mouth, gripping his lips tight enough to hurt, desperate to know what was going on. His mind filled with scenarios. The most optimistic was that Robert Easton had made contact with his dad via the landline to arrange a meeting and he was now on his way.

Three more hurried updates came through as a flurry, the stress clear in the different voices of the team, their inexperience showing perhaps. With the fourth update Joel finally took his hand from his mouth to sigh with relief.

'Vehicle is stopped. We are Rusthall High Street, vehicle has pulled off to park in Hill View Road. Male driver exits vehicle, confirm no other occupants. Standby.'

Joel brought the location up on the mapping app on his phone. It was familiar from the day before, when they had been looking for lunch.

'Driver enters Cheese Pizza . . . approaches counter. Confirmation, male occupant is the target. Now wearing blue jeans, black hooded top and brown boots . . .' Another pause, then another update. The excitement that had been just under the surface of the words was now starting to fade. Joel's

excitement was quick to diminish too as they listened to a very detailed description of Billy Easton picking up a pizza before heading home.

'Seems like a man planning on having a night in.' DS Rose said what they were both thinking and Joel let it fester for a minute or two.

'Do you think he knows where those women are? I didn't ask him outright on purpose. I thought it might make him clam up, make him realise how serious this is for his son.' Joel finally voiced his worst fear. He had had Easton in front of him – what if he could have helped?

'I get the impression he doesn't know his son at all and Robert is acting on his own. No way he would risk using somewhere his dad knew. I think Billy would rat him out if he could.'

'Do you? His own son?' Joel said.

'I think he's devastated. That was how he came across. He'll want to end this before it gets any worse, surely.'

'Do you think Robert will come to see him?'

'I honestly don't know. I think he will want to know what happened at the police station but if he does . . .'

'If he does, what?'

'I think we will have put Billy in a lot of danger.'

Chapter 54

The gate sagged under Joel's weight when he leant on it. They had moved to a different waiting position and the hinges creaked like they were feeling the strain. Joel could relate. DS Rose had chosen the location, a tight strip of tarmac that cut through Broadwater Forest, three miles from Billy Easton's house, as good as anywhere to wait for more activity at that address. Choosing locations was difficult as they needed quick access to the address while also staying out of the way enough that Robert Easton wouldn't drift right past them on his way to visit his dad. They might be in plain clothes and in an unmarked car but they would be screaming *police* vibes to the paranoid criminal.

Joel peered out into a thick forest that was starting to show the beginnings of dusk. As the shadows lengthened, so did the odds of Robert Easton making an appearance at all. Going to see his dad would be a mistake, something Robert Easton had avoided up to this point.

It was almost 8 p.m. Another hour and this operation would be over, and with it all chances of finding those women alive. DCI Kemp's comment about *all eggs in one basket* was already part of Joel's internal dialogue and he was forced to wonder if the fact that he was leaning idly on a gate while time slipped away was down to his failings as a detective. But where else could he be? There was only one other consideration that wouldn't go away. That maybe he should be somewhere with *Escape!* laid out in front of him, poring over it in the finest of detail, reflecting that there was one 'zone' left of the four – *Abandon Ship!* – that was the obvious clue to where they should be looking for their missing women. Joel had asked Eileen to make some enquiries about redundant shipping in Kent and further away, and the result had not been a good one. There was no database for a start, no central place where redundant or disused vessels were listed. There were any number of companies involved in ship breaking, repair or storage. It wasn't just a needle in a haystack; it was worse than that. They didn't even know which haystack to start looking in. And it could only be a huge waste of his resources.

Joel's feeling was that the game was a red herring anyway. At least, it was now. Robert Easton had guided them to make the connection with his dad's game, then used that link to exert control over Joel's investigation. It was a link that had to be broken. Joel felt sure that Robert wanted him to be poring over *Escape!* – that he was supposed to be searching every rusting vessel in a hundred-mile radius. That was the role Easton had for him now. They had to break from what was expected – just like Easton had himself. But doing that had led them here, to the edge of a forest with the sun setting on the only move he had.

'Joel!' He spun towards DS Rose's voice. It was accompanied by the sound of ringing through the car's speakers. He'd left his phone plugged in to charge. It was Eileen.

'Eileen, what have you got?' DS Rose had already pressed to answer as he fell back into his seat.

'Some things you need to know,' came the maddening reply.

'More specific?' Joel said.

'The search at Jessica Harrington's office is done. They couldn't get into the computer system but they *could* get into the filing cabinet. They read out a list of what was in there, all casual, like—'

'Eileen!' Joel cut across, biting his tongue to stop him saying anything more.

'OK! A phone number. Miss Harrington has a stack of appointment books up to 2018. She must have gone digital after that. Joy Harper's phone number was shown against her appointments, but the old one, the one we already had.'

'You didn't call me to tell me that,' Joel said, still holding back.

'I did not. In the back cover is another phone number, labelled just as *Joy*. It could be our woman, but it might not, of course. I haven't called it or done anything with it. I didn't know—'

'That's fine. Send it through, Eileen. Excellent work. Did they find anything else relevant?'

'Yes, actually . . .' The pause was maddening, Joel actually bit his bottom lip to hold back his reaction. 'I don't quite know what to make of this.'

'Of what?' Joel said through gritted teeth.

'They did quite an extensive CCTV review at Miss Harrington's place of work, going back over the week. The waiting area isn't covered, just part of the entrance and the two reception desks. Tuesday, just after 10 a.m., a male appears on that camera, looking like he's come from an area of the building that isn't covered. He walks straight at Jessica Harrington, who's talking to her receptionist, but he doesn't quite make it. He just seems to stop and leave before Jessica notices him.'

'OK?' Joel said.

'The CCTV's not great but you can see what he's wearing, his skin colour et cetera, enough for Major Crime to be very interested. You see, they have a description of a man who has been seen a few times in the area where the homeless man's body was found. This person of interest matches with this person on the CCTV. And how the body was found sounds relevant too. He was in a disused garage with marks around his chest and abdomen consistent with being restrained by a wire or a thin, solid rope and they're obviously aware of our case . . .'

'Wire?' Suddenly one word was all Joel could get out. He was sat straighter, locking eyes with DS Rose, the handle above his open door gripped tightly enough that it might contort and, for a moment it seemed, they were frozen in time.

'It would seem likely. The cause of death looks to be blood clots caused by dehydration and the way he was immobilised, but there will be a full report by the path—'

'And it was Robert Easton, right? On the CCTV, this *person of interest*, that's what you're going to tell me?'

'No, Mr Norris. We do have a positive ID, however. It was Billy Easton.'

Chapter 55

For a moment no one quite knew how to react and there was silence. *Billy* Easton? What was he doing at Jessica Harrington's place of work? And another victim nearby with a cause of death as *dehydration*? That's seven to ten days assuming he was restrained and left to die. This didn't fit at all.

'*Billy* Easton.' Joel was still locked with DS Rose. Her expression was one of confusion turning to panic. No doubt it mirrored his own.

'He was lying. It was all a lie?' she breathed.

'It was so plausible, it can't have been . . .' Joel was floundering, his stomach an instant knot of anxiety, his mind swirling.

'What if it was all true, all the reasons he gave for those people being targeted, for the police being targeted, for not caring about being caught! Only . . .' DS Rose breathed this last word.

'Those reasons were his all along.' Joel finished her sentence, stepping out of the car. He had a sudden urge to stand. 'I let him go.' Joel spoke towards a forest that seemed darker still.

'Sir . . .' Eileen was shrill as she tried to cut back into the conversation via the car's speakers. Joel, in his shocked state, had almost forgotten she was on the line. He squatted to listen. 'Major Crime were intending on heading straight out to arrest Billy Easton for murder—'

Joel suddenly got some focus back. 'He kills them tonight, he told us that, it was all for our benefit. Us against him . . .'

'Us against him?' DS Rose repeated, shock still clear on her face.

'He sat there and told us the game had changed. He told us it was being played against the police. He said the police had been given chances to stop this all the way through, it was our fault they died because we didn't stop them, and something was happening tonight. A *storm!* He was talking to us directly. That was our chance to stop him, there and then . . . He was right in front of us.'

'Jesus . . .' DS Rose's initial shock was starting to drop away. 'We still know where he is. We just need to go and knock on his door. He can't know about the CCTV. Those women might even be there with him, right now.'

Joel was already shaking his head. 'They can't be. We searched his house top to bottom while he was in custody, then we dropped him back there. But this is his big finish. These two women are what he has been building up to – surely he's going to want to be there when they die. He has to go to them tonight!' Joel's energy was returning. Suddenly he was more certain than ever that they were in the right place. Billy Easton would be moving and he was probably waiting for darkness to do it. 'Eileen, did you say Major Crime are coming out to knock on his door? Because they can't, we still have a chance.'

'The last I heard, Mr Kemp was trying to talk them out of it. But I think he's struggling. The garage where the body was found had some other things in it . . .' She hesitated for a moment and Joel seized on it.

'Things?'

'I'm just trying to read what was on the report. A ratchet hand winch, an industrial chain block, a windlass . . .?' Joel heard hurried typing before she continued. 'Which seems to be some sort of mechanical way to drop an anchor on a boat and then retrieve it again. Anyway, they've got skin from it.'

'Skin?'

'This windlass thing has moving parts, seems someone trapped a bit of a skin in there somehow, which means DNA. We didn't have Billy Easton's DNA when they ran the sample—'

'But we do now.'

'From his arrest. They're running a fast-track test. I think if that matches, nothing will stop them. They might already be on their way out.'

'And they know the circumstances, why we're here?'

'Mr Kemp was explaining at length but I'm not sure Mark Hall was in agreement.'

'Of course he wasn't . . . He's been waiting for an opportunity to give me a bloody nose. This CCTV, is there any sign of anyone else or are we saying Billy Easton and Billy Easton alone?

'No mention of anyone else. There is one other thing, but this probably isn't relevant right now,' Eileen said.

'Jesus, what else?' Joel was still struggling to take it all in.

'I ran Billy's Land Rover again. When you said that Robert Easton was using it I thought I would broaden the parameters to see if he'd hit any neighbouring counties. You never know if—'

'Eileen!'

'Sorry! There are two ANPR cameras either side of the Dartford Crossing that come under Greater London. On Thursday at around midday, that Land Rover hit the Kent camera but it didn't hit the other side.'

'Why is that relevant to me?'

'Well, because thirty minutes later, you did the same.'

'What? When?'

'The day you went to see Alison Reynolds. Alison's car was found still parked near to her place of work—'

'So what are you saying, that he snatched her from there, that he was there waiting for her when I turned up?'

'I'm not saying anything for certain, Inspector Norris. Just that you met with Alison, then rushed from there to Billy Easton's home address, and he was otherwise engaged for approximately two hours.'

'Which is time to abduct Alison and get her somewhere else.'

'I spoke to a young lady called Helen Clarke at AR Games, whom you also met. She said that Alison seemed upset after your visit and announced that she would be working the rest of the day at home. She left minutes after you did.'

'And we know she didn't make it home,' Joel said. 'Two hours, with Dartford as your starting point and Easton's home address as your finish. She could be just about anywhere in the county. Following him to them is it. That's our chance. If Major Crime swoop in there to arrest him we're done, we'll never find them.'

'I've sent you that phone number for Joy, sir. I've done my best to find her but I have to say, at this stage, this is all I have. Maybe this is the right Joy and she has some answers for us.'

Joel rubbed his hand firmly over his scalp. 'I hope so. She might be our last hope.'

Chapter 56

'Standby, standby, standby!'

The surveillance team. The voice on the radio excited again. Joel had cut Eileen Holmans off to type out the number he had for Joy but the burst of radio activity stopped him pressing to call.

'Target vehicle is moving away from the address. Passes me at speed. Now making attempts to catch up, standby for direction of travel.'

The urgency stayed in the chatter as the surveillance team suddenly came to life. Those positioned ahead confirmed sightings and that the Nissan Note was now moving considerably faster than on its previous appearance. The team were struggling to keep up and it was just a couple of minutes before they called a *temporary loss*.

'Shit!' Joel exclaimed. He had sat back in the passenger seat and slammed the door, DS Rose had their Ford Focus ticking over and was waiting for an update on where to point it. Now they were faced with a worst-case scenario – losing Billy Easton. It would have been bad enough ten minutes ago, but now he was back as a suspect after being released from police custody earlier in the day, and Major Crime wanted him too.

This was about to look very bad.

'I have the zero back, vehicle remains eastbound, speed remains above limits where possible. Standby for location.'

Joel breathed again, but he lost none of the anxiety as the updates continued. The blue Nissan Note ran a red light as it joined the A26 toward Tonbridge. The surveillance team had hedged their bets, however, and still had a car ahead to pick up the commentary and describe the Nissan flashing across their front. Joel doubted that Margaret Marshall's car had ever been driven like this before.

The next update made Joel's blood run cold.

'This is Zulu Two. We've had a call from Acting Superintendent Mark Hall and will be switching to the main channel for a marked unit to stop the vehicle and effect an arrest for murder. Subject is clearly aware of surveillance assets and is now making off.'

And that was it. Joel brought his fist down firmly on the dashboard, and in the same movement scooped up the encrypted radio to shout his own orders, to remind the *sergeant* leading the surveillance team of the rank structure and to demand they continue. But then he held the radio before his lips, his finger poised over the button. Mark Hall might well be right. The nature of the driving suggested a man running from police rather than driving to where he had two women captive. They were blown out; they might even have been rumbled when Billy had taken his trip out for a pizza. Now Joel had a bigger picture, he concluded that the whole purpose of that trip had been so that Billy could see if anyone was paying him any attention. Billy knew his trip to custody had been filled with lies but he couldn't have been sure if the police knew it too. Now maybe he did.

Joel did now bark into the radio, but only to try and salvage something. 'This is DI Norris, we are making our way and will make the stop. We have lights and sirens and are close to the location.' Joel needed to be the next copper Billy Easton talked to, preferably while wrenching his arm so far up his back that he might finally be able to demand the truth. His phone with the mapping app was still in a holder attached to the dash.

'Standby, standby, standby, vehicle is stop, stop, A26 towards Tonbridge, outside of The Good Luck Chinese Restaurant . . .' Another pause. *'Driver's door is open, single occupant, hood up, subject is out, out. Are we making the arrest here?'* The voice was practically shaking with excitement now. Surveillance teams didn't like showing out to make an arrest and Joel was keen to make it clear that there would be no need.

'We are thirty seconds away!' he shouted above the noise of DS Rose revving the guts out of the Ford Focus. Joel pressed to turn on the grille lights to shift the car in front, then turned them straight back off again as they were let past.

'There it is!'

The Nissan was pulled over untidily, half on the kerb and under a streetlight that was just sputtering into life in the gathering gloom. The hazards blinked, the door fell shut and the form of a tall man with hood up walked quickly out onto the pavement. DS Rose aimed straight for him, the kerb thudding under the wheels to throw Joel off balance as he reached for his door handle. The figure in front reacted by twisting away from the headlights but with palms pushed out towards them like he was trying to protect himself from a blow.

They stopped in time. Joel was already out, already bellowing – the most effective way he knew to prevent a foot chase – and it worked.

'POLICE! STAY WHERE YOU ARE!'

His target didn't move, even dropped to a knee with arms still raised and Joel bundled into him, taking him all the way to the ground.

'OK, OK!' The hood fell back to reveal a panic-stricken face with none of the wrinkles Joel had been expecting.

'Who the fuck are you?!' Joel demanded.

'Jake! I'm Jake, OK . . . I know it's not my car, but I haven't nicked it! The owner asked me to come out and get him a Chinese takeaway, OK! He gave me twenty quid and bought our food too. That's all!'

He looked thirty at the most, scrawny too. Joel was sat on his chest, restricting his movements as well as his breathing.

'Who did?'

'Some bloke, like, two doors down. We only arrived today, OK, Airbnb for a long weekend! I can show you the booking on my phone! I know I was going a bit quick, yeah, but he said if I made it back in ten minutes he would make it fifty quid!'

'Joel!' DS Rose was shouting. He looked up and over to where she was stood by the open passenger door of the Nissan Note. She was holding an envelope.

'What is it?'

'It's just a phone number, nothing else. But the envelope, it's addressed to you.'

Chapter 57

Joel walked away. He had to. Initially he stayed alongside the A26, a quickly darkening ribbon of black beside him, the lights looming above it barely marking the surface with a smear of dirty orange. They shook in a wind now strong enough to shuffle his shirt tails. It already felt like the start of a filthy night, like trouble was coming, cloaked in darkness, and with it, it seemed, confirmation of what he already knew.

Billy Easton had outwitted them. Again.

Joel took an alleyway that led away from the main road and into a housing estate, ignoring the shouts behind him from DS Rose, who still stood with the Nissan, still gesturing with the found envelope while the driver of the car gawped out from the rear of their Focus. He had scooped up his phone; now he unlocked it. The number he had typed out for Joy was still showing. The alleyway brought him out onto a darker, quieter road, lined with houses whose windows were starting to glow. He pressed to call.

'Hello?' Never had such a word carried such uncertainty and confirmation in one word. It was Joy Harper, formerly Joy Easton. It had to be. This was a number she might have only given out to one person, a person who wasn't a gruff-sounding male.

If she hung up, this was all over.

'Jessica Harrington is in trouble. I'm a police officer,' Joel said, hoping he had the order of importance the right way round. He held his breath for the pause that followed.

'Sorry, who is this?'

She didn't hang up. Joel buried his relief to reply. 'Detective Inspector Joel Norris. I am investigating the disappearance of Jessica Harrington and I think you can help me.'

'Jessica . . .'

'This is Joy Harper, right?'

'How did you get this number?' The reply confirmed it.

'Jessica's office. Well hidden, mind, she obviously didn't want anyone to find it.'

'And you're a police officer. How do I know that?'

'I suspect Billy Easton was responsible,' he said. There was no time for toing and froing.

'Billy . . . Did he put you up to this?'

'Listen, Joy, I don't want to know where you are, not right now, this isn't about you. We're running out of time here. I think Billy has Jessica and maybe one other woman. I think he means them harm and you're the only chance I have to find them.'

'Jessica . . . But I haven't spoken to Billy in years, I've made damned sure of that!' Her voice was close to breaking, which Joel took as someone close to slamming the phone down and washing her hands of the call entirely.

'What is he capable of, Joy? You know him better than anyone but I'm struggling to work him out. Is he dangerous?'

'Dangerous!' Joy Harper snorted. 'You think I want to be living like this? You think I want to be the other side of the country, tipping my life upside down, spending my time in hiding to keep us safe? You think that's the life I wanted?'

'Us?' Joel said. 'Is Robert with you?'

'Of course Robert's with me! You think I would leave him down there with that . . . that monster?'

'Where are you, Joy?'

'I thought you said you didn't need to know that?' The strength was back in her voice, bolstered by thick suspicion.

'I tell you what, answer this instead: wherever you are, could Robert have travelled back to Kent in order to commit murder on two occasions in the last week?' Joel might have said too much but he needed a reaction.

'Murder . . .' That one word was enough, the incredulity, the disbelief, the absolute *ridiculousness* of it . . . If there was any doubt left in Joel's mind, it was entirely gone. Robert Easton hadn't murdered anyone. 'Are you serious?' Joy continued, her question genuine. 'He's here with me, has been all week. He's been to work every day, he works in an office, has a manager who will tell you that!'

'Billy Easton, in a police interview earlier today, when accused of murder, told me that Robert was responsible. Why would he do that?'

Laughter. Joel hadn't been expecting that. It didn't sound humorous but fragile, like glass. He gave her time to stumble to a stop. She sniffed and huffed. But she did reply.

'Well, of course he would say that. From the moment that boy was born, Billy was blaming him for anything he could. But it couldn't have been Robert and besides, he simply isn't capable.'

'His police record says different,' Joel chanced.

'And what does it say? That he was aggressive towards me? That he hit me? And do you know why it shows as that? Billy . . .' She was angry now, it was a marked change.

'Billy what?'

'Billy had his own son take the blame!' Her voice was close to breaking, her anger getting the better of her. She took a moment. Joel heard a gulp down the phone like she was fighting her own emotion. 'And not because he was scared of you lot, of being arrested or because he was spineless, it was worse than that.' She gulped again, and this time she couldn't stop the tears leaking into her words. 'It was all a game for him, everything's a game to him. And my boy, my Robert acted out, I know that's what it was. He got arrested for other things too, silly things. It was frustration. His dad used to tie him up in knots, toy with him. He couldn't cope and nor could I!'

'So you left,' Joel said, timing his words so they would be heard around her sobs.

'Do you blame me?' she replied, angry, accusing. 'This is a man that goes into every conversation like it's something to be won. He's exhausting, everything's calculated, everything he says has an ulterior motive, and I was done trying to work out what that might be. Apparently I was in an abusive relationship, and I didn't even know it! Not until we got marriage counselling. And whose idea do you think that was?'

'Billy's?' The word came out in a rush where Joel had been holding his breath. He didn't know how long for. He felt like someone had his stomach in a mediaeval torture device, twisting it slowly tighter and tighter, with a ratcheting sound that kept step with each of Joy's words.

'Of course it was. So then he could say that he was doing all he could when he was talking to Robert, that he was the one trying to hold the family together, but he resented those sessions, every minute, I can tell you that.'

'The referral to the police came from those sessions—' Joel's words were quiet, stripped of all energy, and it was easy for Joy to cut back in.

'Came from me. Jessica got me on my own, told me to get a different phone, a different number, and said she would refer me. She said that there were people out there that could help me get away. They would give advice so he couldn't find me. The only caveat was that the police would have to be told I was taking part in some scheme. They didn't get any other details and I never spoke to anyone. Best thing I did, though. I tried to take Robert with me too but all his mates, everything he knew was down there so he didn't come straightaway. But he soon realised that he needed a clean break too, that he wouldn't be able to have a life so long as his dad was around.' Her tears were gone now, leaving just the anger.

'What happened, Joy?' Joel knew already, but his stomach had ratcheted another notch and three words were all he could manage.

'Robert got a job, a place to live. He was working as an estate agent, something he had always wanted to do. I told him to go for it, if that was what he wanted.'

'He didn't want to take over BTE Games then?'

'Ha! You've got to be kidding. He never wanted anything to do with that, neither of us did. But even when he got away, when he got into something that could be a career for himself, his dad pushed his way in.'

'How?' Joel wheezed out another word.

'I knew he was angry at Jessica. I thought it was just because he'd paid her to fix our relationship and she didn't. He's very black and white like that. But, thinking back, it must have been more. He was obsessed. I think he might have even followed her about for a bit. He told me how she was a home-wrecker herself, how she was having some affair. I didn't care, I told him that. But he found this other woman, this other family that Jessica had apparently ruined and then his obsession changed.'

'To the other woman?'

'I think he was besotted. Robert told me that, he also told me that he followed her too, *stalking*, he said. Billy found out somehow that she was moving and suddenly he was desperate to buy the place next door. My Robert was an estate agent in the area but that place wasn't one of his. His dad had him bullying some other agent to push the sales through. Robert said his dad finally made a play for this woman and it got a bit embarrassing. She knocked him back but he didn't listen – Billy doesn't accept that he can't have things – and this poor woman's daughter had to step in and have a word. I think she told him to back off.'

'Her daughter spoke to him?' Joel's knot was tighter still. Finally something he didn't know. They'd never really got an explanation for why Kelly had been targeted, not one that satisfied him, but this might. It was all falling into place – but too late.

'Robert said so. Can't say I blame her. I think she gave him a few home truths. Sounds like a clever girl to me. I was stupid enough to say yes to him once, but he was different then, he wasn't quite so intense. The more he lost, the worse he got.'

'Lost?' The word was just a squeak now, a dog toy on its last legs, shaken and tossed about in powerful jaws.

'Me, our house, his son, his business. It was a gradual thing but we could all see it slipping away. Of course it was always someone else's fault.'

Joel had to take a minute. He moved the phone away from his mouth to inhale deeply, to focus on his breathing. Then he returned with new strength. 'What happened with his business?'

'Alison Reynolds happened. Billy met someone who played *him* for once. Alison saw an opportunity. Good on the girl. I was entitled to half of that company, you see, and I went for it. Alison came in, propping it up by buying the other half, and from there she worked him over.' The satisfaction was clear, even down a phone line.

'So he doesn't like Alison Reynolds?'

'Hates her. And everything she represents. She ousted him, rejected his vision for the business, told him he didn't know what he was doing. The business world was something else he was trying to conquer and he wouldn't have anyone tell him he was going about it the wrong way. So when he came to them with a new game and Alison turned it down flat . . . I've never seen a man so angry.'

'New game?' Another question squeaked, a sudden anxiety once again gripping his throat.

'*Kismet: The Fifth Day!*' Joy scoffed, her voice suddenly like she was reading the lines from a movie trailer. 'That was what he was calling it. How crap does that sound? I remember when he told me, it was like he'd said the most profound thing any man had ever said. I think I was supposed to fall at his feet. I did, as it happened, but only after I was underwhelmed and he knocked me down with the back of his hand.'

'The fifth day . . . He said that in interview.' Joel had heard of blood running cold, but he'd never really experienced it. Not until that moment, stood out under those streetlights, the gathering wind still playing with a shirt that had come untucked at the back and ruffling the loose part of his trousers to tickle his shins. It came with the realisation that Billy had told him everything, everything he needed. That whole interview was just part of the game and Joel had still been playing his part like a dutiful detective.

'He told you about that game too, did he? I hope you pretended to be impressed at least or you would have lost him there and then.'

'Not the game, no. It was in another context . . . and Kismet . . .' Joel had to pause again. He lifted his eyes to a bright streetlamp shrouded by a whirl of bugs. 'I've seen that too, it's in his garden on some steel sculpture thing . . .'

'You mean the anchor? He's got that in his garden now?'

'Anchor?'

'Kismet was the name of a ship that they were breaking down at Samphire Hoe, years ago. He's always had a bit of a fascination with boats. I think he managed to blag the two front anchors somehow. No idea what he wanted them for. This boat broke down in a storm and ended up on the rocks, heavily damaged. Stayed there for months. In the end they used the Hoe as a place to break it. A local boat repair firm got the job and they based themselves on that Hoe. Still there, last I heard. The fella that runs it, John someone or other, he must be Billy's only friend. I don't think it's much now, two sad little men and a kettle,' Joy scoffed, her hatred never clearer.

'Samphire Hoe?'

'Dover. A big concrete platform at the foot of the cliff, something to do with when they made the Channel Tunnel. Billy had some work down there before BTE. He was a welder then. He worked on the tunnel for a bit and was based on the Hoe so he got to know John at this repair firm and he gave Billy a little work on the side.'

'Boat repair . . .' Joel was almost whispering. 'What was this game, Joy? Did he tell you about it?'

'Just about the last thing he told me. Just before I decided that enough was enough. This was how bad it got: when I left him I took a cab home rather than my own car and I told the driver to call the police if I wasn't back out in five minutes. I made him pull right in front of the window so Billy knew I would be missed. That's not normal, is it? Having to plan a conversation so your husband wouldn't kill you there and then. He told me that if I ever left him . . .'

'The game, Joy, it might be relevant and I'm out of time here. What was it, what did you have to do?'

'Same principle as his precious *Escape!* if you ask me. Something about building boats. Characters are anchored out to sea and they have to roll a dice to build their boat up. You start off on just a wooden pallet and get tools and upgrades as you play. There's a strategy to it but I wasn't really listening. Is this really important right now?'

'How does it end, Joy?' Joel said, ignoring her question.

She huffed. 'You have to build something strong enough to survive the storm that comes on the fifth day. Hence the title. Alison didn't like it, none of them did. That was the final straw before they kicked him out.'

Joel had started walking again, back the way he had come, but he came to a full stop now on heavy legs. The quieter road allowed the sound of the growing wind to shake a squeak out of an overhead power line. A gate bumped against its housing.

'I will need to talk to you again, OK, but I have to go now.'

Joel didn't wait for the reply.

Chapter 58

Joel sprinted back to the Nissan. The hazards were still blinking, the engine running too, a steady chug against the unpredictable gusts of wind, and the headlights raking bright across a takeaway doorway crammed with onlookers dressed as chefs. Joel ignored them to bawl instructions at a marked patrol that had arrived since he had taken his walk and were adding their blue strobes to the show. They were to deal with the driver of the Note, whom Joel now pulled out of the back of the Focus, making it clear that he didn't care how. He plugged his phone back into the car's system, cutting off an inbound in the process, then punching in the number that DS Rose had still been clutching. He left the number on the screen, not yet pressing to make the call until he had got an update from his sergeant and caught his breath. She told him how a patrol had been sent to Billy Easton's address and already forced entry. There was no one there. Joel wasn't expecting anyone. Billy would have slipped out on foot the moment Margaret's car had pulled away and found his way to nearby roads where a taxi could be met or, more likely, where another car could be parked up waiting. It seemed so obvious now.

Joel then gave his own rushed update but it was a garbled message about Samphire Hoe, Dover, an anchor in a garden,

Eileen's ANPR findings and *abandon ship*. He knew he wasn't making much sense. To her credit, DS Rose didn't ask for clarity. She would have seen his finger hovering over the call button on his phone, ready to dial the number that had been addressed to him on the passenger seat of the Nissan. Her focus was on driving the car. Joel's focus was a single phrase: *Four years in the planning*. It was all he could think about. This whole thing, down to the last detail. And he had to assume that this phone call had been part of that plan.

Joel pressed to dial.

'You know how you judge a good game?' The voice that came through loud on the speakers to fill the interior was instantly familiar, but instantly different. It was Billy Easton, only now he wasn't performing, now he was oozing confidence, almost tripping over his own glee.

'Where are you, Billy?'

'A good game is one where you're disappointed when you realise it's coming to the end, despite playing it all night. Have you ever played a game like that?'

'They're still alive then?'

Billy chuckled. 'I think I already answered that question, didn't I? They took it off me, you know, in that hovel of a custody area. The very same envelope you're holding right now. My plan B. Just in case you were clever enough not to let me go, a bargaining chip. I had a lovely little recorded message planned out but look at me now, now I get to answer your call while enjoying the freedom you gave me!'

'You wouldn't have got anything from me.'

'What makes you think I would have asked *you!*' he snapped, the glee changing to fury in a heartbeat, that temper Joy had talked about rearing its head for the first time. For Joel at least. Billy took a moment then continued, more controlled. 'That doesn't matter now. I have to say, I much prefer talking to you out here than in that dark little room. Disgusting place. Not a place for someone like me.'

'Where are they?' Joel didn't want a conversation.

'They are playing their part, just like you are. At least I hope they are. I would be very disappointed if they had upped and died already! They will be struggling by now, however. It is not a pleasant environment.'

'Where are they?' Joel said again.

'Just the key questions, like a good little police officer! Shame you didn't ask these questions of me earlier.'

'Why have me call you? There's something you want, so come out with it.'

'First let me tell you this, DI Norris. Strategy games have been my life so I suggest you think very carefully about your next move. This is where it ends and you get to decide how. Exciting, isn't it?'

Joel didn't reply. This wasn't the time to scream, shout or argue. Billy Easton wanted a reaction, and he'd put a lot of work in to get one.

'Well, I for one am excited. So here it is: you can have my location or you can have the location of Jessica Harrington and Alison Reynolds, but you cannot have both. These are your choices. So what will it be?' The glee was back, thick even when filtered through speakers.

'Why would you give either of those up?' Joel growled.

'Fair's fair, and a game falls apart when you take away the chance of victory. Even if it is just a small victory snatched from the jaws of defeat.' Laughter, enough to bounce round the interior like Billy Easton was sat in the back mocking them in person.

'Fuck you.' Joel pressed to end the call. The car slowed sharply under DS Rose's control. She was staring over at him and he met her glance.

'What the hell was that?' she said.

'The end of the game. I'm not playing anymore.'

'Did we not need to know what he was going to say next?'

'He's not going to give us anything. He hasn't yet, why would he now?'

'Maybe he will, maybe that's what this is all about. You were supposed to pick the women, because that's the right choice and then you have to live with letting him go. Twice.'

'That's what I've done, is it?' Joel spat, his anger now threatening to get the better of him.

'That's not what I'm saying. What I'm saying is that's how he will be looking at it, that's what he's trying to achieve. Call him back.'

'No.'

'What are you doing, Joel?'

'Refusing to play to his rules. That's all we've been doing and look where it's got us. I call him back and he gives us a location that we all drive to and he's still controlling our every move. I know where we need to be going. I'll make some calls. We're going to need support when we get there.'

'And if you're wrong, if he isn't there at all? If no one is?'

'Then we're out of options. And I will have let him go. *Twice*.'

Chapter 59

Joel's hurried Google searches on his phone had revealed Samphire Hoe, near Dover as a 'unique and extraordinary man-made nature reserve'. Putting it more simply, digging a 50-kilometre Channel Tunnel link between Britain and France around thirty years ago had created a huge amount of rubble that had to be deposited somewhere, and the foot of Shakespeare Cliff between Dover and Capel was the chosen place. The result was the reclamation of 45 hectares of the English Channel by building a platform – or hoe – held in place by a sheet-piled wall just over a mile long. Initially the platform was used as part of the construction effort, but once the tunnel was completed, three quarters of the hoe was landscaped to create an undulating nature reserve accessible to the public for walking dogs and spotting birds, with as-far-as-the-eye-can-see views out over the Channel. On a calm, sunny day there was no doubt it would be an oasis of serenity, a sun trap lazily chirping and buzzing with the sound of insects concealed in the wild grass.

Tonight, the wind was rocking the solitary traffic light that granted access to the Hoe through a single-track tunnel. The stark red light stood out from the blackness like a demon's eye. They were on top of Shakespeare Cliff, half way between

Dover and Capel and easily 200 feet above the sea. Not that you would know it. The cliffs rose up another 100 feet, the A20 a flattened strip sliced into it, so that one could barely see the English Channel and had no chance of seeing the platform below. That suited Joel. The fact he couldn't see down meant that no one could see up.

The trail of police cars proceeded. Joel had amassed twelve in total, and a thirteenth had flashed down the other side of the carriageway and would soon slingshot the roundabout on the outskirts of Dover to join the back of the queue, with instructions to block the tunnel when everyone else was in. This was the only vehicular access. He had found online a reference to a steep footpath and had sent two officers to try and find the clifftop end just in case. He'd also spoken to the Coastguard, who would launch the RNLI and their Severn Class vessel to point their huge lamps inland, preventing any movement away by boat. The fact that Billy Easton had had four years to make his plans, and had already slipped through Joel's grasp twice, meant that nothing could be left to chance. Joel would have liked coverage from a police helicopter too, but they were grounded in the strengthening storm.

They were as prepared as they could be.

Now they just needed to be in the right place.

Joel turned a bright orange flare pistol over in his hands, one of four that had had been found in a hurry by a local officer who had warned that it came loaded. He had then gone on to claim to know Samphire Hoe better than anyone. His description did nothing to settle Joel's anxiety: *It's bigger, hillier and much darker than you think. We'll lose each other easy.* The same serious-looking copper had then given a rushed briefing on *how* and *why* you should use the flare and Joel had chimed in with the *when*. He wanted chaos and confusion, he wanted anyone in a building down there to panic and to be flushed out. But he couldn't have confusion among the police. The flare pistol was only to signal if Easton or the women had been located. There hadn't been the time to check for understanding. He'd ordered the officers back to their cars. The next cycle on the traffic lights would be for them. He had made sure the dog handler was the next car behind them. She was carrying a Belgian Malinois General Purpose Dog, or 'land shark' as he had heard it jokingly translated. Whatever Malinois meant, he was their best chance of finding someone quickly.

The traffic light clicked to green, the light flooding DS Rose's determined expression. Joel was forced back in his passenger seat as she roared forward, slamming her palm into the horn to start the siren while Joel pushed the buttons to activate the grille lights. The cars that followed suit were brighter behind. Most of those he had been able to scramble at such short notice were local units, marked with proper roof lights and louder sirens. Their headlights dipped and flashed in patterns too, and the tunnel that had been so dark and foreboding now had icy blue strobes penetrating every inch, while the sirens, trapped under the concave roof, whined and screamed from twelve sources, all out of sync. It was a tangible din, a wall of snarling, flickering sound and light that would burst out the end and onto the Hoe like a ferocious animal. It was everything Joel had demanded.

Joel's car was first to emerge. The slope down through the cliffs was steep, the speed of their car too fast, and the underside scraped where the ground levelled out. To their right were two further tunnels, both with train tracks lolling out of their darkened throats like steel tongues. To their immediate left was a compound, the quarter of the Hoe that was gated off and still in use as part of the Channel Tunnel. It contained the cooling towers that piped fresh air from the surface as well as warehouses for storage, and train tracks that could be used to shuttle supplies between here and the main port at Folkestone. Joel had managed to find aerial shots of Samphire Hoe as part of his hurried research, some from directly above this compound, enough to give a good idea of its layout. He was also sure that this held the boat repair and breaking business that Joy Harper had talked about. The concrete wall that rebuffed the sea had a built-in dip on the east side of the compound, and the water would breach it at high tide to slither across the smooth surface by design, so as to allow smaller vessels to be re-floated, or access to the ocean. It was also where larger boats could dock.

Joel wanted control of this area first.

'There's a gate!' DS Rose said, then swore.

'I want chaos, Lucy, I want the world coming in around him. Take it out.'

'"Take it out", what does that mean?'

'It means you're going too slow, you need a good run-up.'

She understood his meaning. Joel felt the car surge. The siren was still throwing out waves of sound. She spun hard left for the front to swing past eight-foot walls then straighten up for the chain-link gate directly ahead, which was pulled shut and hinged on the left. The sound waves were suddenly shorter and more intense, bouncing back like sonar as the gate rushed at them. Lucy's head turned away the moment before impact, her roar mingling with the sound of the engine.

'FUUUUUUUUUUUCKK!'

The car juddered. Joel slammed his eyes shut too. The momentum was still forwards. Something solid smacked off the windscreen surround and Joel forced his eyes open to a windscreen opaque on his side with cracks and splits. The gate scraped and bucked as it gave, then sparked as it swung away, right to left. Straight ahead the cooling towers suddenly loomed – as did the four-foot solid concrete wall that penned them in. DS Rose had seen it too. She spun the steering hard left and the tyres squealed on the smooth tarmac as the car tried to change direction – but they were going too fast. They had turned enough for the blow to be glancing on the driver's side. Joel was thrown right to take a hard impact on his knee.

He was aware of pops around him as airbags deployed. The bag in the steering wheel flapped and twisted as the wheel flailed out of control. A scraping sound brought them to a stop. The only sound left was the siren. The engine had stalled.

Other cars swept in, their lights and sirens still flashing and blaring. Some of his colleagues already had boots on the ground and the unleashed police dog flashed across their front, his handler lagging behind with hands over her ears. Joel had insisted the noise be left on and it was too late to wonder if that was a mistake as he pushed his door as wide as it would go. The shrill noise was everywhere, reverberating from the flat-sided buildings, vehemently filling the space so that it threw him off-balance as he stumbled to a limping run.

An officer's shouting mingled with a powerful dog bark by the eastern perimeter wall and he headed straight for it, past a building already being swamped by his colleagues. The shouts were beyond it, outside, closer to the water. When he emerged from the building line a massive beam of light erupted from his right to sweep across the bucking surface of the sea. The Severn Class lifeboat he had ordered was right on cue, its deck-mounted lantern like a thick white laser beam that swept across all that was in front of him. Then it stopped, its light now swamping a male figure stood on the very edge of the Hoe, filling a break in the fence, his hands up and facing a dog that looked barely able to contain itself, snarling and barking while edging forward. The cliff face loomed above them here, a huge black wall stretching up to slice the night in half.

The dog handler wrapped a leash around her animal but held their position. The first coppers reached the figure, grabbed his hands, pulled them behind him and cuffed him. The light stayed fixed. Joel sprinted up onto the wall, stopping close enough to see wispy hair being tossed around by the wind, and heavily wrinkled features revealed by the bright light: Billy Easton.

'DI Norris!' Billy smiled, he *fucking* smiled. DS Rose had kept pace. Joel didn't realise just how close she was until she burst past him. He didn't have time to react; she was already on Easton, her right arm swung out, her bunched fist connecting to knock him clean off his feet. The two officers either side were caught out and had to scrabble to get hold of him again. When they sat him up, his eyes were shut and a trail of blood ran from his nose. His lips curled into an even wider smile.

'Where are they?' DS Rose bawled against the wind, which was at its strongest yet as it whipped in unabashed from the sea. More officers bundled onto the thin walkway. The sea was alive below them, flailing and thumping, swirling and hissing. The police sirens were distant but still pulsed out of sync to add to the confusion. Joel heard a distant shout from a uniformed colleague. He turned towards it to see that another male had been detained and was being walked towards him, an officer on each arm making his gait look unnatural.

'You need to learn some manners, little lady.' Billy Easton spat on the ground. 'You think I respond to treatment like that?' Joel stepped across his colleague, lightly taking hold of her arm to stop her moving forward on Easton again.

'He's not going to help us,' he said.

'We found him in the first building.' Joel turned. The two officers were still pushing the stranger towards him. They had made it up onto the wall now and every step closer was revealing the man. He looked a similar age to Billy Easton. His lower half was covered by waders, his top by a thick jacket styled like a shirt, his head by a woolly hat with visible holes.

'I just picked him up! That's all I did! What is this about?' The man was shocked but there was fear mixed up with it. Before Joel could reply, the sea gave its biggest *whump!* yet as the wall took the brunt of a huge wave, leaving just its icy fingers to reach up and over the side and blow across them all. Joel shivered. The air was suddenly thick with salt.

'Do you know this man?' Joel said, pointing at the bleeding Billy Easton.

'Bill, sure I do. I got a call, he said to pick him up. What is this all about?'

'You tell me, *John.*' Joel gave time for a reaction. Billy Easton's ex-wife had mentioned Billy's only friend, and this had to be him.

'How do you know my name?' With the heels of his palms, he wiped his wide eyes clear of another sheet of salty water that blasted over the sides.

'I need to know it for when I arrest you for kidnap and murder, along with Billy here. Where are they?'

'Murder . . .! What are you talking about?'

'Your mate Bill has kidnapped two women. They're supposed to die tonight. If you know where they are, now's the time to tell us.'

The man took a moment. The confusion looked genuine enough. His eyes searched the ground then fixed on Billy.

'What the hell is this all about?' he said. Billy Easton was still smiling but he wouldn't make eye contact with his friend. He didn't respond either. When the man spoke again, he still addressed Billy. 'Does this have something to do with the tribute?'

'Tribute?' Joel jumped in.

'There was a wreck here, a boat that ran aground. It was badly damaged. We were part of breaking it and we kept the anchors. Recently Billy wanted the remaining anchor dropped back near the site as some sort of tribute. I thought it odd, it wasn't like anyone died on the thing. It was a standard job!'

'Where?' Joel pounced and John pointed out over the sea, at an angle back towards the cliff face. Joel tried to follow his direction but all he could see was darkness. He stepped forward to face the lifeboat and raised his hands to signal to them to sweep the water.

The lifeboat crew seemed to understand. The light whipped

across the scenery, looking white hot against the chalk cliff face. Joel watched it sweep. It stopped momentarily on a cave that was largely submerged. There were two stacks of rocks either side of the cave's entrance that were peeking out of the water in places. Something bright glimmered among the closest stack. The lifeboat crew might have seen it too. The light swept back to rest on it. Joel took a few steps closer, his mind taking a moment to make sense of it.

'Is that it?' Joel's voice boomed above the wind.

'Yes,' John called back.

'Can you get to it from here?' Joel said. The bright light had showed glimpses of rocks and the tiniest portion of beach at the foot of the cliff where it met the wall.

'At low tide there's a walkway to the beach. But not like this,' John said. 'You don't think there are people out there?'

Joel did. He was certain of it. He didn't know how exactly, but the game that Billy Easton had seen rejected, the anchor that matched with the one buried into his garden, the final zone from *Escape!* and, most of all, the flash of uncertainty behind Billy Easton's eyes – everything he knew was pointing to this place.

Joel had been holding the flare gun. He shoved it into his waistband so he had use of both his hands as he moved to the gap in the fence that Easton had been dragged out of. It marked steps down to the water, where a depth marker was painted on the side to tell him it was 4 metres. It was the only marker he could see, but he could assume there would be others below, meaning the tide was nearing its highest. Above the marker, the wall lifted at least another three metres. There was a wide shelf that jutted out of it, sloped towards the beach and quickly disappeared under the water – the walkway John had described. It was angled down over a stack of rocks that were surely piled up on purpose to add extra protection from the sea. The beach was sloping too, left to right and steep so it was higher where it met the wall of the

Hoe, as if some of the leftover rubble had been used to build it up. The waves swamped it, but at the highest point the water was rolling back to show a thin walkway against the cliff face.

He had to get closer.

DS Rose shouted to Joel as he walked out onto the steps but the words were lost in the wind and the churning sea. The sirens had stopped, at least. The slope was steeper than he'd expected, the water instantly cold as it rolled along the wall and crashed into his calves to swamp his feet and shins. The ledge was wide but slick underfoot with clumps of seaweed that looked jet-black in the poor light. The ledge ran out almost instantly and he would need to move to the rocks. He identified one large enough to land on, flat-topped and angled slightly towards him. He looked to his right, to where the ocean whumped the Hoe further up, the wave it created bundling towards him to consume the entire ledge. It would consume him too.

Joel jumped.

The landing was slippery, with a sharp edge that collided with his shin. The wave swept in and he had to squat and turn side-on to it to stop himself being swept off. He also plunged his hands down to grip the edge of the rock as best he could. His fingers burned. His nails scraped and threatened to give. All around him was shuffling, hissing blackness, the ocean playing hide and seek with sharp stone edges. For a moment he thought he was stuck, hunkered down to take the punches of the waves and unable to move, as the instant change of direction would involve forces that were almost as strong and threatened to sweep him out to sea. There was the briefest moment of slack and Joel found his feet to leap for another rock, his landing the springboard for another jump. He made three jumps in a row before finally he was able to land on something less threatening.

The beach was a welcome relief. Sodden sand and flat rocks.

The walkway sank under his feet and the cliff face felt slick as he used it for support. Keeping it on his left, he moved down the slope and onto the next rock pile. This one took him back, away from the surface.

He was as close as he could get.

The cave was ahead. He could only see the top but the slope of the beach was steep enough to suggest that it could be as large as a single storey. There was less than a metre exposed above the water line and the bigger waves were concealing it completely.

The white light from the lifeboat fixed on him as he reached the top. A huge wave smashed into the front of the rock pile, its spray soaking him and stinging his eyes, the water cold enough to take his breath away. He gestured again, pointing back to where he had seen that earlier glimmer in the light. When the light swung back to it he was forced to exhale hard again.

Now he was closer, the anchor was starting to give up its secrets.

Chapter 60

It was partly covered by rocks but two prongs were sticking up, each the shape of a bricklayer's trowel but far larger. What he hadn't seen from a distance was the thick chain wrapped around it, with two ends pulled taut to trail into opposite sides of the cave. The chains were both bucking and swinging like something afloat was attached, but the ends disappeared into the cave to be veiled by shadow.

But Joel didn't need to be able to see. He already knew.

There hadn't been time to sort out comms. A pre-planned operation would have ensured the lifeboat was given a police radio so they could talk to each other easily, but they had all had to make do with a hurried phone call on the way to Dover. Now that wasn't enough; Joel needed to get a message to them. He called 999 from his mobile. The Coastguard was the fourth option offered by the bored-sounding operator. Joel battled the wind to hurriedly explain himself, then gave an equally hurried message to pass over to the Dover RNLI Crew. The operator stopped him to say she had direct contact and she could patch him through if that helped.

It helped massively.

Now it was Joel's turn to struggle to hear. The RNLI

Coxswain introduced himself but Joel missed the name. It didn't matter anyway.

'Are you the lunatic out on the rocks?' The voice was male, strong and self-assured, calmer than it should be from a boat dangerously close to rocks on a pitch-black night in a windstorm.

'Yes, I—'

'You're a damned idiot and now you want saving.'

Joel would have to take that on the chin. 'I am an idiot, but it isn't me that needs saving. There are two chains anchored in the rocks. They're attached to two floats with two women attached,' he shouted above the wind. There was a moment's silence that was not entirely unexpected.

'Alive?' The Coxswain's voice had lost none of its calmness.

'I thought I could get there but I can't get any closer,' Joel said, avoiding the question.

'We can't see anyone from here,' the Coxswain replied. 'Are you sure there are people in there? There's a hell of a risk sending someone out to that. We wouldn't even attempt this – unless you're telling me it's a live rescue?'

Joel didn't know for sure but he couldn't quite bring himself to say it. This wasn't the time to doubt his conviction; it had got them this far, he couldn't just call it off.

'I'm sure they're in there.' Joel knew what he was asking.

There was silence on the other end and Joel thought he hadn't been heard. He was still trying to cup the phone in his hands to protect it from the wind. But he had been heard, and the Coxswain was considering.

'Can you see in that cave, from where you are?' The questions were getting maddening now, there wasn't the time.

'No,' Joel replied.

'But you can see the mouth, you have a better angle and you're closer . . .' Another pause, more consideration. Joel actually bit down on his knuckle. 'We can launch the smaller RIB. Two crew, I'll be asking for volunteers and if I don't get any . . .' he said finally.

'I understand!' Joel bawled.

'But you're my eyes down there. Our comms aren't great in these conditions and you're much closer. If they go onto the rocks, or they lose control, you need to call it and we'll haul them back. I'm holding you personally responsible for their safety.' Still calm, but that voice now carried authority. Joel was in no doubt that he meant what he said.

'Understood,' Joel said again.

'We'll be watching you. If they get in difficulties wave your arms—'

'Gun!' Joel blurted, his hand darting to his waistband, 'I have a flare gun . . .'

'Even better. If they're in trouble just make sure you use it.' That threat was back. The call was ended. Now all Joel could do was stare at the lifeboat to see if the call for volunteers got any response. The light shifted to beam directly at the cave entrance. He didn't know what that meant.

A decision seemed to be made. The lifeboat was suddenly a hive of activity. More lights were switched on, this time towards the rear where a Y-Boat appeared. Joel had seen them used in searches before – they were far smaller, flat-bottomed and inflatable for operating in shallow water. Two yellow-hooded figures made up its crew. They both seemed to be focused downwards, perhaps regretting putting their hands up now their headtorches were pointing down towards the black, tumultuous surface. The size difference affected the Y Boat's reaction to the conditions the moment it touched the water. A wave rolled under its flattened hull, lifting it from the rear, pushing the two figures forwards, twisting it a little, and Joel could see them fight to straighten it. Being side-on to onrushing waves meant real trouble.

He could hear the engine now, the sound mingling with the wind to whip over him in gusts. The rocks were arranged in two clear piles either side of the cave's entrance. The rock piles might have been what had caused the cave to form in the first place, acting as a channel for the power of the sea to focus on one spot on the cliff face. But that didn't mean that there weren't rocks they couldn't see in the run-up to the cave.

The Y-Boat straightened and moved to within fifteen metres of the entrance. Joel would have tipped his hat if he'd had one. He'd always had the utmost respect for those involved in sea rescue, but, with the boat riding another huge wave to lurch towards the jagged rocks, his respect went up a notch. These people were fearless.

He watched at the boat bucked and rocked again. The crew were both stood now, stumbling forward in unison as they hit something hard. When they stood back up, an oar jutted out of the side to push against something just below the surface, and the figure at the back fought to lift the engine up out of the water. The ocean remained relentless. It rolled under them to toss the little boat about, then slapped against the cliff face, concealing the cave entrance momentarily.

Its disappearance made Joel stop to think. He had become fixed on finding those women, on being right, locked in a personal battle with Billy Easton – and winning. This was madness. He turned to look back up at Samphire Hoe. He could see DS Rose, still stood with their prisoner. They were all watching with an elevated view. Doubt crept in for the first time. Doubt that anyone could survive these conditions, doubt that those women were even here at all and this wasn't just another Billy Easton misdirection.

The two lifeboat crew were tossed to the floor of the Y-Boat again and they could do nothing to prevent it changing direction, lurching towards the stack of rocks on their right. Two more people in danger now, their safety on him: he had known that even before the Coxswain's warning: *if they go onto the rocks, or they lose control, you need to call it and we'll haul them back. I'm holding you personally responsible.*

The Y-Boat had straightened back up and was just five metres from the entrance, the crew now battling to fix it to something. Joel could see they were both trailing ropes from their waist back to the Severn Class – lifelines. But the next wave was the biggest yet. The boat lifted from the rear, the two crew lurched forward again, the figure at the front tipping forward, grabbing the nose and fighting to stay on his feet. The front of the boat collided with the flat cliff face above where the cave was again swamped. Even if they made it into that cave, there would be no coming out, not alive. Not anyone.

Joel still held the brightly coloured flare gun in his hand and now he pointed it skywards and pulled the trigger. The burst was instant and this time the ratcheting feeling in his stomach was enough to drop him to his knees. He kept his head up to watch as the burning slug soared over the scene and hung in the air, its message clear for all to see.

The rescue was off. Those women were dead.

Chapter 61

It *was* a bright, white light. Just like the books and movies had told her. Only Jessica Harrington wasn't walking towards it, to be slowly consumed by its warm light; she was floating on her back, being gently led, her whole body numb, wrapped in something thick and cossetting. Like the feeling of being laid out in a bath.

But the light hadn't been permanent. It had come all at once, filling every inch of the space, above the water, under the water – even carried in as sparkling froth on the waves. Then it had swept away, and Jessica had panicked, thinking that her chance was gone.

She just wanted to drift into the light.

She was so tired. She had tried to give up, to let it happen, but something deep and instinctive had her fighting, something had lifted her hands back to grapple and scratch at the stone, tearing more nails from her bleeding fingers, something had powered her sore neck muscles to lift her nose out of the water to snatch a breath from the pockets of air where she could find them. Something had refused to let her give up.

It was one image. One memory. She was with Peter and her son and daughter. It was the first time she had introduced her children to her new man. They had been sat out in her garden and she had been nervous, desperate for it to go well, for everyone to get along. And they had. They had drunk wine while the sun set around them. Peter had bought a new firepit and they'd all been gently mocking his numerous failed attempts at lighting it. Steven had got it going in the end. The flames had been quick to grow, to light up their stupid grins. They'd talked about everything and nothing in its warmth. Her daughter had found marshmallows in a cupboard and, to everyone's delight, had promptly burned them beyond recognition. The laughter, the gentle ribbing, the feeling you only get from being part of a happy family after being so sure she would never have that again. It was perfection.

She wanted that. Just once more she wanted to have that.

But the light was back and it was coming for her. The ceiling above her was blurring, she was no longer fighting, no longer gasping for breath. This nightmare, this pain, this life.

It was time to let it go.

Chapter 62

Retracing his steps was just as arduous and Joel's relief was tangible when he reached the sloping platform that would take him back up to Samphire Hoe and his colleagues. He was cold now, the feeling overriding the pain in his knee, shins and fingers, the wind and his soaking clothes conspiring to make him shiver.

'Joel, Jesus, what the hell were you thinking?' Sympathy was not one of his sergeant's strong points. He managed a wry grin.

'That I could do it all, just like always.'

'What was the flare about?' she demanded.

'It was me calling it off. It's too much down there, too dangerous . . .' Joel moved back to lean on the fence marking the edge of the cliff. The wind seemed stronger, his shivering now violent enough to hurt.

'Call it off? I don't think they listened,' DS Rose said, and all at once Joel's gaze was fixed upon the cave again. The smaller boat was gone and, for a few minutes, there was nothing to see. Then there was movement. A blur of yellow, then a fidgeting light – a crew member's head torch. It was angled upwards. They were coming out backwards, holding something, making sure it stayed above the water.

'Joel, he's got someone!' DS Rose shrieked. Joel's hands rose to link behind the back of his head. He felt like bursting into tears. He watched it play out in silence, the yellow bundle now in slow motion, it seemed, while the ocean still pummelled them, hissing a warning on its every retreat. Slowly but surely, the bundle of something was dragged back to be pulled onto the lifeboat.

Joel's phone rang. The number was labelled *Force Cntrl Rm.* He struggled to control his shivering in his haste to answer.

'DI Norris, would you accept talk-through from Coxswain Neil Pope? It's in relation to CAD—'

'Yes!' Joel snapped.

'Putting him through now.'

'Hello, is that the idiot from the rocks?' The Coxswain's voice.

'Neil . . . Jesus, you people are incredible.'

'I wouldn't have gone in there, not sure many would. And then Sally-Anne ignored your signal, ignored me and damned nearly got herself killed.' His calmness was gone, replaced by a clear anger that seemed directed towards Joel. He didn't reply, didn't feel like he was meant to. 'She doesn't give up,' Neil Pope continued, 'and it's like you said, she found two people trussed up in there. She had to get cutting gear for a padlock. We got one out alive . . .' The anger slipped. 'I'm sorry but the other . . . the other's lost, I'm afraid. She didn't get any pulse and she couldn't get her free so that's a body recovery job and I won't let her back out for that. She's not happy but I have to look after my crew. You'll be able to walk it from where you are in a couple of hours.'

'One . . .' Joel had to bite down to catch his emotions. 'That's incredible, I couldn't see anyone coming out of there.'

'Me neither. She should be OK with the right treatment. Deep shock, hypothermia is a risk, dehydration for sure and she's covered in cuts, lost a good few fingernails and she has lacerations just about everywhere really. I can't imagine what it was like in there . . .' Pope faded out now like he was the one struggling with his emotions.

'Is she talking?'

'Barely. We've got a name and a lot of tears. She's quite the fighter but she's exhausted. We're going to take her back to Dover. We'll have an ambulance meet us.'

'Thank you, thank you so much. Your crew, the whole lot, but Sally-Anne . . .' Joel was still fighting his emotions. 'Just thank you.'

'Half a job. We were just too late.'

'What's the name, Neil? Who have you got on there?'

'Says her name's Alison. That's all she's said. Is that who you were expecting?'

Joel took another moment. 'It's more than I dared hope for.'

Chapter 63

Joel was sure to switch his phone off when they finally came away from Samphire Hoe. He left night patrols to secure and guard the scene; the grim task of body recovery would now wait for daylight, and those officers who had lent their time to the operation were sent back to their home stations to complete duty statements. As for Joel, he folded, like a rug that had been rolled up damp, into the back of a marked unit that would take them back to Medway. The recovery of their damaged Ford Focus could wait until morning too. The journey was largely in silence. He and DS Rose were turned away from each other on the rear bench, lost in the flashes and blurs of passing lights. Joel was desperate to focus on what needed to be done next – there was so much – but the gusts of wind that buffeted the side of the car on exposed stretches of road forced his focus to be somewhere he would rather not be. It was a cave. It was dark, with sharp, unrelenting edges, and it was violently flooding over and over again.

Joel could hardly imagine a worse hell.

Medway Police Station lived up to its promise of a shower and a change of clothes. He had assured himself it would make him feel better but it had only made him more comfortable. He wasn't sure what 'better' meant. Certainly the knot of anxiety that had balled itself up in his stomach was still with him, though he was no longer sure why. The job was over. They had found the missing women, the man responsible for that and much more was in a cell downstairs and the evidence was already overwhelming enough that Billy Easton would never see an unobstructed sky again. But something still didn't feel right.

Joel turned his phone back on to instant notifications of missed calls from Mark Hall in his capacity as the Major Crime DCI and acting Superintendent, still covering for Debbie Marsden. There was voicemail from him too, his tone a deliberate combination of patronising and faux-disappointment as he explained that Major Crime would be taking over the interviews of Easton from now on. He stopped short of saying *seeing as you can't be trusted,* but it was clear enough. It was late anyway, close to midnight, and any formal interview with a prisoner arriving at this time of night would be after an eight-hour rest period at least. This timescale removed the point of any protest there and then, but Joel couldn't resist some sort of a reply. He sent a text, knowing it was the best way to get the last word, and made sure it was as non-committal as possible. It said simply: *Just out of courtesy, I received your voicemail.*

Then he took out the card with Tom Lovelock's direct dial on it. He didn't think Lovelock would answer; solicitors weren't on call like that, it was done via a call centre that had a rota of who was covering. The sleepy 'hello' told him it wasn't Lovelock's turn, but his interest was quickly piqued: Billy Easton, Lovelock's first and only murder client to this point, had been arrested again – could he come down? Joel had been confident that he would but the speed caught him out. He was still skulking in the refs room, looking for tea bags to steal from the night duty response team, who had left their cupboard open, when a custody sergeant called him direct. He was instantly curt.

'DI Norris?'

'Speaking,' he said, trying to speak through the stolen biscuit that was crammed in his mouth.

'This is Kirsty Whittaker, down in the dungeons at Medway. I've got a solicitor outside wanting consultation with the murder suspect who was brought in earlier. We were told he was being bedded down for the night. The solicitor's now asking for you?'

'That's right,' Joel sang, 'if a jailer could put them together for a quick chat, I'll be right down.' He cut the call before he could get any protests. Joel took his tea with him and refilled his mouth with digestive. When he walked into the interview room he was still washing it down.

'DI Norris!' Lovelock was cheery, despite looking hurriedly dressed. It was clear he was still enjoying his career-defining moment. Billy Easton was sitting next to him. Some of the confidence he had seen slip away from him out on the edge of the Hoe seemed to be back. 'If you will excuse me, Mr Easton, I need to speak to the inspector here, find out what's been going on.'

'Disclosure, you mean? Let's do it right here, shall we?' Joel snapped and Lovelock's expression instantly changed to a scowl of confusion.

'But officer, the process dictates . . .'

'The process says I don't have to disclose a damned thing so count this as a bonus. Just like I don't have to interview your client again either, and I won't be. I just wanted to tell you that in person.'

'But you have to give him his chance to give his side of the story? That's the system we all work under—' Lovelock began.

'I don't have to give him a *fucking thing*!' Joel hissed. He sat down in the stunned silence that followed. The chair was directly opposite Billy and Joel locked onto him, noting that his lips now had a little curl at both ends, threatening to form a smile. Joel didn't think he would be able to hold himself back if it came. 'I don't have to hear another word that comes out of this mouth. I'm tired of the games and the lies. I only came down here to *disclose* to you that your client has lost, to tell you that he left his skin all over the tools he used to condemn a homeless man to a slow and painful death.'

'Homeless—' Lovelock started to speak, the curl in Easton's lips was gone. Joel cut in to the finish.

'That's right. Your client was captured on CCTV when he was stalking Jessica Harrington at her place of work. It's amazing how silent images can still effectively show a man getting more and more angry. At one point Billy here even crosses the floor like he's going to front her up, but of course he didn't. He'd spent four years planning what he was going to do to her and that might have ruined it all. That's right, isn't it, Billy?' There was no reply. 'Or maybe you lost your nerve, got scared? Easier to watch her from the shadows until she was vulnerable enough . . .' Another pause. Billy's smirk reappeared but nothing else, so Joel continued. 'That wasn't the first time he had been there either, seems he was a regular. But not only there. You see, your client had a homeless man tied to the back of a disused garage nearby. This man was known in the area for begging, but I reckon that Billy here saw someone weak and vulnerable enough to be perfect for his needs, because we know he only goes after the vulnerable.'

'Needs?' Lovelock scoffed, again trying to get a word in.

'Practice,' Joel said. 'That's right isn't it, Billy? There were a couple of restraint options left in that garage, including a windlass, which is something that a man with a fascination with boats might know all about. I had to look it up. It's designed to be used with a boat anchor, its main function to feed out a length of chain into the water and then to bring it back when needed. That's the sort of thing that could be adapted to hold someone tight against a wall, then give them a metre or two of freedom when you wanted to. There was mechanical timer too, that could have worked with the windlass to let you control your victim's distance from the back wall without even being there. And you needed to know you could, didn't you? Did you even know his name?' Joel's sudden change to a question got no reaction.

'Now come on, this is all—' Lovelock's enjoyment was gone and Joel cut him off for a second time.

'From his injuries, from the marks on the floor, we know that he did move forward, at one point he would have been touching distance from the door before you dragged him all the way back. You toyed with him, just to see that you could.' Joel took a moment, he had to, smile or no smile from Billy, Joel wasn't sure he was going to be able to keep it together. 'Was the infra-red sensor method the most successful? Is that why it wasn't in that garage, because you took it out to that fort in Dover?' Another pause, another opportunity for someone else to speak. No one else did. 'I think you always intended for him to die, maybe you were going to put him out of his misery but, when it came to it, you were too much of a coward.' Joel paused, allowing the silence to breathe and grow like it was a whole other entity in the room. 'Seems you got your *strategy* all wrong. Just because some homeless man doesn't matter to you, you assumed he wouldn't matter to anyone else. But someone missed him, someone called and told us the places he used for shelter. You left yourself at that garage and you *even* got yourself seen walking away!' Joel paused, waiting for some sort of reaction to register on Billy Easton's face. It was subtle, but it was there. 'All that planning!' Joel allowed himself a big grin. 'You're not as clever as you think you are. Your ex-wife was right about you, you're just a sad little man.' Joel's chair squeaked as he got back to his feet to loom over the prisoner. Billy kept his head bent, refusing the satisfaction of eye contact, but Joel leant in so close and spat his next words with such force that it disturbed the wispy hair on top of his head.

'You lost, Billy!'

Joel stepped away, leaving the door swinging open behind him as he walked down the corridor, past the questioning looks of the custody sergeant, to make for the fresher air.

And that knot of anxiety, that feeling of his stomach ratcheted tight in a vice – it was gone.

Day 7

Chapter 64

'Hey . . .' Just one word breathed down the phone line at him was enough to convey total exhaustion.

'Lucy, how are you doing?' Joel replied.

The voice at the other end now sounded like it might be accompanying a stretch. 'Awesome. I take it you're my update?'

Joel had sent Lucy home on Friday and begged her to stay away until Monday at least. She needed the rest and besides, Billy Easton was now Major Crime's prisoner while they discussed a homeless man left helpless as the shadow of death inched towards him across a garage floor. To further emphasise his point, Joel had added up the sixty or more hours that his sergeant had been at work the week before, insisting that taking two days off at this stage wouldn't matter. And all the work now required in building their casefile would still be there waiting for her on Monday.

Lucy had thrown it right back at him. *So you're having the weekend off, are you?* she had said.

Of course he wasn't.

Joel wanted to be around just like she did. He wanted live updates as Major Crime came out of that interview room. CSI were still reporting back findings, and witnesses were still giving accounts. He'd pulled rank, insisting that one of them would need to be about for questions – but only one – and he was it. DS Rose had grudgingly stayed away. But he knew she hadn't really.

'I'm sure I remember telling you to get some rest. Two days, that's all I asked, forget about work, see a movie, take a long bath, and then Monday morning all your questions would be answered. Is that not what I said?'

'Something like that,' DS Rose sighed.

'People tell me things, Lucy. CSI tell me when you call them. Major Crime tell me when you call them. The Detention Officer down in custody? He couldn't wait to tell me when you called him!' Joel couldn't stop a small chuckle escaping.

'I can't believe they squealed me up,' Lucy said.

'I can't believe I actually thought you would take my advice.'

'So, are you my update?'

Joel sighed now, resigned. 'I am. Can I come in?'

Lucy took a moment to reply. 'In?' she said.

'In, yeah. Assuming you're at home or this really was a wasted trip.'

'You're at my house?'

'If the address is up to date on your personnel file I am,' Joel said.

'I'll come down.'

Joel stepped back from the double doors that made up the front entrance. He had a coffee in each hand. Her address was just off the main drag that ran through the town of Tenterden. As a first-time visitor, Joel had been delighted to see any number of independent coffee shops with seating areas spilling out onto a wide pavement under freckled shade from mature trees. It was a pretty town.

He hadn't been so delighted at the price, however, or the need for the drink to come with a backstory. He now knew that his coffee was ethically sourced and served in a bamboo cup that would 'return to nature' when he was finished with it. Joel was tempted to tell the beardy barista that he might expect something that had cost him four quid a cup to last a little longer.

The coffee was molten, singeing his fingertips, and he had to relent and balance the cups on the wall until his colleague appeared. When she did it was through a crack where just one of the doors was pulled a few inches open, revealing a single eye laden with suspicion.

'You don't get many guests then, no?' Joel chuckled. DS Rose pulled the door wider. The movement suggested it was every bit as heavy as it looked. 'What an amazing place,' Joel said. He meant it too. The building was a converted church, the outside untouched enough that he had walked past it twice while looking for somewhere residential. Lucy's front door was on the left side of the building, the same side as a tower that stood clear out of a gabled roof. He stepped into an open porch large enough for pews either side. A stone arch loomed above another set of solid double doors, both hanging open. Through them, most of the ground floor was visible. A kitchen island grabbed his attention first, despite being towards the back. The fleck in the black granite work surfaces gleamed in the light pouring through a stained-glass window that dominated the back wall, tantalisingly only showing its lower part; the rest was blocked by a mezzanine floor with a glass edge. Directly to his right and in the double-height part was a living room area with soft furnishings and a plainer, though still large, window that he had seen as he had approached the front. This area stopped abruptly at an exposed stone wall. The developers had managed to preserve the feel of the building while dividing it into several dwellings.

'Small. But it's fine for me. I fell in love with the place.'

'I'm not surprised,' Joel said.

'No need to offer you a drink then,' Lucy said and gestured at the takeaway cups that were still threatening to remove Joel's fingerprints. 'I do have a kettle, you know. I would have made you one.'

'I didn't want to turn up empty-handed.'

'Why would you turn up at all?' Lucy fixed on him like the question was pertinent. Joel had been expecting it and still he didn't really have an answer. He could hardly say he was 'in the area'. Nowhere is in the area of Tenterden, except Tenterden.

He tried it anyway. 'I wanted to bring you right up to date and I was in the area.'

'Of course you were,' Lucy said. Then she pointed at her comfortable-looking living room and its cosy soft seating. 'That area's just for show,' she said, 'I don't use it.' Then she turned away towards the open wooden stairs against the left wall leading up to the mezzanine. Joel followed, aware of a bead of sweat running over his temple. He really needed to put the cups down.

Luckily for him, Lucy went into the first area at the top of the stairs – and here the rest of that window was revealed. The glass in the top half was clear to make the most of the view, and the fact that it rose up through the floor and curved to a point added to the drama. There was no furniture, just an open square of beige carpet. Lucy reached out for her cup, then stood with her back against the thick stone of the window's surround.

'Shit! This is hot, you coulda warned me!' she said.

'I didn't notice.'

There was short period when neither spoke, when both were drawn to that view. Joel stood on the other side of the window, his right shoulder against the glass, the window surround thick enough to support his back. From here he could see the grounds of the church stretching away. There were still some old graves, all overgrown, some at a jaunty angle to make him think of a spoof film set. Joel took a tentative slurp at his coffee.

'What do you have to tell me then?' Lucy said.

'There's not much more. The DNA Major Crime found in

that garage was a match for Billy Easton so he definitely has some explaining to do. I knew that already. When I talked to him in custody and told him it existed, his face changed.'

'Is he having it?' Lucy said.

'He hasn't said a single word since Friday. Unless you count "no comment". Major Crime had a few goes at him then gave up. They're blaming me for tipping him off, of course. It doesn't matter anyway, he was remanded to Elmley and the only time he gets out of there is when they can book him into a nice Category A prison for the rest of his natural life.'

'I assume we caught up with the son?'

'Two detectives from Suffolk Major Crime went out to meet Robert Easton and his mother. They're living in Bury St Edmunds and were only too happy to help. We have good statements from both, a lot of detail, a lot of background. Basically it's what Joy told me on the phone but with some nice extra bits about how much of an arsehole Billy was. They checked out alibis too, of course. Robert couldn't have been involved.'

'That's good to know for sure.'

'It is. Oh, we worked out what happened to our missing survivor from Sandwich Industrial Estate too.'

'I was thinking about that. Did you put an appeal out?'

'There wasn't the need. There was DNA on the wire that was left in the back of one of the trailers. It matched with Bradley Reynolds.'

'Bradley was in that trailer?' Lucy's surprise was obvious.

'He was. His wife has filled in a few gaps but getting all the answers from her is going to take some time. That family's been through hell, and it appears Bradley went through hell twice. Bradley's wife and children were threatened, the wife was abducted to force Bradley to take part for a second time. Her kidnap has been added to Billy's rap sheet.'

'Jesus . . .' Lucy murmured.

'It seems like Bradley attacked Alan Lewis the moment he

got free. He didn't want to take the chance that he might lose the race so he went straight for the jugular as it were. Bradley had two young kids, they meant everything to him and I guess he was doing what he could to get back to them.'

'That didn't work out so well, did it?' Lucy said. Her attention had returned to the view.

'No. Bradley didn't follow the rules. I guess it was set up as a race and it hadn't played out like that. So he was made to take part again, only . . .'

'Only he never stood a chance.'

'He was never supposed to survive, one way or another. They've assigned a family liaison to Bradley's wife and kids, and to Alison.'

'That's good. They're going to need all the help they can get.'

'They are. John Coleman's helping us too.'

'The old man who runs the boat workshop?'

'The very same. He's given up a burner phone that Billy had him keep hold of on Samphire Hoe. It matched the number called when Alan Lewis was killed. Rather than a family member, I think Billy had that phone and took the call when Bradley made it.'

'So that's it then. Write up our reports for CPS, get the case ready for court and onto the next.'

'How do you feel about that?' Joel said.

Lucy turned back into the room but her eyes still lacked focus. 'I feel good. We did good, didn't we?'

'I spoke to your dad too,' Joel said.

'You did what?' Now her focus was sharp – and it was directly on him.

'Walter Jones. I went to see him. Yesterday.'

'Why?'

'A couple of reasons. To see if he was OK, to see if he was pressing charges—'

'He's not, I told you that!' She was angry. She pushed away from the stone to stand upright.

'You did. And the moment I saw his name I knew you were right. You didn't tell me your dad was Walter Jones.'

'So why go and see him then?' she huffed.

'Because I didn't know your dad is one of the most prolific criminals in the county. Because I don't know anything about you at all, really, and I thought maybe he could help me out. Actually, it wasn't the first time I'd met your dad. I looked back and I've done two Theft Act Warrants and three Misuse of Drugs Act Warrants at that address before, all without knowing he had a daughter on the same side.'

'Vetting do.'

Joel held up his hands. 'I know that. I'm not having a go.'

'What are you doing then? My dad wouldn't talk to you. He doesn't talk to police.'

'He did actually. He made me buy him a beer. He took me to that shitty little pub just over the road . . .'

'The Old Buoy!' They both said it together. DS Rose even flashed a smile.

'Cost me three pints of Doombar and something they called a carvery, but definitely wasn't a carvery. He couldn't eat much anyway. He's got a sore face, it would seem.'

'I didn't even know he was out of hospital.'

'He shouldn't be. Discharged himself. They told him he didn't need surgery but would need to stay in for observation and a prescription of painkillers and he was gone. I told him I would have stayed around for the painkillers at least but he says he knows a guy.' Another flicker of a smile. Lucy moved back to her leaning position as Joel continued. 'He took some convincing that I was only there because I was worried about his daughter and I wanted to know a bit more about what was going on in her head.'

'Like he would know,' Lucy scoffed.

'He told me about Hannah Ribbons, about who she really was to you.'

Lucy stared back. Her cheek rippled, her nose twitched but

she didn't respond. Hannah Ribbons: the police officer shot dead as part of their last investigation – their first job together. Lucy had turned up with fire in her belly, looking for justice, and Joel had taken that as the response of a copper who had heard that a friend and colleague had been murdered. But it had been so much more than that.

'You and Hannah were very much in love,' Joel continued. 'Your dad seemed delighted that he was the only one trusted to know about it, but that caused you problems, didn't it? I can't imagine how difficult it was for you.' Joel paused long enough for Lucy to speak if she wanted to. She didn't. 'I stood right next to you at her funeral. We were part of a load of coppers all lined up but out on the periphery, blending into the background, while her family – the people who loved her – grieved together. And we stayed away while they had their own ceremony and went back for a private get-together afterwards. They didn't even know about you, did they?'

DS Rose's nose twitched again. Then words came, but she spoke them facing the window. 'Hannah was married. To a man. It was over, had been for a while and they both knew it, but she hadn't even told her family about that, let alone about me. She was going to, she told me her plans. It wasn't for me to push it.'

'Your dad told me what you said to him. I saw a side of Walter Jones I didn't know existed – and I don't mean the heavily bruised side. He nearly broke down right in front of me. I think I prefer the sweary, difficult old bastard who can't stand the sight of me. You told him that it was like your love never existed, how all memory of it died when she did because there were no other witnesses, no one who knew what she meant to you. But that love *did* exist. And thinking back, from the very first moment we met, I could see what she meant to you. You were a whirlwind. I've never seen someone so passionate. I mistook it for frustration with me. And I stood next to you at that crime scene, when Hannah was lying out

. . . I'm sorry, Lucy. I was so wrapped up in me, I didn't stop to think about you.'

'You don't need to be sorry. You don't need . . . It's been hard but I'm not special, everyone finds it hard when they lose someone. I was coping OK but it all came back when . . . It doesn't matter. It was a setback, that's all.'

'I think it does matter. For you, for us moving forward. We've got something here, the makings of a wonderful team – look what we did this week. And with Eileen in charge there's no stopping us!'

This time Lucy's smile was broader but it still dropped away before it could establish itself. 'I saw Bradley Reynolds shot dead. I saw what that looks like. There was a split second when he saw it coming and it was just . . . terror. Just pure terror. Hannah . . . I can't help but think that Hannah would have looked like that, that she went through the exact same thing. She must have been so scared. I don't want to think of that as her last moment on this earth.'

'Rather than her last moment, maybe you should think about all those other moments you must have had. The happy ones.'

'I've tried. It's been hard. Until recently I couldn't think about her without getting angry. She put herself in that situation, she got herself killed. She cared about those girls and that case more than she cared about her own life, more than she cared about *our* life. That's all I kept thinking.'

'And now?'

'I don't think that anymore, if that's what you're asking. She was passionate, for sure, but she was also very confident in her own abilities. She would never have believed there could be a situation she wouldn't be able to talk or fight her way out of.' Lucy was back staring at Joel now, and she stayed doing so long enough for him to feel the need to prompt her.

'What?' he said.

'Sound familiar?'

'You're saying I'm like that?'

'Yes. And it got her killed. I can't be losing someone else I care about.'

'Don't worry about me.'

'That's exactly what she used to say. And I'm not worried, I just need you to stick around long enough for me to pass my inspector's exam. There could be a vacancy soon!'

Lucy tried to hold it together but the laughter broke through. It did for Joel too. The empty expanse of carpet, stone and high ceiling was an excellent conductor, and their laughter filled every inch of it.

THE END

Acknowledgements

So many people, processes and things are involved in the creation of a book by the time it stands proudly on a shelf, or displays as a thumbnail on your e-reader, or, looking slightly battered and not a little shocked, is propped up on a cobbled-together-table amongst pre-loved teddies in the bright sunshine of a Sunday morning boot fair (depending on where you buy your books). So many people, so much effort, so many hours and so, so many cups of tea that I feel bad making a sweeping statement such as *massive thanks to my publisher* now that it is finally finished. The truth however, is there are too many to name so a sweeping statement it must be. Here goes: Thank you to all at Team Avon. Thank you for continuing this dream of mine, for rolling me in glitter and for sharing my enthusiasm for the humble story.

I would like to reserve an individual mention for Rachel Faulkner-Willcocks, Senior Commissioning Editor at Avon for taking a chance on me (and for going easy on me with the structural edit of *Lethal Game*!), and for Cara Chimirri at Avon, who took up the editorial reigns when no one else would (I made that last bit up) and became the most important person in my world for at least five months as, between us, we did all we could to make *Lethal Game* as perfect as possible.

My wife also deserves acknowledgement. Creating stories was my obsession long before we met, but she still has to live with those restless nights where I constantly click a bedside light on and back off again to hurriedly scribble notes and ideas, or the irregular naked dashes from the shower to the bedroom when inspiration has struck and must be recorded, or, when she's waiting for me because we're watching something together and gets my constant assurances of *just finishing this bit*. Never does she complain.

She does remove the bulb, wrap a towel and start the programme whether I am ready or not, but I adore her for it.

The last thank you is the most important of all as it is for the readers. None of this is possible without you. I love this job; Monday has become my favourite day of the week and long may that continue. But it doesn't without you. Thank you for buying and reading the books, for supporting me with your words of feedback, for the tags, mentions and direct messages on social media, via email and meetings in person – I only hope I manage to reply to each and every method as this is something I find almost as enjoyable as the creation of the stories in the first place.

Almost.

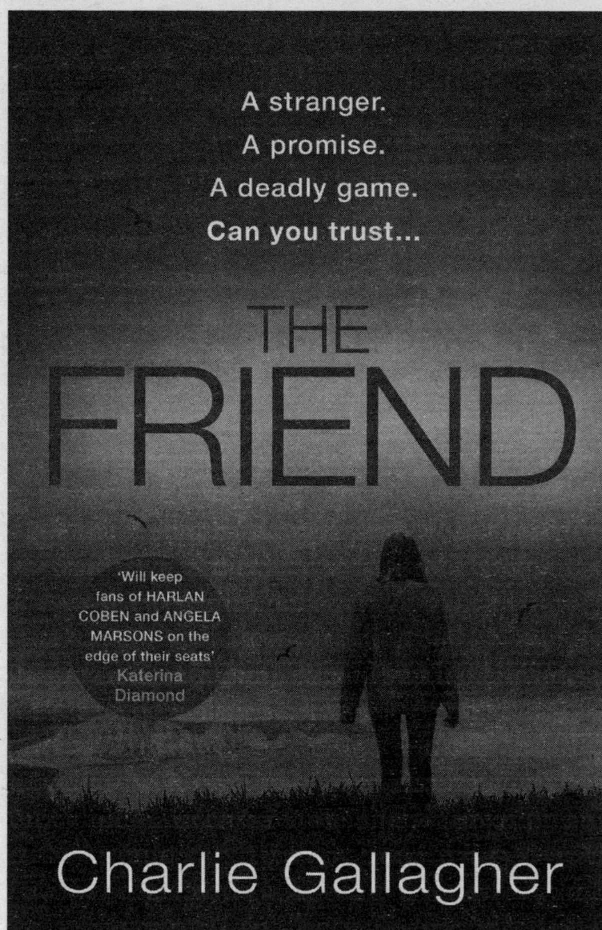
A stranger.
A promise.
A deadly game.
Can you trust...
THE
FRIEND
'Will keep fans of HARLAN COBEN and ANGELA MARSONS on the edge of their seats'
Katerina Diamond
Charlie Gallagher